I0818662

THE HALFADAY CREEK SERIES BY

JAMES B. HENDRYX

Black John of Halfaday Creek

Strange Doings on Halfaday Creek

Skullduggery on Halfaday Creek

The Saga of Halfaday Creek

Badmen on Halfaday Creek

Murder on Halfaday Creek

Adventures on Halfaday Creek

Hell's-a-Poppin' on Halfaday Creek

Visit www.jamesbhendryx.com for more information on forthcoming installments in the Halfaday Creek uniform matching series.

BLACK JOHN OF HALFADAY CREEK

BLACK JOHN OF HALFADAY CREEK

JAMES B. HENDRYX

ILLUSTRATIONS BY
PETE KUHLHOFF

STEEGER BOOKS • 2020

SERIES EXECUTIVE CONSULTANT

Richard Hall

PUBLISHING HISTORY

"Three Birds with One Stone" and "Slang Is Not as Dated as One Would Think" originally appeared in the May 25, 1935 issue of *Short Stories* magazine (vol. 151, no. 4). Reprinted by arrangement with the Estate of James B. Hendryx.

"The Sourdoughs Visit Halfaday" originally appeared in the May 10, 1936 issue of *Short Stories* magazine (vol. 155, no. 3). Reprinted by arrangement with the Estate of James B. Hendryx.

"Whiskers" originally appeared in the September 10, 1936 issue of *Short Stories* magazine (vol. 156, no. 5). Reprinted by arrangement with the Estate of James B. Hendryx.

"The Ghost of Halfaday Creek" originally appeared in the September 25, 1936 issue of *Short Stories* magazine (vol. 156, no. 6). Reprinted by arrangement with the Estate of James B. Hendryx.

"Samson's Luck on Halfaday" originally appeared in the November 25, 1936 issue of *Short Stories* magazine (vol. 157, no. 4). Reprinted by arrangement with the Estate of James B. Hendryx.

"Black John Intervenes" originally appeared in the January 25, 1937 issue of *Short Stories* magazine (vol. 158, no. 2). Reprinted by arrangement with the Estate of James B. Hendryx.

"Black John Files a Stove Leg" originally appeared in the March 25, 1937 issue of *Short Stories* magazine (vol. 158, no. 6). Reprinted by arrangement with the Estate of James B. Hendryx.

THANKS TO

Robert Loomis, Cynthia Whyte, & the Leelanau Historical Society

TABLE OF CONTENTS

THREE BIRDS WITH ONE STONE

BLACK JOHN SMITH returned his empty glass to the bar and eyed the stranger who stood framed in the open doorway of the saloon. The man was tall and angular, smooth shaven, with a thin, sharp nose, a pair of close-set, glittering black eyes. A light pack swung by its straps from the crook of his elbow.

"Good morning, gentlemen," he said. "I trust that I have at last arrived at Cushing's Fort."

"Such trust as yourn has been rewarded, this time," Black John replied. "Step up. The house is buyin' a drink."

The man advanced to the battered brass rail, swung the pack to the bar, and faced the two with a thin-lipped smile.

"My name is Beezely, gentlemen—J.Q.A. Beezely, attorney at law."

Black John regarded the man with interest, "A lawyer, eh? Well, we've had damn near every other kind of a miscreant there is show up on Halfaday, so I s'pose it was only a question of time till a lawyer would come."

The thin-lipped smile widened. "Gentlemen, my appearance on Halfaday Creek may well prove a godsend to you."

"In what way," queried Black John, "could a lawyer be a godsend to a crick?"

"In other words, I may prove a blessing in disguise."

"If the blessin' is as good as the disguise," retorted the big man, "we prob'ly won't have no kick comin'. Smith is my name—

Black John, to be exact. An' the gentleman acrost the bar is Lyme Cushing, proprietor of the fort."

The man regarded the two with interest. "So you're Black John Smith, the king of Halfaday, are you? And you're Cushing? I'm glad to make your acquaintance, gentlemen. I heard about you in Whitehorse."

Black John frowned slightly. "Me an' Cush will admit, fer the sake of veracity, that we're gentlemen without bein' reminded of it every time you open yer head. An' as fer me bein' king of Halfaday—it looks like you'd got off on the wrong foot, to start out with."

"No offense, gent—no offense, I assure you. Quite the contrary! I was merely repeating what I had gathered in Whitehorse."

"On Halfaday," replied Black John, dryly, "what a man gathers he keeps to himself—if he kin. How did you git here? An' why?"

"I hired an Indian in Whitehorse, and we made the journey in a canoe. Devilish trip—that long upstream grind. No wonder you men feel safe from the long arm of the law. My reason for coming is simple. It seemed to be common knowledge in Whitehorse that Halfaday Creek, lying as it is reported to lie, close against the international boundary line, affords a safe haven for numerous outlaws. I was headed for the Klondike—for Dawson. You see, I realized that with thousands of people pouring into the fabulously rich gold field, innumerable disputes would be bound to arise, and the services of an attorney would be in great demand. Therefore, gen—therefore, I decided to locate there and to practice my profession." The man paused momentarily, and toyed with his glass of liquor. "But at Whitehorse I heard of Halfaday Creek, and immediately I changed my plans. You see, g—you see, I specialize in criminal law."

"YEAH," OBSERVED Black John, "quite a lot of the boys along the crick, here, has took a crack at it, too—one way er another."

"I—mean—that I practice criminal law."

"Well, a little more practice wouldn't hurt several of the boys which they undoubtless bungled their job—"

"I practice at the bar—"

"Yeah, I see," interrupted the big man impatiently. "But if you've practiced enough at this one, would you mind h'istin' that drink—so we can go ahead with another? This here licker of Cush's was s'posed to have age enough onto it when it was bottled."

"I have successfully defended some of the most notorious criminals in America," boasted the man, as he rasped the raw liquor from his throat, and refilled his glass. "My fame as a mouthpiece has spread over half a continent. Crooks and super-crooks have paid me thousands, simply as retaining fees, and other thousands to free them when they became enmeshed in the toils of the law."

"Why would you throw up a good business like that, an' hit fer the Klondike?" asked Black John, his blue-gray eyes resting for a fleeting moment on the light pack sack that lay just beyond the man's elbow on the bar.

"As I told you," Beezely replied, downing his second drink, and ordering another round, "I became intrigued with the possibilities of the gold field. But at Whitehorse I heard of Halfaday, and right then I changed my plans. Mining law may be, and doubtless is, remunerative in a high degree. But when the clients are at hand, so is criminal law. And as criminal law is my specialty, why change? First, last and all the time, I am a criminal lawyer!"

"I can well believe it," admitted Black John, his eyes once more on the pack sack. "Of course, it ain't none of our business, what any man done before he come to Halfaday, but I was jest wonderin' what kind of crime it was that headed you north?"

"Let us all be frank—"

"Nope," interrupted Cush, "it won't work. Here a while back, everyone that come to Halfaday wanted to be John—John Smith—till it led to such a mix-up that me an' John invented the name can. It would amount to the same thing, if we was all to be Frank. Drink up, an' I'll buy another."

BLACK JOHN and Beezely grinned broadly, as the latter proceeded. I mean, let's be candid. I first contemplated a change about six months ago, when I became the victim of a disbarment proceeding, the allegations being that I had negotiated for the disposal of certain stolen property—hot bonds, in the vernacular. And, also, that I had been instrumental in the harboring of certain known criminals. The matter of my departure was abruptly precipitated by the fact that, not content with my disbarment, my persecutors, an irate prosecuting attorney, aided and abetted by certain members of the legal profession—my own colleagues, mind you—brought criminal charges against me, and preferred certain charges before the grand jury which, in some manner, they succeeded in sustaining, so that the jury indicted me on several counts—among which were harboring criminals, receiving stolen property, disposing of stolen property, accessory before the fact in several instances of robbery and burglary, subornation of perjury, and several others. Thus, you can readily see that rather than become swamped in endless litigation, I departed from there."

"Yeah," agreed Black John, "under the circumstances, it looks like it was your move, at that."

"You see," further explained the man, "my colleagues at the bar were actuated purely by motives of jealousy. They realized that I was getting, what in their opinion, was far more than my share of the criminal practice, and they took that cowardly means of putting a successful competitor out of business. The prosecuting attorney acted merely out of spite. I had beaten him so many times—won verdicts of acquittal so often against him, in cases that he had proclaimed were ironclad—that he held a personal enmity toward me. It was the malicious revenge of a small soul."

"An' you wasn't guilty of none of these allegations, I s'pose?" queried Black John.

"Well, yes—and no. I will enumerate. On the harboring of criminals count, for instance—I certainly did know where certain criminals were in hiding. In fact, in numerous instances where I had accepted a retainer, I had arranged in advance for their hide-outs. I considered it a duty that I owed to my clients. And I had to know where they could be reached for matters of conference.

"As to the receiving and disposition of stolen property—how is a criminal lawyer to be paid except from the proceeds of a crime? The fruits of crime are the only property with which the criminal can pay. And as for the disposal of such property—it is a well known fact that the sooner a man gets hot bonds off his hands, the better it is for him.

"In regard to subornation of perjury; of course it was necessary for me to instruct my clients and their various witnesses what to say on the stand—and what not to say. How else could a man establish an alibi for a client when, as a matter of fact, that client was at that particular time engaged in committing a burglary or a robbery?

"As to the matter of being an accessory before the fact; I never really plotted any crime—in its entirety. It is true that in certain instances, I did hint to clients of certain profitable jobs they could pull, and advised them as to how to go about it. I advised them as to what evidence is admissible, and what is not. And I coached them in regard to the destruction of valuable clues confusing or destroying evidence, and in fact, in numerous matters having a direct bearing upon the success of the enterprise. An attorney, my friends, who has not the best interest of his clients at heart, is sorely remiss in his duty."

"Jest a good, square-shootin' lawyer, tryin' to git along," agreed Black John, "An' this here advisory service—was it; gratuitous? Er was there a fee attached?"

"Oh, no fee! No fee, at all! Of course, an attorney can not be expected to render his services for nothing. I always arrange with the client for a remuneration somewhat commensurate—"

"My God," exclaimed Cush. "What-with them big words you use, you an' John ought to git along fine!"

"—commensurate to the service," continued Beezely, ignoring the interruption. "The payment to be made out of the proceeds of the venture, generally upon a percentage basis. I never could bring myself to accept a flat fee for these prearranged jobs, because if my client, or clients, were unsuccessful in the venture the poor fellows would be out of pocket."

"Looks all fair an' reasonable," admitted Black John. "It looks like if a man had a lawyer like that, he could go ahead an' pull most anything."

BEEZELY'S BEADY black eyes snapped appreciatively, and the thin lips smiled. "And you don't know the half of it, my friend! For after the job is pulled there is old J.Q.A. Beezely, with the hideout all arranged, and ready to take over all the hot stuff and dispose of it to the best advantage; ready with a roll to cool the heat by certain judicious payments to policemen and politicians—sometimes, even, to prosecutors or judges. And finally, if worse comes to worst, to defend his client at the bar of justice!"

"You must of been a comfortin' thought to such as was criminally inclined," opined Black John, tossing off his liquor, and ordering another round. "But the facts is, P.D.Q.—"

"J.Q.A.," corrected the attorney. "Named after John Quincy Adams, one of the greatest characters in American history."

"Oh—one of them historical names, eh? I trust this here Adams was dead before you was named after him."

"Long, long before. He was one of the earlier presidents."

"As I was goin' on to say, up to now we never had no lawyer on Halfaday—never felt the need of none. We ain't got many laws on the crick, an' sech as we have got, none of em's brittle."

"Brittle?"

"Yeah, you know brittle—ones that's easy broke. Our laws is few, but tough an' durable. Not wantin' the police hornin' in on us, we keep the crick moral by the simple expedient of hangin' anyone that is found guilty of murder, larceny in any form, claim-jumpin', er general skullduggery. Our verdicks is reached by the vote of miners' meetin's, an' the meetin' ain't called till we're practically sure the culprit is guilty. There ain't no crime on Halfaday."

"But," queried Beezely, in apparent surprise, "what do you do here on Halfaday for a livelihood?"

"We're miners. Halfaday is a gold camp."

"Why, I understood, at Whitehorse, that it was a community of outlaws."

"I wouldn't know about that," replied Black John. "Of course, what any man done before he come to the crick ain't none of our business, an' it's barely possible that some of the boys might of infringed some law, somewheres, in their past."

After several moments of silence, Beezely smote the bar with his fist. "I've got it!" he cried. "What Halfaday needs is organization. Leave it to me! We've got a wonderful opportunity here—with the rich Klondike gold field within striking distance. Leave it to me—J.Q.A. Beezely will work out the details. Halfaday Creek looks like a permanent home for me,"

Black John nodded, his eyes once more on the pack-sack. "Yeah," he agreed, a bit grimly, "It shore does, Beezely—it shore does."

II

OTHER DRINKS WERE had. One Armed John strolled in with a nice string of fish which Beezely, pretty well oiled by that time, purchased for a five dollar bill.

"Now," he stated, holding the string up to admire it, "if we only had some means of preparing these, we could have a good old-fashioned fish-fry."

Old Cush nodded. "I feel kind of fish-hongry, myself," he admitted, and turned to One Armed John, "Take 'em out back an' gut 'em," he ordered, "an' give 'em to the klooch. Tell her to fry 'em good an' brown an' fetch in here along of some boiled spuds, an' some bread."

"In the meantime," suggested Black John, his thoughts on the thick roll that Beezely had returned to his pocket after peeling off One Armed John's five, "there ain' nothin' in the book that says we couldn't be passin' away the time with a little stud."

"Ah—stud—a great game—a great game, indeed!" cried Beezely, with enthusiasm. "By all means, let us play. It seems, my friends," he beamed, "that at last my peripatetic feet have borne me to a safe haven amid congenial surroundings."

"What did you say ailed 'em?" inquired Cush solicitously.

"Ailed them? Ailed what?"

"Why, yer feet. I've got some corn medicine that my third wife had. Yer welcome to try it. Her feet ailed her somethin' fierce. She claimed it done 'em good."

"There ain't nothin' the matter with Beezely's feet," explained Black John. "What he meant was that at last, he figgers he's lit in a spot he likes."

"Oh," grunted Cush. "Why in hell didn't he say so, then? Them big words you educated folks uses only leads to the confusal of them that don't understand 'em. Wait till I dig out a deck of cards."

"Yeah," said Black John, "an' you better toss me a sack of dust out of the safe; an' fetch along one of yer own too, an' the chips. This here game is liable to git good. I'll fetch the bottle an' glasses, so you won't have to be jumpin' up all the time servin' drinks."

AS CUSH swung open the door of the old fashioned iron safe, Black John noted that the beady black eyes of the attorney seemed fairly to bulge from their sockets at sight of the tiers of neatly piled gold sacks, and the thick packets of paper currency that nearly filled its interior. As a gold sack thudded onto the bar before Black John, Beezely reached out and lifted it in his hand.

"Gosh, it's heavy for the size of it!" he exclaimed. "About how much gold would you say that it contains?"

"Oh, somewheres around eighty ounces," Black John replied.

"And gold is valued at about twenty dollars an ounce, isn't it?"

"Twenty, sixty-seven at the mint," replied Black John. "It passes around here for sixteen."

"Nearly thirteen hundred dollars in this little sack!" the other exclaimed. "Why, there's a sizeable fortune in that safe."

"Yeah," replied Black John indifferently. "Mostly it's in bills, though. There ain't a hell of a lot of gold in there, now. It's too bulky, takes up too much room, so every little while we take a batch of it down to Dawson an' trade it off fer big bills. Must be dost to half a million in the safe, all told."

As the game proceeded the chips piled steadily up in front of Beezely as both Cush and Black John consistently lost, so that when they cashed in, as the Indian woman deposited the platter of fried fish on the bar, the lawyer was some fifteen hundred dollars to the good.

"Just a little run of luck," he smiled, as he counted up his chips, "and if it's just the same to you, I'd rather have paper money than gold. Your turn next," he added, as he wrapped the bills Cush counted out on the bar around his roll. "And now we'll attack the fish—they certainly look appetizing, fried to a golden brown. That Indian woman of yours must be a wonderful cook."

"She's all right," Cush admitted, "once I got the idee into her head. But it was a hell of a job to learn her. When she first come, her notion of makin' bread was to slop a dipperful of water into the top of the flour sack an' mix around in it with her hands, an' then lift out everythin' that stuck together an' lay it on the top of the stove to bake. But she finally ketched on, after I'd shoved her face in the mess, three er four times. You can learn a klooch, if you've got patience."

"Now in the matter of an abode," began Beezely, after the last of the fish had disappeared, and he had cleansed his fingers and lips upon a handkerchief. "I was wondering if there is an empty cabin of some sort that I could occupy until such time as I may procure a suitable habitation of my own?"

"Well," replied Black John, "there's several shacks along the crick that's been abandoned, fer one reason er another. Some of 'em's on pretty good claims, too. My cabin's right close, an' I've got an extry bunk. You better jest throw in with me till you can look around a little. Bein' as yer residence on Halfaday is liable to be more er less permenant, you don't want to make no hasty mistake. Come on over an' you can make yerself to home, an' we'll come back, later. Some of the boys'll be driftin' in this evenin', an' we can mebbe git up a game of stud."

Beezely readily accepted the invitation and, swinging his pack sack over his shoulder, he followed Black John out the door, where he paused and glanced toward the well-beaten trail that slanted steeply downward to the landing.

"The Indian who brought me turned back a few miles down the creek, as soon as we came in sight of the fort," he said. "I came on alone from there, and when I got here I was too tired to carry my pack up the bank. This sack I have here contains only a few—er—personal belongings."

"Hold on a minute, an' I'll git yer pack," said Black John, and stepping down the trail, he returned a moment later with a well filled pack sack. He then led the way to his cabin, on the bank of the creek a short distance above the fort. Swinging the door open he motioned for the other to enter, and following him in, deposited the pack sack on the floor and indicated a bunk made up with clean blankets. "That's yourn," he said. "Jest throw yer stuff in under it, an' make yerself to home." As he spoke, Black John set a bottle and a pair of glasses on the table and indicated a rude chair. "Draw up," he invited, "an' we'll have a little drink whilst you go ahead an' explain what you meant by this here organization you mentioned. I figgered it would be better to kind of talk it over here—on account of Cush.

"Mouthy, eh?" asked the lawyer as he seated himself and filled his glass.

"Well—no, I wouldn't say Cush was exactly mouthy. Fact is, he don't run off at the head no more'n the average mud turtle. But he ain't no hand to grasp new idees, unless they're set before him in words of one syllable er less. He'd be pesterin' us with questions, an' besides that, some of the boys might drift in, an' interrupt the flowin' of our thoughts."

"Quite right," agreed Beezely, "I much prefer to talk man to man. A long and varied experience at the bar has taught me the danger of a witness. Now I mean to cast no aspersions, but let us assume, man to man, that we have here on Halfaday Creek, at least the nucleus of an extremely potent mob."

"Meanin'?"

"Meaning that there are men here who would not balk at well, for instance—robbery. Provided, of course, that the venture were well planned and carried out at some point far enough away from Halfaday so that no suspicion would fall upon any resident of the creek."

"W-e-e-l-l," replied Black John, drawing the word out reflectively. "I don't know as I'd go so fer as to say that any of the boys would actually an' personally participate in no major crime. There's some, mebbe, that I might suspect would possibly wink at some minor infringement of the law. But fer the sake of argument we'll assume that the material you would be needin' could be sifted out."

"Quite so. Of course, I realize that I can make no headway in this matter without your approval and coöperation. The plan is very simple. Merely that we select a few—say a dozen or twenty men among whom would be specialists along different lines, and organize them into a mob. You would be in command at this end, while I would go on to Dawson and look the ground over—find out where gold or currency is concentrated in quantities sufficient to interest us, and then case the job—find out all about the conditions under which it is held, and the habits and character of its custodians. This information I would relay here to you, and your part would be to select the proper men for the job and send them down to me. In the meantime, of course, I would have established myself as an attorney in good standing, so that no suspicion could possibly fall upon me, or upon anyone seen consulting me. The job would be pulled, and later the proceeds divided, all members of the mob participating in the profits. Of course, we would have to provide a fund—a fall fund—which I would have at my disposal, for fixing the police, and in the event that something should go wrong, conducting the defence. How does the idea appeal to you?"

BLACK JOHN hesitated, apparently in deep thought. "This here fall fund that you would have," he asked at length, "would want to be a fairly good jag of ready cash, wouldn't it?"

"The more, the better. A mob with cash enough behind it can pull anything."

"An' where would we raise this here fall fund?"

"Why, we would assess each member of the mob. Everyone would have to kick in with his share."

"S'pose there would be some of the boys that wouldn't have enough to kick in?" Beezely's thin lips smiled. "I guess we won't have to worry about that. I saw enough in that old safe there in the saloon—gold and packages of bills—to finance a dozen mobs."

"Yeah," agreed Black John, "there's considerable wealth in there, but—" He paused, and regarded the other with a smile. "An' I don't aim to cast no aspersions, no more', than you did. Fer all I can see yer motives is upright an' honorable as mine is, but you can see as well as I can, that if we dug the fall fund put of the safe, us Halfaday Crickers would be furnishin' all of it—an' you'd have the handlin' of it, an' share in the profits of these here ventures. What I'm drivin' at is—would you be in position to put up a part of this fund?"

The attorney's smile widened as he indicated with a jerk of his thumb, the small pack sack that lay on the bunk behind him. "No offence, I assure you. And regarding my ability to put up my share, I will tell you that in that bag I have exactly ninety-six thousand dollars in currency."

"You mean," exclaimed Black John, "that you've got that much on top of the roll yer carryin' around in yer pocket?"

"That flash roll is mere spending money—chicken feed. There's not more than six or eight thousand in it. Are you satisfied? What do you say?"

"Well," grinned Black John, "knowin' the Northwest Mounted Police like I do, an' Corporal Downey in partic'lar, I'd say that if our fall fund was twice as big as what we could make it, we couldn't even spit on the sidewalk in Dawson without gittin' pinched. In fact, Beezely, the whole scheme is cock-eyed. A mob like that wouldn't git nowheres in the Yukon. It's all right down in the States, where you can shift around amongst crooked policemen, an' politicians, an' prosecutors, an' judges—but down here it's different. There ain' no politicians, an' the Mounted is policemen, prosecutors, an' judges—an' they ain't crooked."

"Every man's got his price," Beezely retorted.

"Yeah?" grinned Black John, "Well, when you find Corporal Downey's price, would you mind lettin' me know what it is?"

"If you think the scheme is cock-eyed, why were you so interested in knowing whether or not I could put up my share of the fall fund?" asked the attorney.

"Merely fer yer own good," the big man replied. "An' mebbe fer our good, too. You see, when you come in to Cush's I seen that you took good care that yer small pack, yonder, didn't git no further than arm's reach away from you at no time. Whilst we stood at the bar, it was right beside yer elbow, an' when we went over to the table to play stud, you laid it beside yer chair. So I figgered that it contained somethin' of value. I didn't like to say nothin' over there, on account of One Armed John er the klooch might of listened in, so I invited you over here. The invitation stands—you can stay here as long as you like until you find a location of yer own—but I wanted to warn you that if you had anythin' of much value in yer pack, you better deposit it in Cush's safe. You took notice, I suppose, that the safe ain't exactly empty—there's better'n a half million in it, right now—an' that's because it's the only place on Halfaday where a man can keep his gold er his cash where it will be absolutely safe, an' where he can git it the minute he wants it. It's a damn good, four-bolt safe. There can't no one bust into it. Just between me an' you, I don't mind admittin' that there's certain characters on the crick whose morals in regard to property is open to question. An' I'd hate like hell to see one of 'em git their hands on yer ninety-six thousan', or yet on the roll you've got in yer pocket. Not only you'd lose the money, but you'd immediately an' rightly report the loss to the police, an' we'd have 'em up here on the crick, snoopin' around till they found who done it. Like I told you, we keep Halfaday moral."

"How about hiding the stuff some place?"

Black John grinned. "You could try cachin' it if you want to. But as the Good Book says, when in Rome do as the roamers do. You seen fer yerself that Cush's safe is the repository fer the wealth of Halfaday—an' there's a reason. Several has tried cachin' their stuff, but somehow no matter how careful they was, it always turned up missin'. If a man is suspected of havin' a cache, he's a marked man, an' there ain't no minute that there ain' someone's eyes on him. If they can't locate it no other way, they watch him till he goes to it. Mebbe he goes to it only once—when he's pullin' out of Halfaday—but that once is enough. Sometimes we find his body; an' sometimes we don't—but in no case do we ever find his property. Of course, if it was only me an' Cush that know'd you had the money, that would be different. But there's One Armed John, an' there's the klooch. They seen what me an' Cush seen—an' don't fergit it. An' from the time you walked out of that saloon until such time as you've deposited yer property in the safe, there'll be eyes on you every minute."

"Do you mean—now?" asked Beezely, with a swift glance about the room, "You mean that someone is watching us now?"

"Well, not here in the cabin, but you can bet on it that someone is watchin' the door, an' they'll know if you carry that small pack when you go out er not—an' I shore don't want that much wealth cached around here. My advice is to carry it back an' stick it in the safe—an' most of that pocket roll along with it. I wouldn't advise carryin' around no more than a thousan' at the outside. There wouldn't hardly no one stoop to murder a man fer a mere thousan'."

BEEZELY TOSSED off his drink and rose nervously. "Let's be getting back to the saloon," he said. "I'm obliged to you for giving me this tip. You think we can make it, do you? That is—there's no danger of anyone bumping us off between here and there?"

"Oh hell, no! There won't no one pull nothin' whilst I'm around. It's the stuff that's pulled while I ain't here that's got me worried. Fetch yer pack, an' we'll be goin'."

The man stepped to the bunk, loosened the straps of the two packs, and hastily slipped a package from the smaller into the larger one. Then he secured the smaller pack, and accompanied Black John to the saloon, keeping close beside him all the way, as his beady eyes darted swift glances into the bush on either side of the trail.

Old Cush set out bottle and glasses as the two entered. When the glasses were filled, the attorney loosened the straps of the sack he had set upon the bar.

"I have considerable cash here," he said, addressing Cush, "and my friend advised me to deposit it in your safe. I wish you would take it, and if there is any charge I'll be glad to pay it." As he spoke he lifted out packet after packet of bills of large denomination, and piled them on the bar.

"There ain't no charge," Cush replied, his eyes widening at sight of the ever increasing pile. "Count it, an' I'll give you a receipt."

The counting took some time, and at its conclusion, the man pulled the thick roll from his pocket and counted off seven thousand more. "There you are," he said, "one hundred and three thousand, in good cash." He paused and frowned, as his eyes lingered on the pile. "And it should be more than double that!" he snapped. "I left Chicago in a hurry with plenty of hot bonds on my hands—and hit Seattle without having made proper connections. The result was that I was forced to dispose of them to those damned coast crooks at a terrible sacrifice. I wanted to deal quickly, and the dirty thieves took advantage of me. But—I'll square the account, sometime!"

Black John shook his head solemnly. "Tch, tch, tch," he uttered, "Don't it beat hell how some folks carries on? It's almost enough to make a man lose faith in human nature."

"Sure it is," agreed Beezely indignantly. "I could have got twice that amount out of those bonds if I could have stayed on for a few days in Chicago, or had time to slip down to Frisco. It's a damn shame how they'll take advantage of a man. But of late it seems that every man's hand is against me. Why, gentlemen, I haven't even a relative in the world to turn to!"

III

WITH HIS MONEY locked in Cushing's safe, Beezely shared Black John's cabin, spending his days roaming up or down the creek inspecting the abandoned claims that the big man described to him, and his evenings in playing stud in the saloon.

One morning, a week after Beezely's arrival, Cush asked Black John an abrupt question as the two stood drinking together at the bar. "How do you like yer lodger, John?"

Black John grinned. "Oh, about as well as the average man would, I s'pose. Why?"

"Nothin'—except that it looks to me like he could of found some place to suit him before this. Here, he's been pokin' around amongst all the empty shacks on the crick fer a week."

"Yeah, he went way up that feeder to look over Whiskey Bill's old shack, today. I was tellin' him about it last night."

"Olson's old cabin, down the crick, is the best of the bunch—best claim, too."

"Yeah, that's what I told him, but when I told him about Olson, an' Stamm, an' some of the others that's sojourned in it, he claimed it was too unlucky to suit him."

"Huh," grunted Cush, "with his luck, it don't look like he'd have to worry none. He ain't made a damn losin' at stud, yet. Wins every night. Just shoved ten thousan' more in the safe fer him this mornin'!"

"H-u-m, that makes a hundred an' thirteen thousan', don't it?"

"Shore it does. An' I'm jest wonderin' if he ain't crooked."

Black John's grin widened. "Why, Cush! Shorely you wouldn't suspect a lawyer that would do all he done fer his clients, of crookedness, would you?"

"Well, I don't know. About the cards, I mean. It looks like he's got just too damn much luck fer one man to have. But we've never ketched him at nothin'. An' several of the boys has been watchin' pretty close, too. Tellin' you about me, I've never seen no man yet, which he had a couple of snake eyes set right up agin' a thin nose, that I'd trust him very fer. This here Beezely, every time he opens them hard, thin lips of his'n, I expect to see a forked tongue snick out an' in. An' another thing, I don't like the way them eyes sort of lingers on the safe, neither."

"Oh, he's just kind of interested in the safe, I guess. He's got quite a lot in it."

"Yeah," answered Cush dryly. "Well—so've we."

A form darkened the doorway, and a man stepped hurriedly into the room and advanced to the bar. Both saw that he was one Booker T. Breckenridge, a name-canner who had appeared on Halfaday some six months before, and located a claim up the creek. He was a quiet man, who minded his own business. Black John rather liked him.

"Hello, Book," he greeted. "Jest in time to j'ine us in a drink. Cush is about to buy one."

Old Cush, slid a glass toward the newcomer, and entered a round of drinks against Black John in the day book. Breckenridge downed the drink and turned to the big man.

"Can I see you a few minutes alone?" he asked. "It's important."

"Why, shore. Jest step on over to my cabin." When the two were seated Black John filled and lighted his pipe. "What's on yer mind?" he asked abruptly. "I ain't seen you around fer a couple of weeks."

"No, I been workin' pretty hard up on the claim. That stuff's gittin' better as she goes down. What I wanted to tell you—I come up out of the hole this mornin' to crank up my bucket, when who the hell was standin' there but Old Quince Beezely, the crookedest damn skunk that ever walked on his hind legs! An' what's more, he claimed he was stoppin' with you."

"Yeah," admitted the big man, "Beezety's stoppin' here till he can look him up a location."

"Location—hell! He's got his location, all right."

"Goin' into Whiskey Bill's old shack, eh? Well, that ain't such a bad proposition, if a man was to work it right."

"Goin' into Cush's safe!" exploded the other. "Old Quince never got his claws on an honest dollar in his life."

"What makes you say he's crooked?" asked Black John mildly. "He told me he was a criminal lawyer."

The other's lips twisted into a wry grin. "He is," he said. "Both. An' the reason I say he's crooked is because it's the God's truth. He's crooked, an' he's smart—so damn smart that if he hadn't been crooked, he could have cleaned up a million."

"Then he ain't smart," grinned Black John.

"That's right, too—in a way. What I mean, there wasn't a mouthpiece in the country that could keep a guy out of stir like Quince Beezely could. He knows all the tricks—an' invented new ones. He'd have a jury wipin' the sympathy out of their eyes fer some stiff that bumped off his gran'mother fer her insurance money. He'd grease everyone from the cops to the judge, an' fix the jury, to boot. He'd git a yegg out on bail so he could pull some job that would pay fer his defence. Not only that, he'd lay out the job fer him, an' case it, an' then dispose of the stuff—an' then he'd git the guy off when he come to trial. An' not only that, but he'd work on the parole board fer some guy that was already doin' a stretch. Oh, he was a lulu, Quince was—until he got to playin' both ends against the middle."

"Yeah," observed Black John, "he told me that he always had the best interests of his clients at heart."

"AN' THAT'S a damn lie, too," retorted the other. "Here's one he pulled a year ago—jest before I come away. He laid out a big mail robbery job, an' got a mob together that was the tops. The job was pulled. The boys took that mail car like Grant took Richmond, an' made a clean git-away to a bungalow Quince had rented over on the west side. There was about twenty-thirty thousan' in cash, an' bonds that run right around a quarter of a million. Quince took over all the stuff—the cash for the fall money, in case anything went wrong—an' the bonds to dispose of when the heat cooled.

"Well, somethin' went wrong, all right. Two nights later the cops crashed the hideout an' gathered in the whole mob. One dick got knocked off—an' that made two murders, countin' the mail clerk. What happened? Quince had tipped off the bulls—see? But up to then the mob didn't know that. They laid their hard luck to Dopey Dick Fliegle, cause he had slipped out to the corner that night to git a paper. The boys didn't worry none. They figgered they wasn't so bad off. Old Quince would sure clear 'em at the trial. But Quince didn't. He lost every one of them cases. The whole mob—there was six of 'em—got life, an' Quince got the cash an' the bonds.

"The boys tumbled, then. They squawked their heads off down in Joliet. But you know how much weight a guy's squawk carries when he's in stir fer the long stretch—an' not a friend on the outside. They laughed at 'em."

Black John's brow knitted in a frown. "Didn't they have no connections—no pals on the outside—that would sort of take care of Beezely fer double-crossin' 'em?"

Breckenridge laughed shortly. "I told you Quince was smart. He handpicked that mob. He knows every damn crook in the country. There wasn't a damn man in it that wasn't in bad fer double-crossin' some pal, er turnin' state's evidence, er somethin'. There wasn't a crook in the country that didn't laugh with the screws when they heard the squawk. They'd even laughed harder if the mob had got the rope. Most of 'em didn't believe Quince had crossed 'em up, an' them that did said it was a damn good thing—an' liked Quince all the better."

"H-u-m," Black John grunted, "but even so, what a man done before he come to Halfaday ain't none of our business. It's what he does after he gits here that interests us. You mentioned, a while back, somethin' about Cush's safe."

"Only that Quince figgers on takin' it, is all," grinned Breckenridge.

"How do you know?"

"I know because he told me." The man's voice became suddenly hard. "Git an earful of this. There's plenty on me back in the States, an' Old Quince knows it; he knows a lot more about it than even the cops do, an' they know plenty. I'm wanted on a rap that's good fer the long stretch, an' not a chance of beatin' it—see? When I hit here an' draw'd that name out of the can I figgered I'm all set. I like it here. I believe I've got a good thing up the crick, an' I want to stay with it. I'm on the up-an'-up, here on Halfaday. I ain't claimin' I always will be, nor none of that crap. Mebbe I will; an' mebbe I won't. Anyhow, it's the first time in years that I ain't be'n lookin' over my shoulder. Now Quince shows up. He lamps me the minute I lamps him—see? He figgers I'm right down his alley. He knows there ain't no box made that I can't git on the inside of. He tells me how much is in that old can of Cush's, an' how you guys all think it's the nuts. Hell, that can wouldn't stop me fifteen minutes! I could kick a hole in it anywheres, an' you can hear them damn old tumblers rattle clean acrost the room. Quince, he claims he's got the latest thing that's out in the way of a jointed can-opener."

"Yeah," agreed Black John. "I was lookin' it over. I seen him lift a package out of one sack an' stick it another the day he come, so one day when he was off down the crick, I looked it over. It seems like a useful tool. A man could git a hell of a leverage with it, when all them parts was screwed together."

"Sure, but I wouldn't need no tool to crack that box. Hell, I could go over there right now an' git into it as quick as Cush could. Quince can case a job, all right, but when it comes down to doin' the work, he'd be jest like any other punk—thinkin' a man would need a can-opener fer a job like that! It makes me laugh. Claimed he had a bottle of soup, too."

"Soup! You mean he's got nitro glycerine in that bottle? Cripes, I thought it was some kind of licker!"

THE OTHER grinned. "If you take a drink of it, don't set down hard fer a while. But layin' the kiddin' aside. Quince means business. I didn't say much, jest let him go ahead an' talk. He's figgerin' on pullin' the job Sunday night. He claims that the boys will prob'ly play stud all night Saturday, an' Cush will close early on Sunday night. Claims that's what they done last week. Says we ought to be in the clear by midnight Sunday."

Black John nodded. "Yeah, he's about right, at that."

"He claimed there was enough paper in the box so we wouldn't have to bother with the gold; it would be too heavy."

"We?"

"Sure—me an' him. He's rung me in on the job, see? I told him right flat that I wouldn't have nothin' to do with it. You guys has been on the level with me. An' like I said, fer the last six months I ain't been lookin' over my shoulder. But Quince just grins when I tells him that. 'You'll begin lookin' over yer shoulder agin, damn quick,' he says, 'whether you take on this job, er not. The police in Dawson will have yer prints, an' a damn good description—an' a long record. An' I can help 'em out with more, plenty more. They'd appreciate a tip on where yer hidin' out.'" The man paused, and ran his fingers nervously through his hair. "An' the hell of it is, he's right. But I'll be damned if I'll pull that job! I come damn near killin' Quince where he stood, but I know'd what a miners' meetin' would do about that."

"Yeah," agreed Black John. "We don't encourage murder on Halfaday."

"It looks like I'm on the spot, no matter which way the cat jumps."

Black John combed at his thick beard with his fingers. "Oh, I don't know. It's only Wednesday. There's quite a bit of time to figger, between now an' Sunday night. Why not just let him go ahead an' pull the job, the way he's got it figgered out?"

"Pull the job!" exclaimed the man. "Hell, it won't be him pullin' it! It'll be me! He'll be damn good an' careful not to show up in it. You know damn well what a miners' meetin' would do to a guy caught robbin' that safe! An' Old Quince would be the first one to grab the rope. Damn if I'll git mixed up in any job on Halfaday. I'll take it on the lam, first."

The blue-gray eyes of the big man met the eyes of the other squarely. "I've got my faults," he said with seeming irrelevance. "But double-crossin' a pal ain't one of 'em. An' I'm advisin' you to go ahead."

The man's eyes held Black John's long and searchingly. "O.K.," he said. "I'll take a chance. I better be hittin' back now. Quince went on up the crick. He told me I better think it over. Said he'd stop late this afternoon fer my answer. Where'll I see you before Sunday night?"

"Saturday night, like Beezely said, there'll be a stud game. Beezely'll be settin' in it. At ten o'clock I'll drop out an' go out back. You be waitin' there."

"O.K. I'll be seein' you."

A few minutes later, when Black John strolled into the saloon, Old Cush regarded him searchingly as he set out the bottle and glasses "What did he want?" he asked.

"What did who want?"

"Why, Breckenridge, of course. Who'd you think I meant?"

"Oh—him. Cripes, I'd fergot he'd even been down here. Why, he run in amongst some rocks in his shaft an' wanted to borrow, my pick."

"Borry a pick? What was so damn private about that?"

The big man shrugged. "Why, damn if I know. You know how some folks is—kind of secretive that-a-way. Hell, Cush, you don't think I'd lie to you, do you?"

IV

THE FOLLOWING MORNING Beezely took leave of Black John. "I'm obliged to you," he said, as he departed from the cabin with his pack, "fer the tip about depositing my money, and for your royal hospitality. I only hope that I may, someday, be permitted to return the favors. I rather like that place of Whiskey Bill's, and I may like mining. At least, I've decided to stay here until fall. The life in the open will do me good. In the meantime, I shall endeavor to get down to the fort at least on Saturday nights for the stud game. I shall, of course, keep in touch with you, and should you reconsider that matter of organization we can doubtless embark in a very prosperous enterprise. If not, in the fall, I think I shall move on to Dawson and open an office for the practice of law. I engaged a man I ran across up the creek—Breckenridge, he said his name was—to assist me in moving my supplies up the creek in my canoe. He will doubtless be waiting for me at the fort. Good-bye, my friend. I'll be toddling along, now. I have a long trail ahead of me—and a rough one."

"I'll say you have," muttered the big man, as the other turned from the door. "Mebbe not such a long trail, but a damn rough one."

Promptly at ten o'clock on Saturday night, Black John temporarily checked out of the stud game and stepping out the door, passed around to the rear to find Breckenridge waiting for him in the black shadow of the storeroom.

"Got yer plans all laid?" he asked.

"We did have, but we've got to change 'em, or there's sure as hell goin' to be a murder on Halfaday."

"Who," asked Black John, "would murder who?"

"Peanuts Landowski an' the Duke will murder Old Quince. Listen—did Quince give you the low-down on why he had to get out of Chicago?"

"Yeah, he claimed that he'd got disbarred, an' besides that, there was a matter of some indictments the grand jury found agin him. Spite work, he claimed it was, amongst the prosecutor an' some other lawyers."

"Disbarments an' indictments—hell!" scoffed the other. "That old fox would of beat all them raps with his eyes shut. But his eyes wasn't shut, by a damn sight, an' when he picked up his newspaper one mornin' an' seen where there'd been a jail-break down at Joliet, an' Peanuts Landowski and the Duke was on the loose, he know'd it was either lam er croak, fer him. An' he know'd, too, that Joliet ain't no hell of a ways from Chi. So he gathers what's loose an' handy, an' fades. You see, Peanuts an' the Duke is two of that mob he double-crossed, an' take it from me, either one of 'em's plenty tough. An' no one knows that any better'n Old Quince Beezely. It was Peanuts that blasted that cop when they took the mob, an' the Duke has knifed two guys that I know of. He's a killer," added the man, with a shudder. "He kills jest fer fun—er else he's nuts, er somethin'. These guys was both knifed in their own house when the Duke was h'istin' their wife's jewelry—an' there wasn't no need of it. An' in the hang-outs the Duke bragged about it, an' laughed."

"An' you think these two characters is on Halfaday?" asked Black John. "That they followed Beezely here?"

"Think! I know damn well they're here. I talked to 'em. As fer followin' Quince—partly they did, an' partly they didn't. It's like this, when they crashes out of stir there's eight of 'em in it, an' two screws is bumped off. They scatter, an' it takes Peanuts an' the Duke two days to make Chicago, on account they got to git clothes, an' heel themselves. The heat's on, an' they see by the papers how five of the boys ain't had no luck. One is shot, an' four is back in Joliet—two in the hospital.

"Peanuts an' the Duke knows they're takin' a big chance, but they try to git to Old Quince. The Duke was tellin' me about it; an' believe me, if you could see his eyes when he told it, you would hate to be Old Quince Beezely—if he found you er not! He claimed he'd of carved Quince up if he know'd he'd walk on the trap the next minute—an' he would. But they couldn't find Quince, an' Chicago was pretty hot fer 'em—what with neither one of 'em standin' in too good with the boys, an' all. So they reads in the papers about this here Klondike, just like I done, an' decides to fade out here. They figgered if there was gold here like the papers claimed, there'd be pickin's. They finances themselves with a couple of jobs on the north shore, an' lams.

"In Seattle they run acrost Old Quince's trail. They got to git rid of some stuff from them two jobs they pulled, an' they find out how Quince had took a big loss on a lot of bonds—the bonds that they'd got on the mail car job.

"Well, if a guy is in Seattle, turnin' off his stuff at a loss, it's a cinch he's hittin' fer the Klondike—like everyone else in Seattle is, except a man would live there. So Peanuts an' the Duke takes on a new hope about Quince. But when they git to Dawson, Quince ain't there—an' no one has saw him. They hangs out at the Klondike Palace an' meets all the boys that's on the make around Dawson, but no one has saw Quince—but he might be out on some crick. So they hangs around, an' cases some jobs, but they don't pull nothin', an' some of the Dawson boys puts 'em hep to that old can of Cush's. They claimed it could be took like takin' candy from a baby. Claimed they damn near took it one time, but the job went wrong on account that a fat guy which they sent on ahead to case the job, sold 'em out, an' they was scairt they was goin' to git hung by a miners' meetin', but the miners' meetin' turned 'em loose on account of no evidence, an' they hung the fat guy themselves, on a crick back in the mountains."

Black John nodded thoughtfully. "So, that's what become of him, eh? I kind of mistrusted they would, at that. But go ahead with yer story."

"Well, there ain't much more to tell. None of them Dawson Boys wanted in on the job, but they told Peanuts an' the Duke how to git here, an' that there wasn't no cops here, nor nothin', so they decided to come up here an' take the box alone."

"How come they got in touch with you?"

"That was by accident. You see, Old Quince, he's been mosе-yin' up an' down the crick, casin' it, while he's pretendin' to look fer a location, an' he looks over a cabin, down the crick that used to belong to some guy named Olson, er some Swede name like that, an' he figgers that this cabin would be a good place fer him to wait in while I was pullin' the job. Then I would come down there with the stuff, an' we could pull right out fer the big river, with a good start. So today, I takes them supplies Quince bought off'n Cush—the ones I was supposed to help him up to Whiskey Bill's shack with the other day—an' who in hell do I walk into but Peanuts an' the Duke. They jest got there this mornin' an' is figgerin' on hangin' out there till they kin case this job. Well, they both know'd me the minute they lamped me, an' knowin' that a job like this is right down my alley, they votes me in. I try to duck it, but settin' there lookin' at the Duke kind of fingerin' that long bladed knife of his whilst he was tellin' about Old Quince, I didn't put up no hell of an argument—jest kind of stalled along. I sure as hell hate a knife, an' I hate the way the Duke handles one—kind of lovin' like, while he touches the blade here an' there with a little hone. So I'm counted in an' we leaves it that we'll wait a few days an' kind of case the job, an' the git-away, an' all."

"Did you tell 'em about Beezely bein' on the crick?"

"Hell no! I know you don't favor murder on Halfaday, an' the way they feel about Quince, there's no tellin' what they'd do. They didn't even know about the supplies I took down there. When I seen someone was in the cabin, I left the supplies in the canoe, an' when I come away I shoved up the crick a ways an' cached 'em in the brush, canoe an' all, an' come on up the foot trail."

"That's good," approved Black John. "You done right."

"But it leaves me in a hell of a spot—a damn sight worse than before. If I don't throw in with Quince, he'll turn me in. If I do, I git hung by miners' meetin'. If I don't throw in with Peanuts an' the Duke, I git that long thin blade shoved between my ribs, an' if I do, there's that hangin' again."

Black John grinned. "Yeah," he agreed, "it does look kind of 'out of the fryin' pan into the fire' as the Good Book says, no matter which way you jump, don't it? In such case, if I was you, I'd pursue a middle course."

"What do you mean? Damn it!" the man suddenly exclaimed, "You know, since I been up here, workin' that claim of mine, I've felt better'n ever I felt since I was a kid. I like it—like takin' out that gold. I like to look at it, an' feel of it—an' I like to think that it's damn good an' clean. It's mine—an'—an'—oh, hell! I don't know. Seems like I've kind of got a different slant on things, I guess. I was feelin' fine till that damn old Quince showed up—an' now these two guys. I know'd 'em all before, back there in the States, an' while I never really, what you could say, liked 'em—they seemed sort of all right. But now, listenin' to 'em talk an' all, I can sort of see what a rotten lot they are. But that don't git me nothin'. 'Once a crook; always a crook' is a true sayin', I guess. No matter where a man goes, he can't git away from 'em."

"Oh, I don't know, son," Black John replied. "I guess mebbe it'll work out all right in the long run. Hell, I used to be more er less shady in my ethics, myself—an' look at me now! You jest go ahead an' do like I said—sort of let things drift. Cush will close up early Sunday night, but you won't have to rob the safe. Beezely'll be down the crick—waitin' till you git there. Jest go ahead like he planned it, an' let nature take her course."

"But he'll hit for Olson's shack to wait. An' that's where Peanuts an' the Duke are!"

"Yeah, that's what you said."

"But they'll kill him sure as hell—jest as soon as he sticks his nose in the door!"

"That," said Black John dryly, "is merely a conjecture—simply an expression of opinion on your part. To twist an' old sayin' around if better comes to best, an' they should happen to knock him off, I wouldn't know of no one that needs it more—except, mebbe, the two that killed him, would you? If they knock Beezely off, that will be their business. But in doin' so, they'd be committin' a murder—an' that would be our business. Murder ain't condoned, on Halfaday. We'd have to call a miners' meetin'.

An', if they was found guilty, it looks like we might go the Good Book one better, an' kill three birds with one stone, instead of two."

V

THE STUD GAME lasted all Saturday night, with the result that business was dull at Cushing's Fort on Sunday. At ten o'clock Cush barred the doors, and took his rifle from its accustomed place, put out the lights, and letting himself out the back door, headed for Black John's cabin, a short distance up the creek. "Wonder what in hell give John the notion of a moonlight moose hunt tonight?" he grumbled. "Any more meat than what we got on hand would spile, weather like this. I told him that, an' he jest kind of grinned. Chances is he's got somethin' else on his mind. You can't never tell what John's thinkin' by what he says."

In the cabin were Black John, Red John, Long John, and Breckenridge. The big man glanced at his watch.

"Come on," he said, "we'll be goin'. Breckenridge says Beezely went on down the crick twenty minutes ago. We don't want to be in too much of a hurry, nor yet we don't want to be too late, neither."

"What in hell we follerin' Beezely fer?" asked Cush, falling in directly behind Black John on the narrow foot trail down the creek. "Where is he headin'?"

"That," replied the big man, "is more or less a matter of conjecture. Some theologians hold that—"

"What in hell's all them big words got to do with it?" interrupted Cush impatiently. "Why can't you come right out an' tell me where Beezely's goin'?"

"Because, I don't know myself. I ain't made up my mind, yet, whether to accept the good old Presbyterian theory of instant damnation, er the milder one put out by the Catholics—with a sort of half-way house between. Then there's the doctrine of utter annihilation; that's well thought of by some, an' would undoubtless be a comfort to many."

"You mean Beezely's dead?" exclaimed Cush. "If he is, how in hell could he be goin' down the creek?"

"Well, he could be floatin' down, if he was dead," grinned Black John. "But he ain't—not jest at this minute—unless he's travelled faster'n what I think he has."

"You mean, we're goin' to kill him?" cried Cush. "Is that why we're all fetchin' our rifles? Cripes, John, we can't do that! If he's pulled off somethin', we can call a miners' meetin'. We don't want no unlegal killin's on Halfaday!"

"Hell, you know as well as I do, I wouldn't kill no one. We're goin' to call a miners' meetin'—in case the facts warrant one. We're goin' down here a ways to arrest a couple of fellas, in case a murder should have come off."

"But what's Beezely got to do with it?"

"Well, speakin' in a dramatical way—he's cast in a roll. One might almost say, he's the protagonist—"

"Why—the damn cuss! Is that some form of skullduggery, John?"

"Yeah," replied Black John. "In his case, it seems to embrace about every form of skullduggery there is."

HARDLY WERE the words out of his mouth than the silence of the night was split by a long, thin scream, then another that ended abruptly—eerie, bloodcurdling screams, they were—screams of mortal terror and agony. The five men stopped in their tracks, in the profound silence of the moonlit night.

Old Cush, his eyes gleaming wildly, stared into the face of Black John. "My God," he cried, "it's down there jest around the next bend—at Olson's old shack! I'm goin' back. I always know'd that shack was unlucky."

"Yeah," agreed Black John dryly, "that's what Beezely claimed. An' I've got a hunch that mebbe he was right. We'll go on down an' see."

Pushing on to the edge of the little clearing that surrounded the cabin, the five concealed themselves in the thick brush, their eyes focused on the oblong of lamplight that showed through the open door, not more than thirty feet distant from where they stood. Low voices could be heard from the cabin, and part of a man's posterior could be seen as he evidently stooped over something on the floor.

Presently the man straightened up, and a moment later he backed out the door, closely followed by another man, walking forward. Between them they supported a limp human form—the dead body of J.Q.A. Beezely.

At a whispered word from Black John, five rifles were cocked, and five men stepped from the edge of the bush into the clearing, their guns covering the two who had stepped from the cabin.

"You can lay him down there," said Black John in a hard, brittle voice. "We'll 'tend to the buryin'. An' then you better reach high, er some of these guns is liable to go off."

"Who the hell are you?" demanded the larger of the two men, truculently. "An' what the hell you buttin' in here fer?"

"The name is Smith—Black John, fer short."

"Oh, so you're the guy that tried to hang them Dawson boys the time you claimed they was up here to crack a box, eh?"

"Yeah, I'm him—er one of 'em. I rec'lect we bungled that job, on account of Corporal Downey comin' along just at the wrong time. An' besides, them boys hadn't committed no murder—till after they'd got off the crick."

"An' this ain't no murder either. We had to bump this guy off in self defence. You've no witness that we didn't."

"That's right," grinned Black John. "What did he attack you with—his toupée?"

"He pulled a gun on us. That's what he did!"

"Tut, tut, Duke."

"Duke!"

"Well, Peanuts, then. It don't make no difference, except fer the head slabs. Mr. Beezely put up with me fer a week er so, an' I happen to know that he didn't have no gun."

"Where the hell did you git them names?" demanded the man, peering toward the five, but not glimpsing the face of Breckenridge who was purposely, keeping behind Black John.

"We didn't git 'em—they're yourn," replied the big man. "Where you got 'em ain't none of our business, no more'n it's any of our business whatever you done before you come to Halfaday. After you got here, though, what you done is our business—like murderin' Beezely an' aimin' to rob our safe. You've compounded yer felonies, by addin' murder on top of skullduggery."

"It's a damn lie!" cried the man, his face contorted with rage. "You can't prove a word of it."

"Oh, yes he kin, Duke," said a voice, as Breckenridge stepped out from behind the big man. "An' he can prove that you threatened to kill old Quince Beezely on sight, too."

"Dink McQuire!" screamed the other, as with a swift movement a long blade gleamed in the moonlight as he drew back his arm. There was a loud explosion, and the man pitched forward upon his face.

Black John, standing a pace or two in front of the other, never turned his head. "Everyone throw a fresh shell in his gun," he ordered. "The miners' meetin' will have to investigate this fresh killin'. An' it would be better if we wasn't to find no empty shell in anyone's gun. Come on, now—we'll be takin' this other one along before somethin' definite happens to him."

The man, Peanuts, and the two bodies were searched, Black John deftly retaining only a small scrap of paper—which was Cush's receipt for Beezely's deposit. Magnanimously, he turned over to Long John some thousand dollars in currency.

"Just divide that up amongst you three," he said. "Me an' Cush wouldn't care to participate. There wasn't nothin' found on Beezely, these others havin' prob'ly frisked him before carryin' him out. An' there wouldn't be no use to bother the public administrator with it—on account of them names not bein' no help in huntin' out heirs. We'll go on back, now, an' stick Peanuts in the hole. We'll call the miners' meetin' fer tomorrow afternoon."

VI

WITH THE PRISONER deposited in "the hole," a narrow subterranean cell beneath the storeroom floor, and a barrel of pork rolled into place on the trap, the others dispersed, leaving Black John alone with Cush.

In silence Cush set out a bottle and two glasses, and each poured a drink. Cush was the first to speak. "So it was Breckenridge put you on to this here racket, was it?" he inquired. Pausing suddenly, he lowered his chin, and peered at the other over the square rims of his steel spectacles. "So that was what he wanted to speak to you private about t'other day—when you claimed he'd come down to borry a pick?"

"A pick did I say, Cush?"

"Yeah, you claimed he'd run onto some rocks in his shaft, an' he wanted to borry a pick."

"Oh, yeah—I rec'lect of givin' you some sort of an evasive answer. But I fergot that I'd mentioned a pick."

"What difference does that make?"

"Why yeah, what difference does it?"

"What I mean—ain't that when he told you?"

"Oh, shore. I didn't want to worry you none. You see, he told me that Beezely was aimin' to rob the safe."

"Beezely! Cripes sakes, you told them other fellas it was them that was aimin' to rob it."

"Yeah, they was—but that was after. They wasn't even on the crick, then."

Cush shoved his spectacles to his forehead in a gesture of resignation. "It's too damn mixed up fer me," he said wearily. "I don't seem to grasp no holt of it."

Black John grinned. "Jest open the safe," he said. "An' grasp holt of that package of Beezely's, an' set it out here on the bar.

When Cush had complied, Black John lifted it, and began to remove the bands from the various packets of bills. "A hundred an' thirteen thousan' dollars in good currency," he said. "An' you rec'lect Beezely told us he didn't have a relative in the world! It's hell, ain't it, Cush, when a man ain't got no relative to leave his property to? It kind of looks like his fall-fund had fell, at last. Ah, well—it jest goes to show that honesty is the best policy in the long run. Come on, we might's well git it divided up—share an' share alike, Cush—just like we let them other three boys divide up what we found on them others. Trouble with Old Quince Beezely, he didn't have no ethics."

THE SOURDOUGHS VISIT HALFADAY

BLACK JOHN SMITH turned from the bar, where two empty glasses and a bottle gave mute evidence that the day's activity had begun, to face the three men who stood grinning in the open doorway.

"Well, I'll be damned if it ain't the sourdoughs!" he exclaimed. "By God, I know'd it was only a question of time till you old reprobates would be seekin' the sanctity of Halfaday! But I figgered you'd kind of trickle in, one to a time, fer individual infringements of the law. What sort of mass crime did you commit—tip over somebody's backhouse? Come on in. Cush is buyin' a drink. We jest been havin' our mornin's mornin'."

Old Bettles, dean of the sourdoughs, glanced at the clock and shook his head disapprovingly as the three advanced to the bar. "Here it is nine o'clock, lackin' of fifteen minutes, an' you jest havin' yer mornin's mornin'. Cripes—we've been five hours on the trail!"

Black John grinned, as old Cush set out the glasses. "Oh, shore. There's been times when I've had to git an early start an' pick 'em up an' lay 'em down pretty fast, too. Like them first few days immediately subsequent to that army payroll job. But now that my conscience is clear, I kin kind of take things easy. How much of a start do you figger you've got on Corporal Downey?"

"Downey sent his regards to you fellas when we told him we might swing around here," said Swiftwater Bill. "Me an' Moose-hide, an' Bettles heard of a proposition on a crick up this way, an' bein' as we'd heard so damn much about Cushing's Fort, we figgered we'd swing around an' make a social call."

"That's fine!" exclaimed Black John heartily. "Yer shore welcome, an' we'll do our damndest to show you a good time. You see, we don't git many strickly social calls. What I claim, all Halfaday needs to make it a fine place to live is good society, an' along about this time of year, mebbe a little more water in the crick."

"Yeah," grinned old Bettles, filling his glass from the bottle, "but when you come to think of it, that's all hell needs to make it a fine place to live—good society, an' more water."

"We've always got plenty of water in the spring when the boys is sluicin' out their winter dumps," defended old Cush lugubriously. "Take it along, like now, in August, we don't need no more water'n what we got. Trouble with John, he ain't never quite satisfied. I'll bet he'd change the ten commandments, if he could."

"Yer damn right I would," agreed Black John. "There's some of 'em that's irreverent an' immaterial, an' not a one of 'em mentions claim-jumpin' as a major offense. As fer as Halfaday is concerned, they could be revised to good advantage."

"August is a damn pore month, anyway," opined Old Bettles, as he contemplated the little beads that rimmed his glass of whiskey.

"In what way?" asked Moosehide Charley. "Cripes, the weather's been fine ever sence we started out on this trip."

"Yeah," agreed Bettles, "an' that's one of its main troubles. Everyone's busy, either workin' his claim, er prospectin' fer new ones. Take most any other month an' it's got somethin' to recommend it. Most of 'em's got stormy weather that fetches the boys in fer a jamboree, er else a hollerday of some sort—an' some months has got both. But look at that calendar there on the wall—not a damn red letter day in the hull month, an' it a long one, at that."

SEEMS LIKE Worshin'ton's birthday used to come sometime along in August," said Moosehide.

"I disremember it that way," said Swiftwater Bill. "Seems to me like it come in the winter."

"I don't rec'lect," Bettles cut in, "but it wouldn't cut no figger, nohow. The Yukon's in Canady, an' Canady's British—an' their calendars shore as hell wouldn't brag up Worshin'ton's Birthday, no matter what month it come in. Cripes, George Worshin'ton would be lucky if they didn't leave off his birthday altogether. Them Mexicans is the ones to have hollerdays. I put in a couple of years prospectin' down in Mexico, an' every month has got from two to a dozen hollerdays in it, account of saints dyin' off. It's a good way to have it. It gives a man a chanct to git caught up with his stud, an' his drinkin'."

"What's a saint?" asked Moosehide.

"Oh, he's some fella that's dead. It tells about 'em in the Good Book, er somewheres like that. Someone which he was stoned to death, er b'iled in oil."

"Stoned to death, an' b'iled in oil! How come?"

"Oh, it was jest one of them quaint old customs they had them days," Bettles explained. "If someone didn't believe like the rest of 'em, they'd either b'ile him up in a big kittle of oil, er tie him up to a hitchin' post an' throw rocks at him till he was dead, er mebbe they'd feed him to a lion. Then he become a saint. It's a kind of title."

"Huh," grunted Swiftwater Bill, "it looks like the title was damn hard come by."

"Yeah," admitted Bettles, "but look what it done fer the rest of humanity. Folks don't have to work that day."

"They could keep on workin' fer all of me. There ain't never goin' to be no Saint Swiftwater."

"Seems to me," said old Cush, as he set out a fresh bottle, "that I rec'lect there was a Saint Valentine, an' when his day come we use' to send ornery pitchers to the school maim, an' what girls we

didn't like. Them pitchers cost a cent apiece, an' it would make the girls mad as hell when they got one."

"Shore—I rec'lect that!" exclaimed Swiftwater. "An' there was some of them pitchers fer what girls you liked—all made up fancy with hearts, an' pigeons, an' paper lace. Them kind cost a nickel, an' some of 'em even a dime, where I come from."

"Yeah," said old Bettles, "seems if I kin rec'lect some sech doin's, too. But this here Saint Valentine would be fer too piddlin' a saint to git drunk over at this late day. An' besides his day comes in the winter, too."

"Cripes!" exclaimed Moosehide. "It looks like they all come in the winter!"

BLACK JOHN grinned. "Why, shore—that's reasonable. You kin see how it was, bein' cooped up in the house in the winter, what with the long evenin's, an' all—them folks got to augerin' about politics, an' religion, an' sech like. Take it in the summer, when the fishin' was good, an' there was horse races an' ball games to go to, no one would give a damn what these here saints believed. But in winter—that's different. They prob'ly didn't have no decent saloon to go to, so they sort of killed time with a saint-b'ilin'. It helped to pass away them long winter evenin's."

"How about this here Saint Vitus's dance?" queried Moosehide. "When does that come off at?"

"Hell, that's a disease; an' not no *fiesta!*" exclaimed Bettles.

"It's too damn bad we ain't got no local saints," said Swiftwater. "I'm beginnin' to feel in the mood to celebrate somethin' er other. Even a small saint would answer the purpose, as fer's I'm concerned." He appealed to Black John. "Accordin' to the talk, you've dealt out a hell of a lot of justice here on Halfaday. Didn't none of these here events come off in August, so we could celebrate it?"

"W-e-e-l-l, yes. I rec'lect it was along in August, a year ago, that we hung One Eyed John Smith, wasn't it, Cush?"

"It was in the summer, sometime. I disremember the exact date. I know the ground dug easy. Yeah—we could call it August. But Cripes, John—One Eyed wasn't no saint, anyway you look at him."

"Oh, I don't know. Of course, we didn't stone him to death, nor b'ile him in oil, nor neither we didn't feed him to no lion. But in case of an emergency like the present, he might be made to do. When a crisis arises, a man's got to meet it. I hereby proclaim this Tenth day of August to be Saint Smith's day, an' order an appropriate celebration to commemorate it."

"Saint Smith, somehow, ain't got the right kind of a sound," objected Bettles. "Seems like a saint ort to have a fancier name than Smith."

"Well, Saint One Eye don't sound so good, neither," opined Swiftwater.

"We can't call him Saint John," said Cush, " 'cause there's another Saint John. It would lead to confusion. I got a Bible. My last wife was religious. I read in it, now an' then, when business is slack. It tells about him in there."

"That's so," agreed Black John, gravely. "An' come to think about it, it ain't the last name they hitch the title to, nohow. No matter if it don't sound quite up to snuff, Saint One Eye it's got to be. I hereby amend the proclamation, an' change the Tenth day of August to Saint One Eye's Day."

"Hooray!" cried Swiftwater Bill. "I'll buy the first drink in honor of Saint One Eye!"

"Saint One Eye," grunted Old Cush disparagingly as he filled his glass. "If you ask me, One Eyed John would make a hell of a saint."

"If One Eyed could only know about the honor we conferred on him," grinned Black John, "he'd turn over in his grave. But it's jest as well he don't, er he'd try to cash in on it, somehow. A post mortem honor is the only kind One Eyed John could of got away with."

"What did you hang him fer?" Bettles inquired. "If a man's celebratin' a Saint, he'd kind of like to know what he was guilty of."

"Damn if I rec'lect," replied Black John. "It was ondoubtless some malfeasance, er other. Do you remember, Cush?"

"No—but heer comes One Armed John. He might know."

ONE ARMED JOHN was duly presented to the sourdoughs from Dawson, but he couldn't remember the offense for which One Eyed John had been hanged. He seemed surprised that the deceased had been elevated to the rank of a saint.

"Beats hell how a man's luck kin change," he opined. "Why, One Eyed John was the orneriest damn man on Halfaday!"

"Oh shore," admitted Black John. "But if a man needs a saint right quick he's got to use the ones that's handy. These boys has been out in the hills fer the last three weeks, they want to celebrate, an' One Eyed John was the only saint we could think of, which we hung in August. Of course, if a man was to pick his saint, he wouldn't hardly select One Eyed John. But, this here constitutes an emergency. Drink up, boys—I'm buyin' one."

"We'd ort to have a big feed along with our celebration," suggested Swiftwater Bill. "We killed a young moose, a couple of miles back. If anyone will go with me, we could fetch in a lot of good fresh meat."

"I'll go," offered Black John. "We'll fetch a couple of pack sacks full an' Cush's klooch kin bile us up a big stew. Come on, Swiftwater, so we kin git back quick. Hooray fer Saint One Eye! He's done more good in the last fifteen minutes than he ever done in his whole life! It jest goes to show that all any man needs is a little encouragement."

A HALF an hour later a man entered the door, and advanced to the bar. "Come on up the crick!" he exclaimed. "There's a man damn sick up there in his cabin. It's Grover Harrison. I'm afraid he's goin' to die. It's them damn musheroons he et."

"Musheroons!" exclaimed Cush, untying the white apron from about his middle. "It's more'n likely they was toadstools! What in hell did he eat 'em fer?"

"He claimed they was good to eat. He stopped in to my claim an' offered me some, but I didn't like the looks of 'em. That was last evenin'. This mornin' I went over to his shack on the next claim to mine, 'cause I didn't see him around his shaft, an' found him layin' in bed so damn sick I'm afraid he'll die."

"I'll go up there an' see what I kin do," said Cush, "but I shore as hell don't know no anecdote fer musheroon p'izen."

"God, we've got to do somethin'!" exclaimed the man. "Grover was the best friend I've got. Why we was jest like brothers! We even wrote out our wills, so in case one of us was to die the other one would git his claim, an' all his stuff."

"I'll go 'long with you," offered Old Bettles. "We kin take a couple of quarts along. What I claim, whiskey's the best medicine a man kin git—no matter what ails him. If we kin git two, three quarts down him, chances is it'll kill that there p'izen."

"It might help," admitted Cush doubtfully. "But when a man's time comes, he's goin' to die, no matter how much licker he drinks." Slipping some bottles into a pack sack, he tossed the apron to One Armed John. "You tend bar till we git back," he ordered. "We might be quite a while, if that man ain't dead. If John an' Swiftwater gits here first, tell 'em where we're at. John might know some anecdote we could feed him along with the licker. He's pretty handy, that way."

II

TWO HOURS LATER, Black John and Swiftwater returned to the fort, turned over a hundred pounds of choice moose meat to the Indian woman with instructions to prepare a big stew, and entered the saloon to find One Armed John presiding behind the bar.

"Where's Cush an' Old Bettles?" Black John demanded.

"Some fella come in an' claimed another fella et some musheroons, an' got sick," explained Moosehide Charley. "They went up to see what they could do about it."

"Chances is, they can't do nothin'," opined Black John. "Who was the fella?"

"The one that is claimed to have et the musheroons is that there Grover Harrison that came to Halfaday along in the spring," explained One Armed John. "An' the one that come an' told us about it is Benjamin Cleveland. He come to Halfaday pretty quick after Harrison, an' he located him a claim right next to Harrison, who had moved into Robert E. Grant's old shack."

"Ain't that jest like a damn name-canner—to git p'izened on a saint's day!" exclaimed Black John. "Not that his demise will throw no hell of a gloom over the crick—but in hot weather he won't keep an' it's a nuisance to bury him."

"What's a name-canner?" asked Moosehide Charlie.

"It got so that every malefactor that reached Halfaday give out that his name was John Smith," explained Black John. "That was all right with us till we run out of descriptive adjectives like One Eyed, One Armed, Long, Short, Pot Gutted, Black, Red, an' so forth. We seen that it was bound to lead to confusion, so about that time we hung One Eyed John, an' amongst his effects which he left was a hist'ry book. So me an' Cush copied the names out of it on slips of paper, takin' care to use the wrong front names with the right hind ones, an' then we put the slips in that there molasses can on the end of the bar. Now when someone comes we invite him to draw him a name. So if you meet up with anyone on Halfaday which he sounds historical, you'll know he's a name-canner—an' not one of us Mayflowers."

"It's a damn good scheme," approved Swiftwater Bill. "I'll buy a drink in honor of Saint One Eye. There's one good deed he done fer Halfaday, anyhow. He give you the name can!"

"That's right," agreed Black John. "We'll elect him Patron Saint of the crick—even if his good deed was entirely inadvertant, as you might say, it not happenin' till after he was hung. Drink hearty, boys—here's mud in Saint One Eye's good eye!"

"I s'pose," suggested Swiftwater, "that we'd ort to go up there an' see what we kin do. I don't s'pose Cush is no doctor, an' I know damn well Old Bettles ain't. Cripes, one time down to Forty Mile, Mrs. McSweeny's baby got the colic, an' Bettles wanted to give it half a pint of whiskey—an' it only six weeks old!"

"He took three quarts up to give this fella," said Moosehide. "Claimed whiskey will cure anything, if you take enough of it—said it would kill that musheroon p'izen."

"In such case," grinned Black John, "the most helpful thing we could do would be to begin diggin' the grave. Three quarts will kill Harrison before it does the p'izen."

Behind the bar One Armed John shrugged. "If you wanted to do somethin' helpful, John, it wouldn't hurt to kind of give this here Benjamin Cleveland the once-over."

"What do you mean?"

"Meanin'," replied One Armed John, "that mebbe Harrison et some musheroons—an' then agin, mebbe he didn't. There's other kinds of p'izen kills men besides musheroons."

"You think that mebbe Cleveland p'izened him?" asked Black John, in astonishment.

"I ain't thinkin' he did; er he didn't. He could of. An' when a man like him could of, it's more'n likely he did. I know you don't favor murder on Halfaday. I'm jest tellin' you."

"You mean, you know this Cleveland?"

"Yeah, I know him, all right. Only his name ain't Cleveland—it's Bill Snook."

"But—why would he p'izen Harrison?"

"To git his claim, an' what other stuff he's got. It wouldn't be the first time he's done it. I don't claim to be smart, like you—but when he said somethin' about wills, an' musheroon p'izen, I know'd damn well he was up to his old tricks. The police, downriver, both sides of the line, has tried to git the goods on him, but they never could prove nothin'. He'll prob'ly git away with it agin."

BLACK JOHN nodded slowly. "He might," he admitted grimly. "We'll see. Any murder's bad. But p'izenin' is the worst form of murder there is. I'd shore hate to see it got away with on Halfaday. S'pose you go ahead an' tell us what you know. In the meantime leavin' the bottle where it's handy to reach."

"The first I know'd Snook it was in a camp on Birch Crick. Him an' a fella name of Buck Huston was pardners. They'd located a couple of claims down the crick a ways, an' one day Snook come bustin' into camp hollerin' that Huston had shot hisself. He took on somethin' fierce, claimin' Buck was his best friend, an' all he had did fer him, an' how he'd ruther it was him that was dead instead of Buck. Claimed Buck come back from a hunt an' stood leanin' on his rifle, an' his dogs was friskin' around him, an' jumpin' up on him, an' one of 'em must of ketched his toe on the trigger of Buck's rifle an' pulled it off, an' the bullet went plumb through Buck's chest. We went up there, an' shore enough Buck had been shot right off'n the end of his rifle. He laid there dead as hell, an' the rifle jest like it had dropped out of his hands when he fell, jest like Snook claimed. We buried Buck, an' then Snook filed his will with the public administrator, which it left Snook everything Buck owned, incloodin' the claim, which was a pretty good one, fer them parts. He showed his own will, too, which it left Buck all he owned, in case it would be him that died off first. A constable come up an' looked around, but he couldn't find nothin' that would prove Buck hadn't got shot like Snook claimed he had, so that was the end of it. But there was plenty of us know'd that Buck Huston wouldn't never of stood leanin' on a cocked rifle, with a bunch of dogs jumpin' around him—not no other time, neither.

"Then, there was a flurry on a crick near Circle, an' the bulk of us stampeded there from Birch Crick—Snook along with the rest. He hooked up that time with Fatty Eckinrod an' they done pretty good until one day Snook come into Circle, snifflin' an' sobbin' about Fatty gittin' ketched in an ice jam on the river an' squished. He showed up with another one of them wills an' claimed all Fatty's stuff. That's over on the American side, an' we told the U.S. marshal about that time on Birch Crick, an' that other will. He done some lookin' around, but Fatty was somewhere under the ice, an' nothin' to show it wasn't an accident. So Snook got his stuff, too. But we know'd different, 'cause Fatty was a good riverman, an' he wouldn't git ketched in no ice jam unless he was shoved in. It looked like the best luck a pardner of Snook could have would be that his claim wasn't no good.

"The next one was the Bird Man. He wasn't no pardner of Snook's, but Snook was guidin' him. That was on the American side, too. There wasn't much doin' that summer—no new strikes nor nothin', an' I was tendin' bar down to Eagle. This here Bird Man, he was some scientist from the States an' he come into the country fer to git samples of all the birds there was. He'd shoot anything that wore feathers, from a hummin' bird to a swan, an' skin it an' save the hide. An' besides that he took samples of all the kinds of flowers, an' grass an' weeds he could git holt of an' saved 'em. Most of these here scientists is huntin' rocks, but the

Bird Man didn't give a damn about rocks—birds an' grass was his weakness. Snook, he hired out to guide him, an' they'd be gone out along the cricks fer a spell, an' then they'd come into Eagle, an' the Bird Man would spend a few days, sortin' out what he'd got, an' packin' it away in boxes.

"One time they come in an' the Bird Man had a lot of toadstools which he'd picked, an' he claimed they was good to eat. He took 'em to Pop Bascom's restaurant an' told Pop to cook 'em. Pop allowed they was p'izen, but the Bird Man claimed they wasn't, so Pop went ahead an' cooked 'em, an' the Bird Man set there in the restaurant an' et 'em, an' a lot of us set around watchin' him to see if he would die. But he didn't—an' I'll bet he et a quart of the damn stuff.

"Besides these ones Pop cooked, he fetched in some other kinds. But he cooked them hisself, separate, an' et jest a little bit of each kind—one each day. He claimed that he suspicioned they might be p'izen ones, so he was tryin' 'em out. One kind did make him sort of sick to his stummick fer a while, but he hadn't et enough to kill him, an' he got all right, next day.

"I s'pose that's a damn good way to find out if a thing is p'izen. But it takes guts to do it—an' what I claim—who would give a damn if it was p'izen, er not? There's plenty other stuff to eat besides toadstools.

"Well, about a month after that, Snook came bustin' into Eagle one day, an' claimed the Bird Man was sick as hell out in the hills. Old Doc Smedly went out an' found him sick, all right—so damn sick Doc couldn't do nothin' but jest set around an' watch him die. Couldn't git no medicine down him. He'd throw it up before it could take holt.

"Snook claimed that the Bird Man had cooked up a mess of them toadstools, er whatever it was he et down to the restaurant, so we wasn't surprised to hear he'd got p'izened. But when they fetched the body in, an' we found out it didn't have no more'n about ten dollars an' some change on it, we begun to wonder if it was musheroons, er somethin' else, that killed the Bird Man.

Because we all know'd he carried a roll with him—an' the most of us remembered about Buck Huston, an' Fatty Eckinrod.

"We told Doc about it, but he claimed that the only kind of p'izen there was that he could of got holt of was strychnine, fer to p'izen wolves with, an' he claimed it worn't strychnine p'izen the Bird Man died of—the symptoms was different.

"So we buried the Bird Man, an' some society er museum er somethin' back in the States sent on some money fer to ship back his samples, an' that's all there was to it—except you can't never make me believe the Bird Man died of eatin' musheroons. He know'd too damn much about 'em to eat a p'izen kind—an' his pockets bein' damn near empty when he always carried a roll."

"How come," queried Black John, "that if you was all these places where this here Snook was, he ain't recognized you on Halfaday?"

"Oh, hell—I was different, them days. I had two arms, an' no whiskers. An' my name was a little different, too."

"WELL," OPINED Moosehide Charley, "if a constable, an' a doctor, an' a U.S. marshal couldn't ketch this damn cuss at his murders, it looks like he'd git away with another one, too."

"Oh, I don't know," grinned Black John. "I've saw constables that wasn't none too wide between the ears, an' doctors, too. An' my own experience down around Fort Gibbon, in the matter of that army pay-roll, wasn't nothin' that would put me in no awe of the acumen of U.S. marshals. Off hand, from what One Armed has told us, I'd say that if this here Harrison didn't p'izen hisself with musheroons, like Cleveland claims, he'd been fed a dose of arsenic."

"Arsenic!" exclaimed Swiftwater Bill. "Where in hell would he git arsenic in this country?"

"My guess would be that that roll of bills wasn't the only thing this here Snook, alias Cleveland, took off'n that Bird Man. You see, I happen to rec'lect the Bird Man—er another one jest like him. He come upriver from the coast whilst I was sojournin' around Fort Gibbon. He was an interestin' sort of a cuss. I got acquainted with him, an' I kind of liked him. He hired him a Siwash fer a guide down there, an' he'd come in every little while with his specimens, jest like One Armed claimed he done at Eagle, an' I'd help him sort 'em an' pack 'em away. He'd explain all about the different kinds—most of which I've fergot. But I ain't fergot that he dusted them bird skins with arsenic an' plaster of Paris. The arsenic, he explained, preserved the skins, an' kep' the bugs out of 'em, an' the plaster blotted up the grease an' the blood. He had plenty of arsenic with him, an' Snook could of got holt of it easy enough."

"By God, John, I believe yer right!" exclaimed Swiftwater Bill, with enthusiasm. "An' now we'll see fer ourselves how this justice works out, that we've been hearin' about down to Dawson! They all claim down there, that no man kin git away with a crime on Halfaday. When will you call yer miners' meetin', John?"

"Well—we've got to go slow. We don't never make no mistakes on Halfaday—because you can't never rectify a dead man. I liked that Bird Man. He was a damn nice fella—if it's the same one. I—"

"He was kind of littlish, an' red-headed, an' he didn't wear no hat," cut in One Armed John.

"That's him to a T. Perfessor Amadon, his name was."

"That's him! I rec'lect the name, now you've spoke it."

"H-u-u-m-m, he was a friend of mine," mused Black John, half aloud. And Swiftwater Bill noted a steely glint in the blue-gray eyes, as the big man added, "What a hell of a way to die!"

"Do you know arsenic symptoms?" asked Moosehide.

"No, but I know strychnine symptoms," Black John replied. "We'll have to git along with them. We'll go up the crick, now. You go to Harrison's shack? I'll show you the one. Stick around there an' keep this Snook, er Cleveland, there on one pretext er another. Don't say nothin' about us comin' back with the meat. Let 'em think we're still out in the hills. Jest tell 'em you come up to see if you could do somethin'—fetch Bettles up some more whiskey, er somethin'. Me an' Swiftwater'll slip on to Cleveland's tent, on the next claim to Harrison's, an' look around a little."

LEAVING THE saloon, the three proceeded rapidly up the creek for three or four miles, when Black John halted and turned to Moosehide. "Harrison's in the first shack around this bend," he said. "Go on up there an' do like I said, an' me an' Swiftwater'll slip around through the brush to Cleveland's. When we git through there we'll go to Harrison's, like we jest come up from the fort."

Arriving at the tent. Black John threw back the flap and entered. "We'll find out, now, if that damn cuss has got any arsenic in his outfit," he said.

"I wouldn't know it if I seen it," said Swiftwater.

"It's fine white crystals, somethin' like sugar, only finer ground. I used to help the perfessor mix it with the plaster of Paris an' sprinkle it on some of them skins which he hadn't done a thorough job on whilst he was out in the bush—in the field, he called it, like it was a cow pasture, er somethin'. But that was jest his way of speakin'. An' he had the damnedest names fer the commonest kind of a bird or a flower. A woodpecker wouldn't be a woodpecker to him. It would be a rhinohinkus spoodukus Canadensis, er some sech a name as that. Cripes, if Cush thinks I use big words, he'd ort to know'd that perfessor!"

"Mebbe I better stay outside an' kind of keep a lookout in case this here Cleveland would come an' ketch us goin' through his stuff," suggested Swiftwater.

"It ain't necessary," replied Black John, his arm thrust to the shoulder into a duffel bag. "In case we should find he's got arsenic, an' he started to do somethin' about it, it would ondoubtless only serve to hasten his doom. If we don't find none we might have to resort to certain methods to make him tell where he's got it cached—an' it might as well be here as anywhere. He's got a six-gun, anyhow," he added, examining a loaded pistol which he withdrew from the duffel bag and laid to one side. Presently he withdrew his arm from the bag again, and Swiftwater saw that the huge fingers gripped a stout tin with a small screw top. He looked on with interest as Black John removed the metal cap and poured about a teaspoonful of a white crystaline substance into his palm. Without a word the big man replaced the cap, and after transferring the crystals from his hand to an empty gold sack, pocketed the sack, and returned the tin to the duffel bag, being careful to replace it where he had found it in the extreme bottom of the bag.

"The stuff in that can was arsenic, wasn't it?" asked Swiftwater.

"Such is prob'ly the case," Black John replied. "It looks jest like what the perfessor claimed was arsenic, an' it's in the same kind of a can he carried it in, an' the label says it is."

"The dirty skunk!" exclaimed Swiftwater. "That cinches the case agin him!"

Black John shook his head. "No, not yet. Like I told you, on Halfaday our verdicks has a permenant effect on a man's career. We don't want to make no mistakes. I ain't shore this is arsenic. If it is, I ain't shore that arsenic is p'izen. It's got that reputation—an' the perfessor claimed it is, an' he ort to know. But all that's only hearsay. Besides, admittin' that it's arsenic, an' that arsenic is p'izen, that ain't sayin' that Harrison didn't eat some musheroons that p'izened him. An' even if he didn't we've got to find out if, beyond a reasonable doubt, Cleveland could of give him a dose of arsenic. On Halfaday we don't call our miners' meetin's till I'm damn good an' shore a man is guilty. Even a pardner-killin', p'izonin' coot like this here Snook is entitled to all the breaks he kin git—an' he generally needs 'em. Come on, we'll slip over to Harrison's cabin, an' see what luck Old Bettles an' Cush had with the whiskey."

III

CIRCLING BACK, THE two approached Harrison's shack from the direction of the fort. The door opened abruptly to Black John's knock, and they entered the single room to see four men huddled together staring down at a still form on the bunk. A tin cup, and a half emptied bottle of whiskey stood on the table.

"Hello, John," Cush greeted. "This here Harrison, he's dead. He et some musheroons he found an' they was p'izen."

"Yeah, One Armed John told us about it when we got back with the meat, so we come on up to see if there was anything we could do."

"Wouldn't of been a damn thing you could have done even if you'd got here in time," said Old Bettles. "We done all anyone could. Fetched along enough whiskey to cure him, if we could of got it down him. There on the table's all there is left out of three quarts—but I'm doubtin' if even half a pint of it stuck. You can't cure no one if he can't keep his medicine down. He died jest a couple of minutes ago. Guess he was p'izened, all right. A man's a damn fool to eat them toadstools."

"He might of got holt of some wolf p'izen by mistake," suggested Black John. "Did he git all rigid, an' twitch around, like he was throwin' some kind of a fit?"

"No, he jest laid there cold an' sweaty, like. He wasn't, what you might say, conscious. He moaned about his stummick hurtin' turrible. An' he was awful sick to it. He kep' mumblin' fer a drink, an' when we'd give him the whiskey, he couldn't hold it down."

"Did you try givin' him a drink of water?"

"Hell, no! It takes somethin' a damn sight stronger'n water to cure a man as sick as he was. When whiskey can't fetch 'em around, nothin' kin. 'Tain't the fault of the whiskey," added the oldster, with conviction; "it would cured him if he could of kep' it down."

"Well, he's dead now—no matter what ailed him," said Black John. "You boys go on back to the fort, an' we'll call a coroner's inquest to set on him. Swiftwater an' I'll fetch down the corpse in his canoe."

"Pore Grover," sniveled the man known as Cleveland, "he's the best friend I ever had. We was sech good friends that each one of us made out a will, leavin' all our stuff to the other one. I'll stay with you two boys an' help fetch him down to the fort."

"You'll go along with the rest, like I said," ordered Black John. "Me an' Swiftwater kin handle him. We'll have a canoe load, as it is."

"What's the idee of an inquish?" asked Cleveland. "We all know what he died of."

"We like to do things up reg'lar, on Halfaday," replied Black John. "An inquest will give you a break, at that. It will establish his death as a matter of record, in case the public administrator would git suspicious about his will."

"Guess yer right," admitted the man. "Let's go down an' git it over with. Pore Grover. It's too bad it had to be him that went first. I almost wisht it was me that got p'izened."

"Sometimes," said Black John, "a man gits his wish. An' sometimes, he don't. It's owin' to how his luck runs."

"Come on," urged Old Bettles, "let's be gittin' along. Here we got a saint's day to celebrate—an' we've wasted more'n half of it a'ready!"

"Jest remember," said Cleveland, turning to Black John, as they left the shack, "that any property you might run acrost belongs to me."

"You don't need to worry none," replied the big man. "We do things right on Halfaday. You'll git what's comin' to you—an' don't you fergit it."

WHEN THE others had gone, Black John glanced at the face of the body. "He never died of strychnine," he opined. "I've saw several that did, an' their face is always draw'd up in a grin. But he had tea, an' meat, an' rice fer his breakfast, this mornin'—and one of 'em was p'izened."

"Prob'ly the tea," suggested Swiftwater. "Mebbe Cleveland come over here an' slipped some arsenic in his tea when he wasn't lookin'." Picking up the empty teacup, he carried it to the doorway and held it to the light, as he poked among the damp leaves with a forefinger. "Shore he did," he exclaimed. "There's some of that white stuff in the bottom of the cup!"

Black John joined him, and peered into the cup to see nearly a quarter of a teaspoonful of the white crystaline substance. "It ain't the p'izen in the bottom of a cup that kills a man," he said. "It's the p'izen in his belly."

"Shore it is," admitted Swiftwater, "but what I claim, enough of it dissolved to kill him, an' there was this much left. Like when you put sugar in yer tea—if you put in quite a bit, there's gen'ally some left in the bottom of the cup after the tea's drank."

"Set the teapot on the stove an' build up the fire, an' we'll soon know," said Black John. "If arsenic will dissolve in hot tea; yer prob'ly right. If it don't; yer wrong."

Removing a bit of the white substance that he had taken from the tin in Cleveland's duffel bag, Black John poured some hot tea into a cup, added the arsenic, and stirred it slowly. Apparently none of it went into solution. "Score one fer the defense," he said, and returned to continue his scrutiny of the table. "I believe I've got it," he announced directly. "Rice is white. Arsenic wouldn't show up on rice—an' he'd eat it without ever noticin'."

"Shore, he would!"

"But," continued Black John, "how would it git on his rice? A man don't dish out his rice an' leave it settin' around to git cold whilst someone sprinkles p'izen on it. An' how did the p'izen get in his tea?"

"Why, Cleveland might of been here when he started to eat, an' watched his chanct to p'izen his grub."

"On Halfaday we convict a man fer what he done; not what he might of done."

Swiftwater Bill frowned. "It's all right to be careful, John," he said. "But it looks to me like yer carryin' carefulness too damn fer. That damn cuss ain't never goin' to admit that he p'izened this man's grub. Yer givin' him all the breaks."

Black John nodded. "An' he's goin' to need all the breaks he kin git, when I git this thing figgered out. There's damn few murders got away with on Halfaday. Go ahead an' hunt around the shack whilst I try an' dope this business out. The way Cleveland spoke, he must believe there'd be somethin' worth while here in the way of property."

After some minutes of search Swiftwater returned to the table, where Black John stood in apparent contemplation of the dishes. "There ain't nothin' here except his reg'lar outfit," he opined.

"Hunt up his ax," said Black John, without removing his eyes from the table, "an' pry up that third puncheon from the wall. When you stepped on it a minute ago, I seen it move a little. This here is an old floor. The puncheons hadn't ort to be loose."

Swiftwater complied, and a moment later he reached into an aperture beneath the loosened puncheon and withdrew a thick packet. Hastily removing its canvas wrapping, he disclosed several packets of bills which he proceeded to count. "Cripes! There's eighteen thousan' dollars," he announced, "an' they've got bank bands on 'em!"

Black John glanced at the packets which the other laid on the table. "Yeah," he said. "They're ondoubtless the fruits of some crime. It's an American job—so we don't have to worry none about it. It ain't none of our business what a man done before he come to Halfaday. He was a fool to let Cleveland know about them bills, though!"

"But what'll you do with 'em?"

"Put 'em in escrow."

"What? Put 'em where?"

"In escrow. That's the legal way of handlin' funds like that. You see, it wouldn't be no use to turn 'em over to the public administrator because he couldn't never locate no heirs—Grover Harrison bein' merely a synthetical name, as you might say. Of course, Cleveland would be entitled to inherit 'em, under the will, but the chances is he ain't goin' to have time to spend 'em nohow. In sech cases, it's customary to hold 'em in escrow fer a reasonable time. If at the end of that time no one has called fer 'em, they revert to the finder, which in this case, is you an' me. I'll fetch your share down, next time I go to Dawson—in case they ain't called fer. But we'll be goin' now. Wait till I do up my evidence."

"You mean, you've doped out how Cleveland got that p'izen onto the rice?"

"Cleveland didn't do it. Harrison p'izened his own rice—an' his own tea, too."

"P'izened his own rice!"

"Shore. All Cleveland done was to mix the arsenic up with Harrison's sugar, here in this can. Then when Harrison come to eat, he spooned it out of the can onto his rice, an' into his tea, too." As he spoke, Black John poured some of the contents of the half filled tin that had served Harrison as a sugar bowl, into his hand, and carried it to the light, where both could plainly distinguish the poison crystals mixed with the sugar.

RETURNING THE mixture to the tin, Black John poured it out onto a piece of paper, made it into a package, and pocketed it. Then he refilled the can with fresh sugar from a cloth bag which he found on a shelf.

"We'll load Harrison in the canoe now, an' git goin'," he said. "No use keepin' the boys waitin'. An' besides, we'll be wantin' to go ahead with our celebration."

"You'll call the miners' meetin' first, won't you? You shore as hell can't claim you ain't got the goods on that damn skunk now, kin you?"

"Well, we've got a motive in them bills, an' we've got the intent to p'izen in tracin' that stuff from Cleveland's pack, to Harrison's belly—an' we've got a dead man. The only thing we ain't shore of is that them there white crystals is p'izen."

"Ain't shore they're p'izen! Harrison's dead, ain't he?"

"Lookin' at him from here, I'd say he has that appearance."

"Well, what more do you want?"

"I couldn't ask fer nothin' better—in view of his probable character. But on Halfaday we don't never take nothin' fer granted. You believe that stuff is pi'zen, I believe it's p'izen, but that don't make it p'izen. I'm goin' to make shore. I've got a couple of old dogs that's all crippled up with rheumatism. I've been goin' to put 'em out of their misery fer quite a while, but kep' puttin' it off. We'll try out this stuff on 'em, an' then we'll know fer shore."

"Looks like one dog would be enough," said Swiftwater.

"Nope. Half a job is no job at all. One dog gits a dose of the stuff that was mixed with Harrison's sugar. That'll show if the stuff he et on his rice was p'izen. The other gits a dose of the stuff out of Cleveland's pack. That'll link Cleveland up with it. We'll hold the inquest first, an' jest make it a matter of form. Then we'll turn Cleveland loose, an' try out this stuff on them dogs. After that we'll govern ourselves accordin'."

Swiftwater Bill eyed the big man with approval. "No wonder Corporal Downey claims you do a good square job up here, John. By Cripes, you as good as know this man is guilty—yet you're shore givin' him all the breaks."

"Oh shore. We give 'em the breaks, all right. I wouldn't like to see no innocent man git convicted on Halfaday. Downey might think we was careless." He paused and slipped the packets of bills into the front of his shirt. "Git holt of Harrison's feet now, an' we'll lay him in the canoe."

As they were about to shove off, Black John hesitated. "Hold on a minute till I slip back to Cleveland's tent," he said. "I jest happened to think that I left that there six-gun of his layin' out on the floor. I'll stick it back in his pack. There ain't no use in him knowin' anyone was prowlin' around there."

"Better fetch it along with you," suggested Swiftwater. "He might take a notion to use it on someone when we come back to git him—if them dogs dies."

Black John shook his head: "Cripes, Swiftwater—that would be larceny! We hang men fer stealin', on Halfaday. Of course if Harrison had been shot, we might be justified in takin' the gun along fer evidence. But there ain't no shootin' involved in this case. It's a good gun, an' I wouldn't mind ownin' it, but when a man lets his ethics git to slippin' on him, he's in a hell of a fix. No—I'll jest slip the gun back where I got it. I ain't lookin' fer Cleveland to put up no resistance, nohow."

IV

THE GROUP THAT awaited the arrival of the body at Cushing's Fort had been augmented by the presence of a dozen or more residents of Halfaday who, having dropped into the saloon during absence of the men up the creek, had remained out of curiosity. For One Armed John, from behind the bar, had hinted of certain mysterious doings on the creek.

"Some of them sourdoughs from Dawson is here. They claimed they wasn't on the run—jest a kind of a socialistical call on account they was in this part of the country. An' them an' Cush an' Black John is aimin' to throw some kind of a celebration on account of One Eyed John gittin' hung."

"Hell," snorted Red John, "it must of been a year back when we hung One Eyed!"

"Shore it was," agreed Pot Gutted John. "A year, jest about now. Looks like it's a damn stale hangin' to be celebratin' about!"

"Well, I didn't jest git the straight of it, myself," admitted One Armed John. "But seems like they made some kind of a deeciple, er—er—apostle—er—saint, er one of them old Bible characters, out of One Eyed, on account of his hist'ry book. An' they aim to celebrate his day. The celebration would of been good by about now—the way they was startin' out—but that damn Benjamin Cleveland come along an' claimed Grover Harrison had p'izened hisself eatin' toadstools."

"Why would he eat toadstools?" asked Long Nosed John.

"Cleveland claimed he thought they was musheroons. But," he added darkly, "mebbe he didn't eat neither one."

"What would he have et, then—that p'izened him?"

"That's what Black John an' Swiftwater Bill has went up to see. Cush an' Old Bettles went up to Harrison's to see if they couldn't do somethin'. I never know'd Old Bettles was a doctor—but he talked like he know'd how to cure folks. They took along three quarts of licker to give him, an' Black John sent Moosehide Charley up with another quart. It looks like Harrison had a good chance to pull through—if he don't die."

"You say Black John an' Swiftwater went up to see what p'izened him?" asked Pot Gutted John. "You mean—they think mebbe some one done it a purpose?"

One Armed John waxed noncommittal. "There can't no one tell what Black John thinks; er what he don't think. You boys knows damn well that he don't favor no one runnin' off at the head. So, personal, I ain't sayin' no more. Except, mebbe, that Black John might of got an inklin' of some kind that this here Benjamin Cleveland ain't got no sweet-smellin' past."

So the men of Halfaday lingered, and later when Cush returned, accompanied by Old Bettles, Moosehide, and Cleveland, they still lingered, Cush having explained that despite all efforts to save his life, Harrison had died. "An' you boys better stick around," he added. "John claims we'd ort to hold an inquest on him. Personal, I know damn well the man's dead. I stood there an' seen him die, an' I've got the first one to see yet that onct he was dead, he didn't stay dead. But you know how John is—likes to have everythin' done up reg'lar. Him an' Swiftwater'll be along d'reckly with the corpse. They're fetchin' it down in Harrison's canoe. An' meanwhile, the house is buyin' a drink." Stepping behind the bar he donned the apron which One Armed John relinquished, and set out bottles and glasses. "This here drink," he solemnly announced, "is in honor of Saint One Eye."

"Saint One Eye!" scoffed Pot Gutted John. "What I claim—One Eyed John would make a hell of a saint, in any man's language."

Cush shrugged. "Any saint in a pinch, Pot Gut—any saint in a pinch. You know Black John. If he deems a saint is called fer, in order to celebrate his day, by God, he'll produce a saint, even if it's only a home-made one! I'll give him credick fer tryin' to think up a bony-fido saint which his day come in August, but there didn't seem to be none handy, so recollectin' that it was August when we hung One Eye, he up an' proclaims him the Patron Saint of Halfaday—"

"What's a Patron Saint?" asked Red John.

"Damn if I know," replied Cush wearily. "Except that One Eye is one. I don't know half the words John uses, nohow."

"A Patron Saint," explained Old Bettles, downing his liquor, and refilling his glass, "is jest like you'd say—a Patent Saint. He's Halfaday Crick's own, particklar saint, an' there can't no other crick claim him—"

"Damn' few cricks would want to," grunted Pot Gutted John. "We wouldn't have to take out no patent to keep him."

"What good does a saint do a crick, anyhow?" demanded Short John.

"Cripes," explained Bettles, "they're a damn good thing to have! Every time their day comes along, you celebrate it. If every crick in the Yukon was progressive, like Halfaday, we wouldn't practically have to do no work at all. We'd have even them Mexicans beat fer shif'lessness. Drink up an' I'll buy another. Long live Saint One Eye!"

"He could stay a long time dead, an' it would suit me," grunted Cush, dourly. "It seems kind of triflin'—grow'd men standin' around gittin' drunk over a make-shift saint like him. But

August is a kind of a long month, at that," he added, as he refilled his own glass. "Listen—I hear someone hollerin'. It's Black John. Go on down, boys, an' help him an' Swiftwater up the bank with that corpse."

V

AFTER THE BODY had been carried into the saloon and deposited on the floor, a round or two of drinks were had, and Black John thumped the bar for order.

"Gents, the solemn festivities attendin' the celebration of Saint One Eye's Day, havin' been rudely interrupted by the apparent demise of our esteemed citizen, to wit, an' namely, alias Grover Harrison, it becomes our dooty to hold a coroner's inquest to inquire into such death, an' make it a matter of record. Cush, bein' a dooly app'inted coroner, he'll now go ahead with the inquest. He'll app'int Red John, Short John, Pot Gutted John, Long Nosed John, One Armed John, an' me, as a jury. Fer the first witness, he'll call alias Benjamin Cleveland, him bein' an alleged friend of the deceased, an' the last person to see him alive, an' in good health. Step out here in front, Cleveland, an' take off yer hat, an' hold up yer hand. Do you swear to tell the truth, the hull truth, er any part of it, s'elp'e God?"

"Shore."

"What's yer name?"

"Benjamin Cleveland."

"Are you a bony fido resident of Halfaday Crick?"

"Yes."

"Cush, as coroner, wants to know if yer acquainted with the deceased, to wit, alias Grover Harrison?"

"He was the best friend I ever had."

"Cush would like to know what, in your opinion, was the cause of his death?"

"Well, yesterday evenin' he stopped in to my place an' he had a small pail of what he claimed was musheroons with him. He offered to divide 'em up with me, but I didn't want none of 'em. They looked like toadstools to me."

"What's the difference between a musheroon, an' a toadstool?"

"Why—damn if I know. Musheroons is s'posed to be good to eat; an' toadstools is s'posed to be p'izen."

"But what does a toadstool look like?"

"Well, I couldn't say—jest what one looked like."

"What Cush is tryin' to git at," explained Black John patiently, "is how could a musheroon look like a toadstool to you, if you don't know what a toadstool looks like?"

"Why—the damn things didn't look good to eat. I wasn't takin' no chances. I figgered they might be p'izen—an' now I know they was."

"How do you know that?"

"Well, Cripes—look what they done to pore Grover!"

"Yeah," admitted Black John, with a glance at the deceased, "it looks like somethin' done aplenty. We'll have to admit, yer p'int seems well took. Go ahead—when did you next see the deceased?"

"This mornin', when I didn't see hint monkeyin' around his shaft, I went over to his shack to see what ailed him. He was sick as hell, an' I know'd it was them musheroons, so I come hell-bent down here for help."

"Did he tell you it was the musheroons?"

"No, he was too sick to tell anythin'. Cush, an' this old man, here, they went back with me, an' we tried to git whiskey down him, but he died."

"That'll do. Next, Cush'll call Old Bettles."

BETTLES HAVING been duly sworn and identified, testified to the fact that he had been present at Harrison's death.

"In your opinion," asked Black John, "could his death been caused by him eatin' musheroons er toadstools?"

"I don't know nothin' about neither one of 'em," Bettles answered. "An' if what they done to this here corpse is a sample of what they kin do to a man, I don't want to know nothin' about 'em, except to let 'em alone. Somethin' he et shore raised hell with him, an' fer all I kin see, it might's well be toadstools as anythin' else. When lib'ral doses of whiskey won't fetch a man around, he's in a hell of a fix."

"That's all," announced Black John. "An' now, if the jury will take a good look at the corpse, an' satisfy ourself that he's dead, we'll render a verdick to the effect that the deceased come to his death by reason of somethin' he et havin' a deleterious effect on his system. All in favor signify by sayin' 'Aye.'"

The verdict was unanimous, and Black John, aware that the eyes of One Armed John were fixing him with a stare of disapproval, dismissed the jury in the name of Coroner Cushing.

"An' now," he continued, "in view of the heat, an' the flies, an' all, we'll go ahead an' bury the deceased. We won't need to dig no new grave on account of havin' the one on hand that we dug fer Pot Gutted John the time we thought he'd broke his neck fallin' down his shaft. He got well on us after we'd went to all that trouble, but we won't begrudge him none, pervided he'll loan it to Harrison."

"There ain't no property I've got that I'd part with happier," grinned Pot Gutted John. "It won't cost him a cent. Let's go ahead with the buryin'. Passin' that open grave allus kind of gives me the creeps, anyhow. Them rocks in the bottom never looked comfortable. I'll be glad to see it filled up."

The obsequies over, the men returned to the saloon where, after a few rounds of drinks in honor of Saint One Eye, Black John and Swiftwater Bill slipped unobtrusively out the back door and hastened to Black John's cabin where he prepared the two doses and fed one to each of two old dogs. Twenty minutes later, with both dogs showing unmistakable evidence of poisoning. Black John mercifully dispatched each with a rifle bullet through the brain.

As the second shot sounded, One Armed John appeared around the corner of the cabin. "What the hell you doin' over here?" he asked, eyeing the two dead dogs.

Black John grinned. "I was jest puttin' them two old crippled dogs of mine out of their misery," he explained. "What's on yer mind?"

"Cush sent me to hunt you up. The klooch has got a hell of a big feed all cooked up, an' besides that, some of the boys is whisperin' around that they don't believe that there Harrison et no musheroons."

"Their belief is well founded," admitted Black John.

"I don't believe he did, neither—knowin' that damn Bill Snook, like I do. Didn't you find out nothin' about that there arsenic you was tellin' us about?"

"Yeah—I found out plenty. Me an' Swiftwater has jest concluded the evidence. We know, now, that Cleveland p'izened Harrison. He mixed arsenic in his sugar."

"Then why in hell didn't we hang him when we had the chanct?" asked One Armed John.

"What do you mean—had the chanct?"

"Why, you never said a damn word about no arsenic when he was standin' there tellin' that damn lie about them musheroons. If you know'd about it, an' I'd told the boys what I know'd about Snook, previous, we could of hung him right then! An' now he's gone. Claimed he didn't have no heart to stick around celebratin' on the same day his best friend died. So he pulled out—said he was goin' up to his claim."

"Trouble with you fellas is yer always gittin' yer functions mixed. That was a coroner's inquest we held today—an' we couldn't of hung no one fer nothin'. Besides, me an' you was both on the coroner's jury. We couldn't of testified. It wouldn't of been legal. It takes a miners' meetin' to hang folks—not a coroner's inquest. An' the quicker you birds learn them legal distinctions, the better it'll be fer all of us.

"Me an' Swiftwater has got the goods on Cleveland, now. So we'll go ahead with the big feed, an' when we git through we'll call a miners' meetin', an' if there's any occasion fer it, we'll hang Cleveland at our leisure."

"But—what if he wouldn't be at his claim? What if he's skipped out?"

"Why would he skip out? The inquest didn't implicate him none. He'll be at his tent when we want him. Go ahead an' tell Cush that me and Swiftwater'll be along as quick as we wash our hands."

ENTERING THE cabin, Black John drew the packet of bills from beneath his shirt. "I'll jest put this here property in escrow before I fergit it," he said, slipping the packet between the blankets of his bunk. "I like fer everything to be done legal. By the way, Swiftwater, did you put back that puncheon like you found it?"

"Yeah, I put it back. But hell, John—that won't make no difference. He prob'ly know'd where Harrison kep' them bills cached. Prob'ly waited till he found out before he knocked him off. I'm bettin' he'll come b'ilin' down to the fort, demandin' that property, under the terms of the will."

"He might," admitted Black John, "but I ain't lookin' fer him to. I'll take that bet—fer a round of drinks. Come on, let's be gittin' over to the saloon. I'm hungry as hell. I'll bet Cleveland's hungry, too. I've got a hunch he'd ort to bottled up his grief an' stayed an' et here."

Kettle after kettle of savory moose stew disappeared, as other residents of Halfaday drifted in, and whiskey flowed like water as the big feast progressed. It was nearly ten o'clock when Black John once again pounded on the bar for order.

"With all due respect fer Saint One Eye, the Patron Saint of Halfaday, we've got to call a halt in his celebration in order to perform a solemn dooty. You all have ondoubtless heard of the demise of our esteemed name-canner, alias Grover Harrison, an' them of us that was here at the inquest, will rec'lect that the verdick of the jury was that he'd died of somethin' he et. We also rec'lect that another name-canner, to wit, alias Benjamin Cleveland, testified that the substance which caused his death was some toadstools. Now, gents, I don't claim that toadstools won't kill folks. They might, er mightn't, as the case may be. But I'm statin' it as a known fact that no toadstool killed Grover Harrison. Havin' learnt somethin' of this here alias Cleveland's past record, through a word er two let fall by our valuable citizen, One Armed John, me an' Swiftwater slipped up an' done some investigatin', which we follered up with an experiment that proved conclusively that Harrison died from arsenic p'izen havin' been mixed with his sugar by said alias Cleveland, with felonious intent—namely, to cause the death of said alias Harrison, so Cleveland would inherit, under a will, the property of the deceased, consistin' of his claim, an' what personal property would be found layin' around.

"Therefore, gents, I deem it necessary to call a miners' meetin' to try this here alias Cleveland fer the lowest form of murder. An' I deem it advisable to hold sech meetin' before we git any drunker'n what we are. I hereby app'int Red John an' Long Nosed John an' Short John, a committee of three to go fetch this here alias Cleveland, er what's left of him, back to this saloon, where he will be give a chanct to offer whatever defence fer his act that he kin think up. Also, they're to fetch back the sugar can on Harrison's table, an' the one on Cleveland's, jest as they be. After that, if we deem it necessary, we'll hang Cleveland, an' go on with our celebration."

THE THREE men named departed, and in the saloon the celebration proceeded. Pot Gutted John demonstrating to all and sundry his proficiency in tying a proper hangman's knot in a length of new rope.

It lacked only a few minutes of midnight when the three who had been dispatched to bring Cleveland in appeared wide-eyed in the doorway.

"He's dead!" exclaimed Red John.

"Shot hisself plumb through the head!" added Short John.

"The pistol he done it with is layin' right there beside his hand—an' there's powder marks on the side of his head where he helt the gun clost," added Long Nosed John. "It looks like he'd et his supper, an' was took awful sick jest before he done it," he added. "An' here's them sugar cans, Harrison's was empty."

In the silence that followed Swiftwater Bill glanced toward Black John, who had listened to the report apparently in deep thought, as he combed at his beard with his fingers. Finally, the big man spoke.

"Shot his self, eh? Yeah—I rec'lect he had a pistol. Me an' Swiftwater found it when we was huntin' fer evidence. An'—you say it looked like he'd be'n took sick before he done it?" He paused, and suddenly, his hand came down upon his thigh with a mighty slap. "By Cripes, I've got it! He p'izened hisself—that's what he done! An' havin' had the chanct to see a couple of other men go that road, he shot hisself ruther than go like they did. An' I don't know as we should blame him, at that."

"But," cut in Old Bettles, "why should he p'izen hisself?"

"I don't hardly believe he done it apurpose," Black John replied. "You see, me an' Swiftwater found where he'd mixed up arsenic with the sugar in Harrison's sugar can, so I took out that there lethal mixture fer evidence an' refilled Harrison's can with sugar, like it hadn't be'n disturbed. I didn't want we should hang Cleveland ontil we was plumb shore that the stuff was p'izen, so we fetched some of it up an' tried it out on them two old dogs of mine, which I've be'n aimin' to kill. We found it was p'izen, all right. But while we was still down to Harrison's, I know'd that Cleveland would be at large, an' I figgered he'd hit back there an' dump out that sugar can so's to git rid of the evidence. But I figgered he wouldn't dump out his own sugar can. So jest before we started fer here with the corpse, I slipped over to Cleveland's tent, an' throw'd the sugar out of his can, an' put in the mixture that I'd took out of Harrison's. In that way, I figgered the evidence would be safe till we wanted to use it. An', gents, he done jest like I figgered. Here's Harrison's empty can—an' here's the p'izen mixture I cached in his can. In the meantime, though—it seems like the damn fool must of et some of it."

"Yeah," agreed Bettles solemnly, "that's jest about what come off. An' if you ask me, I'd say that the damn skunk got jest what was comin' to him. I realize, now, what Corporal Downey means when he talks about the eternal jestice of Halfaday Crick. The only kick I've got comin', is that this thing bobbed up on a saint's day. Look at the clock—it's lackin' jest one minute to twelve! In one more minute, gents, our celebration will be all shot to hell!"

"No," grinned Black John, glancing at the clock, "come to think about it, it was jest a mite after midnight when we hung One Eyed John, that time. How about it, boys? Am I right; er wrong?"

A noisy chorus proclaimed that he was right, whereupon Black John pounded on the bar for order. "Owin' to a slight mistake in time havin' been made," he announced solemnly, "an' bein' loath to curtail even a modicum of the honor due to our Patron Saint One Eye, I hereby proclaim that this day shall be carried over to inclood tomorrow."

"Huh," grunted Cush, as he set out bottles and glasses amid loud cheers. "One Eyed John a saint—an' a double one, at that! Kin you beat it?"

"I doubt if it could be even tied," grinned Black John. "An' now, belly up, boys! Swiftwater Bill is buyin' a round, in payment of a little bet we made. Drink her down, boys! Here's to Saint One Eye—the good ol' Saint of Halfaday!"

WHISKERS

WARM SPRING SUNSHINE flooded the little valley of Halfaday Creek which harbored the little community of outlawed men who were wont to foregather at Cushing's Fort, situated on the verge of a high bank that commanded an unobstructed view of several miles of the creek, in convenient proximity to the Yukon-Alaska border.

It was mid-forenoon when Black John Smith strolled through the open doorway and approached the bar as Old Cush removed, from the back bar a bottle, two glasses, and a leather dice box which he set out on the bar.

Black John picked up the box, rattled the dice, and cast them. "Three fives," he announced. "I'll leave 'em in one."

Peering through his square-rimmed steel spectacles, Cush verified the cast, and gathering the dice, shook the box, and spread them with a flourish.

"Four treys," he boasted. "Trouble with you, John, yer allus sendin' a boy to do a man's chore." Gathering the dice he cast again. "An' four sixes right back at you. See what yer law of averages yer allus talkin' about, kin do to them in one shake."

Black John eyed the four sixes sourly as he returned the dice to the box. "The drinks is on me," he announced, as he regarded the two pairs that showed after the cast. "But after this you keep yer thumb away from in front of that box when you throw."

"My thumb! What in hell's a thumb got to do with it?"

"I don't know. But it looks like you been practicin' up on some kind of shenanigan. It don't stand to reason a man could throw four of a kind in one throw, twict in succession. The law of averages—"

Old Cush chuckled audibly, as he shoved the spectacles from nose to forehead, and set the dice box on the back bar. "Yer law of averages is jest like any other law—it works all right ontil someone comes along an' breaks it. Looks like you slep' kind of late, this mornin'."

"Yeah, the stud game didn't bust up till around three o'clock. The boys plays later now that the spring clean-up's about over."

"Looks like four, five hours would be enough fer a man to sleep. I been up sence seven and I got the bar chores done."

"Well, that's good. I come to remind you that it's about time I was takin' some dust down to Dawson to exchange fer bills. The safe's gittin' crowded agin, what with all that new gold. It's a nice day, an' I'll be startin'. Weigh out a couple hundred pound of dust, an' I'll throw my outfit together."

II

BLACK JOHN, LIKE many of the residents of Halfaday Creek, banked his dust and his money in the huge iron safe that stood back of the bar at Cushing's Fort. Each spring after the clean-up, it had become customary to remove most of the accumulated dust to Dawson and exchange it for paper money, and by unanimous consent this duty had devolved upon Black John Smith, the dictator of Halfaday, and a man known to be scrupulously honest in his dealings with his fellow outlaws—providing, of course, that such outlaws were themselves on the up-and-up with their fellow members of the community.

Black John, however, was canny. While he banked most of his wealth at Cush's, he always had a goodly sum in his own private cache which consisted of certain sealed glass jars buried deep in the mud at the bottom of the spring where he kept his meat.

Patience and quiet observation had enabled him to locate the caches of nearly all the residents of Halfaday who did not bank with Cush. These caches remained Black John's secret, and were never molested so long as their owners remained in good standing on the creek. But let a man break the code—and the contents of his cache almost invariably disappeared.

No one else on the creek, not even Old Cush, suspected that Black John had a cache, as he was careful never to visit the spring unless it was to fetch a pail of water, or a cut of meat, or to deposit some meat for cooling.

Returning from the saloon for his stampeding pack, he visited the spring and returned to his cabin with fresh meat for the trail, and also a package wrapped in moose-hide that contained a thousand ounces of dust. This he placed in the bottom of his packsack. Returning to the saloon, he gave Cush a receipt for thirty-two hundred ounces, which the two carried down the steep bank to Black John's canoe and deposited in a packsack amidships.

"So long, an' good luck," said Cush, as the big man stepped into the canoe. "I'm glad it's you an' not me that's headin' fer Dawson with better'n fifty thousan' in dust, what with all the chechakos that's pilin' into the country."

"I don't figger any chechakos would try to bother me," Black John grinned. "The worst could happen, I might lose part of it to them sourdoughs in a stud game. But I've got more'n enough to make it good—if I lose the whole works."

With plenty of water in the creek the portages were few and short, and the big man took keen enjoyment in the swift, smooth course of the canoe between banks lined with the young green of birches and aspens and the blaze of countless wild-flowers.

Half way down the White River he camped, cached the gold, and spent four days prospecting a small tributary he had long suspected of harboring a pay streak. But the result was disappointing, and he gave it up after failing to find any spot where the top gravel promised wages.

ARRIVING IN Dawson shortly after noon, two weeks from the day he left Cushing's, he drew his canoe from the water, shouldered his pack containing two hundred and sixty-two and a half pounds of dust, and half an hour later, with an empty pack-sack dangling from his shoulder, and sixty-seven thousand, two hundred dollars in bills of large denomination in his pocket, he entered the Tivoli saloon to be tipsily greeted by Old Bettles, who stood at the bar with Swiftwater Bill and Moosehide Charley.

"Hello, John! How's everything on Halfaday?"

"Belly up," invited Swiftwater. "I'm buyin' a drink. And how about the four of us startin' a stud game? Camillo Bill an' Burr MacShane'll be in this evenin'. They went up to look over a proposition on Bonanza."

"Stud would suit me fine," grinned Black John. "Come on buy yerself a stack of chips, an' we'll git started."

III

THE STUD GAME, as always when a card game for high stakes started among the sourdoughs, drew its gallery of kibitzers from among the idlers and the casual visitors to the saloon. Early in the evening, when the four had been joined by Camillo Bill and Burr MacShane, the onlookers were crowded three and four deep around the table behind the chairs of the players, who with hat-brims drawn low over their faces to shade their eyes from the glare of the hanging lamp, played on in silence, save for an occasional short-clipped word, or a call to the bar for drinks.

Thus it was that no one noticed two men who entered the saloon hurriedly, stepped to the bar, swallowed a couple of quick drinks, and turned to leave. Nor did anyone notice that one of these men, glancing casually toward the card game, halted suddenly and, clutching his companion by the arm, pointed toward one of the players. Nor that the two advanced to the outer edge of the rim of onlookers, stared fixedly at this player for a full minute, then turned and passed hurriedly from the room.

Fifteen minutes later the two returned accompanied by Corporal Downey, of the Northwest Mounted Police. Then everyone noticed them as the three paused at the edge of the crowd and one of the men pointed a shaking finger at Black John, as his voice rose shrill with excitement:

"That's him! That's the damn cuss that robbed us! Robbed us of a thousan' ounces—an' hit right fer here to play our money in a stud game!"

And the other, no less excited than his partner, plucked at Corporal Downey's sleeve:

"Grab him, officer! An' look out! He's got a big revolver hid in the front of his shirt!"

To state that everyone now noticed the two strangers is describing the incident mildly. Everyone in the Tivoli stood, goggle-eyed, as glances shifted from the two men with the officer to the face of Black John, who, with the other players, had looked up as the hysterical outburst disturbed them.

Many of those in the room knew Black John personally, and nearly all knew him by reputation as the "King of Halfaday Crick", an appellation that clung to him along the big river, despite his repeated denials of any leadership over the outlaw community. They knew, also, that he was famed far and wide for his iron-bound determination, backed up at times by summary and high-handed measures, to keep Halfaday Creek free of crime. Also they knew that his efforts had met with marked success. And now they were hearing Black John Smith, the notorious king of Halfaday, himself accused of a crime by a couple of unknown chechakos! To most minds the idea was preposterous. To the minds of all the situation was dramatic. And in the death-like silence that followed the accusations, men strained forward tensely to see what would happen.

Black John smiled, showing white, even teeth behind the heavy black beard as his blue-gray eyes scrutinized first one, then the other of his accusers. "Jest when, an' where," he asked, in an untroubled, level voice, "was this here incident supposed to have took place?"

"You know where it was!" cried one of the men. "An' you know when! You opened the door of our shack up on Hunker an' pulled a gun on us when we was weighin' up our dust night before last. An' then you tied us up, an' beat it! You can't bluff out of it—nor lie out of it! There was others seen you besides us."

Old Betties chuckled tipsily as he glanced at Black John. "Ain't you ashamed, John—robbin' them chechakos! Give 'em back their dust, an' let's git on with the game."

Swiftwater Bill, after a scornful scrutiny of the two accusers, turned to Corporal Downey, who stood beside the two, a puzzled smile on his lips.

"Throw 'em in the jug, an' let 'em sleep it off," he suggested.

The young officer's smile faded as he shook his head. "They ain't drunk," he answered. "They really believe John done it."

"Well, you don't believe it—fer Cripes' sake?" asked Burr MacShane, eyeing Downey sharply.

"No. Knowin' John like I do, I don't believe it. I believe these men are mistaken in their identification. But—they're makin' charges. They claim they've got other witnesses that seen the robber. It was bright moonlight that night, an' they claim that two other men on Hunker passed a stranger on the trail to these men's shack before the robbery—an' another man seen him leavin' the shack after the robbery. He didn't think nothin' of it at the time, not knowin' of the robbery till damn near mornin', when these men freed themselves."

"Chechakos is all damn fools!" exclaimed Camillo Bill, eyeing the two in disgust. "I wouldn't believe a hull damn crick full of 'em under oath."

"You ain't a goin' to arrest John on the say-so of a couple of yaps like them, be you?" demanded Moosehide Charley.

Downey nodded. "There ain't nothin' else I can do," he replied. "Unless these men withdraw the charge."

"We don't withdraw it!" cried one of the men.

"Not by a damn sight we don't," echoed the other. "He's the one that done it, all right. Cripes, you don't think we could be wrong, do you, when we both of us looked into that face over the top of a gun—an' then had to set there an' let him tie us to the bunk poles? I'd know the damn skunk if I seen him in hell. I couldn't never fergit them whiskers."

Corporal Downey turned to Black John. "I guess you'll have to come along down to detachment, John," he said. "Maybe them other witnesses will know the difference between you an' the man they seen. I hate to arrest you, but I've got to. It prob'ly won't take long to clear the matter up, onct we get at it."

"All right," replied the big man with a grin. "If it's whiskers they want, I guess I fill the bill. But it's hell to git pinched on a winnin' streak." He counted his chips and cashed them in. "Twenty-four hundred an' thirteen dollars to the good," he announced. "I s'pose it was them odd thirteen dollars that brought me bad luck." He rose from his chair, as the on-lookers made way for him, and grinned ruefully at the sourdoughs. "So long, boys. Come down to the jail an' see me sometime."

"Jail hell!" exclaimed Camillo Bill. "Hey, Downey—cut out this nonsense! How much bail do you want? There's enough of us here at the table to put up a million in cash—if you think John 'll skip out."

"I ain't got no authority to accept bail," Downey explained. "If he's remanded fer trial, the bail can be arranged later. In the meanwhile, he'll have to come along. That's the law."

"An' you know me, boys," Black John grinned. "Always ready to work hand in glove with the law. I'll be seein' you later."

AS THEY stepped out onto the street both accusers were careful to keep Corporal Downey between themselves and Black John.

"You better search him, officer," urged one of the men, "I tell you, he's armed!"

"Yeah?" replied Downey, without according the man a glance. "Well, the police was doin' business before you was here to tell 'em."

In his little office at detachment. Corporal Downey took the two men's statements, and sent them to bring in their other witnesses—the three men who claimed to have seen the bearded stranger in the vicinity of the robbed shack. When they had departed. Corporal Downey turned to Black John.

"Well—you've heard what they had to say. How about it?"

"Offhand," replied the big man, "I'm inclined to believe they was robbed. The man that done it was prob'ly hidin' behind a stand of whiskers that put 'em in mind of me."

"Where was you night before last?"

"About fifty, sixty mile upriver, campin' on the far side."

"Alone?"

"Shore I was alone. You don't suppose I'd be messin' around with none of them damn chechakos that's clutterin' up the river, do you? Cripes, if anyone had robbed me that night—they'd got 'em a real haul. I was fetchin' down a load of dust to trade in fer bills. Cush's safe was gittin' clogged up till he couldn't hardly git no more in it."

"How much gold did you have with you?"

"Forty-two hundred ounces. It fetched sixty-seven thousan' two hundred dollars." Reaching into his pockets, Black John tossed several thick rolls of bills onto the desk. "Count it up, an' give me a receipt fer it," he said. "I ain't takin' no chances of gittin' my pockets picked in yer damn jail. You'll find that twenty-four hundred an' thirteen dollars along with it that I won in that stud game—barrin' a few dollars I blow'd fer the drinks. Oh yes—an' here's the big revolver them chechakos claimed I had in the front of my shirt. They was right about that, anyway. What with all that dust I fetched downriver, I figgered I'd better go heeled." As he spoke the big man opened the front of his shirt and withdrew a forty-five Colt which he laid beside the money on the desk.

Downey's face clouded. "The fact is, John," he said, "you ain't got no alibi. An' if these other three witnesses should identify you as the man they seen that night on Hunker, I'm afraid I'm goin' to have to hold you till this case is cleared up."

Black John nodded. "Shore you will," he agreed. "An' if them other three ain't got no better eyesight than them two that claimed I robbed 'em, the chances is they'll swear I was the one they seen. An' as a matter of fact, I ain't never set foot on Hunker Crick in my life."

That night Black John slept in a cell at headquarters, and the next day he faced the three witnesses from Hunker, all of whom unhesitatingly identified him as the man they had seen in the vicinity of the robbed shack, at the approximate time of the robbery. Also, there were two other men who said they had seen Black John lurking about the shack of an abandoned claim a mile or so below the robbed shack, during the late afternoon preceding the robbery.

A formal charge of robbery was placed against the prisoner. Constable Peters was dispatched to Halfaday Creek to check up Black John's story that he had come to Dawson to exchange gold dust for currency. And Corporal Downey, himself, visited Hunker Creek and then started a check-up of every suspicious character in and about Dawson.

Black John remained in his cell, reading the books and magazines furnished him by the sourdoughs, playing solitaire, kidding the policemen, and enjoying three huge meals a day.

IN DAWSON Black John's arrest was viewed from different angles. The sourdoughs, to a man, were convinced of his innocence. They ridiculed the idea that Black John would stoop to the common robbery of a pair of chechakos, but recognized the fact that Corporal Downey was pursuing the only course open to him in holding the prisoner during investigation of his case. At first, the other residents of the big camp were inclined to treat the matter as a joke, but as the days passed, with apparently no progress being made in the solution of the crime, men began to express the opinion that maybe there was something in the accusation. After all, they argued, Black John was an outlaw, wasn't he? Heretofore he probably had refrained from robbery merely as a matter of policy, and because of his realization of the efficiency of the Mounted Police. It was common knowledge that he had committed a robbery in Alaska. Various accounts of that episode were repeated in the saloons and magnified to include the robbery of practically the whole United States Army of its payroll, including the Civil War pension funds. This whispering campaign was cleverly fostered by Cuter Malone, proprietor of the notorious Klondike Palace, a low dive patronized by chechakos and tin horn gamblers. Cuter had good reason to hate and fear Black John, who despised him and had been instrumental in hanging several of Cuter's minions who had had the temerity to pull some crime on Halfaday. Black John was known to have stated publicly, and in no uncertain terms, that should Cuter, himself, ever show up on Halfaday, he would be hanged forthwith—on general principals, but technically for some violation of the so-called Skullduggery Act, a special provision invented by Black John for the punishment of any hangable offence not included under murder, robbery, claim jumping, etc.

So Cuter gladly fostered and abbetted the growing doubt of Black John's innocence.

IT WAS nearly three weeks later that Constable Peters returned from Halfaday. Next morning Black John faced Corporal Downey across the flat top desk in the little office.

"How much dust did you say you was fetchin' down from Halfaday?" he asked.

"Forty-two hundred ounces."

Downey's brow puckered, as he eyed the other through narrowed lids, and picking up a scrap of paper from the desk, he drew it slowly back and forth between his fingers. "Do you recognize this?" he asked, abruptly, holding the paper up for observation.

"Shore. That's the receipt I give Cush for the dust I fetched down."

Downey nodded. "An' it's made out for thirty-two hundred ounces—not forty-two hundred, as you jest stated. Cush told

Peters that the receipt is correct. Said he helped you carry the stuff to the canoe."

"Yeah, that's right," agreed the big man. "That's the exact amount we took out of the safe. The rest was some dust of my own that I had cached."

"A thousand ounces," reminded Downey, "is exactly the amount those two men were robbed of."

"Why—so it is!" exclaimed Black John. "Ain't that a coincidence fer you? Makes it look kind of bad fer me, too, don't it? Like I was really the one that held them two chechakos up."

"I thought you always banked your dust and money in Cush's safe."

"Yeah—a lot of 'em thinks that. Cush, he thinks so, too. But what I claim—a man hadn't ought to keep all his eggs in the one basket, as the Good Book says."

"Another thing," continued Downey. "Peters made the trip back from Halfaday in eleven days. He says he didn't hurry—jest kept pluggin' along. Now I know that you're a lot faster than Peters. Admit that you took your time, and that the water was about the same as now, you should have made the run in ten or eleven days. Is that right?"

"Oh, shore. I could make it in eight, if I hurried."

"You arrived in Dawson on the second of June. Cush told Peters that you left the fort on the seventeenth of May."

"Well, mebbe. I didn't give no heed to the date. Cush is prob'ly right. He notices them things more'n what I do."

"That," continued Downey, "leaves three or four days unaccounted for—even admitting that you took your time."

"Yeah, so it does. Well the fact is, I shoved up a crick an' done some prospect pannin'. I stayed up there four days. But I didn't run onto nothin', so I come on down. Looks like that item don't help my case none, neither," he grinned. "Say, Downey, if you keep on pilin' up the evidence agin me, you'll almost have *me* convinced that I pulled that chechako job. It shore looks from here like I ain't gittin' the breaks in this case."

"It sure does," agreed Downey, his lips pressed tight. "Is that all you've got to say?"

"Well, there don't nothin' occur to me, at present. Except, mebbe, that it looks like I'm in a hell of a fix. But you know that as well as I do. Looks like it was up to you to hustle around an' git me out of it."

"I'm workin' on the case," replied the officer. "But so far, the harder I work, the deeper you get in. An' here's another thing. A U.S. marshal showed up last night, with a couple of deputies. He's got a warrant from Circle City for the arrest of one John Smith, for a robbery and murder pulled off near Circle a month ago. A prospector was murdered and robbed of six hundred ounces. He stopped at Forty Mile, and fixed up the requisition papers with the inspector. The two men with him are witnesses, who claim to be able to identify the man who shot this fellow when he robbed him. The marshal deputized them to help him make the arrest. He mentioned that old pay-roll robbery, too. Said information had reached him that the man who pulled that robbery was livin' on Halfaday Creek under the name of John Smith. He is wonderin' if the same man didn't pull both jobs."

"Nope," replied Black John. "He didn't. I pulled the payroll job, all right. But this here murder an' robbery, is somethin' else agin."

"Where were you on or about May first?"

"May first—that's a little better'n a month ago, ain't it? Well, let's see. I was off on a moose hunt along in there—yes, it would be jest about that time. I swung off into the mountains an' done a little prospectin', too."

"How long were you gone?"

"Oh, four, five weeks—some sech matter."

"Long enough," suggested Downey, "for you to have gone down to Circle City, and returned."

"Well—yes, I could go from Halfaday to Circle an' back in a month. It would crowd me a little—but I could make it."

"These men from Circle are waiting in the other room. They heard we had a prisoner named John Smith locked up, and they'd like to look you over."

"Well—tell 'em to come in. I'm here, ain't I?"

The men were ushered in by Constable Peters, and the moment the two deputies laid eyes on Black John, they both asserted positively that he was the man who had committed the Circle City crime. They emphatically declared that there was no possible chance that they were mistaken. Whereupon, the marshal demanded that the prisoner be turned over to him at once.

Corporal Downey, himself, escorted Black John back to his cell. "I'm sure sorry, John," he said. "But—I've got to honor those papers. There's nothin' else I can do. Tell me, John—man to man—are you guilty?"

"Guilty as hell—of the payroll job. Never heard of the other one, nor the Hunker Crick job, neither. That's straight goods, Downey. But unless you git busy as hell an' find out who did do it, it looks like I'm due to hang in Circle. I've got a hunch that when you locate the Hunker Crick robber, he'll turn out to be the one that pulled the Circle job, too. Git to work now, an' hunt you some whiskers!"

IV

THE MARSHAL AND his two deputies had come upriver from Circle City on the regular steamboat, and planned to leave with their prisoner on the downriver boat which was due on the day following. Arranging with Downey to hold their prisoner until boat time, the three proceeded to make the rounds of the saloons where, with each succeeding drink, the marshal boasted the louder of Alaska justice—and of how his prisoner, the notorious Black John Smith, would receive short shift, once they got him to Circle City.

"Yep," he boasted in the Tivoli, "the judge is due in Circle the fourteenth, an' court'll set on the fifteenth an' what with the evidence we've got, it won't take more'n a couple of hours to convict him, an' in the afternoon, we'll hang him higher'n hell. That's the way we do things in the U.S.A., gents. Betcher life—over in Alasky we don't fool. An' this here Black John Smith—he's got it comin', too. Yessir—when that there prospector got murdered on Wood Crick, jest a little ways out of Circle, they sent fer me. I was up to Fort Yukon, an' I hopped on the next boat an' come up to Circle. Didn't take me no time to round up my witnesses an' find out that the man that done it had hung around the saloon fer a day er two an' give the name of John Smith. Then I begun to hear rumors that a guy by the name of Black John Smith hung out on Halfaday Crick over here in the Yukon, an' that he was supposed to be the one that pulled that army payroll job down to Fort Gibbon quite a while back. The witnesses claimed the man that murdered the prospector had a heavy black beard—an' that's the way this here Black John was claimed to look, too. So I says to myself, 'It's the same man, b'God—I'll go git him!' So I deputized the two witnesses, an' was hittin' fer Halfaday Crick, after stoppin' off in Forty Mile an' fixin' up my papers with the inspector, an' when I got here I finds out that Corporal Downey's already got him arrested." The man paused and surveyed the listeners magnanimously. "Yer Mounted Police over on this side ain't so bad. They've got a lot to learn, but they're pretty good, at that, fer a bunch of young fellers."

"Yeah," grinned Burr MacShane, "we think they're pretty good."

"Oh sure. They're all right—like I said. But they're mostly English, an' the English is a lot slower'n what we be, over on the American side. Somehow they ain't got the zip.

"It's a damn good thing," observed Camillo Bill, "that Downey saved you the trouble of showin' up on Halfaday Crick. Cripes—Black John would of took you apart an' tied knots in the pieces—you an' yer deputies, too."

"If yer a sportin' man," suggested Old Bettles, "I'll lay you even money, up to a couple thousan' ounces, that the three of you won't never git Black John to Circle. An' I'll give five to one, you won't never hang him, if you do."

"Hell," cried Moosehide Charley, "I'll go you even money, you won't never git him out of Dawson!"

"I'd like to take part of that, too," said Swiftwater. "I'll give odds you don't never git him on the steamboat."

TAKING THEIR cue from the attitude of the sourdoughs, others in the crowd muttered threats and forebodings until the two makeshift deputies began to show decided signs of uneasiness. Even the marshal, sensing the undercurrent of hostility, abruptly turned the conversation into safer channels. At supper time the three officers repaired to the Gem Restaurant.

"Tellin' you about me, I don't like the looks of things," confided one of the deputies, as they waited to be served.

"What d'you mean—'looks of things'?" demanded the marshal.

"That's what I mean. Jest like I said. This here Black John has got too damn many friends in this man's camp to suit me."

"Yeah—an' they ain't chechakos, neither," added the other.

"S'pose he has?" blustered the marshal, pointing importantly to his badge of office. "I'm a U.S. marshal, ain't I? An' you two is deputies, ain't you? I guess these Canucks ain't goin' to raise no rookus of no kind that'll git 'em in bad with the old U.S.A.! Hell—we got the papers that says we kin take this here Black John back with us, ain't we?"

"Yeah," admitted the first speaker, "but if you ask me, a paper is a hell of a thing to go up agin a moose rifle with, in case any trouble is started."

"Listen," argued the marshal, albeit with a trifle less confidence. "Do you know what would happen if anything was to harm us in discharge of our duty?"

"No," the deputy replied, "I don't. An' the hell of it is—I never would."

"Well, I'll tell you what would happen—the hull U.S. Army an' Navy would come up here an' blast these damn Canucks clean off'n the map—that's what! It would be an international incident."

"Yeah, it might be," admitted the other without enthusiasm. "But I don't hanker to be no international incident—an' a dead one to boot. Prospectin' suits me. I wish to hell I hadn't never saw that murder. I'd like to be back on Wood Crick, right now."

"Me too," agreed his companion. "I ain't no hero—an' never was. I'm quittin', er resignin', er whatever you call it, right now. There's too damn many of these here Dawsoners to suit me—an' they've got a look in' their eye. The odds ain't right."

"Gittin' cold feet, eh?" taunted the marshal.

"Yeah—mebbe. But if I quit now, they'll warm up agin. If I don't, an' them sourdoughs does what they look like they wanted to do, by God, they're liable to stay cold."

"D'you really figger they aim to start somethin'?" asked the marshal a bit uneasily. "They did look kind of ugly. An' wantin' to bet, an' all. They was offerin' odds, too."

"Shore they was. Why wouldn't they? What could the three of us do agin' a big camp like Dawson?"

"An' that ain't all," added the other deputy. "A guy told me, confidential, that all them Halfaday Crick outlaws would be on our neck by tomorrow. He claims all them pals of Black John's is aimin' to slip aboard the boat tomorrow, jest like common passengers, an' when we git downriver a ways, they'll jest nachelly toss us over the rail, an' take Black John back to Halfaday. I've saw enough right here in Dawson to chill my feet. An' these is all middlin' law-abidin' men. Hell, we ain't saw nothin', yet—them Halfaday Crickers is outlaws!"

"There's the Mounted Police," countered the marshal uneasily. "They'd be bound to help us."

"Yeah, that's what I told this guy, but he claimed that there wasn't only three, four of 'em in Dawson, right now—an' besides, he slipped me the word that this here Corporal Downey, which is at the head of 'em, is a friend of this here Black John. An' like as not, if anythin' was to start, they'd be busy as hell doin' somethin' else."

"This guy was prob'ly lyin'," suggested the marshal lamely.

"He looked to me like a man that was tellin' the truth. Old Bettles his name is, an' he's one of them sourdoughs. It was him wanted to bet them couple thousan' ounces we'd never git Black John to Circle. He ain't no damn fool. He wouldn't resk no two thousan' ounces, onlest he was shore."

"That's right," admitted the marshal, a worried look in his eyes. "An' there was plenty of others wantin' to bet. They was offerin' odds, too. What I claim, when they begin offerin' odds, a man wants to look out."

"Shore he does. What we better do, is to hit back fer Circle, an' leave this here Black John where he's at. You kin report that you couldn't find him. Hell, these Canucks has got a robbery on him—let them handle him."

The marshal frowned. "I can't do that. Them papers is all made out. They'll know damn well I located him. I'll lose my job."

THE OTHER shrugged. "Well—suit yerself. If you lose yer job, you could go back to saloon-keepin'. If you lose out tryin' to take that hombre back to Circle, you can't go back to nothin'—you won't even be goin' back. Believe me—it's a chore I wouldn't want to tackle single handed."

"Single handed!"

The other deputy nodded. "Yeah, that's what it'll amount to. We've quit."

The marshal's eyes widened in sudden terror. "Listen—you boys can't go back on me that-a-way. It ain't legal. You can't quit!"

"Who says we can't? We already done so."

"Listen," said the marshal, his eyes lighting with an idea. "I been thinkin'. You boys leave this to me!"

"Oh, shore. We done that, already."

"But that ain't what I mean," persisted the harassed marshal. "Listen, you claimed these Halfaday Crickers was aimin' to pile on that boat tomorrow? Well—let 'em!"

"Yeah," replied a deputy dryly. "We aim to."

"What I mean," continued the marshal, ignoring the interruption, "we won't be on the boat."

"Yer damn right we won't."

"We'll already be a good ways downriver. It's like this—I'll slip out after supper on the q.t., an' pick up a couple of canoes, an' I'll git an outfit of grub, an' some blankets, an' along about midnight, we'll slip Black John down to the river an' hit out fer Circle. We'll have start enough before anyone finds out we're gone so there couldn't no one overtake us. An' if them outlaws gits aboard the steamboat tomorrow, figgerin' on overtakin' us that-a-way, we'll camp an' lay in the bresh till the boat goes by. We'll have plenty of time to go ashore an' git hid when her smoke shows up, an' we kin gag Black John so he can't holler."

"Them sourdoughs back in the saloon would git onto it," objected one of the deputies. "If we didn't show up there this evenin', they'd suspicion somethin' an' go on a hunt fer us."

"No, I figgered on that. You boys go to the saloon, an' mix around whilst I'm tendin' to gittin' the outfit together. You kin tell 'em that my licker throw'd me down. Tell 'em I drunk quite a bit today, an' by suppertime I got sick, so I went to bed to sleep it off. Then at midnight you boys pertend to be soused yerselves, an' claim yer goin' to bed, an' then slip over to the police office, an' we'll slip our prisoner down to the river an' hit out. You two kin git in one canoe, an' I'll take Black John in the other one. That way's better'n gittin' a big canoe. He might tip us all over. This way, if he tips ourn over you two kin fish us out."

Plainly not relishing the arrangement, the two deputies finally agreed to the marshal's plan and, supper over, they proceeded to carry it out.

AT MIDNIGHT the three confronted Corporal Downey in his office.

"We've come fer the prisoner," said the marshal. "We're pullin' out."

Downey eyed the obviously nervous trio in surprise. "Pullin' out!" he exclaimed. "The boat ain't due till around noon tomorrow—er, today, rather," he added, glancing at the clock.

"Yeah, but we ain't waitin' fer the boat. We're pullin' out now. We don't like the looks of things."

"Don't like the looks of things? What do you mean?" asked the officer, eyeing the men closely.

"Well, there's a lot of talk around the saloons. They're claimin' we won't never git this here Black John to Circle."

"Who's claimin' that?"

"A lot of 'em is. They're sourdoughs, too. We wouldn't paid no heed if it was chechakos said it."

Corporal Downey grinned. "You don't want to pay no heed to those old badgers, either. They're tryin' to kid you. Go on to bed. It's their idea of a joke."

"Joke—hell! They're bettin' on it! A man don't try to put up good dust onlest he's shore. If we wait till tomorrow there'll be trouble. Them Halfaday Crickers is aimin' to be on that boat an' take him away from us."

The Corporal's grin widened. "There won't be any trouble," he said. "An' outside of Black John, there ain't a Halfaday Cricker within two hundred miles of here. I tell you those old timers are stringin' you. Don't get jumpy. I'll see that you get your man onto the boat."

"Yeah, but there ain't only three, four of you police in camp, an' there's a hell of a lot of other folks—not to mention them outlaws. If they was to ondertake to git him away from us, you couldn't do nothin', even if you—" The man broke off abruptly in evident confusion.

Corporal Downey's keen blue eyes narrowed slightly, and there was no smile on his lips as he said, "Well—go on. Even if I—what?"

"Why—er—what I meant," stammered the flustered marshal, "the facts is—one of my boys, here—someone told him—er—anyways it don't make no difference. I didn't believe him, nohow."

The young officer opened a drawer in the desk and shoved a paper toward the marshal. "Jest sign a receipt for the prisoner, an' I'll deliver him to you right now," he said coldly. "You can take him to Circle any way you want to."

The receipt was signed, and a few moments later, the three American officers disappeared into the night with the manacled prisoner between them. Left alone in the office, Downey chuckled to himself.

"Those damn sourdoughs sure must have spilled those birds an earful. Prob'ly told 'em the police would throw in with the Halfaday Crick bunch an' take Black John away from 'em. They sure had 'em scairt stiff—whatever they told 'em." Then he added thoughtfully, "Maybe they wasn't so far wrong in their bettin', at that. I'm kind of wonderin' now—if those three damn fools ever will get Black John to Circle City."

V

PROCEEDING BY A roundabout course to the river bank just below the saw mill where the marshal had concealed two canoes, one of the deputies spoke:

"What did I tell you? See how he tried to git us to wait over an' take the boat? That was to give them Halfaday Crickers a chanct to git on it, an' take him away from us. It was a smart trick. No one could of blamed the police—they wouldn't of been on the boat."

"Shore," agreed the marshal. "I seen through his scheme right on the start. He couldn't fool me! D'you notice how firm I was in demandin' that he should turn over the prisoner right then an' there, an' no foolin' about it? Yessir—an' d'you see how quick he done so, after givin' me that one look in the eye? He know'd his game was up. He seen at a glance that I wasn't no man to monkey with. We won't have no trouble, now. You boys jest leave things to me. Hell—as soon as I'd ketched on to what was goin' on, I outguessed the hull kaboodle of 'em—them sourdoughs an' the Halfaday Crickers an' the police, to boot. What I claim, if a man's app'inted marshal, he wants to be one—an' not no damn coward. 'Course I ain't blamin' you boys fer gittin' cold feet. You ain't no reg'lar marshals, nohow, only dupties, you ain't had no experience."

Arriving at the river bank the canoes were placed in the water, the supplies loaded, and the marshal ordered Black John to take his place forward as he settled himself in the stern and shoved off.

"You boys foller along behind," he ordered, addressing the deputies, "an' keep yer eye peeled. "If any canoes begin follerin' us, blast hell out of 'em with them rifles. One of you kin be shootin' whilst the other paddles. I don't expect no trouble—but you can't never tell." He turned to Black John who was regarding him with a grin. "An' you, you better not try no monkey business—like tippin' the canoe over, er somethin'. I kin swim, an' you can't with them handcuffs on. An' besides, the first crooked move you make, I'll wham you over the head with this paddle."

"There ain't goin' to be no canoe-tippin', nor paddle-whammin', if I kin help it," smiled the big man reassuringly. "Cripes, fella—I'm a damn sight more anxious to git to Circle City than you are to git me there! The fact is, I ain't guilty of the job you're takin' me back there fer, an' when the case comes up it won't take me no time at all to prove it. This here Hunker Crick case that

Downey had me in fer is different. I ain't got no alibi fer that one. How the hell could I have—when I pulled the job? Yes sir—you don't need to worry about me tryin' to git away! Like I said, I'm anxious as hell to cross that boundary line. Onct I git over in American territory, I'll breathe free. They ain't got nothin' on me over there that they kin make stick. Here in the Yukon, it's different. Hell—I'm the last man in the world that wants to git rescued!"

"Well now, that's fine," said the marshal, evidently vastly relieved, and as evidently determined to foster the complacent attitude of his prisoner. "Fact is, we ain't got sech a hell of a case agin you. Couple of fellas claimed they got a kind of a glimpse of the fella that knocked this guy off, but they could easy be mistaken. It prob'ly won't be so hard fer you to prove you didn't have nothin' to do with it. An' that there old army payroll job—the marshals that worked on that, claimed the guy that done it got drowned tryin' to cross the river on the ice. I don't s'pose you had anythin' to do with that, did you?"

Black John roared with laughter. "Hell, fella—do I look like a man that could rob an army? I'm askin' you—do I?"

The marshal joined in the laughter. "No, I can't say as you do. I guess you won't have no trouble beatin' that case, neither."

"Shore I won't," agreed Black John, "an' believe me, I'm obliged to you boys fer showin' up jest when you did. I was in a hell of a fix, there in Dawson, without no way of beatin' that case. Yer friends of mine—you bet! If ever I kin do you a good turn, jest call on me. You'll find out I ain't a man that fergits his friends."

FOR FIVE hours the two canoes proceeded rapidly with the current, Black John regaling the marshal with stories, and listening with uproarious appreciation to the stories told by the officer whose many years of saloon keeping had furnished him with an almost inexhaustible fund. As early daylight brightened, the big man turned frequently to scan the river in the rear, each time expressing satisfaction that there was no pursuit.

"I was kind of afraid that mebbe some of the boys would figger they'd be doin' me a good turn by tryin' to foller along an' take me away from you. But Cripes—that's the last thing I want! We've got Forty Mile to pass yet—an' all the police that's there." He paused and laughed. "An' here I be—goin' plumb out of the country, legal, right under their nose, an' they can't do a damn thing about it. That's a good one—they signed the papers theirselves that takes me clean out of their jurisdiction. I guess that's puttin' one over on 'em—eh?"

"I'll say it is," agreed the marshal. "An' I don't mind bein' a party to it. Them Mounted Police thinks they're damn' smart. How about landin' fer a bite of breakfast? I'm hongry as hell."

"Suits me," Black John replied. "An' how about takin' off these damn handcuffs while I eat? You know damn well I ain't goin' to try to make no git-away this side of the line. An' with my hands fastened behind me this way, it's damn uncomfortable. My arms is numb clean to the shoulders."

"Why—shore. I don't see no reason to keep you chained—anyways this side of the line. Like you say, if yer so hell-bent to git out of the country, why would you try to pull anything? After we cross the line I kin slip the cuffs back on—you might make a try then."

Black John grinned. "You're the doctor. I won't blame you none fer takin' precautions over on the Alasky side. Fact is, you couldn't hardly do nothin' else. You might git criticized fer fetchin' in a prisoner wanted fer murder without you had him handcuffed. A man in a responsible position, like you, has got to watch his step."

A landing was effected, the canoes pulled clear of the water and concealed in some brush, and the four proceeded into a thicket, built a fire, and prepared breakfast. The meal over, the marshal yawned prodigiously:

"I could do with a little sleep," he said. "Didn't git none last night. Guess we'll camp fer a couple of hours. Couldn't no one see us from the river, nohow. If anyone was follerin', they'd slip right on past." He turned to one of the deputies. "You set here an' stand guard fer an hour, an' me an' Bill will take a snooze. Then you wake Bill up, an' you kin go to sleep."

"Yeah," retorted the deputy, "an' you git two hours sleep to our one. To hell with that—I'm jest as sleepy as you be."

"Me, too," chimed in the other. "I couldn't stand no guard. I can't hardly keep my eyes open as it is."

"Well, damn it! Yer my deputies, ain't you?" snapped the marshal.

"Yeah," retorted one, "but yer the marshal. Yer gittin' more pay'n what we be—an' besides it's yer job. We don't lose no job if this guy gits away on us—we're through anyways when we git to Circle."

Black John grinned. "Go ahead, boys, an' all take a nap. Hell I'll stand guard—an' if any damn cusses comes along an' tries to rescue me, I'll blast hell out of 'em. We've got three rifles here. They couldn't effect no rescue in the face of them."

The marshal blinked sleepily and grinned. "But hell—we couldn't do that! Who ever heard of the officers all goin' to sleep an' leavin' the prisoner stand guard? It wouldn't work. What in hell would you be standin' guard of?"

"That's so," grinned Black John. "I hadn't thought of that. I like you boys, an' I was jest tryin' to help you out a little."

"I've got it," said the marshal. "I'll handcuff you to a tree—put the chain around the trunk so you kin lay down fairly comfortable, an' we'll all take a sleep!"

THE OTHERS, even the prisoner, agreed, and five minutes later Black John lay listening to lusty snoring in three different keys. He grinned to himself as he figured his chances of escape. The tree to which he was chained was too thick to whittle through with a pocket knife, even if he had had one, and the light camp ax was well out of reach. Nor could he slip the chain up the trunk and over the top, too many branches. Neither could he reach the marshal to steal his keys. He studied the handcuffs, and decided that he might possibly pick them with a piece of tin or wire—but he had neither. So he settled himself for a nap with the thought that there would be plenty of time before reaching the international boundary line at Eagle.

Sometime later he awoke at a slight sound, and opening his eyelids just a slit, he saw the marshal sitting up, rubbing his eyes. The man consulted a thick silver watch, and roused his deputies by shaking them lustily. Black John feigned sleep.

"Come on, boys—wake up. Time to git a-goin'. We've slep' damn near three hours."

The men returned slowly to consciousness and they, too, sat up.

"Ain't sech a bad sort of a guy," opined one. "You wouldn't think a guy like him would murder anyone, would you?"

"No, mebbe not," admitted the other deputy, "but he did—an' you bet, if I was the marshal, I wouldn't of took off them handcuffs, even fer him to eat."

"You would if you know'd what I do," retorted the marshal. "Marshalin' is jest like anythin' else—a man's got to use his head. Not only I took off them cuffs fer him to eat, but I'm takin' 'em off agin so he kin help paddle. It's like this—" the man paused, and lowered his voice. "He claims he kin beat the case we've got agin' him in Circle, an' that army job, too. Claims he never pulled neither one of 'em. But we know he did—at least the Wood Crick murder—"

"Shore he did. Hell, me an' Bill here seen him plain as day."

"I know all that, an' I know it won't take hardly no longer'n to pick a jury before we'll have him convicted an' hung—but he don't know it. I let him think we didn't have much of a case agin him. You see, he admitted he was guilty of this Yukon job that the police had him in fer, an' he couldn't beat that one—so he's hell-bent to git out of the Yukon an' over into Alasky, where he thinks he'll git turned loose after the trial. He'll paddle like hell to git to the line, an' we kin make better time. Onct we git to

Eagle, though, believe me them cuffs goes back on his wrists—an' he won't be gittin' no favors from there on to Circle. What I mean, it takes brains to kid a man along so he'll paddle like hell to git to his own hangin'. He ain't got a show in the world of beatin' that case onct the jury hears what you boys has got to say. Go wake the damn fool up—an' we'll be movin' along."

Black John was awakened after much shaking, and the cuffs unlocked by the marshal who returned both cuffs and key to his pocket.

"I ain't botherin' to put them cuffs back on," he smiled. "Two men can git a hell of a lot more out of a canoe than one. If we make good time we ought to fetch Eagle sometime durin' the night—an' then you'll be safe acrost the line."

"That's right," agreed the big man, picking up a paddle. "Come on—let's go. I'll feel a hell of a lot safer onct I git out of the Yukon."

THE CANOES made better time. Forty Mile was passed without a stop, and toward the middle of the afternoon, when a smudge of steamboat smoke showed far behind them, the marshal headed for shore. Again the canoes were concealed, and again, in the cover of the brush, a meal was prepared and eaten. Black John wondered at the air of genuine relief with which the three officers watched the boat pass and disappear downriver.

The two deputies stepped into their canoe and shoved off. As Black John was about to take his place, he spoke to the marshal. "We could make better time," he suggested, "if I was to take the hind paddle. I'm heavier'n what you be, an' the damn canoe don't travel good with the bow way down in the water. Ain't you noticed how hard she steers?"

"I'll say I have," agreed the other, "bein' as I've been the one that done the steerin'. I believe yer right. Head paddlin's easier, anyhow. Let me in the front, an' we'll give them two deputies a race. They was kind of growlin' about us not making better time. But by God, from now on they've got to paddle!"

"Yer damn right," agreed Black John heartily. "Let's go. I won't breathe easy, till I git across that line where I know them Yukon police ain't got no authority."

The canoe shoved off, and swung in beside the other whose occupants were holding her in an eddy a few yards below.

"Hey," called the marshal, when the craft come alongside, "you guys was bellyachin' about us holdin' you back—what'll you bet we don't beat you to Eagle?"

"Bet you ten dollars you don't," offered one of the deputies.

The marshal promptly accepted, and the other deputy turned to Black John. "How about you? I'd like to git in on that easy money, too."

The big man grinned. "I'd like to bet all right—but I ain't got the ten. Them damn police up to Dawson took what change I had on me, along with my knife an' gun. It looks like easy money to me. I figger me an' the marshal here ought to paddle circles around you two."

"Is that so!"

"Shore it's so," grinned the marshal. "An' jest to make it some object to you to git down an' paddle, I'll take you on fer a ten, myself. Come on now—last one to touch the Eagle landin' loses."

The two canoes headed diagonally out into the current, and the race was on. At first, the marshal paddled furiously as the other canoe drew slowly ahead, but Black John steadied him down.

"Take it easy," he advised. "This here's a long race. It ain't goin' to be won by sprintin'. Let them damn fools wear 'emselves out right on the start, an' we've got 'em. They can't hold that lick up fer very long. We'll jest shove along steady, an' let 'em tire out—an' then we'll begin leanin' on the paddles a little harder an' slip past 'em like they was tied to a tree."

An hour later, with the other canoe only a speck in the distance as it disappeared around a wooded point at a bend of the river, the marshal spoke.

"Hey, we don't want to let the boys git too damn fer ahead! Don't fergit—I got twenty dollars on this race."

"Don't you worry none about them twenty dollars," reassured Black John. "At the clip they've been goin', they're gittin' tired, right now. We can pass 'em any time we want to. Did you notice how they hung way out in the middle of the river, goin' around that bend? Not only they're tearin' out the bone at the paddles, but they're travelin' two miles to git one, to boot."

"What d'you mean—two mile to git one?"

"Well—that's a wide bend, ain't it? It's a damn sight further around it, if you hold out there in the middle like they did, than it is if you cut in clost to the p'int, ain't it? Don't you rec'lect yer geometry?"

"My which?"

"Yer geometry—that you learnt in school—angles, an' segments, an' arcs, an' chords, an' all that stuff."

"Oh—like that. No, I didn't fool with that stuff. I quit in the sixth grade. What I claim, onct a man gits his education, it ain't no use he should go on crammin' his head full of stuff like that. Hell, I was makin' eight dollars a week in a paint shop when them other kids in my grade was still goin' to school yet. An'—look at me now. I'm a U.S. marshal—an' hell only knows what they're doin'."

"That's right," agreed Black John, grinning broadly at the man's perspiring back. "But you've seen bows an' arrows, ain't you?"

"Shore I have."

"Well, take the bow—the two ends of it is a certain distance apart—but you'd travel further to git from one end to the other if you followed the bow, than you would if you followed the string, wouldn't you?"

"Why—shore. The string's shorter."

"All right—then we won't travel so far if we start in now an' cut clost to that p'int than if we held out in the middle, will we?"

"That's right, we kin cut off quite a bit—onlest the river runs faster in the middle, er somethin'. I ain't much used to this here canoe work. I've mostly tended bar, an' run saloons. I ain't been a marshal only goin' on three months. They's prob'ly some tricks I ain't onto yet."

"Oh shore. There's bound to be," grinned the big man. "But you're learnin'—fast. Hell, take this here trip yer on now—I'll bet you'll pick up quite a few tricks."

"What I claim—a man ain't never too old to learn—if he uses his head. I can see now, we ought to gain damn near half a mile on them boys—the way we're headin'." The canoe was fast approaching the wooded point around which the other canoe had disappeared, and Black John was holding her well in. "I wouldn't go too clost," cautioned the marshal. "We might hit a rock."

"No rocks on this p'int. Speed her up, now—an' leave the steerin' to me. We'll shoot around this bend like a bat out of hell. When them birds sees us comin', they'll know they're licked."

The canoe shot ahead under the paddle strokes and it suddenly became apparent to the laboring marshal that if it held to its present course it would only miss the point by a matter of inches. The gravelly point was now only ten—five—three canoe lengths away. He turned his head in sudden alarm just as Black John, with a twist of his paddle sent the frail craft crashing onto the gravel with a force that pitched the marshal forward on his face, half out of the canoe. In an instant Black John was upon him, pinioning his arms, dragging him clear of the craft. A few moments of struggling, and the marshal lay glaring up into the grinning bearded face, his hands secured behind him with his own handcuffs.

"What the hell!" he roared, his face purple with rage. "You damn fool, you ain't across the line, yet! Them Yukon police will be pickin' you up."

"Not," grinned Black John, "without a certain amount of trouble. An' as far as crossin' the line—the last place I want to show up in is Alasky. Hell, man—you can't blame me fer not wantin' to git hung, can you?"

"Listen," said the marshal, regaining something of his composure. "You ain't in no danger of gittin' hung."

"Yer damn right I ain't—as long as I keep out of Alasky."

"I mean—we ain't got no good case agin you. You kin beat it easy. Come on, unlock these cuffs, an' let's git agoin' before some Yukon policeman comes along. We ain't got hardly nothin' on you at all over to Circle."

"Yer a damn liar!" retorted Black John. "I heard every word you told them deputies when you thought I was asleep. As a matter of fact, I didn't have nothin' to do with yer damn murder over there, but you'd shore as hell hang me fer it if you got me back there. I ought to knock hell out of you fer a damn dirty double-crossin' skunk—but it wouldn't be but damn little satisfaction beatin' up a man that was handcuffed."

"What you goin' to do with me?" asked the man, his voice dropping into a whine, as he stared up into the frowning face of the other.

"Jest teach you a few of them tricks you claimed you wasn't onto yet. Hell, you ought to be glad this here excursion turned out like it did. Look at the experience yer gittin'."

"Where's them damn deputies?" sniveled the marshal. "Why'n hell didn't they stick around?"

"What—an' lose them twenty dollars?" grinned Black John. "You ain't got no kick comin'; it was yer own proposition, this race—an' then bettin' on it. They're a good three, four miles downriver by now—an' goin' like hell. Looks from here like yer out that twenty."

"I was a damn fool to ever take them cuffs off'n you!" snarled the man.

"Yeah, it was a kind of an error in jedgment, at that," grinned Black John. "A list of the mistakes you've made would make a damn good record of this journey. But you ain't been a marshal fer long."

"By God, you can't leave me here to starve!" the marshal cried, as Black John proceeded with his preparations which included throwing the rifle and the bunch of keys far out into the river.

"Nope. You ain't in no danger of starvation. I'm jest makin' me up a light pack of grub, an' seein' we ain't got no pack-sack, I'll make one out of yer coat, here."

"Hey—give me that badge! I'll prob'ly catch hell if I lose that."

"Jest tell 'em it was stole off'n you. I'm keepin' it fer a souvenir—that an' the fact that I might find use fer it sometime. It's the only thing I'm takin', except the coat an' a little grub."

The pack made up, Black John lifted the man and laid him in the canoe. "You'll git to Eagle, all right," he said. "Prob'ly be a little late to win yer bet, but you'll git there. Jest holler when you go by, an' someone'll come out an' git you—that is, unless them deputies git worried an' start back upriver huntin' you. That don't seem likely, though—in view of that twenty dollar bet."

"But hell, man, a steamboat might hit me!" cried the marshal as Black John shoved the canoe out into the current. "I can't paddle with my hands behind my back!"

"Damn few men has been hit by steamboats," called the big man as the canoe floated downstream. "It's a chance you've got to take. So long—I'm hittin' back into the hills!"

VI

BLACK JOHN MADE his way swiftly afoot, holding close to the bank of the river. It was near midnight when he reached Forty Mile, and after some maneuvering, stole a police canoe, and headed on upriver. Toward mid-forenoon, he drew the canoe from the water, concealed it in the brush, ate a cold breakfast to avoid showing smoke, and proceeded to sleep till early evening. Then he resumed his upriver journey, arriving at the Indian village of Moosehide, some four or five miles below Dawson in the early morning. Placing the paddles in the canoe, he shoved it out into the river, and unseen, made his way to the shack of Owl Man, an Indian whose life he had once saved at the risk of his own. The Indian was delighted to see him.

"Ba Goss, me—I'm ain't'ink I'm no see you no mor'. I'm seek in ma head 'bout dat. Yes'day in Dawson dey say you gon' down Circle City—git hung."

"You don't want believe all them rumors you hear," grinned the big man. "You got a pair of shears?"

"Got—w'at?"

"A pair of shears—scissors," explained Black John, making scissoring motions with his fingers at his beard.

The Indian grinned as he nodded his comprehension. "My sister got. Me go git. Liv' no far. You cut off w'iskers, huh? No look lak Black John no mor'. Mans t'ink mebbe-so som' nudder man, huh?

"That," agreed Black John, "is the impression I'm strivin' to foster. You got a razor?"

"No—no razor got. My sister got no razor. No Injun got no razor."

"Well, go git them shears, an' hurry back here with 'em—an' don't say nothin' to no one about my bein' here, er I'll throw you back in the river where I pulled you out of, that time."

The Indian returned shortly with a pair of shears, and Black John asked abruptly, "You got any money?"

The man nodded. "Got money. You want?"

"Shore I want it! How much you got?"

"Got hondre seex dolla. Got 'bout forty-wan ounce dus'."

"Git it," ordered Black John, and when the Indian returned from another room with a greasy sack, the big man counted it, and handed the Indian some bills. "I'm borrowin' this, savvy? You'll git it all back, an' plenty more along with it. Yer workin' fer me from now on till I fire you—savvy? But you keep yer mouth shet, an' don't let a damn soul know I'm back here. Go to Dawson an' buy a razor, an' a shavin' brush, an' some soap, an' hustle back here with 'em. In the meanwhile I'll git to work with these shears. An' when you go, don't fergit to put that padlock on the door an' lock it—I don't want no damn Siwashes buttin' in on me."

THE MAN departed, and Black John seated himself at the table, propped the cracked and distorted mirror before him, and proceeded to shear off his heavy black beard. When the Indian returned a couple of hours later, he finished the job with brush and razor to the vast amusement of Owl Man who stood watching each motion.

"There," grinned Black John, as he scrutinized himself in the mirror. "I wonder who the hell I look like, now?"

"Look lak damn chechako," chuckled the Indian. "No mor' Black John—damn chechako."

"That's a good idea. By God, I'll act like one, too. All I got to rec'lect is to do what a sourdough wouldn't—an' ask damn fool questions every time I open my mouth. I shore wish Old Cush could see me. He'd realize what a hell of a good lookin' young fella I used to be!"

"Too mooch look w'ite on de face," observed Owl Man, regarding the big man critically.

"That's right," Black John agreed, peering into the mirror at the contrast presented by his weather-browned forehead, and the white skin of his lower face. "I've got to lay around here in the sun fer a few days an' pick up a tan. You kin tell the Siwashes that I'm some chechako that's hired you to guide me on a prospectin' trip—an' I'm hangin' around waitin' fer my pardner to show up. In the meantime, you go up to Dawson an' hang around the saloons an' let me know when the word gits back that I got away from that marshal. You savvy?"

The Indian nodded. "W'at de p'lice git you for? Mans say Black John rob chechakos on Hunker. Mor' mans say Black

John keel man an' rob heem down Circle City. Me—I'm say dat de dam' lie!"

"Couldn't make you believe I'd pull jobs like them, could they. Owl Man?"

The Indian shrugged. "Mebbe-so keel mans—mebbe-so rob 'em—but you no git ketch."

"Oh, that's it," laughed Black John. "Well, in view of yer touchin' vindication of my character, an' yer firm belief in my rectitude, I'll tell you that I didn't have a damn thing to do with neither one of them robberies. But someone pulled 'em. An' from what certain witnesses say, the one that done it must look a hell of a lot like me. An' he's smart enough, er lucky enough, to keep out of the way of the police, too. Corporal Downey's no damn fool. He had to arrest me, an' hold me fer that Hunker Crick job, but he don't believe I done it—even after he'd worked on the case an' turned up a lot of evidence that got me in deeper an' deeper. An' he had to turn me over to them Americans, when they showed up with their papers fer that Circle job. Ever since he arrested me he's been huntin' the man that looks like me—a man with a heavy black beard—but he ain't found him—er hadn't up to midnight, night before last.

"While I was in jail Bettles an' the rest of the boys come to see me every day, an' they told me that Cuter Malone was spreadin' it around that it was me done them jobs, all right. He got a lot of folks believin' it. Cuter, he hates me—an' he's got damn good reason to. My hunch is that he knows who pulled them jobs, an' is either keepin' him hid—er knows damn well where he's hidin'. He figgers that if he could git me off'n Halfaday, an' git someone else in there, he'd git control of the crick. Then, with what he's got on some of the Yukon wanted's that's up there, he'd have things, his own way—after buyin' Old Cush out er gittin' him knocked off.

"When word gits back to Dawson that I busted loose, I figger he'll pass it along to this bozo that done them jobs, an' tell him to pull another, an' then hit fer Halfaday, knowin' damn well that

I can't go back there, with the police both sides of the line hot on my tail. That's the first place they'd hunt fer me.

"An' onct Cuter's man gits up there, it wouldn't take him long to convince the boys that they'd better play along with Cuter Malone. I've had a hell of a time keepin' 'em lined up on the side of rectitude.

"So as soon as you slip me the word that news of my git-away has reached Dawson, I'll slip up there an' hang around the Klondike Palace, like some green chechako would, an' mebbe I kin ketch me an earful. Cuter an' his mob wouldn't be so damn careful what they said in front of a chechako, 'specially one that was dumb as hell, an' half soused, to boot. Meanwhile I'm goin' out an' expose my face to the sun, after burnin' up these here whiskers. If Downey was to come prowlin' around here an' run onto that beard he might git suspicious—knowin' that me an' you is friends." Black John paused, and fixed his gaze on the face of the Indian, who had been listening with the utmost attention. "You savvy what I've told you, eh?"

The man nodded. "Me, I'm fin' out when mans say you git 'way—com' back, tell you 'bout dat."

"That's right. Git a goin'. You prob'ly won't hear nothin' till tomorrow er next day, but it won't hurt to make sure. An' you better take yer canoe up an' fetch back grub enough fer a couple of weeks stampedin' trip. We're liable to be pullin' out of here damn sudden, when the time comes."

VII

IT WAS IN the afternoon of the second day thereafter that Owl Man reported that news of the escape had reached Dawson.

" 'Merican p'lice coom tell Cop'l Downey you git 'way on heem."

Black John grinned. "Come back himself, eh? Has the word got out? Do the boys know it yet?"

The Indian grinned. "De sourdough dey know 'bout dat. In Tivoli dey laugh lak hell on de 'Merican p'lice. He mad lak hell. T'ree 'Merican p'lice coom back."

"Did you hear what they said in Cuter Malone's?"

"Cuter, he mad, too. Den, bye-m-bye he ain' so mad. He say Black John no kin go back Halfaday Crick no mor'. Lot of mans talk. Me, I'm come 'way—tell you 'bout dat."

"That's right. Owl Man—you done fine. I'm goin' to Dawson now. You stay right here. I ain't acquired no tan, but my face is burnt red as a lobster. Anyway, it don't show white like it did. I guess it'll git by. No one looks twict at a damn chechako nohow. It's a good thing you're about my size. I've borrowed a pair of overalls an' a shirt off'n you, so no one would recognize, my clothes. That damn fool marshal wouldn't notice 'em—but Downey might. Remember, now—you stay right here in yer shack, er within spittin' distance of it, till I come back. It might be an hour—er it might be a week. An' keep that stampedin' pack handy. When we go, we're liable to start in a hurry."

Black John, an unimpressive figure in patched shirt and faded overalls, pushed open the door of Cuter Malone's Klondike Palace, approached the bar with an air of diffidence, and in a voice slightly thick from evident indulgence in liquor, ordered a drink.

He filled the glass, clumsily slopping a portion of the whisky on the bar. As the frowning bartender mopped it up, he grinned foolishly:

"Jes' li'l ac'cent, brother. Have one on me."

The bartender's scowl relented somewhat,' as he tossed off a short one and shoved the customer his change. "That's all right. You want to be a little careful—whisky costs money in this man's town. Jest get in?"

"Yeah, got in s'mornin'. Me'n my partner. He's over to 'nother s'loon—Tivoli. We got kind of soused. He's over there yet. I says hell wish stickin' 'roun' one place—wan' to she the town. Nice place you got—lot of girls, eh?"

"Yeah, plenty of girls. We got anythin' a man wants here—women, cards, roulette, faro. We aim to show the boys a good time."

"Tha's right," assented Black John, staring vacantly around, and spotting Cuter Malone leaning against the safe at the far end of the bar in earnest conversation with three characters whom he recognized as habitués of the place. He swallowed his liquor, and moved away from the bar, to stroll aimlessly about, looking into the dance hall, and inspecting the idle roulette wheel, and the faro layout which some half a dozen chechakos were giving a desultory play. After a few minutes, he strolled again to the bar, this time taking his place close beside the men who were in conversation with the proprietor.

He beckoned to the bartender. "Give me 'nother li'l drink," he ordered, "an' have one yerself—an' ask these ge'men what they want. Drinkin' 'lone's too damn lonesome. After while I'm goin' to take a whirl at the wheel—feel kin' lucky today."

The bartender set out bottle and glasses, and Malone and the others joined in the drink. Malone bought another.

"Newcomer, eh?" he asked. "Well, stick around. We'll show you a good time here. There won't be nothin' doin' with the wheel, though, till after supper. Jest make yerself to home."

Black John mumbled an appreciation of the hospitality, and relapsed into silence, toying with his glass. Presently, the four resumed their conversation, evidently paying no further heed to the half drunken chechako, whose attention was centered on his drink.

Ten minutes later the men dispersed, and, downing his liquor, Black John sauntered about the place for a while and unobtrusively slipped out the door. As he strolled aimlessly toward the Tivoli, he grinned to himself. He had not learned much from the occasional words that reached his ears. However, he had heard his own name mentioned repeatedly, also Halfaday Creek, and knew that the four had been discussing some definite plan.

"Hadn't ought to be long before my namesake an' double will be pullin' another job. Then he'll hit fer Halfaday, where, accordin' to reports, I don't dare to be."

Momentarily he stiffened, then resumed his slouchy walk. Coming directly toward him down the street was Corporal Downey. Here, he realized, was to be the supreme test of his disguise; if Downey didn't recognize him, nobody would. As the officer was about to pass, Black John stopped him, eyeing the uniform with undisguised admiration. " 'Scuse me, Cap'n, you in the p'lice?"

"Yes," answered Downey, eyeing the tipsy chechako with bored tolerance. "Anything I can do for you?"

"Yeah—that is, mebbe you c'n tell me good place to go to dig me some gold. Been out here on a crick, but wasn't no good. Hell of a lot of sand, an' no gold. My pardner quit on me so I come to town. Got a li'l drunk, but I'm good fella, all right. Tell me where's good crick, an' I'll buy li'l drink."

Downey grinned. "There's a lot of good cricks," he explained. "What you chechakos ought to do, is to hire out for wages till you get onto the hang of it. There's tricks in gold diggin', same as anything else. Go get yerself a job somewheres."

Black John blinked as he considered the advice. "Guess that's right, Cap'n. Much 'blige—come on over to s'loon, an' I'll buy a drink."

"No thanks. I'm busy. See you some other time, maybe. So long, an' good luck."

THE OFFICER hurried on, and Black John proceeded to the Tivoli, where he found the marshal, flanked by two huskies he had never seen before, loudly explaining to a bunch of grinning sourdoughs, for the hundredth time, how Black John had effected his escape.

"Yessir; if them two damn fools I had fer deputies had minded their business it would never of happened. They wouldn't hold up like I told 'em to—keep their canoe dost behind mine. They went on ahead. I had him handcuffed, an' he claimed he had to git out on shore fer a minute. Well, if he had to, he had to, so I landed—an' the next thing I know'd I was handcuffed, an' he was loadin' me in the canoe an' shovin' me off. What happened, he'd brought them cuffs down on my head an' knocked me out. Then he took the keys out of my pocket an' onlocked 'em an' slipped 'em on me. I hadn't ought to have cuffed his hands in front of him, but I'm a humane man, gents. He claimed they hurt him the way I had 'em—behind him. So I changed 'em, an' that's what I git fer it. Believe me—next time he don't git no favors. An' I fetched a couple of deputies this time that'll tend to their business. Them other ones was more witnesses than deputies, anyhow—I fetched 'em along to identify the prisoner."

Black John had edged in between Bettles and Swiftwater, jostling each of them. Both gave him a dirty look, but paid no further attention to him.

"Well," chuckled Bettles, "you got him identified, didn't you? You'll know him agin if you see him."

"Yer damn right I will! I'd know them whiskers if I seen 'em in hell. An' believe me, the next time I git holt of him I'll keep holt till he's hung!"

"Who you huntin', mister?" asked Black John, awkwardly shifting his stance to bring his heel down on Swiftwater Bill's toes.

"Look out where yer steppin', you clumsy loon!" cried Swiftwater, giving the offender a shove that nearly bowled over Old Bettles, who in turn pushed him against the marshal, with the remark that, "there ought to be a law agin' chechakos mixin' around where folks is, anyhow."

With a well simulated grin of drunken good nature, the offender retired to a chair, satisfied that his disguise would answer his purpose.

"Beauty," he observed philosophically to himself, as he eyed the sourdoughs and the irate marshal, "ain't only skin deep, as the Good Book says. But it seems like friendship an' animosity don't even git past a man's whiskers."

Black John hung about Dawson, mingling unobtrusively with the men in the saloons and listening to the talk which ran mostly to the escape of Black John Smith from the American marshal and his deputies. He listened with amusement to a hundred garbled accounts of the incident, and enjoyed hugely the preposterous speculations that were rife, as to what could be expected of the notorious outlaw in the future. Some predicted a series of crimes that would spread a veritable reign of terror throughout the Yukon. Others opined that the North had seen the last of Black John. While still others believed that he would slip quietly back to Halfaday Creek until the excitement blew over. This latter opinion was fostered by Cuter Malone, who further stated that, with as few police as there were in the country and as busy as they were, Black John was now in a position to organize the Halfaday Creek outlaws into a gang that could openly defy all authority. He pointed out that since the outlaw was now facing definite charges on both sides of the line, he would have everything to gain and nothing to lose by such procedure. This theory, with its apparent plausibility, was generally accepted throughout the camp. But Black John noted that the sourdoughs shook their heads, and for the most part reserved their predictions. As for the police—they, too, reserved their predictions, and went silently about their business.

ABOUT NOON on the third day after Black John's return to Dawson, a wild-eyed prospector catapulted into the big camp with the story of how he had been held up and robbed, at the point of a big revolver, of seven hundred and twenty-one ounces of dust that he was bringing in for deposit. The man was a sourdough named Riley who had a claim on Bonanza. The hold-up had occurred on the Klondike, just below the mouth of Bonanza, and Riley stated unequivocally, and in no uncertain terms that the lone bandit was no other than Black John Smith. He had known Black John by sight for more than a year, having seen him in Dawson on numerous occasions. There was no chance that he was mistaken in this identification. In fact, the bandit openly admitted his identity when Riley told him he knew him. Not only that, he had told his victim to tell Corporal Downey, and all the rest of the police that from now on they'd better stay off Halfaday Creek.

This announcement created intense excitement in Dawson. Black John had hurled defiance into the very teeth of the Northwest Mounted Police. What would the police do now?

In the Klondike Palace, Cuter Malone and his henchmen openly opined that the police would not call the bluff. In the Tivoli, the sourdoughs shook their heads and wondered. It was up to Corporal Downey. What would Downey do?

Toward the middle of the afternoon Black John formed one of a group of chechako hangers-on who occupied chairs ranged along the wall of the Tivoli when Corporal Downey entered and sauntered to the bar where some of the sourdoughs had foregathered. Abrupt silence had greeted the appearance of the officer—a silence that told more plainly than words that he had been the subject of discussion. Old Bettles shoved over to make room for him.

"Looks like Black John's runnin' hog-wild," commented Swiftwater Bill, by way of opening conversation.

"Sure looks like somebody is," grinned Downey.

"D'you reckon he'd hit fer Halfaday?" inquired Moosehide Charley.

"He might," answered the officer. "I'll swing around that way an' see, after he's had time to get there—if we don't pick him up somewheres else first."

"Goin' up alone?" asked Burr McShane.

Downey grinned. "Hell—there's only one of him, ain't there?"

"Yeah," chimed in the marshal, "but he's warned the police to stay off'n Halfaday. An' how about that gang up there?"

"There's only one gang," Downey replied. "An' besides, Black John ain't got no authority to order the police where to stay away from. I've got a constable up on Bonanza workin' on this last robbery. If he don't turn nothin' up in a week er so, we'll go up to Halfaday an' kind of look around."

"We!" exclaimed the marshal, his eyes widening. "You mean *me?*"

"Sure. You want him worse'n I do. You've got a murder charge agin him, besides a robbery—an' that escape. All we've got is a couple of robberies. Hell—you want to get yer badge back, don't you? I would, if I was you. There wouldn't hardly anyone know you was a marshal without that badge."

The marshal gulped and swallowed. "Mebbe," he ventured hopefully, "that Constable will pick him up on Bonanza."

"He might, at that."

"But if he don't, it'll be all right to take my deputies along, too, won't it?"

"Oh, sure. We won't be makin' no secret about the trip. Jest go on up an' get our man, if he's there. Fetch along anyone you want to. It's all right with me."

"What with bein' wanted both sides of the line, I don't believe he'd dare to show up on Halfaday," suggested the marshal eagerly. "I'll bet that warnin' he give was jest a bluff."

"Yeah?" drawled Old Bettles, eyeing the uneasy marshal, with a grin. "It's plain to see, brother, that you ain't never played no stud with Black John. When yer damn near shore he's bluffin', is jest the time he ain't. But anyways, you fellas'll be dyin' doin' yer duty—an' that's somethin'. Would you like fer the remains, if any is found, to be shipped back to Circle? Or Fort Yukon?"

VIII

BLACK JOHN LEFT the Tivoli and made straight for the Klondike Palace where he found in earnest conversation with Cuter Malone the same three men who had been talking with him just after his escape had become known.

Making no attempt to overhear them, he bought a drink, stepped from the room, and struck out for Moosehide at a rapid pace.

An hour later he surprised Owl Man in his shack. "Come on—throw the stuff into the canoe, an' well git agoin'! I've got a hunch that this hombre that looks like me will be hittin' fer Halfaday, if he ain't done so already. If he has, he ain't got no hell of a start an' we kin slip past him on the river. I want to be waitin' fer him on the White, an' kind of look him over. Well hit acrost an' hug the other bank."

TOWARD NOON of the sixth day thereafter Black John, who was seated comfortably among some rocks screened by a clump of bushes at the foot of a portage on the White River, turned his head and called to the Indian, who was dozing on his blanket.

"Here comes a canoe," he said, "an' I mistrust it's the party I'm lookin' fer. You go back in the brush a ways an' wait till I holler fer you. Go back fer enough so you can't see nor hear nothin'. What goes on here ain't no one's business but mine—an', of course, the party's I'm speakin' of. We won't be needin' no witness."

Black John picked up Owl Man's rifle which rested against a rock close beside him, made sure it was loaded, and settled back to scrutinize the approaching canoe. It contained a single occupant who, a short distance below, shifted from paddle to pole and after a survey of the fast water ahead of him, headed for the portage trail straight toward where the man with the rifle was waiting.

"Well, I'll be damned," muttered Black John, as he stared at the lone canoeman. "Unless them bar mirrors all lies like hell,

I can't blame them fellas that got robbed fer claimin' it was me that done it. He shore as hell looks like I used to before I shaved off my whiskers. I'm wonderin'," he grinned, "if he'll try to make me believe he's me?"

The canoe grated on the coarse gravel, and the man stepped ashore, stooped, and pulled it a little higher. As he straightened and turned to study the foot rail, he found himself looking squarely into the blue-gray eyes of a huge, smooth-shaven man with a sunburned face. The man stood squarely in the trail, the barrel of a rifle lightly cradled in the crook of his elbow.

For tense seconds they stood, looking into each other's eyes. Then the bearded one frowned. "Who the hell are you?" he demanded. "An' what you doin' here?"

The smooth-shaven one noted that the canoeman's right hand was creeping slowly toward his shirt front which bulged near the waistline to show the outline of a heavy revolver. Casually the muzzle of the rifle shifted and came to rest on a direct line with the bearded one's heart. The creeping right hand dropped to the man's side.

"I'm jest some chechako that's restin' up a bit before tacklin' the portage," Black John replied. "Who are you? An' where the hell you headin'?"

"Chechako, eh!" The frown darkened, and the man's voice boomed threateningly. "Well, I'm Black John Smith—does that mean anything to you?"

The blue-gray eyes widened in surprise. "Black John Smith! You don't mean the Black John Smith that's king of them outlaws up on Halfaday Crick, do you? The one the police had in jail fer a robbery, an' give him up to a U.S. marshal fer to take down to Circle an' hang him—an' he busted away from the marshal! You don't mean *him!*"

"The hell I don't," thundered the man. "An' it was a marshal an' two deputies. Not jist a marshal. An' that ain't all; I've hung more chechakos on Halfaday, than I've let live—see?"

"What did you hang 'em fer?" queried Black John, the inquisitive chechako eagerness in his voice.

"Just fer bein' chechakos!" boomed the man. "Swing that gun off'n me, an' git to work an' help me pack this stuff over this portage. Yer lucky as hell I'm lettin' you live. We're bad men up on Halfaday—outlaws. We'd jest as soon kill a man as look at him. We're tough—hard—see?"

"Yeah, I see," Black John replied, a slow grin twisting the corners of his mouth, as he thumbed the hammer of his rifle to full cock, while its muzzle still covered the man's heart. "An' it seems like when anyone gits as tough as what you claim to be, it's time someone pinned his ears back. Fact is, yer too damn rough a character to suit me. I won't feel safe as long as I know a hard guy like you is packin' a belly gun. Jest pull yer shirt out of yer pants an' let the gun drop to the ground—bein' damn careful you don't make no grab fer it in transit, as a railroad would say."

"What!" roared the astounded man, his eyes on the muzzle of the rifle. "Who the hell do you think you are?"

"I'm the same chechako you been talkin' to all along, an' I don't aim to git potted with no six-gun. Pull yer shirt out like I said an' let that gun drop—an' do it now. 'Cause if this rifle lets go, like it's bound to within the next few seconds, there's goin' to be a hole right through your middle you could throw a dog through."

ONLY FOR an instant did the man hesitate, as his eyes met the gray-blue eyes that gleamed, cold as ice. Then deliberately the man drew the front of his shirt from his trousers, and allowed a forty-five six-gun to drop to the gravel.

"Now," continued the man with the rifle, "you walk out on the p'int there; go clean to the end of it an' set down in plain sight, where I kin keep an eye on you till I git through runnin' through yer outfit. I don't dare to trust a man as hard as you claim to be out of my sight. If you was as lucky in them hold-ups as what folks claims, you ought to be packin' considerable dust along with you. If I take that dust off'n yer hands, you won't need no help to pack the rest of yer stuff over the portage. I don't like to do this, you understand. Fact is, I'd heard Halfaday was a good crick to locate on, an' I was headin' up there to try an' make me an honest livin'. But if you men up there is as tough as what you claim, I don't want nothin' whatever to do with you. So I'll take what dust you've got, an' go somewhere's else."

"You mean," snarled the man, his eyes glaring with hate, "that this is a stick-up?"

"You ought to know, if anyone does," replied Black John. "From what folks say, yer pretty handy at it yerself. 'Course, I don't claim to be no professional at it—like you. There'll prob'ly be some little mistakes I'll make that you'd notice—me bein' jest a chechako. An' I'd take it kind of you if you'd sort of p'int 'em out, as I make 'em. You see, bein' as this here dust you've got is, what you might say, the fruits of crime, I don't feel no compunctions about takin' it—'specially as you've practically deprived me of a livelihood by scarin' me off Halfaday. Git along, now—an' go out on the p'int, before I have to kill you—like you done that prospector down to Circle. I wouldn't have no compunctions about that, neither."

The man obeyed, muttering curses as he backed along the narrow spit of sand.

Black John laughed. "No matter how tough a guy is, he don't look nothin' but funny with his shirt tail out. I'll bet even them outlaws would laugh, if they could see you, now."

It took him but a few minutes to locate the man's gold—fifteen small heavy moose-skin sacks of it—which he promptly transferred to his own packsack. Thrusting the man's revolver beneath his own shirt, he secured his rifle and regarded him with a frown.

"Near as I kin figger, from the talk around Dawson, you ought to have a little better'n twenty-three hundred ounces. The American marshal claimed you got six hundred ounces off'n the prospector you murdered over around Circle City, an' them two birds claimed you robbed 'em of a thousand ounces on Hunker. Then there was that last job near the mouth of Bonanza—"

"How the hell could you know about that?" exclaimed the man suddenly.

Black John grinned. "Why wouldn't I? This here Riley you robbed, he shore didn't make no secret of it. Hell, everyone in Dawson know'd it ten minutes after he hit camp. Man, I'm tellin' you—he squawked!"

"But—what I mean—I didn't hang around long after pullin' that job—how in hell could you git here ahead of me?"

"The answer," grinned the big man, "is simple. I come faster."

"You ain't no chechako!" exclaimed the man. "Who the hell are you? Mebbe we kin deal."

"Who I ain't, er who I am, ain't neither here nor there. An' as fer dealin'—we've already dealt. If I seem to have got slightly the better of the deal, don't let it sour you none. You got to remember that you won out on them last three deals you made—an' a man can't expect all the breaks. Besides, if you look at it right, this here deal is an even break fer both of us—our losses on it is almost identical. Think of my deep chagrin in gettin' less than a twelve hundred ounce profit, when I had every reason to expect better'n twenty-three hundred ounces. To say that I'm disapp'inted in you is statin' the case mildly. You ain't livin' up to yer reputation—by a damn sight! You ought to be ashamed of yerself. You ain't hardly no more than a common piker." Black John stemmed the torrent of profane objurgation that interrupted his words. "Of course, there might be some mitigatin' or extenuatin' circumstances—like folks exaggeratin' yer take on them three jobs, er the fact that you had to split with a pardner. Bein' as these was all reported as one-man jobs, the pardner, if any, would be a silent one. An' that's prob'ly the answer—Cuter Malone has collected his split."

"Cuter Malone!" cried the man, staring wide-eyed at the speaker. "What the hell do you know about Cuter Malpne?"

"It would take too long to tell it."

"Who the hell are you, anyhow?"

Black John grinned broadly. "Names don't cut no figger in this country—it's faces that counts. Like I told you—I'm jest some chechako tryin' to git along. But we've wasted time enough, already. I don't want to detain you no longer'n what's necessary. I'm retainin' yer dust, an' yer rifle an' revolver. I know you must be anxious to be gittin' back to Halfaday Crick amongst them hard guys, so you'll feel to home. It must be kind of degradin' fer a tough hombre like you, the notorious king of the outlaws, to be associatin' with any common chechako he happened to meet up with on a river. I can understand that it would be right humiliatin' if anyone was to come along an' catch you at it. But I don't see no one comin', an' if you git agoin' right away, you'll prob'ly be spared the mortification. I'll promise not to mention the matter to anyone, if you don't. Sorry I can't help you over the portage with the balance of yer stuff, but I know you realize that it would be folly fer me to let go of these guns even fer a minute under the circumstances. There's times, you know, in this country, when a man is forced to forego the amenities, even at the risk of bein' thought crude an' boorish. So long, King—next time you hang a chechako, think of me."

IX

IN SULLEN SILENCE the bearded man packed his outfit over the short portage trail and launched his canoe above the rapids. Black John watched until he disappeared around a bend of the river, and then called to Owl Man who appeared promptly:

Black John regarded him sternly, albeit with a twinkle in his eye. "Either you didn't go back in the brush as fer as I intimated; or else you come like hell when I hollered. Did you perchance see or hear anything that went on?"

The native shook his head. "No—no see—no hear. Me sleep. Wake oop fas' w'en you holla."

"You must of had a damn comical dream then—accordin' to that grin on yer pan. But whatever it was, you better fergit it. You're hittin' back to Dawson in a few minutes, an' git this straight—you've got to git word to Downey that Black John Smith is headin' up White River. Don't tell Downey yerself. He'd figger it was a phony tip, because he knows yer a friend of mine an' wouldn't talk if you had seen me. There must be some of them constables around Dawson that don't know you, ain't there?"

Owl Man nodded. "Cop'l Downey know me. Cons'ble Peters know me. Mor' p'lice don' know me."

"All right, you slip one of them others the tip that I'm headin' up White River. Tell him you was campin' at the mouth of the White an' saw me go by. If he asks yer name, lie to him an' slip away. All Siwashes looks alike to them rooky constables. He'll pass the word to Downey, an' Downey'll come up to Halfaday an' git this bird that looks like me. Mebbe the American marshal'll come along, too, if his guts'll permit it. You savvy what I told you?"

The Indian repeated the instructions, and glanced toward the canoe concealed in the bushes. "Only wan canoe. W'at you do?"

"You take the canoe. I'll hit fer Cush's afoot. I know a short-cut that'll git me there a good day ahead of this double of mine. I want to kind of wise Cush up to what's goin' on, before he does something drastic. Git goin' now. Here, hold on—what was it I borrowed off'n you?"

"Wan hondre seex dolla—forty-wan ounce dus'."

Reaching into his packsack Black John drew out two heavy sacks which he tossed to the Indian whose eyes fairly bulged from his head as he hefted them in his hands.

"Too mooch dus'!" he exclaimed. "Wan sack plenty. Wan sack too mooch dus'."

Black John interrupted him with a frown. "Quit yer damn quibblin'!" he growled. "Them sacks runs right around eighty ounces apiece. What I borrowed would run around forty-eight er nine ounces. The rest is wages an' interest—savvy? An' don't stand there an' give me none of yer back talk, neither, or I'll throw you back in the river where I pulled you out of that time. If I hire a man it ain't none of your damn business what I pay him. Shut up—an' git a goin'. I'm takin' grub enough with me to see me to Cush's."

SHOULDERING HIS pack, Black John struck diagonally into the hills, and five days later, he descended into the valley of Halfaday, some half a dozen miles below Cushing's Fort.

Pot Gutted John and Red John paused in their labor to eye the big smooth-shaven stranger who had halted beside their shaft.

"Is this Halfaday Crick?" asked the man. "An' could you tell me where I'll find Cushing's Fort?"

"Yeah, this is Halfaday," Pot Gutted John answered. "An' you can't miss Cush's. It's about four mile up the trail. Figgerin' on locatin' on Halfaday?"

"Well—I might, if I like it here. The name is Smith—John Smith."

Red John grinned broadly. "So's ourn," he replied. "That there's Pot Gutted John—on account of him bein' that shape. An' I'm Red John, on account of my hair an' whiskers is that color."

"But," interrupted Pot Gutted John, "the name ain't allowed no more on the crick. Old Cush, he'll fix you up out of the name-can."

"The name-can?"

"Yeah, there got to be too damn many John Smiths on the crick. It's a kind of a handy name to think of, if a man wants a name right quick, an' most everyone that come to Halfaday claimed they was named that. So when we hung One Eyed John one time, he left some book behind. An' Black John an' Cush copied a lot of names out of it an' stuck 'em in a can—an' now when anyone comes along an' says his name is John Smith, he's got to draw some other one out of a can."

"Good idea," grinned the big man. "You mentioned a Black John? I wonder if he could be the Black John Smith that they say is under arrest for a robbery, or somethin' down to Dawson?"

"Yeah, he's the one. But he never pulled no robbery down there. He's too smart to pull a job like that. There was a constable up here talkin' to Cush about it. He says the fellers that got robbed claimed Black John done it, but hell, them damn chechakos don't know one man from another nohow. Downey'll turn Black John loose pretty quick. He's bound to. Downey ain't no damn fool; he knows Black John wouldn't pull no job fer no thousan' ounces—an' he wouldn't."

"Accordin' to the talk in Dawson, Downey had to turn this Black John over to a U.S. marshal an' a couple of deputies that come to Dawson with papers. He's wanted fer a murder an' robbery over on the American side—Circle City, er somewheres."

"Well, I'll be damned," chuckled Pot Gutted John.

"It'll be fun hearin' him tell about it," grinned Red John.

"You don't seem to be very much worried about it," the smooth-shaven man said. "Ain't this Black John a friend of yourn?"

"Shore he is! But why the hell should we worry? We ain't tryin' to take Black John nowheres. That marshal an' them deputies is the ones that's got to worry. There ain't no three men livin' that's goin' to take Black John nowheres he don't want to go."

"Well, I'll be movin' along," said the big man. "I'll be seein' you later, if I decide to locate somewheres on the crick. So long."

As Black John passed on up the trail he chuckled to himself. When he reached a point within half a mile of the fort, he stepped from the trail, seated himself comfortably on a rock, produced a piece of wrapping paper from his packsack, fished the stub of a pencil from his pocket, and proceeded to write a note which he carefully folded and placed in his pocket. Then he resumed his journey, halting uncertainly some ten minutes later in the doorway of the saloon, to eye the somber-faced man with a drooping yellow mustache, who stood behind the bar intently reading the Bible spread open before him.

The man looked up as the shadow darkened the doorway, peering over the top of his square rimmed steel spectacles. Deliberately he closed the book, set it on the back bar, and set out a bottle and two glasses.

"Come on in, stranger," he invited. "The house is buyin' a drink."

"Is this Cushing's Fort?" asked the man, as he advanced to the bar, and swung the packsack from his shoulders.

"Yeah, this is the place."

"An' are you the proprietor?"

"I'm him."

"Sometimes known as 'Old Cush?'"

"Yeah, but I ain't no older'n some of the rest of 'em, at that."

"My name's John Smith. I—"

"Not on Halfaday, it ain't," interrupted the somber-faced one. He indicated a tin molasses can at the end of the bar. "Jest help yerself to a name," he said. "The name of John Smith has already been took—too many times."

The big man smiled good naturedly. "Oh, yes—I stopped and talked to a couple of men a few miles down the trail, and when I told them my name, they explained about the can. They said I couldn't use the name 'John Smith' on the crick."

"They was right."

Moving over to the can Black John thrust in his hand and drew out a slip of paper. "George Cornwallis," he read aloud.

The somber-faced one nodded. "Drink up, George," he invited. "The last man that draw'd that name got hung."

"Here's how. I hope I'll have better luck," grinned the other, swallowing his liquor.

"It's hard to say. You might."

"Fill 'em up again," said the big man, tossing a sack onto the bar. "An' if you're Old Cush, I've got a letter fer you."

"Who from?"

"All I know is an Injun that claimed his name was Owl Man, slipped it to me when I told him I was hittin' fer Halfaday. He says to give it to you, an' no one else. Here it is," the man removed the paper from his pocket and slipped it across the bar.

Cush took it, held it to the light, and studied it intently through his spectacles. "That's John's writin'," he muttered to himself, "an' Owl Man is a friend of his'n. But—I wonder what kind of tom-foolery he's up to now?"

"What's that?"

"Nothin'," replied Cush bluntly. "Except his writin' is hell to read. John, he kin talk big words till hell wouldn't have it, but he can't even write little ones so anyone kin read 'em without studyin' an hour."

"Mebbe I could help you," suggested the other.

Cush eyed him fishily. "If John had wanted everyone to know what he'd wrote down, he'd of put it in a newspaper," he said, and folding the note, slipped it between the leaves of the Bible on the back bar.

"Could a man locate on the crick?" asked the other.

"Help yerself," replied Cush. "There's some shacks up the crick that's empty. Move into one till you find somethin' you like."

"Thanks, I believe I will," replied the other, and an hour later, he left the fort after purchasing supplies to last for a couple of weeks.

WHEN HE had gone, Cush retrieved the note, and pondered it intently. "It's bad enough readin' printin' with these here specs, but readin' writin' is hell," he grumbled to himself as he smoothed the paper out on the bar and bent over it, moving his lips as he slowly read aloud.

Cush—
Some damn cuss that claims his name is John Smith an' looks like me, pulled off three robberies an' a murder. The victims, except the murdered one, an' some witnesses claims it was me that robbed 'em. Downey arrested me on a complaint an' then had to turn me over to a U.S. marshal who showed up with papers—one robbery an' the murder bein' pulled off somewheres around Circle. This marshal an' a couple of deputies started to take me to Circle, but they didn't have much luck at it. So I'm on the run till Downey arrests the real robber. That won't be long because he's hittin' fer Halfaday. Him an' Cuter Malone, believin' I won't dare to show up there, are figurin' on organisin', the boys into a gang of bad actors. When this bird shows up let him claim his name is John Smith an' let him move into my cabin. Slip the boys the word to string along with him till Downey comes, which won't be long, because he's already got the tip that he's hit fer Halfaday. Wish I could be there to see the fun when Downey picks him up.

(Signed) John."

Old Cush folded the note with a sigh, and slipped it between the leaves of the Bible. Then, shoving the spectacles to his forehead he shook his head forebodingly. "Things ain't never dull where John's mixed up in 'em," he murmured. "He kin git into the damndest jams I ever see. But he allus gits out of 'em—an' most times with a profit. It must be 'cause he thinks faster'n most folks—even the police." He was about to pour himself a drink, when the doorway darkened for an instant as a man strode into the room. Old Cush stared, slipped the spectacles back to his nose, and peered into the bearded face in undisguised astonishment, as the man faced him across the bar.

"This is Cushing's Fort—an' you're Old Cush," he announced, abruptly, and paused as though expecting a reply. But no reply came; the solemn faced man behind the bar simply stood peering through the spectacles. "Well," rasped the other, "don't stand there gogglin' like a dummy! Am I right; er wrong?"

"I wouldn't wonder."

"You wouldn't wonder—what?" demanded the man with a scowl.

"If you was."

"If I was—what? Right; er wrong?"

"Both."

"How the hell could I be both?"

"Right this time; wrong most of the time."

"Is that so!"

"I couldn't say."

"Look here," rasped the man, "don't try to git funny with me, you damn old moss-back! My name's Smith, John Smith—an' from now on Black John Smith, see?"

"There's already one Black John Smith on the crick," replied Cush mildly.

"That's right—an' I'm him. The one that used to be here won't be here no more. He's prob'ly plumb out of the country, by now. The police both sides of the line is huntin' him. He ain't got the guts to show up here—nor nowhere's else. He's afraid the police'll nab him. An' if he did show up, an' run into me—he'll wish to God the police had picked him up. Tellin' you about me—I'm hard!"

"Yeah?"

"Yeah—an' if you've got any sense you'll string along with me, see? You've got a good thing here, they tell me, an' you kin keep on havin' a good thing—if you watch yer step. You'll have a better thing than you ever had while the other Black John was here. Trouble with you guys was, you didn't have no guts. How many outlaws is here on the crick?"

"I couldn't say."

"Well—there's forty, er fifty, ain't there?"

"I wouldn't know."

"Well, that's what Cuter—that's what I've heard. That's the talk down around Dawson, an' I've got reasons to believe it's straight goods. A hell of a bunch of outlaws, I'd say, workin' claims like a bunch of damn chechakos, when there's a hundred cricks in the country full of chechakos—an' sourdoughs, too—that's jest hollerin' to be robbed. An' only a hundful of police on this side of the line, an' you might say none at all on the other side. Trouble is, you ain't had no one that know'd how to organize. Take me, I know. Split the boys up into small mobs an' put 'em on different cricks, with a connection in Dawson to keep cases on the police, an' act as a kind of a clearin' house—switchin' the mobs around from one crick to another, an' all that. Hell, the police won't never even suspect Halfaday, an' if they did, they wouldn't git time to come up here, we'd keep 'em so busy on other cricks. If they did, it would be jest too damn bad fer 'em, that's all. I've warned 'em to stay off Halfaday! Do you git the idee?"

"It sounds easy," admitted Cush. "Did you think it out by yerself?"

"Well, me an' one er two others that's smart enough to know a good thing when they see one. How does it strike you?"

"All of a heap."

"Yer damn right! Hell—there ain't nothin' to it. We'll take this country like Grant took Richmond. Ain't you goin' to buy a drink?"

"Oh—shore," Cush replied, sliding a glass across the bar and indicating the bottle. "The house allus buys the first one. I'd plumb fergot—listenin' to them plans of yourn. Drink up."

"Well," demanded the man, as he swallowed the liquor and refilled his glass, "ain't you got nothin' to say? No questions to ask, er nothin'?"

"I was jest wonderin' about this here Grant you spoke of. Has he still got it?"

"Got what?"

"Why—Richmond, didn't you say he took?"

"Hell—no!" exclaimed the man in disgust. "Richmond's a city, you damn fool. The Gover'ment's got it, of course."

"Oh—I was jest wonderin' if that ain't what would happen to the Yukon, if we was to take it."

"Hell, ain't you got no brains, at all?"

"I couldn't say. Not many, I guess—accordin' to Black John."

THE MAN grinned. "He was right fer onct in his life, anyhow. By the way—do you handle guns?"

"Pretty good. Black John's about the only one on the crick kin outshoot me."

"I mean—do you sell 'em?"

"Oh—yeah. I got a few rifles in the storeroom."

"How about revolvers? I had bad luck comin' up the White. I landed at a portage, an' a damn cuss throw'd a rifle on me, an' lifted my own rifle, an' my revolver, an' better'n eleven hundred ounces in dust."

"You don't say! I wonder who done a trick like that?"

"I wish I know'd. Claimed he was jest a chechako, but he didn't act like one. An' his eyes didn't look like no chechako's eyes I ever seen. He never give me a break."

"Well, you can't hardly blame him fer that—tough as you be. What did he look like?"

"He was a big smooth-faced guy—big as I am. Kind of red-faced, an' he had sort of blue eyes that could look plumb through a man."

"Did he come on up the White?"

"He better not! I'd know him if I ever seen him agin. He claimed he was goin' back to the big river. Why—d'you think you know him?"

"No. Only—folks don't allus go where they claim they're goin'."

"How about a revolver?"

"I don't sell none. I got one of my own, but I'm apt to be needin' it any time."

"Where the hell can I locate, here on the crick? You got extry rooms upstairs?"

"Nope. You claim Black John ain't never comin' back. Why don't you take his place? It's a good cabin, right handy to here—jest up the trail a few rod. You can't miss it—it's the first one you come to."

"That'll suit me fine," agreed the man. Guess I'll go throw my stuff in there an' kind of look the place over. See you later."

When the man had gone, Old Cush shook his head dolefully. "It beats hell," he muttered, "some of the folks that's runnin' loose. Guess I better lock up an' go tell the boys what John said in his letter—'fore some of 'em knocks this tough guy off. Downey wouldn't like that. He'd claim we was hasty." As he struck off down the creek he grinned to himself. "This here smooth-faced man that fetched John's letter—he must be quite a fella, after all—'leven hundred ounces ain't so bad."

X

NEARLY TWO WEEKS passed, during which the self-styled Black John hung about the fort getting acquainted with the men of Halfaday who, following Cush's instructions, accepted him at his own valuation. He even broached his plan of organization to several of the men, who accepted it with apparent enthusiasm. He established a credit of drinks and supplies which Cush readily granted, grinning to himself as he charged the items against Black John's account.

Then one morning when the saloon was empty save for Cush and the pseudo Black John, four men appeared suddenly in the doorway. Three of them carried rifles which were immediately trained upon the bearded man who stood before the bar. The fourth wore the uniform of the Northwest Mounted Police.

One glance at the menacing rifles, and the bearded one reached high with both hands. Corporal Downey advanced, flanked closely by the riflemen. With a sly wink at Old Cush, the young officer paused directly before the man with the elevated hands.

"John Smith," he said, "you're under arrest, charged with the robbery of two men on Hunker Crick, and another near the mouth of Bonanza. It is my duty to warn you that anything you say may be used against you. Lower your hands now—an' try these on."

As the man's hands were lowered, the young officer slipped the cuffs on his wrists. "It is my duty, also, to turn you over to these American officers in compliance with the law."

"American officers!" cried the man, a look of terror in his eyes. "Not by a damn sight, you don't turn me over to no American officers! Listen, I'm guilty of them two robberies on the Yukon side. I robbed them two chechakos in their shack on Hunker—I took a thousan' ounces in dust off 'em. An' that guy on Bonanza—Riley his name is—I took him fer seven hundred an' twenty-one ounces."

"That checks," grinned Downey, "right to the ounce. Where is this dust? You got it cached?"

"No, I ain't got it, I was stuck up an' robbed comin' up here. A big smooth-faced guy done it. He claimed he was a chechako. I'm willin' to plead guilty, an' take my medicine on the Yukon side, but I didn't have a damn thing to do with that Wood Crick job. I don't know nothin' about the murder of that prospector."

"Who said anything about murderin' a prospector? No one's mentioned Wood Crick, er a prospector, either."

"I heard about it in Dawson," cried the man. "But you ain't goin' to pin that murder on me. It was the other Black John done it!"

"Oh," grinned Downey, "so there's two to Black Johns, eh? Do you mean to tell me you ain't the same Black John Smith that I had locked up in Dawson, an' later turned over to this American marshal?"

"Sure I ain't! I never seen you before—nor that marshal, neither. It was the other Black John you guys had—an' it was him pulled that murder near Circle." Corporal Downey turned with a grin to the United States marshal. "He sure looks like the same man I turned over to you. How about it?"

"I'll tell the world he's the same man! The damn dirty double-crossin' coot!" He glared at the manacled prisoner. "Worked me pretty slick, that other time, didn't you—claimin' you was hell-bent to git over to the American side, cause you know'd you could beat the case—an' then knockin' me cold an' makin' yer git-away?"

"I tell you I never seen you before," shouted the prisoner. "You got the wrong guy. There's another Black John. Ain't there, Cush?" He turned suddenly and appealed to the sombre-faced one who stood behind the bar, an interested spectator. "You tell 'em! There is another Black John, ain't there?"

Old Cush deliberately shifted his quid, and spat into a box of sawdust. "I couldn't say," he replied, eyeing the man steadily. "Yer the only Black John around here."

"It's a lie! It's a damn lie! Yer framin' me," cried the man, his voice rising almost to a scream. "I never seen none of you before. Take me to Dawson. Ask Cuter Malone—he knows!"

The American officer leered at the hysterical man. "Oh, yeah? Take you to Dawson, eh? Take you down where all them sourdough friends of yourn kin git you away from me. Not on yer life. You got away from me onct—an' onct is enough. Where in hell's my badge? Fork it over!"

"I don't know nothin' about yer badge. I tell you I never seen you before. It wasn't me got away from you. I ain't got no sourdough friends."

"Aw, hell," snorted the marshal, in disgust, "don't play me fer a damn fool! I'd know them whiskers anywheres. Don't try to pull that fool stuff on me. Come on along—I'll have plenty time to search you fer that badge. We ain't goin' to risk no trip down the Yukon—not when we're this dost to the Alasky line, we ain't." He turned to the deputies. "Fetch him along, boys; we'll slip him acrost the line before these Halfaday Crickers go on the warpath. Downey here, he's agreed to stick around an' keep 'em good till we git a start."

Corporal Downey spoke as the two husky deputies seized the prisoner's arms. "Better jest slip yer own cuffs on him. I might be needin' mine."

"Sure," assented the marshal, producing a pair from his pocket. "An' I'm lockin' his hands behind him, instead of in front. That's a trick you ought to remember," he added with a superior smile, as he returned the young officer's cuffs.

"You better take plenty of supplies along," cautioned Downey. "It's a long way to the nearest tradin' post on the American side—a hell of a long way, an' the goin's rough."

"Oh, we've got all the supplies we'll be needin'," replied the other. "Come on, boys, yank him along. If he won't come peaceable, a few good swift kicks from behind'll make him step up. I'll tend to that part. You keep holt of his arms."

And so the squirming, cursing, protesting prisoner was hauled out through the doorway, and headed toward the gulch that Downey had indicated as leading to the line, only a mile or so distant.

WHEN THEY had disappeared Corporal Downey turned to Old Cush, who had set out the bottle and glasses. "How about it, Cush?" he asked. "Ain't Black John showed up on the crick?"

"Nope," answered Cush, "he ain't. An' that's a fact, Downey. I ain't saw John sence that day he left here with that dust to take it down an' trade it fer bills. What do you want him fer—seein' how that damn cuss confessed to them robberies?"

"Well," grinned the officer, "there's a matter of some sixty-nine thousan' dollars in bills we're holdin' fer him. I was jest goin' to suggest to him that he better stop in fer it when he gits time."

"Did you relly figger Black John pulled them hold-ups?"

"No, I didn't. But after seein' this other fellow, I don't know as I blame them witnesses none fer claimin' it was him. Damn if I believe I could tell 'em apart if I was to see 'em together."

"Me, neither," agreed Cush. "That day he come stompin' through that door braggin' how tough he was, I'd swore it was Black John—that is, till I heard him talk, I would."

"I sure hated to turn John over to that marshal that night. They might have convicted him over there—especially if we hadn't been able to pick up this other one before the trial. It's no cinch he wouldn't have been convicted in Dawson, on the evidence, either. I've heard of men havin' doubles before, but that's the first time I ever saw it."

"Listen!" exclaimed Cush. "Sounds like shootin'—back in the hills over on the American side."

"Good God!" exclaimed Downey. "You don't suppose some of the boys here are try in' to rescue him, do you? Surely, even the dumbest of 'em must know that damn four-flusher ain't Black John."

Cush shook his head, and wangled a fresh chew from the corner of his plug. "No," he said. "It wouldn't be none of the boys. They all know'd he wasn't Black John. An' he ain't no one anyone on the crick would waste any shells over. Fact is, I seen blood in that marshal's eye when he was talkin' to that damn skunk. An' besides, I seen they never figgered on goin' very fer with what grub they had."

"You mean," exclaimed Downey, staring incredulously, "that they—they've murdered that poor devil?"

Cush shrugged. "They won't call it that. They'll claim he tried to git away on 'em—or attacked 'em, er somethin'. At that, they prob'ly give him as much show as he give that prospector he murdered, an' look at the trouble they saved theirselves takin' him clean' back to Circle!"

"But good God—they're officers, policemen!"

Again Cush shrugged. "Policemen is jest like anyone else—there's a damn sight of difference in the breed of 'em."

"But they're paid to bring a prisoner in—not to kill him!"

"Their pay goes on jest the same—either way."

The conversation was interrupted by a huge, smooth-shaven man who stepped into the room and advanced to the bar.

"Why hello, capt'n!" he exclaimed, thrusting out his hand. "What you doin' way up here? Last time I seen you was in Dawson. Bet you don't rec'lect me, at that."

"Why, sure I do," smiled the officer, shaking the proffered hand. "You stopped me on the street one day, and asked me where you could find some gold. I believe I advised you to get a job till you got onto the hang of things."

"That's right! That's jest what you said. I was a little bit soused that day, so I didn't pay no attention to that there advice, figgerin' you'd prob'ly feel different about it when I sobered up. So—"

"What?" interrupted Downey, eyeing the man with a puzzled frown.

"Yeah—you know yerself, capt'n, that you can't put no confidence in what a drunken man says, an'—"

"But," grinned the officer, "I wasn't drunk when I gave you that advice."

" 'Course not—but I was. You can't believe what a drunk hears, no more than what one says, so I took that there advice with a dose of salts, an' come on up here. I figger I'm goin' to like it on Halfaday—onct I git acquainted."

Old Cush slid a glass toward the newcomer. "The house is buyin' one," he said. "Corporal Downey, meet George Cornwallis. But—it looks like you'd met before."

"Oh shore, but I didn't tell him my name, that time. Drunk as I was, it prob'ly wouldn't of sounded much like 'George Cornwallis', if I had. It's faces that counts—not names, anyhow. Ain't that so, Capt'n? Take you police now, I bet you don't never fergit a face, onct you've got a look at it. Spottin' me the minute I come in here proves it. You know'd right where you seen me before—an' what the both of us said."

"I wouldn't say I never forget a face—I've prob'ly forgot thousands of 'em—but a man sort of gets into the habit of rememberin' a lot of 'em. It often comes in handy."

"I'll bet it would," agreed the other. "By the way, I heard some shootin' a few minutes ago—back a ways off the crick. Someone must be huntin'. Mebbe I could git a piece of meat off'n him. I ain't had no time to hunt sence I come here. Been' busy findin' a location."

"I don't think you want none of the meat they've killed," observed Cush. "Fact is, some American marshals jest crossed the line a while back with a prisoner. He claimed he was a tough hand."

"You mean, mebbe this prisoner attacked 'em, an' they shot him?"

Cush replied. "If they shot him they'll be back d'rectly."

"What was his name?"

"He claimed it was Black John Smith."

"Prob'ly a good thing if they shot him," observed Cornwallis. "I heard about him down to Dawson. They tell me this Black John was a bad actor. From what they say, I'll bet he's give you plenty of trouble, ain't he, Capt'n?"

Downey nodded. "That man has," he replied. "But, at that, they shouldn't have—"

The sentence was interrupted by the entrance of the marshal, followed by his two deputies. "Well, his hash is settled!" the marshal announced loudly with a broad wink at Corporal Downey as the three ranged themselves before the bar. "Belly up, boys—I'm settin' 'em up to the house."

"Meanin'?" inquired the corporal, meeting the other's glance squarely.

"Meanin' that Black John Smith won't never rob no more armies, nor murder no more prospectors, nor stick up no more chechakos. He's deader'n a nit—right now."

"You killed him?" asked Downey incredulously.

"Shore as hell we killed him!" boasted the marshal. Then, with a broad grin, he added, "He tried to git away on us. He pulled that git-away stunt jest onct too often—see?"

"Yeah," answered Downey, "I see."

"Well, come on, boys! Set out the glasses, barkeep. What you goin' to have?"

Both Corporal Downey and the smooth-shaven man stepped slightly back from the bar. "I ain't dry," said the corporal, his eyes still on the marshal's face.

"How about you?" asked the marshal, shifting his glance to the big man at the officer's side, as the smile faded from his lips.

"Dry as hell," replied the smooth-shaven one, contempt showing in his blue-gray eyes, "but partic'lar who I drink with."

The marshal shrugged. "Suit yerselves," he grunted, and turned to Cush. "The barkeep'll have one, anyhow. Right?"

"Wrong," said Cush, leaning against the back bar as the three downed their liquor.

"What the hell's the matter with you guys, anyhow?" demanded the marshal. "Here we come clean up here an' take a bad actor off'n yer hands, an' put him where he won't never bother no one no more—an' you practically insult us fer it." He turned to Downey. "I s'pose you'd of let him git away on you, eh?"

"No. I'd have taken him in to stand trial."

"Oh, you would, eh?" sneered the marshal. "Well, you've learnt somethin', then, in the way of policin'."

Downey nodded. "That's right," he admitted. "Only on this side of the line we ain't supposed to murder prisoners."

The man's face flushed. "Murder?"

"That's what we'd call shootin' down a handcuffed prisoner, over here. The officer that done it would be hung. An' he should be, too."

THE BIG man beside the corporal cleared his throat roughly. "This here murder," he began, "while it didn't come off exactly on Halfaday Creek was undoubtless committed in the immediate vicinity thereof, an' in sech case, would rightly come under the jurisdiction of a miners' meetin'. Of course the fact that it occurred on the Alasky side might complicate matters, in case anyone was minded to quibble." The big man paused, a twinkle in his blue-gray eyes as he was conscious that at the sound of his voice, both Old Cush and Corporal Downey were regarding him with open mouths and eyes that seemed to fairly pop from their heads. He turned to the astounded Downey, and continued, "So if the Yukon law would turn his back on the incident, an' head back to Dawson, we'd call a miners' meetin' an' go ahead an' hang about three so-called American marshals fer the crime of murder."

A look of sudden fear flashed into the marshal's eyes, as he appealed to Corporal Downey. "Don't go!" he cried. "Yer bound to stay here an' protect us! I've heard of these hangin's on Halfaday Crick! We're in a hell of a fix! We've jest killed the king of these outlaws, an' they'll hang us shore as hell! You can't go away an' leave us. We demand protection!"

"All right," replied Downey, his face purple with suppressed laughter, "I'll do my damndest. But I wouldn't advise you men to go back down the crick. You'd better get supplies here, an' hit straight for the line—where you crossed yer prisoner—an' then hit for the Tananna. There's only one of me, an' there's lots of outlaws here, on the crick—so you'd better not delay startin'. I'll keep this man under surveillance so he can't spread the word about the murder of Black John Smith. If that once got out on the crick, no one could foresee what would happen."

"I kin," scowled the huge man, "an' my advice is, that if you birds don't want it to happen, you'd better begin pickin' 'em up an' layin' 'em down as fast as yer conscience dictates—an' keep on doin' it fer as long as yer legs holds out. We ain't never hung a U.S. marshal on Halfaday—but a lot of the boys would delight to."

Half an hour later, after Cush had turned over supplies that would last them for ten days, the three took a hurried and fearful departure. When they had gone, the big smooth-shaven man turned to Corporal Downey with a grin:

"How about a little drink, Capt'n? The house is about to buy one. Ain't that right, Cush?"

"Well, I'll be damned!" breathed Old Cush, as he set out the bottle and glasses. "To think that you'd ever be able to fool me! I wouldn't never believed it."

"Oh, you wasn't so hard to fool, but Downey, here—what with the police trained to recollect faces, an—"

"You go to hell!" laughed Downey, "John, you'd have made a great actor."

"Oh shore—always wanted to be one, too. But actors don't move around as fast as I've had to, sometimes. I'm shore glad that Army pay-roll job is wrote off the books fer good. It was kind of botherin' me. Of course," he added, with a grin, "that marshal might hear that Black John Smith is back on Halfaday agin, but he won't hardly believe it. An' it ain't likely he'd come up an' investigate, if he did."

"I guess yer right," agreed Downey, his eyes on Black John's face. "But I was just wonderin' about that dust that the dead man took off those prospectors? He claimed he was stuck up an' robbed down on White River, by a big, smooth-faced chechako."

"He did, eh?" queried Black John, with undisguised interest. "Well—there's a job fer you, Downey. Policin' must be hell—first yer out huntin' fer a man with whiskers, an' the next thing you know, yer huntin' a man without none. It must be right discouragin', at times. Well, here's luck to you! An' speakin' of whiskers— I've got to git to work an' grow me a new stand of 'em."

"Yeah," grunted Old Cush, as he swallowed his liquor, and refilled his glass, "an' see that you don't fergit to put that there name you draw'd back in the can neither."

THE GHOST OF HALFADAY CREEK

ONE MORNING, A week after the killing of the pseudo Black John Smith by a United States marshal and his two deputies, Old Cush grinned across the bar as Black John scratched irritably at his heavily stubbled jowl.

"You put me in mind of one of them tramps that used to come beggin' a handout off'n my ma when I was a kid back there in Minnesoty. It's kind of funny about them tramps. There wasn't none of 'em which his beard had grow'd out long, an' none of 'em was shaved smooth, an' none of 'em looked like they'd shaved yesterday, er the day before—they allus had about a week's stand of whiskers on their face. I can't figger out why that would be."

"Well," replied Black John, "off hand I'd say it was because they hadn't shaved fer a week."

"But," persisted Cush, "why was it allus a week they hadn't shaved? No matter what time of year it was, nor which way they was goin', they allus had about a week's len'th of whiskers on 'em. They looked like hell."

"There's the answer. The worse they looked, the more likely they was to git a hand-out. Them bums wasn't no fools'. A long series of careful experiments, extendin' back over a certain number of years, had proved that a week's stand of whiskers was the proper amount to coax the biggest hand-out from a housewife. Hoboin' is a profession, same as anything else. There's tricks to it."

"Y-e-a-h," replied Cush, his forehead furrowed with doubt, "but hell, John, what would they do the next week? The next week they'd have a two weeks—"

"Listen, Cush," Black John interrupted, "You know jest as well as I do them hoboes lives a hand-to-mouth existence. Cripes, if they stopped to figger where they was goin' to eat the next week, the next day, even, they wouldn't be hoboes. An' if they wasn't hoboes they'd either shave every day, er else they'd grow a beard like respectable folks does, an' wouldn't have to be lookin' fer no hand-out. If you'd use yer head you could figger them things out fer yerself, instead of pesterin' me with 'em. At that, though," he added, scratching once more at his jaw, "they shore must have lived a miserable existence, if their week's stand of whiskers itched like mine does. They're sharp as needles, an' stiff as wire. My face got a hell of a sunburn after I shaved my beard off, that's prob'ly what makes it itch. I'll shore be glad when them whiskers grows out long enough to bend a little. I've got to sleep flat on my back."

"That there fella them marshals murdered that claimed he was you—I wouldn't of thought two fellas could look so much alike. Yer shore you ain't got no brothers, er nothin' like that?"

Black John grinned. "I've got two brothers an' a sister—but this fella couldn't of been none of them. My youngest brother, he found steady work on a chain gang down in Florida, er mebbe it was Georgia. Everett, his name is. Seems like he didn't have no ethics to speak of. Us older boys done what we could fer him, but he was a kind of black sheep—he was always gittin' caught. My older brother's a preacher, like pa. I come damn near bein' one, too, but I couldn't see no future in it. My sister married a professor; an' it's your turn to buy a drink."

"I wouldn't think she'd of married no perfesser," opined Cush as he shoved the bottle across the bar.

"Why not?"

"Well, I don't know. They might be all right, but I never seen none that I'd want fer my sister should marry him—playin' the pyanner nights in them dance halls where all them girls is hangin' around, an' all. I—"

"Why, you damn fool, that ain't the kind of a professor I mean! This fella is a professor of history in one of the biggest universities in the country!"

"Oh," replied Cush doubtfully. "That might be different. But at that, it looks like she was takin' a chanct. Them perfessors is prob'ly all more er less alike."

The two were interrupted as One Armed John burst into the room, his eyes wide with horror. "My God, Cush," he cried, with hardly a glance at the stubble-faced man who stood at the bar. "Black John's killed!"

OLD CUSH regarded him with a grin as he slid a glass toward him. "Drink up," he said, "an' tell us about it."

"Don't laugh!" cried the excited man. "It ain't nothin' to laugh about! It's true! I seen him myself—jest a few minutes ago! Someone sneaked up an' shot him through the back, four, five times. He's layin' there in a snowbank that ain't melted yet, in a deep coulee, jest a little ways acrost the line. I seen him, I tell you, an' he's deader'n hell!"

"Who is this Black John! An' how long's he been dead?" asked the big man who stood beside One Armed John at the bar.

"Who is he? He's the best damn man that ever hit Halfaday—er any other crick! He's got more guts an' more brains in a minute than anyone else has got in a year! Ain't that so, Cush?"

"W-e-e-l-l," drawled Cush, "John's got a pretty good head on him, most times."

"Pretty good head! I'll say he had a pretty good head! Cripes, he done all your thinkin' fer you—an' the rest of the boys, too. What we goin' to do, Cush, now he's gone?"

"Bury him, I reckon, same as anyone else," Cush replied.

"Shore we'll bury him," agreed One Armed John. "We'll give him the damndest funeral Halfaday ever seen! But—it looks to me like yer takin' it damn ca'm. How we goin' to git along without him?"

The big, stubble-bearded man grinned.

"No one ever died yet," he opined, "that couldn't be got along without. How would I do—to sort of take this party's place?"

One Armed John flashed the speaker a glance of contempt. "You! Who the hell are you?"

Gray-blue eyes twinkled above the black stubble. "Smith, is the name. John Smith—Black John, I'm called, owin' to my whiskers bein' sort of dark-like, when they've grow'd out."

At the sound of Black John's familiar voice. One Armed John stood as one suddenly bereft of his senses. His mouth sagged open, his eyes seemed to protrude from their sockets, and he shook as with a violent chill. "John," he finally managed to gasp. "Is it really you, John?"

"Why, shore it's me," grinned the big man, "barrin' a few whiskers. Cripes, One Armed, git holt of yerself. You'd ort to use yer head. What the hell would I be doin' layin' dead on a snowbank up some coulee. It wouldn't make sense."

"But—but—someone's layin' dead up there. I tell you I seen him. Only a few minutes ago—I run like hell when I seen fer shore who it was—an' I never stopped till I got here. If he ain't you, by God, he's yer ghost—er yer brother, er somethin'. He looks jest like you used to look!"

"Where you been fer the last week?"

"I made me a prospectin' trip, over on the American side. Been gone damn near two weeks.

Black John nodded. "That's why you didn't know about them U.S. marshals murderin' that fella that looked like me. They arrested him, an' then shot him, ruther than have the bother of takin' him to jail. That was a week ago. What kind of shape is he in?"

"Oh, he's good an' fresh, yet," replied One Armed John. "Might's well of been killed this mornin' fer all you could tell.

He's layin' on his face in that snow, an' that deep, narrow coulee's cold. I've got to go back up there. I throw'd my pack away so I could run."

"There ain't no hurry," said Black John. "Wait till tomorrow, an' we'll git some of the boys an' go up there an' bury him."

"All right. I'm goin' up to the shack, now, an' cook me up a meal of vittles. I'm hungrier'n hell. So long."

An hour after One Armed John's departure, a form darkened the doorway, and both turned to glance at the stranger who stood peering into the room.

"Is this Cushing's Fort, on Halfaday Crick?" the man demanded in a strident tone as he stepped into the saloon.

"Yeah," answered Black John, "this is the place."

"The house is buyin' one," said Cush as he slid a glass toward the man, who had halted before the bar.

"I heard about this place up to Whitehorse," the man said as he poured his drink. "Fella claimed you was all outlaws up here. How about it?"

"I wouldn't know," Cush replied, filling his own glass.

"You wouldn't know! Well, who the hell would know, if you don't?"

"I couldn't say."

The man turned a glance of impudent appraisal on Black John. "You look like you'd fill the bill, all right. What the hell are you on the run fer—steal some farmer's sheep?"

Black John shook his head. "No, I never got no sheep. I figgered around to, one time—it was down in Indiany—but it looked too resky. I got sixteen hens one night, though—out of a hen house right near Fort Wayne. I took 'em in town an' got seven dollars fer 'em off'n a butcher. Next day the police was huntin' all over hell fer the one that done it, but they never ketched me—I was too slick fer 'em. Then over to Muncie I got away with damn near a hul wash off'n a line—I got twelve dollars an' thirty cents fer that stuff off'n a pawn shop man in

Indianapolis, an' in South Bend I stole a bicycle an' rode it clean through to Chicago, an' sold it fer twenty-six dollars."

The man grinned contemptuously. "Jest left a broad trail of crime clean acrost the state, eh?"

"Oh shore," replied Black John complacently. "I'm like that. I ain't never been ketched yet. But it was in Chicago I pulled my big job. I was on a street car. A woman was settin' in one of them seats, an' she punched on a button, an' the street car stops, an' she gits off, an' I sets down there—me bein' standin' alongside of her on account of all the seats bein' full of folks—an' I looks down there on the floor an' damn if there wasn't a pocketbook layin' there damn near a foot square, where it had slid off'n her lap when she got up. I stuffed it in under my sweater when no one was lookin', an' then I got off after I'd rode a few blocks, an' I ketched another street car an' rode to near where my room was.

"**YOU SEE**, when I decided on a life of crime I hired me a room out on South Clark street. I give two dollars a week fer it—six floors up, it was, an' at the back of the house, so the police wouldn't know where I was at.

"So I goes to my room, an' locks the door on the inside, an' opens this pocket-book, an' there was four hundred an' eight dollars an' seventy-six cents in it, an' some other stuff that wasn't no 'count. Well, I seen right away how with that amount of money missin' they'd prob'ly arrest damn near everyone in Chicago till they found it. So I hid the pocketbook in under the mattress an' went down stairs, jest like nothin' had happened, an' hit out fer the depot. I didn't dast to even give the man back his key. I throw'd it away.

"I guess word had got to the police about the robbery, all right, because I'll bet damn near every policeman in Chicago was out on them streets an' all of 'em looked right at me, too, but I jest went on past 'em, like I wasn't in no hurry, an' none of 'em arrested me. I don't know yet, whether they figgered I wasn't the one that done it—er whether they was afraid to tackle me.

"Anyhow, I went to Minneapolis on a train, an' then I bummed my way to Seattle, an' when I heard about gold bein' up in this country I come up here. I'm jest like you—when I hit Whitehorse an' heard about how Halfaday Crick was the hangout fer all the outlaws, I says 'that's the place fer me,' I says—an' here I be."

"Have you pulled any big jobs sence you hit the gold country?" asked the man, with a wink at Cush.

"No, I ain't got around to it yet. I figger on takin' it easy fer a spell, till that trouble in Chicago gits a chanct to kind of cool off. I figger if a man's smart he won't try to pull off too many big jobs."

"Guess yer right at that," laughed the man. "Fill 'em up, barkeep. I'm buyin' one." Producing a roll, the man peeled off a new bill and laid it on the bar.

Black John eyed the roll in undisguised admiration. "Gosh!" he exclaimed, "you've got a sight of money! Be you one of us outlaws, too?"

"Us outlaws!" snorted the man contemptuously. "Where do you git that 'us'? Yer no outlaw. Yer nothin' but a hen-stealin', shimmy-snatchin' bum. Take a look at yerself in the mirror."

Glancing into the mirror, Black John ran his fingers over his black stubble. "It ain't no use a man should waste all his time shavin'," he said. "An' if you don't think I'm a reg'lar outlaw, how about that big job I pulled in Chicago?"

"What big job?"

"Why I jest got through tellin' you about it—them four hundred an' eight dollars an' seventy-six cents I got out of that pocketbook."

The man threw back his head and laughed. "Chicken feed!" he scoffed. "Hell, I wouldn't bother to lean over an' pick it up off the floor! Bank jobs is my specialty—an' now an' then a payroll, if I know it's goin'to be good. See that twenty there on the bar? Well, I've got two thousan' of them double sawbucks hid in the bresh down by my shack. This here roll I got on me is jest spendin' money—there ain't more'n six, seven hundred in it."

Black John was regarding the man with a look of incredulous awe. "Two thousan' twenties," he said. "Gosh, mister, that's forty thousan' dollars!"

"You kin count," grinned the man, "even if you can't git away with nothin' but hens, an' bicycles, an' didies."

"Oh, I'd steal money out of a bank, too," replied Black John, "if I got the chanct. But I never had no' luck findin' one open when there wasn't nobody around."

"Nobody around! Good God! Neither did anyone else! Walk right in, like I do, an' stick a persuader under their nose an' tell 'em to fork it over. The business end of a forty-five looks a damn sight more important to a bank teller, right at the moment, than a barrel of other folks money—so he shoves it acrost as fast as he kin git holt of it."

Black John shook his head slowly from side to side. "Looks like it would be awful resky," he opined. "S'pose the bank man would have a gun? Er mebbe he might holler, an' a policeman would come. Take it with hens an' washin's—a man kin steal 'em at night when there ain't no one lookin'. You spoke about havin' a shack. Have you moved in on the crick?"

"Yer damn right I have. Found a shack a few miles down the crick that was, empty an' throw'd my stuff in. I come on up fer to git some grub."

"Is it on the high side of a bend, in a little clearin' acrost the crick from a willer flat?" asked Black John.

"That's the place. The shack's abandoned, ain't it?"

"You mean," asked Black John, "that yer goin' to live there, in that shack? Stay there nights, an' all?"

"Sure. What's the matter with it?"

"Oh, the shack's all right. Olson, he put up a good cabin down there. An' I guess you could call it abandoned. No one lives there. No one would."

"Why not?"

"On account of all them ghosts."

"GHOSTS!"

"Yeah, you know—ha'nts. Seems like everyone that lived in that shack never had no luck. Olson, he got hung, an' Miller's pardner got shot, an' Stamm's woman shot Stamm in there, an' a lawyer name of Breezely got stabbed. Folks claims the place is onlucky—they claim it's on account of them dead men comin' back to kind of git revenge on the ones that killed 'em."

"Did they git their revenge?" scoffed the man.

"No, 'cause there wasn't no one there to revenge on. But they've been seen walkin' in the clearin'—the ghosts has."

"Did you see 'em?"

"Who, me? Not by a damn sight. I wouldn't git that clost to the damn place at night—not me."

"I guess there won't no ghosts bother me none," said the man. "In the first place there ain't no sech thing as ghosts. An' even if there was, they couldn't hurt no one. If these folks that is scairt of ghosts would stop an' think a minute they'd see what damn fools they was. If there was any sech thing as a ghost, he wouldn't be nothin' but—but air, er somethin' like that, an' he couldn't *do* nothin' to no one, but scare him—an' if the party wasn't scairt, that's all there'd be to it. No ghost ever hurt you, did there?"

"Me? I'll tell the world he didn't. He would have to ketch me first—an' it would be a damn lively ghost that could do it if I got a start. Folks is foolish that claims there ain't no ghosts. I know there is." Black John paused and regarded the man seriously. "My folks comes from Pennsylvany," he said. "My pa's got a hex book. I know all about it. I kin hex folks, an' after I'm dead, I know how to come back an' git revenge. No one better fool with me."

"You damn fool hill-billies is four hundred years behind the times," sneered the man, "what with yer ghosts, an' hexes, an' them fool things."

"Is that so!" bristled Black John in a highly offended tone. "Well, you might be a brave man, mister, but there's things you don't know, an' I'm a-tellin' you right here, I won't never fergit about you makin' light of my folks. If I die before you I'll come back an hex you shore as hell. I'll show you if there's ghosts, er not!"

"Come right along, hill-billy," grinned the man. "I'll be waitin' fer you. An' if you should die before I do I'll take delight in spittin' on yer grave jest to show folks what I think of you." The man turned to Cush. "What the hell do the boys do up here on the crick between jobs?" he asked.

"Oh, most of 'em works their claims."

"Is there really gold on the crick?"

"Shore there's gold. Take that there claim you're on—it's a damn good claim. If it wasn't fer everyone bein' scairt of it, someone would be workin' it, right now. Trouble is, John here, has got 'em all scairt, what with believin' in ghosts, an' all."

"Well, he can't scare me." He turned to Black John. "Jest tell them ghost friends of yourn that there's a bird livin' in that shack now that ain't afraid of the ghosts of all the dead men that ever lived. Tell 'em to come on down an' see me, some night, an' I'll thumb my nose at 'em."

Black John's eyes widened in horror at the sacrilege. Solemnly he raised his hand, and with his forefinger traced a mysterious sign on his forehead, a circle within a triangle, as he muttered the unintelligible words of some weird ritual.

The man laughed derisively. "Go to it, hill-billy! By the way, what do you do up here where there ain't no hens an' panty-waists to snitch?"

"I work my claim part of the time," Black John replied. "But mostly I like gamblin'. I'm a gambler."

"A gambler!" the man sneered. "What do you do—toss pennies at a crack in the floor?"

"No. There ain't no pennies on the crick—an' besides, I like stud better."

"Stud! Hell, you can't play stud!"

"I kin so," defended Black John. "I bet you can't play none yerself!"

"How much you got to lose?" retorted the other. "What little's left out of that four hundred dollar haul you made in Chicago?"

"No sir! I got about eight hundred dollars in my cabin. I got a pretty good claim, an' besides, I make money gamblin'. If you would play a game of stud I would go an' git my money. Cush here would play too, so's to make it three handed. Two handed ain't no fun."

"Go git yer roll, hill-billy. I jest as soon take your money as any one else's. I'll give you somethin' to hex me fer."

When Black John had departed for his cabin, the man grinned at Cush. "Kin he play any at all?" he asked.

"Oh, he ain't so bad. He plays along about even with the boys, I guess. Wins sometimes, an' sometimes he loses. He shore likes to play, though."

"Has he got any tricks?"

"Any which?"

"You know—does he know anything? Kin he handle the deck?"

"You mean cheat?"

"Sure?"

"No. He don't cheat. Cheatin' don't go here on Halfaday. We've hung men fer cheatin'."

The man shrugged. "Suits me. I guess I kin out-guess a bum like him without usin' no tricks. If I can't, I'd ort to lose."

Returning, Black John stepped behind the bar. "You fetch some glasses an' a bottle of licker," he said to Cush, "an' I'll fetch the cards an' chips. Ain't no use in jumpin' up from the table every time we want a drink."

Cush acted as banker. Black John produced a roll of bills, each bought a stack of chips, and the game proceeded. Again and again the stranger bought stacks and at the end of a couple of hours, he shoved in his last chip, turned up his hole card and nodded, as Black John turned his.

"That's good," he said. "You cleaned me, this time. But you ain't seen the last of me, yet. I'll be back here tonight fer revenge."

"Revenge is a good thing," opined Black John, gathering in the chips, "if a man kin git it. But make it tomorrow afternoon instead of tonight. My eyes is weak. An' besides I've got a little job to do over on the American side. Be shore an' fetch some money when you come tomorrow."

The man glared angrily across the table. "Money! You don't need to worry about me fetchin' money. I won't need no hell of a lot of money to take you! You had fool's luck today. There wasn't a damn one of them big hands we played that I hadn't ort to won, if I'd got any breaks at all. No one but a damn fool would of bet them hands like you did. You was rotten with luck—that's all."

Black John nodded. "Well hell, if a man ain't got no luck, he hadn't ought to gamble. I think jest like you do, only the other way around—no one but a damn fool would of bet them hands of yourn like you did. Come on back tomorrow, if you ain't afraid of losin', an' I'll show you."

"I'll be back," cried the man angrily. "There can't no hill-billy make a fool of me! Go over on the American side an' steal someone's shirt off his clothesline tonight. I'll give you a run fer yer money, tomorrow."

II

WHEN THE MAN had gone Old Cush regarded Black John with a look of disapproval. "It kind of looks to me like yer slippin', John."

"Slippin'?" queried the big man, pouring himself a drink. "Why I don't know, Cush. What makes you think so? I took him fer his roll, didn't I?"

"Usin' marked cards in a friendly game of stud, ain't so good. You know damn well, John, we keep them markers fer cases where we need 'em—like when we know damn well some cuss is cheatin' on us an' we can't ketch him at it. Then we run them markers in on him an' git our money back, an' whatever of his'n we kin get along with it. But here you go, right on the start of a game, usin' 'em. I wondered why you fetched the cards an' chips to the table yerself instead of lettin' me fetch 'em. I was plumb ashamed when I seen you had them markers. It ain't right, John—an' you know it. We could of took that short-horn with a reg'lar deck."

Black John grinned. "Well, we might of, an' then agin we might not. I'll admit, Cush, that to a casual observer like you, the propriety of springin' markers on a man right on the start is open to question. An opinion based on the hypothesis of ethics, alone—"

"Listen, John, it takes a damn sight more'n jest a lot of big words to jestify doin' what you done. Stringin' a lot of big words together that don't mean nothin' ain't never goin' to make me believe you was right—without you've got some damn good reason fer it."

"The reason," replied Black John, "is simple. I wanted to git that bird's roll—every damn cent of it. An' I wanted to git it in sech a way as he would think I was a damn fool. In order to do that, an' make it convincin', I had to know exactly what every card was that had been dealt. We could have took him, as you say, with a reg'lar deck. But he plays a pretty good game of stud. To take him in the usual run of luck an' cards would have made us play a better game than he did. No man gives a damn if he gits beat by men that's jest as good, er a little better than him. But it makes him mad as hell to git beat by someone that plays his cards like a damn fool. An' not only it makes him mad, but, knowin' damn well he kin outplay such a bird, he's plumb anxious an' eager fer revenge."

"But what would you want to bust him fer? An' why did you want to make him mad?"

"I didn't want to bust him. You heard him say he had forty-thousan' in his cache. Hell, Cush, if what little we took off'n him in that game was all he had, I'd of handed it back to him. I wanted to make him mad so he'd be hell bent for revenge. An' I wanted to take all them bills off'n him so he'd have to go to his cache fer more. I want to locate that cache. I'll be slippin' down the short way directly an' watch him go to the cache an' dig out another roll. I kin give him half an hour's start an' beat him to Olson's."

"But cripes, John, you don't aim to rob his cache, do you?"

Black John frowned darkly. "Did you ever hear of me robbin' a cache?" he demanded.

"No," admitted Cush. "But I never seen you run no markers in on the start of a game, neither. You know, John, you been gone quite a while—what with bein' in jail in Dawson, an' them U.S. marshal's havin' you, an' all. I figgered mebbe yer morals might of slipped, bein' so long away from Halfaday."

Black John grinned. "I don't know's I blame you none fer suspectin' anyone that had been associatin' with them marshals—but you don't need to worry none, Cush. I come through the ordeal onscathed. My ethics is as pure, an' as ontrammeled by the thought of personal gain as they ever was. I'll prove that to you by promisin' that if I ever set in a stud game with that bird agin, I'll deliberately lose to him the exact amount I won off'n him today. I wouldn't want nothin' like that on my conscience—takin' a few dollars off some bird with markers! It's too pifflin' a sin to be guilty of."

"Then why would you want to know where his cache is at?"

"Jest in case he was to leave the crick in a hurry, an' would fergit to stop an' remove its contents. You know damn well, Cush, that if a man would deliberately leave a crick without expressin' no intention of comin' back, then whatever in the way of property he leaves here would revert to the finder."

"But hell, no one would go away from a crick an' leave forty thousan' dollars in a cache!"

"Mebbe not," agreed Black John. "I jest said in case he should. The fact is, Cush, I don't like that hombre. He's bragful, an' I can't help but feel that he holds me in some sort of contempt, from little things he said."

"Well, why in hell wouldn't he? You talked like a damn fool to him, tellin' him about stealin' washin's off'n lines, an' hens out of coops, an' bicycles, an' old women's pocketbooks! An' about believin' in ghosts an' ha'nts, an' hexin' folks, an' all that stuff. Why wouldn't he think you was a damn fool?"

The big man grinned. "The reputation of bein' a damn fool never hurt no one. I shall endeavor to prove that postulate. As I said, I don't deem this hombre to be no ornament to Halfaday. Besides bein' bragful an' snobbish, I suspect him of criminal tendencies. The quicker he's off the crick, the better it'll be fer all of us. Take it, from certain things he said, an' from certain things One Armed said, I've been kind of puttin' two an' two together ontil an idee had occurred to me—mebbe not a full-fledged idee, but at least the germ of one, which if properly fostered should produce results. In other words, I believe I see the rudiments of a drayma shapin' themselves in our destiny."

"I don't know a damn thing yer talkin' about, except that drayma part—an' when it comes to draymas, you kin count me out! I won't have nothin' to do with no drayma! Two, three times you've pulled draymas on me, that if anything would of went wrong with 'em, I would be in a hell of a fix. Onct I would be dead, like if them fellas had shot me, that time. Or else I would be married to that damn hellion that claimed her name was Goldie! No sir! No more draymas fer me! If you want to ring in One Armed John, er any of the rest of the boys, that's their hard luck, but I won't have nothin' to do with it."

Black John laughed. "But hell, Cush. This here is a comedy. No one gits hurt in a comedy."

"They can't if they keep out of one," replied Cush somberly. "But git this—I don't want nothin' to do with no drayma, no kind, no place, an' no time."

"Comedies is sometimes successful, financially," observed Black John.

"How much would there be in one?" asked the canny Cush, after a moment of consideration. "Dammit, there's been a couple of times when I haven't went in with you on some deal, that I wished I had."

"The profit would, of course, depend entirely on the success of the venture. Think it over. I've got to be goin' now, er that bird might beat me to Olson's."

III

BLACK JOHN RETURNED to the saloon about the middle of the afternoon. Old Cush set out the bottle and two glasses as he entered the door.

"Did you have any luck?" he asked.

"Oh shore," replied the big man as he poured his drink. "He went to his cache pretty quick after he got back. I figgered he would. Mad as he was, an' thinkin' about that revenge, an' not havin' anything else to do, he went an' dug up them bills. Reg'lar chechako cache—jest a hole dug in the sand in the brush alongside of the clearin', an' the bills in a cloth bag. Hell, the first few rains would soak 'em so they's be in a hell of a shape. He shore don't have much respect fer my stud game—near as I could see, he didn't take out no more'n about five hundred dollars. Figgers that would be enough to clean me with, I s'pose. You goin' to play along with me? Er is yer feet still cold?"

"Well, I might—if you give me yer word I don't stand a good show of gittin' shot er married. An' if the deal ain't shady—"

"Shady! Look here, Cush. You know damn well I wouldn't have nothin' to do with no shady transaction. Hell, ain't I always tried to keep Halfaday moral? Ask anyone. Ask Corporal Downey. This here's a sportin' proposition. There ain't no danger of yer gittin' shot er married. I'm playin' the leadin' role, but there's a couple of minor parts that's got to be played by someone, an' it might as well be you an' One Armed John. I'm willin' to let you in, share an' share alike. We kin pay One Armed fer his time, at goin' wages. Large amounts of money is a temptation to him to stay drunk longer'n what's good fer his health. What do you say?"

"All right. What do I do?"

"Loan me a pair of shears."

"A pair of which?"

"Shears—scissors. Ain't you got no shears?"

"I don't keep none in the store. There ain't no call fer 'em. Seems like my wives always had 'em layin' around, though. Mebbe I kin find some. I'll look."

Stepping into his living quarters, Cush returned a few minutes later with a pair of scissors which he handed to Black John, who pocketed them. "Don't lose 'em," cautioned Cush. "I borried 'em off'n the klooch. She claims she wants 'em back. Red er white, women's all alike. If a man uses somethin' of theirs they squawk like hell, an' don't give a man no peace till they git it back."

"I'm goin' up to One Armed John's," said Black John, swallowing his drink. "I'll be back after a while."

Proceeding up the creek a mile or so, Black John paused before the door of a shack from which issued a thin cloud of dust. One Armed John stepped out, broom in hand.

"Jest reddin' up a little," he explained. "Beats hell how the dust sifts in when a man goes away an' leaves his shack empty. Seems like it gits dirtier'n if a man stays to home."

"That's right," agreed Black John. "Did you ever do any barberin'?"

"Barberin'? You mean shavin' folks?"

"Well, that, an' cutting hair, an' trimmin' whiskers."

"No, I wouldn't be no good at that. I'd be afraid the fella might wiggle, an' I'd cut him, er somethin'."

"This fella won't wiggle," grinned Black John. "He's dead—er that is, you claimed he was."

"Me!"

"Yeah—he's that fella you claimed was me. He is dead, ain't he?"

"Shore, he's dead," replied One Armed John. "But cripes! I wouldn't bother no corpse! What do you want him barbered fer?"

"Well," Black John replied, "it seems jest too bad not to. You see, One Armed, durin' his life that pore fella strove to look like me. Now, I'm kind of sentimental that-a-way, an' it seems to me that if that was his aim an' ambition, it's jest too damn bad that he should be thwarted in death. You see, it wasn't his fault that I cut off my whiskers—at least, he never know'd it was his fault. Now I figger that if he yearned to look like me in life, he would yearn to look like me in death also. Don't that stand to reason?"

"Why shore, John, I s'pose that's so."

"Well then, the least we kin do fer the pore fella is to see that his life long wish is gratified, ain't it?"

"Why I guess so, John. But I never know'd you was so—er—kind of tenderhearted, like that."

"Oh, shore, One Armed. It's the way I was raised. No matter how old a man gits, er how fer he travels—er how fast—he never fergits them early teachin's. He might ignore 'em, but he never fergits 'em. So I got to thinkin' about that pore fella layin' there, not lookin' like me at all, when he wanted to, so I decided that the least we could do fer him was to trim them whiskers of his'n down till he does. Ain't that right?"

"Yeah—if a man looks at it that way. But—why don't you barber him yerself?"

"There's two reasons. In the first place, I don't know where he's at. An' in the second place, I couldn't do no real good job. You see, I don't know jest how I look. I might trim them whiskers a little too long, er too short. In sech case the pore fella would go to his grave not lookin' like me, which, in view of his yearnin's would be the nature of a major catastrophe."

"**IS THAT** what folks is that's buried without lookin' like you?"

Black John grinned. "In this case, yes. In a broader sense it would apply to a man who was buried with his life-work onfulfilled. I couldn't never rest easy thinkin' about it, if we was to bury him without doin' our damndest to fulfil his wish. Could you? When so simple an act of kindness as trimmin' a stand of whiskers would set things right?"

"Well, I hadn't give it no thought. I guess yer right, though. You gen'lly are. But I never know'd you was soft-hearted. It jest goes to show you can't tell nothin' about a man by his looks."

"What do you mean—looks?"

"Oh, I didn't mean it like you think!" One Armed John hastened to explain. "What I mean, a man sort of thinks of women bein' soft-hearted—an' you don't look like no woman."

"That's all right," laughed Black John. "Yer dead right about women bein' more tender-hearted than men—some women. It was a woman I learnt my tenderheartedness from. Yeah—my old gran'ma, back there in the Pennsylvany mountains. I kin see the old lady now, settin' there in the cabin, the light from the fireplace sort of playin' over her features, lightin' 'em up—an' me a little kid, settin' there by her knee. 'Johnny,' she says, kind of softlike, shiftin' her old clay pipe to the other corner of her mouth, an' spittin' in the fire, 'Johnny—always be kind to corpses,' she says. An' it's a lesson I never fergot."

"I never know'd you was from them Pennsylvany mountains, John."

"Shore I am—a hell of a ways from 'em. I was jest tellin' a fella about 'em this mornin'. That's prob'ly what made me think about my old gran'ma, back there in that cabin. It must of been—I never did think of her before. It makes a great background fer a man, a gran'ma like that, don't it?"

"Why—yeah, I s'pose it does. My gran'ma didn't smoke."

"Well, don't you go holdin' that agin her, One Armed. Mebbe she never learnt to. You don't want to blame no one fer what they never learnt. If she was a good woman other ways, it wouldn't make no difference."

"She was mean as hell to me. That's why I run away."

"We'll git off together sometime, One Armed, an' have a good talk about our gran'mas, if you'd like to. But right now, we've got a corpse to clip. Come on—you do the clippin', an' I'll set there fer a pattern."

"Should I fetch a shovel along so we kin bury him when we git him clipped?"

"No, we won't bother to bury him till tomorrow. Mind you, I ain't expectin' you to put in yer time fer nothin'. I'm payin' you wages fer the next couple of days. Let's go."

One Armed John led the way to the coulee where the corpse lay, exactly as he had described it, face down on a sodden snowbank in a deep, cold ravine. Rolling the cadaver on its back, One Armed gingerly began his task under the watchful eye of Black John, who posed at intervals, turning his head this way or that, whereupon after a critical study, One Armed John would go industriously on with his snipping. At the end of a half hour the task was completed to the satisfaction of both. One Armed John surveyed his handiwork with pride.

"That's a damn good job, if I do say it myself. Why, you two fellas look so much alike that I wouldn't give a damn fer the difference—except he's dead, an' you ain't."

"Yeah," grinned Black John, "but when you come to think about it, that makes quite a lot of difference."

"Oh, shore. There don't everyone git the chanct to see how he's goin' to look dead. What I mean—you ain't goin' to make sech a hell of a bad lookin' corpse, John, as corpses go. I'll bet if some of the boys was to come along now, they wouldn't know which one to bury. Even yer shirts is alike, barrin' his'n bein' all bloody there in front."

"A good p'int," observed Black John, eyeing the body critically. "Jest one of them little touches of realism that helps to put a good drayma acrost."

"What?"

"I mean," explained Black John, "that me an' Cush is puttin' on a sort of a show—a play, you know. You an' Cush an' one other fella appears in the first scene. This here corpse is property."

"Property! You mean—like a claim?"

"No. Anything you use in a play is called property."

"Use! I've saw considerable corpses, take 'em first an' last—but I never seen none *used.* Before, we've allus jest buried 'em."

"An' that's the use yer goin' to put this one to—you an' Cush, an' this stranger. Now listen, One Armed—an' I don't want you buttin' in with a lot of questions, neither. You do an' say jest what I tell you to do an' say, an' tomorrow night I'll give you two ounces of dust—an' that's more'n you'd make foolin' around fishin' in a week. You rec'lect how you come bustin' into Cush's this mornin' an' claimed you'd found me shot dead up this coulee?"

"Shore I do."

"Well, I want you should do that same thing right over agin, jest like you done it this mornin'. Tomorrow afternoon is the time, about two o'clock—you come bustin' into the saloon, an' claim you found me dead in this coulee. But instead of braggin' me up like you done to Cush, you say it's a damn good thing I'm shot because now folks'll prob'ly quit missin' things along the crick."

"Yeah—an' Cush would bust me one on the head with his bung starter fer sayin' them things agin you!"

BLACK JOHN grinned. "No he won't. Cush is in on this play, jest like I told you. He'll agree with you, an' he'll say somethin' about me bein' a damn fool fer believin' in ghosts, an' the like of that." The big man paused and regarded the other with a fixed stare. "Do you believe in ghosts?" he asked abruptly.

"Well, no I don't know as I do. I ain't never seen none that I know of. I've heard some damn funny noises now an' then. An' one time it was jest gittin' dark, an' I was comin' up the crick down there by Olson's old shack, an' I seen somethin' slip out of the clearin'. It looked kind of graylike. It might of been a moose, but—"

"Did you go over an' see if this thing left any moose tracks?"

"Who—me? Hell, no! It didn't quite look like no moose. An' what with all the folks that's been killed around there, I didn't fool around there none. I come hell-a-tearin' up the crick to Cush's."

Black John nodded solemnly. "An' that's the wisest thing you ever done, One Armed. Because you wouldn't have found no moose tracks. No sir. What you seen was a ghost—one of them gray ghosts, which is the worst kind of ghosts there is. The white ones ain't so bad—they show up plainer—but they're mostly wimmin ghosts. The gray ones is the ones to look out fer."

"Some claims there ain't no sech thing as ghosts," ventured One Armed John, a half fearful, half hopeful note in is voice.

"Jest let 'em go on claimin' that," replied Black John, nodding his head forbodingly. "They'll find out, sometime. Don't you never think that them gray ghosts don't know who believes in 'em an' who don't. They know everything. Why wouldn't they? Jest stop an' think."

"Why—why—shore, John—why wouldn't they?"

"You bet they know—an' they go easy on the folks that believes in 'em. It's the ones that scoffs at 'em, an' denies that there is sech things that them gray ghosts is layin' fer, like this stranger that'll be in Cush's tomorrow. He claims he ain't afraid of all the ghosts there is, an' he scorns 'em an' makes fun of 'em—an' on top of that, he's livin' right in the worst ghost hole on Halfaday. He's moved into Olson's old cabin!"

"My Gawd, John!" cried the man, his eyes rolling in terror. "Is—is there really ghosts? You're smart. You'd know."

"Listen, One Armed, have I ever lied to you? That is, that you know of?"

"No."

"Well, you ain't goin' to know it now, neither. Listen. If I told you there was ghosts, wouldn't you believe me?"

"Shore."

"An' if I was to tell you that I know a lot of 'em, personal, an' know how to talk to 'em, what would you say? You know there's times on the crick when I've come acrost with information about folks that no one know'd but me, don't you?"

"Shore I do. You know damn near everything that's goin' on."

"Well—" Black John paused and regarded the man impressively. "Where would I git this here information, if them gray ghosts didn't tell me? Where would I? Jest think it over."

The man's face had gone chalky white and his staring eyes rolled from the speaker to the corpse on the snow and held there in horrid fascination. Noting the glance, Black John continued: "Yeah, he's one of 'em, now—this man that looks like me. But, he won't harm you none, One Armed. He knows you done him a favor, snippin' off them whiskers. An' he knows you're goin' to do him another tomorrow—helpin' Cush an' that stranger bury him. He'll tell them other ghosts, an' so'll I—an' they'll all be friends of yourn, too. You don't need to worry. But that stranger, livin' like he does, down there to Olson's an' scoffin' at 'em like he does—he's the one to worry. At that, though, me an' the gray ghosts is givin' him one more chanct. If he treats this here corpse with respect when he helps bury him, they might relent. But if he don't—"

Black John paused ominously, and One Armed ventured a question in a voice that faltered with terror: "Wha—what—what'll happen to him, John?"

Black John shook his head sadly. "Who knows? Them gray ghosts has mysterious ways of their own—ways they won't explain even to me. But if we don't see this fella no more after tomorrow night, me an' you will know that the gray ghosts has took their revenge."

"You—you shore they ain't mad at me fer—fer kind of doubtin' 'em—up to now?" quavered One Armed John, beseechingly.

"Not if you go through with this here buryin' jest like I told you, they won't. Them gray ghosts is reasonable—they won't harm no one on account of an honest doubt. They'll be watchin' you, an' if they see you help bury their pal here, an' if they hear you try to persuade this stranger that there's ghosts, an' that he ortn't to scorn 'em—then they'll know fer shore you're their friend—an' they'll look out fer you same as they do fer me."

"B-but—I—I don't want to talk to 'em, John. I—I like 'em, all right. I—I'll do anythin' to help 'em out. B-but I don't want to talk to 'em—like you. I—I wouldn't know what to say."

"It ain't necessary," reassured Black John. "Them gray ghosts ain't gabby, nohow. There ain't many folks they'll even speak to. I'll tell 'em how you feel. They'll onderstand. Come on, now we'll pick up them whisker ends an' hide 'em, an' you git yer pack that you throw'd away this mornin', an' we'll go."

"Should we roll him over on his belly, like we found him?"

"No. Leave him lay like he is. It'll help explain them tracks there by him that you made when you clipped him. You kin tell Cush an' the stranger that you messed around there, rollin' me over to see if I was really dead. Remember, now—if you want to keep on the good side of them gray ghosts, you've got to do jest like I told you. Don't let on but what you think this corpse is me—an' don't say nothin' about clippin' no whiskers. That would be the worst thing you could do—it would make them ghosts madder'n hell. Jest act like you done this mornin'—an' don't fergit that slurrin' remark about me bein' a sneak thief—an' then help bury this fella, jest like you believe it's me. Cush'll do likewise. Come on, let's go."

The two parted on the creek. One Armed John heading up toward his cabin, while Black John returned to Cush's, where he spent the next two hours in instructing Old Cush in his role of the following day.

"I'll be goin' to supper now," he concluded. "I won't show up tonight—jest in case the stranger should take a notion to come up. I told him I was goin' to take a little trip over on the American side, an' I wouldn't want him to think I'd lie. You got everything straight, have you—about tomorrow?"

"Why, shore. There ain't much to remember. I act like I'm kind of worried about you not showin' up. Then when One Armed comes bustin' in claimin' you're shot over on the American side, an' makin' slightin' remarks about you. I'll come back with another one, an' then say how you believe in ghosts—an' let on like I kind of half-believe in 'em myself. An' then I'll say how we better slip right up there an' bury him—an' we do so. That's all, ain't it?"

"Okay," approved Black John. "You've got it down pat. So long. See you tomorrow evenin'."

IV

SHORTLY AFTER NOON the following day, the stranger from Olson's shack stepped into Cush's saloon and advanced to the bar.

"Where's that damn hill-billy that thinks he kin play stud?" he demanded, his glance sweeping the room.

Old Cush set out a bottle and two glasses. "I don't know," he replied gloomily. "He ain't show'd up today. I'm kind of worried about him. Drink up—it's on the house."

"Worried? Why would you be worried?"

"Well, he gen'lly stops in here first thing of a mornin'. He ain't been in yet—an here it is way past noon."

"He's prob'ly asleep yet. He claimed he was goin' on some kind of a trip over on the American side last night. Where does he live? I'll go wake him, if it ain't too fer. I aim to git my money back."

"He ain't to his shack," replied Cush. "That's why I'm worried. I went over there this mornin' to see, an' agin this noon, an' he ain't been there. I'm afraid mebbe somethin's happened to him."

"Mebbe some one took a shot at him," suggested the man. "He was prob'ly over there on some petty larceny job, an' got ketched at it. Hell, an' he had the nerve to call himself an outlaw! Sneak-thief—that's all he was, any way you look at him."

"Well," defended Cush half-heartedly, "John wasn't sech a bad sort of a fella. Little light fingered, mebbe, if he seen a good chanct. But he wasn't bad hearted."

"Wasn't bad hearted, hell! What I claim, a man that'll steal hens, an' washin's off'n lines, an bicycles, an' old women's pocketbooks is worst hearted than one that steps right in an' robs a bank. The man that does that has got guts. He's takin' a chanct. The sneak-thief ain't nothin' but a coyote. The bank robber is a real wolf."

"Yeah," admitted Cush, "bank robbin' is prob'ly a higher form of thievery. But, it's jest like any other business—everyone can't git to the top. There's big ones, an' little ones in every business."

"That's right," approved the man. "Brains, that's what counts—brains, an' the guts to back 'em up. Is he the only kind of outlaws you've got on Halfaday?"

"Well, no, there's some of the boys that's prob'ly pulled bigger jobs than John. 'Course, I don't know nothin' about none of 'em, only what I hear, now an' then. It don't pay a man in my business to know too much about his customers."

"Yer dead right about that," agreed the man. "You've got brains. You ain't like this Black John, as you call him. He ain't nothin' but a cheap-skate hill-billy, an' never will be. A man kin tell that by jest lookin' at him. It's enough to make a man laugh—all that talk about ghosts, an' hexes, an' the like of that."

"Quite a few folks believes in 'em," said Cush. "John, he don't play a bad game of stud, though."

"Bad game, hell!" snorted the man angrily. "He plays about the worst game I ever seen played!"

"Well," reminded Cush, "he took your roll."

"Yeah, but how'd he take it? He took it by makin' big bets on fool hands—hands that anyone with any sense would of turned down, er at the most, jest called on. But he set there like a damn fool, raisin', an' raisin' on em. It was fool's luck, that's all. I'll show him up next time we play—an' don't you fergit it!"

A man suddenly catapulted into the room. He was a one armed man, and his eyes were wide with horror.

"Black John's shot!" he shouted hoarsely. "Shot an' killed, deader'n a nit—over on the American side!"

"Shot!" cried Old Cush excitedly. "How do you know he's shot?"

"I seen him, that's how! He's layin' on a snowbank down a deep coulee. I seen somethin' layin' there, an' I dumb down to see what it was, an' it was a dead man—an' when I rolled him over, it was Black John. I fooled around there a few minutes to see if he was really dead—an' he was. His shirt was all blood. He was shot in the back, four, five times. He was cold, too, like if he was shot sometime last night." The man paused, and Cush slid a glass toward him.

"Have a drink," he said. "I wonder who could of shot him?"

The one armed man shrugged. "I don't know. There's some tracks on the snow, but they was all blurred up. Mebbe he'd lifted somethin' off'n someone over there. You know, sometimes he'd steal, if he had a good chanct." The speaker added this last with a wary eye on Old Cush, as though half expecting an assault with a bung starter. He heaved a sigh of relief when Cush agreed.

"Yeah, there prob'ly won't be so many things missin' along the crick, now he's gone. But there ain't no use speakin' evil of the dead. What we've got to do is slip up there an' bury him." He turned to the stranger. "You wouldn't mind helpin', would you?"

"Who, me? Help bury that damn four-flusher? Not by a damn sight, I won't. The wolves kin have him, fer all of me. Damn him, I'll never git my money back now!"

Cush regarded the man reflectively. " 'Course," he said, "we can't make you help, if you don't want to. But bein' a stranger, this-a-way, I guess you don't quite onderstand about us, up here. You see, a lot of the boys is outlawed, fer one reason er another—like robbin' banks, an' the like—an' we don't want the police snoopin' around the crick. You see, them Mounted Police, down to Dawson, has got the descriptions of almost every robber down in the states. The American police sends 'em up. They've picked up quite a few that was wanted in the States, on them descriptions. If we was to leave this here corpse lay where it's at, it wouldn't be long till someone else found it. Then he'd tell some others, an' they'd shoot off their mouth, till the police would soon hear that there was a murder up on Halfaday. Then they'd come snoopin' up here—an' they'd stay till they got their man. An' in the meanwhile, the chances is, they'd git about half the other men on the crick along with him. They'd fetch them descriptions along an' look all the boys over whilst they was at it. That would make it mean fer lots of folks. So the best thing we could do is to sneak out, jest us three, an' bury this corpse, before news of the murder gits spread around. A lot of the boys is gabby about sech things. They ain't got no sense. They're like Black John—they shoot off their mouth too much. But us three wouldn't never talk. No one would know about the murder but us, an' the one that done it—an' he ain't goin' to talk, you kin bet on that. What do you say? Will you help?"

"SURE, I'LL help!" exclaimed the man. "Yer damn right I'll help! Knowin' how things is, I'd be a fool not to. We don't want no police nosin' around here. Come on, lets git it over with. An' by God, if he's got that roll on him, I'll take out what he won off'n me, an' well divide up the rest. Besides, it'll give me the chanct to spit on his grave, like I told him I would—him an' his ghosts an' hexes!"

"You better not do nothin' like that," warned One Armed John in an awed tone of voice. "He'll come back an' hex you, shore as hell. An' he'll bring them other ghosts along with him. They all hang together, ghosts does. An' them gray ghosts is hell."

"Gray ghosts!" snorted the man. "I thought all ghosts was s'posed to be white."

"That's where yer wrong. Black John, he knows about ghosts an' things like that, an' he told me all about 'em. It's women ghosts that's white. Men ghosts is gray. Black John knows. He talks to 'em, an' they tell him things."

The stranger laughed uproariously. "Tell him things, do they? Well, where he's at now he kin set right down amongst 'em an' git him an earful. Mebbe they'll tell him about me spittin' on his grave. Come on, rustle some shovels an' we'll be goin'. Where's this place at?"

"It ain't fer," One Armed John replied. "Only about a mile er so acrost the line."

"Let's git through as quick as we kin," said Cush as he locked the saloon. "I've got to git back. Someone might be wantin' somethin'."

One Armed John led the way to the coulee where a shallow grave was dug, and the corpse lowered into it, after the stranger had gingerly searched the pockets and found them empty.

"The one that knocked him off prob'ly frisked him, onlest you did when you found him," he added, turning on One Armed John.

"Not me!" exclaimed the one armed one. "When I rolled him over an' seen who it was, I come away from here, hell-a-whoopin'. I wouldn't of took a dollar off'n him, if he'd had a million.

Not off'n him, I wouldn't. Not with him standin' in with all them ghosts!"

The grave was filled, and the surface tramped down and levelled. "An' now," grinned the man with an air of bravado, "I'm goin' to do what I told him I'd do, in case he died before me. I'm agoin' to spit on his grave." Working his jaws rapidly for a few moments the man pursed his lips and ejected a brown stream of tobacco juice that landed squarely in the center of the newly made grave. "There," he said, "that's what I think of him—an' all the rest of his damn ghosts, too. If they don't like it let 'em try to do somethin' about' it. I'll be waitin' fer 'em with a six-gun."

One Armed John had viewed the sacrilege with horror. "I wouldn't be standin' in your shoes fer all the money in the world," he said. "A six-gun ain't worth a damn agin a ghost. Nothin' is."

"Listen," sneered the man, "if there's anything to a ghost—bone, er muscle—anything that could hurt a man, then a six-gun'll stop him. If he ain't nothin' but air, er gas, er shadows, er somethin' like that, the bullet wouldn't have no effect on him, but he couldn't do a man no harm, neither. That's common sense, ain't it. Besides, there ain't no sech a thing as a ghost."

"The hell an' there ain't!" cried One Armed John in a tone of deep conviction. "I seen one myself. I know! One evenin' it was, jest on the edge of the dark. In that clearin' down to Olson's old shack, where all them fellas has been killed. I seen him plain as I'm seein' you now. He slipped into the bresh."

It seemed to Old Cush that the stranger's manner lost something of its bravado at the earnestness of One Armed John's direct assertion. The sneering tone was absent, and it seemed almost as if there was a note of anxiety in the man's voice as he asked:

"You say you seen one, yerself—down there?"

"Shore I did," replied One Armed John, and added in an awed tone, "an' it was one of the gray ones."

The laugh that greeted the statement seemed a trifle forced, as the man replied. "Hell, it was prob'ly a moose you seen—er mebbe a wolf."

One Armed John regarded the man fixedly. "A moose," he said in the solemn, subdued tone commonly assumed in discussing the supernatural, "would leave a moose track in that soft sand. An' a wolf would leave a wolf track. But a ghost don't leave no tracks."

"Poppycock!" snorted the man with a forced attempt at his previous bravado. "All this talk about ghosts is enough to give a man the creeps. Come on. The job's done. Let's git to hell out of here. I need a drink."

BACK IN the saloon several drinks were had, and as it was getting late in the day, Cush invited the man to linger.

"Stick around a while. I'll have the klooch fetch us in a bite to eat. Some of the boys'll prob'ly drift in after a while, an' we might git up a game of stud."

The man glanced a trifle uneasily toward the door. The sun had set, and in the little valley of Halfaday shadows were deepening. "No thanks," he replied. "I'll be gittin' back down the crick while I've got daylight. Some other night, when I know the trail better. I might lose it in the dark. I've got quite a piece to go."

"Where do you live at?" asked One Armed John.

"Four, five mile down the crick," the man replied. "I moved into an abandoned shack down there. Olson's, I believe they said it was."

"Olson's!" breathed One Armed John, eyeing the man in horror. "Why—why— Olson's is where I seen that ghost! A gray one, it was, right on the edge of the dark. I wouldn't go down there fer a thousan' dollars, er a million, er a billion. Yer a brave man, mister," he added in a voice of profound respect. "I'm atellin' it to you now—'cause I won't never be seein' you no more."

"Shut up!" cried the man testily. "Always fetchin' in about them ghosts!" He turned to Cush. "Give me another drink.

Better slip me a bottle, too. I might not git back up fer a couple of days."

"I'll say you won't," murmured One Armed John, forbodingly. "You ain't comin' back from where you're goin'—never no more."

The man departed hastily with a curse, and a few minutes later Black John sauntered into the room. "Hello," he greeted. "Did you git my namesake an' double properly planted?"

"Yeah," Cush replied, sliding a glass across the bar. "We buried him, all right."

"How about it?" grinned Black John, turning to the one armed man. "Did our friend show proper respect fer the corpse?"

"John," replied the man solemnly, "he talked plumb scandalous about ghosts—even the gray ones. An' he up an' spit on yer grave—er I mean, the man's grave which we buried."

Black John nodded. "It is much as I feared," he said, a note of sadness in his voice. "Well, the pore fella. He had his chanct, an' it looks like he failed miserably. Them gray ghosts is shore outraged."

"John!" cried the one armed man, his eyes fixed in horror on the big man's front. "Why—yer all blood! Yer shirt—all down the front of it! Look—it's—it's jest like—that other man's shirt—the one we buried!"

Black John stared down at his shirt front in well feigned surprise. "Well, so it is," he said in an awed tone. "Jest like that pore dead man's shirt. Now how could that blood have got there? It wasn't there a while ago. I kin swear to that. It must be, somehow, because him an' I was so much alike." He paused and shook his head in resignation. "It must be the doin's of them gray ghosts," he said. "A man can't always onderstand 'em. Their ways is mysterious as hell. Come on, One Armed, let's me an' you take a walk."

"A walk?" queried the other, his fascinated gaze still on the blood-smeared shirt. "A walk—where to, John?"

"Well, I thought we'd sort of stroll down to Olson's clearin'. We kin take our time, so we'll git there right on the edge of the dark. It would be kind of interestin' to see what them ghosts will do to—"

"Olson's clearin'!" cried One Armed John in a voice that was a quavering squeal. "Me—go to Olson's clearin'—an' git there on the edge of the dark! Jest me an' you alone? An' all them ghosts around there—an' all of 'em mad as hell! If you git me down there tonight, er any other night, you would have to kill me first!"

"Why, it ain't you an' me they're mad at, One Armed. Like I told you yesterday, they're friends of ourn. You might be passin' up the only chanct you'll ever git to see the ghosts work on a man. They might dissolve this here stranger into thin air. Did you ever see a man dissolved into thin air, One Armed?"

"Cripes, no!" shrilled the man. "An' I don't never want to! I don't want to see no one dissolved into nothin'! I don't want to see no ghosts at work! I don't never want to see no more of 'em anywheres! I—I—like 'em, all right," he added hurriedly. "You tell 'em I like 'em, John. But I—I don't want to see 'em. It's jest that I ain't use' to 'em."

"Oh, that's all right," soothed Black John. "They onderstand about them things. Lots of folks is like that. They don't hold it agin a man." He turned toward Cush with a wink. "How about you, Cush? Let's me an' you go down there. One Armed, he'll stay an' tend bar."

"Yer damn right I'll stay!" offered One Armed John eagerly. "Not only that—I'm stayin' clean on through till tomorrow. I'll sleep on the floor. I ain't goin' home tonight. What with them ghosts runnin' loose, I might meet one of 'em comin' down the crick—one that was late, er somethin'."

"Well," replied Cush, with evident reluctance. "I'll go along, John, if you want I should. I'd jest as soon pass it up, though. But I claimed I'd play along with you on this. It's the last time, though. No more draymas fer me. An', if you ask me, you've got a hell of an idee of a comedy. I'm scairt, right now. Come on, let's go. But, I'm takin' my shotgun loaded with buck along—jest in case."

ONE ARMED JOHN donned with alacrity the white apron Cush turned over to him, and a few moments later the two men disappeared down the trail.

"How in hell did you git all that blood on you?" asked Cush as they proceeded along the creek.

"I knocked over a young moose this afternoon when you fellas was over on the American side, an' rubbed his liver around on my shirt. Jest a touch of realism, Cush. You rec'lect that corpse's shirt looked about like this."

"I don't like this here drayma," grumbled Cush. "What with buryin' corpses, an' all this blood, an' talk about ghosts, an' all. You've got One Armed jittery as hell. Even that stranger that didn't believe in ghosts, he went down the trail kind of lookin' over his shoulder. I ain't feelin' none too pert, neither. A comedy, like you claimed this was, is s'posed to be comical, ain't it? An' I ain't saw nothin' funny yet. It's jest like all them other draymas of yourn—all the fun I git out of 'em is to be scairt as hell till they're overwith. I won't go in on no more of 'em no matter how much I would make. What in hell do I do when we git down there to Olson's—crawl in some hole an' poke a ghosts out, er somethin'?"

"No," grinned Black John, "from now on, you've got merely a passive part. The part of a mere spectator. You done your heavy work this afternoon."

Arriving at Olson's, the two took up a position in the brush at the edge of the clearing. The evening was warm. Yellow lamplight glowed at the window, and the open door of the shack.

"We'll wait here a while," whispered Black John with a grin. "Ghosts does their best work right on the edge of the dark." Taking a small round tin box from his pocket he removed the cover and peered at its contents. Old Cush craned his neck, and stared at the salvy surface that gave off a luminous glow.

"What in hell's that stuff?" he asked.

"It's some of this here luminous paint. Some of the boys down to Dawson was tellin' me about it, so I got some. They claimed it was good stuff to touch up yer gun sights, an' along the top of the barrel, fer night huntin'. It's got phosphorus in it. I ain't had no chanct to try it out yet."

"But hell, John, you claimed there wasn't goin' to be no shootin' in this here drayma!"

"No, I didn't claim no sech thing. I claimed that you didn't stand in no danger of gittin' shot—nor married, neither. An' you don't."

"But—what you goin' to shoot with? You didn't fetch no gun along. When I seen it wasn't in under yer shirt was when I decided to fetch my shotgun. I wasn't comin' down here without nothin'."

"I ain't goin' to do no shootin'. I figger the party in the cabin might, though. Sh—sh—sh—don't make no noise—that's the third time he's come to the door to look around. Seems like he's kind of oneasy, er somethin'. The dark's about right now. Hold on till I git this stuff on, an' we're all set fer the show."

Dipping his forefinger into the luminous paint, Black John traced a triangle on his forehead. "Now, Cush," he said, "stick your finger in an' make a circle inside of that triangle. Don't you rec'lect? It's the sign I made on my forehead when he was makin' light of them ghosts in the saloon yesterday. Just another little touch of realism, Cush—they all help."

Cush complied, and when he had finished, Black John demanded, "How does it look? Does that paint show up good?"

Cush nodded. "Yeah, it glows out right plain in the dark. It looks like hell, John. God, it would scare the devil hisself!"

"Set tight, then—an' don't make no move. If he comes to the door an' begins blastin' at me with a six-gun, don't pay no heed to it, jest set there an' watch. We don't want no murder here. I'll holler if I need help, an' then you kin use yer own jedgement. But don't do nothin' till I yell."

"But cripes, John, is he goin' to be shootin' at you? S'pose he hits you?"

Black John's grin widened. "He'll hit me every shot, Cush—onless he's too damn scairt to hold the gun stiddy. But he can't hurt me none. Jest remember, Cush—you can't shoot a ghost."

The next moment he was gone, melted into the shadows of the bush. Left alone, old Cush craned forward and strained his eyes to peer into the clearing. Presently he saw a dark form appear and take a position directly in front of the door, and about fifteen paces distant from it. The next instant the silence of the night was broken by a long, weird groan. Again the hollow groan sounded, and Cush felt the hair prickle at the back of his neck. A figure appeared in the doorway—a silent figure, the figure of a stranger. The man seemed to stiffen, to be held rigid in his tracks by some unseen force. By the lamplight, Cush could see that his eyes were staring wide at the apparition that confronted him in the clearing. Then slowly the apparition raised an arm, and a long finger pointed squarely at the man in the doorway.

"Revenge," moaned a sepulchral voice. "Revenge against the man who dared spit on my grave. Revenge! Revenge!" Then a moment of silence, and a peal of horrible, demoniac laughter. Louder and louder it rose, until the figure in the doorway staggered back, and clawed wildly at its eyes as though to rid them of the horrible spectacle. Then, it was gone—to reappear an instant later, a six-gun in its hand. Deliberately, the man raised the gun, and as he did so, the apparition in the clearing moved slowly forward. It seemed not to walk, but to float, slowly, inexorably toward the man in the doorway, the finger still pointing.

There was a blinding spurt of yellow flame from the muzzle of the gun, and a report rang loud. The apparition raised the hand of the pointing finger slowly to its mouth, from which it seemed to take some object. The next instant, with a slow deliberate movement, it pitched the object so that it hit against the chest of the man in the doorway, and fell to the floor with a sharp thud. The man recoiled slightly and glanced downward. Staring in horror at the object, he fired again. Again the apparition went through the same motions, and another object struck squarely in the center of his chest and thudded on the floor. Once more the man fired, and the performance was repeated. Then suddenly with a wild scream of terror, as the apparition slowly advanced, the man hurled the gun to the floor, leaped from the doorway, darted around the corner of the cabin, and crashed into the underbrush, shriek after shriek of horror rending the silent night.

Old Cush stepped into the clearing as Black John turned to face him, a broad grin on his face. "He's goin' like hell, Cush, fer a man that ain't afraid of ghosts, ain't he?"

"But, John—them shots! Why in hell didn't he hit you?"

Black John grinned. "He did," he said. "Never missed onct. But it didn't hurt none. Only little plugs of paraffine. You see, I come down here whilst you-all was buryin' that corpse, an' pulled the bullets out of the shells in his gun. I plugged the ends of the shells with paraffine off'n his candle, put the bullets in my pocket, put the shells back in the gun an' left it handy. Then, when I got all ready out here, I held 'em in my hand—an' when he'd shoot, I'd toss back his bullet, like I was takin' it out of my mouth. It was havin' his own bullets hit him in the chest, an' drop back to the floor that got his goat. An' all things considered, you can't hardly blame him none.

"Come on, we'll dig up his cache an' divide up that forty-thousan'. Somehow, I don't believe that man's comin' back. Listen—you kin still hear him smashin' through the bresh, an' screamin'. The sounds of his flight has got a permenancy to 'em, that jestifies the assumption that he's abandoned this claim fer good."

SAMSON'S LUCK ON HALFADAY

OLD CUSH, PROPRIETOR of Cushing's Fort, the log trading post and saloon that served the little community of outlawed men that had sprung up on Halfaday Creek close against the Yukon-Alaska border, laid aside his account book, shoved his steel-rimmed spectacles from nose to forehead, and set out a bottle and two glasses as Black John Smith entered the door.

"I seen in the Bible where I was readin' in it a while back about some Swede, I guess he was, by the name of Samson, which he was so damn stout that a lion come at him an' he grabs holt of this lion with his hands an' twists the jaw off'n him an' kills him."

"Yeah," Black John replied, "I rec'lect that story. But you got to remember, Cush, mebbe it was some old lion, er a little one, er one that mebbe was ailin'."

"Humph," grunted Cush. "He was able enough to be huntin' his vittles er he wouldn't of come at the Swede. By God, if a lion would come at me he'd have a foot race instead of a fight to worry about, even if he was so old his last pup was already a grandfather. An' speakin' of jaws, this here piece in the Bible goes on to say how in some war they was havin' them days this Samson grabs up the jawbone of an ass an' slews twenty er thirty thousan' enemies with it. If it wasn't right there in the Bible damn if I'd believe no sech talk. I ain't never been in no wars, but it looks to me like that would be a damn good day's killin' if a man had a Gatlin' gun, let alone a jackass'es jaw. Cripes, it looks to me like this Swede had plenty of guts to go up agin all them

swords an' spears with only the jawbone of an ass, which a man wouldn't figger to be no deadly weapon, even in times of peace."

"Oh I don't know," grinned Black John. "Didn't you ever listen to a political speech?"

"What's politics got to do with the jawbone of an ass?"

"It sets a lot of 'em in motion an' the effect is deadly on them that's got to listen. I ain't deridin' this here Samson none. If he done all er any part of what's claimed fer him he was a damn good man—below the collar.

"But it looks like whatever he had comin' to him run to muscle instead of brains the way he fell fer that skirt."

"You mean that there Della, er whatever her name was?" asked Cush, pouring his second drink. "Well—I ain't blamin' the big Swede none fer fallin' fer her. My last wife had a book of Bible pitchers, and I keep it on a shelft in the other room. When I read along about these different folks in the Bible, I look 'em up in this book of pitchers. They ain't all in there, but most of the important ones is, an' it makes it more interestin' if a man knows what they looked like. This here Della's in there. She had more on than what Eve had in the way of clothes, but she's a damn sight better lookin' than Eve, even at that. A man don't want to be too hard on this here Samson—livin' like he had to amongst all them old characters like Adam, an' David, an' Soloman, an' Henry the Eighth. Adam started it, an' the rest jest nach'ly trailed along. Cripes—I've fell fer four different ones, myself! An' none of 'em, except mebbe it was the second one, was anywheres near the looker this here Della was."

"Oh, I ain't blamin' him fer fallin' fer her, so much as lettin' her gyp him after he'd fell. That's where his lack of brains come in—not the fallin'! Cripes—my younger days was jest one long series of falls. But, somehow, I always managed to land on my feet."

"Yer lucky," grunted Cush. "The first three times I lit otherwheres. The last time was all right—but she up an' died on me. Yer smart, all right, John. But you ain't so old but what some woman will git you yet. Then you'll be wise as well as smart. Look who's comin' in the door."

BLACK JOHN turned to greet young Corporal Downey of the Northwest Mounted Police. "Hello, Downey! Shove up agin the bar. The house is buyin' one. Is this here a business call? Er are you jest seekin' surcease from the sinful along the big river?"

"A bird named Britton is my main worry, at present," replied the officer, filling the glass that Cush slid toward him with professional accuracy. "He's supposed to be loose somewheres in the Yukon with sixty thousan' dollars that never reached its proper destination. It seems he stood up an express car in Idaho. Accordin' to our information it was a well planned job. He worked in cahoots with a woman—a good lookin' jane that played up to the express messenger for a month or so an' finally persuaded him to let her make a trip with him. Then, at the proper time she either opens the door to the car, or forces him to open it, and lets this Britton in. The rest was easy, they got away with a bank shipment of sixty thousand but somehow they had to knock off the messenger to do it. That hooks a murder on 'em besides the robbery. This man, Britton, is an ex-con from Stillwater, Minnesota. One of the mail clerks recognized him as he left the train, an' we've got a good description from the prison records. We ain't got a line on the woman, except that she was a good looker. Britton was supposed to have crossed the line into British Columbia, and there's reason to believe he managed to ship for the North. He's a smallish man—five foot six, blue eyes, sandy complexion, reddish-brown hair, with a small V-shaped scar at the outer corner of his left eyebrow. He's a smooth talker, has worked along with con-men an' queer shovers, an' he's plenty cultus if he's cornered. Got a stick-up record half as long as this bar. Guess he deserves it, too. Because he answers the description of a gent who stuck up a prospector single-handed a couple of weeks back, just below Whitehorse. He was goin' outside an' this bird stands him up for thirteen hundred ounces—all the dust he had. He's back in Dawson, now—startin' all over. I'd sure like to get that cuss. He'd do plenty of time for that job, an' when he got it served, we'd turn him over to Idaho for the murder."

"Yeah," agreed Black John, "sech a character as you've depicted sure constitutes a menace to those of us who strives to live in rectitude. You say he stood that prospector up single-handed? The woman didn't show in the play?"

"No. It was a lone job. I've checked up with Tagish, an' the Passes, an' the only women that's came in lately with men are accounted for. Of course there's plenty of gals tricklin' in fer the dance halls, an' such, an' she might have got in with them—but the chances are they split up, an' she stayed in the States. Haven't had any newcomers on Halfaday that would answer Britton's description, have you?"

Black John shook his head. "Nope. Newcomers of any description is plumb absent fer better'n a month back, which would let this here Britton out, if he pulled the prospector job. No one on the crick answers such description as you give. I'm sorry we can't help you out, Downey. You know we always aim to work hand in glove with the police in sech matters."

CORPORAL DOWNEY grinned. "I know, John, that you've helped me out several times, an' I sure appreciate it. But generally it's in some roundabout way."

"Well hell, Downey—you got to remember that the ways of these here criminals is devious in the extreme. An' likewise, you've got to remember that what a man done before he come to Halfaday ain't none of our business. After he gits here though his morality has got to protrude like a bump on a log er he finds himself in the same kind of difficulty as any other corpse would be. I'll give you my word that in case this here Britton shows up on the crick, I'll proceed along the lines that my conscience, an' the ethics of the case demands. Further than that, I can't make no promise. Except I might add that sech a character as would stoop to murderin' a man in what you might say, cold blood, in that express car, wouldn't be no one we'd care to have settle down on Halfaday permenant."

"Well," Downey replied, "I'll be goin' back, now. I'll appreciate anything you can do for me. I'd sure like to get that prospector's dust back for him. That twenty thousan' he'd gouged out of the gravel looked like a fortune to him. He was tellin' the boys in the Tivoli jest the night before he hit for the outside about how his wife an' kids would be waitin' for him, an' how he'd have enough to start up in some business back there in the States. Then he come back, an' it made him plumb sick to have to write an' tell 'em how he'd lost his dust, an' they'd have to keep on waitin' till he could make another stake. He was game, though. Started right in to work a location Swiftwater Bill let him have on shares over on Quartz Crick. It's too damn bad."

"Yeah," agreed Black John. "Of course that express job, barrin' the murder of the messenger, could be viewed as a sportin' proposition—the odds agin the success of sech enterprise bein' heavy. It shore don't give me no pain in the pants if some bank loses some money. But this here prospector is different. A man's got to think of his wife an' them kids. Jest keep yer eyes peeled back there in Dawson, Downey. It might be that between the two of us we could do 'em some good."

II

A WEEK PASSED, and one afternoon Old Cush closed the Bible he had been reading, inserted a playing card between its leaves to mark his place, returned it to the back bar, and regarded the stranger who had paused momentarily in the doorway. As the man approached across the floor Cush appraised him through his square-rimmed steel spectacles. Instantly, the words of Corporal Downey recurred to him "five foot six—blue eyes, sandy complexion, reddish-brown hair, small V-shaped scar at the outer corner of his left eyebrow." Halting before the bar, the man swung a pack from his shoulders—a pack that thudded heavily as it struck the floor.

"Is this Cushing's Fort on Halfaday Crick?" he asked abruptly.

"Yeah, this is the place," replied Cush. "What you goin' to have? The house is buyin' one."

The man regarded the four or five bottles ranged in a row on the back bar. "I see you've got connyac there. Give me a shot of that."

Gravely Old Cush set the bottle labelled *cognac* before the man and shoved him a glass. When he had poured his drink, Cush filled his own glass from the same bottle.

"Here's mud in yer eye," said the man, downing the liquor. He smacked his lips and returned the glass to the bar. "Hell—that ain't connyac—it's whisky!" he scowled.

"Yeah," agreed the unperturbed Cush, "all them bottles is filled out of the same bar'l. That there name is jest the name of the bottle—not what's in it. We don't go in none fer fancy drinks on Halfaday. It's bothersome, besides bein' bad fer the guts. If a man don't like whisky he could go down to the crick an' drink water—if he was that dry."

"Oh, whisky's all right," replied the man. "I was just surprised that you'd have connyac way out in a place like this. Fill 'em up agin."

"The surprise didn't hurt you none, an' has ondoubtless wore off by now," observed Cush as he refilled his glass. "Be you aimin' to locate on Halfaday?"

"Well—that's accordin'. I might—an' then, agin, I mightn't. I heard about this place down to Whitehorse. It's claimed yer all outlaws up here—an' that would suit me fine." The man paused and winked. "I'm an outlaw, myself. This party that put me wise to this place, he told me to hunt up Black John Smith, an' everything would be jake. Where'll I find this Black John?"

"You wouldn't hardly be able to find him," replied Cush. "John, he hit out in the hills, mebbe it's a week ago, to prospect a crick some Siwash told him about. I'm lookin' fer him back most any day. If you want to see him you better wait around till he comes."

"Where kin I stay?"

"Well—there's One Eyed John's cabin. We hung One Eyed a while back, an' it's empty."

"Hung him? What fer?"

Old Cush wrinkled his brow and scratched at his ear with a gnarled thumb nail. "Damn if I rec'lect. It was prob'ly fer somethin' he done. We aim to keep the crick moral so the police won't come snoopin' around. What a man done before he come to Halfaday ain't none of our business. But after he gits here—that's different. Quite a few of the boys learnt their lesson by gittin' hung. Not but what the lesson come too late to do them any good—but it shore helps with the others."

"How many lives on the crick?"

"Oh—quite a few."

"Are they all outlaws?"

"I couldn't say."

"You ain't puttin' out much in the way of information," grinned the man. "Well—that suits me. I'm the same way, myself—except when I know I'm amongst friends—others that's in the same boat I'm in, you know. The less a man says the further he gits in our game. Ain't that so, brother?"

CUSH SHRUGGED. "Women runs more to talkin'," he opined.

"You said it, brother. An' it's mostly on account of a woman I'm here. She was a swell dame. Been on the make around Frisco with a bunch of junkers when I cops her off 'em an' puts her in the big money. I takes her to Seattle an' steers her up agin an express messenger, an' she hooks him fer fair. Then, when he spills it that there's a bank shipment, she gets him to let her make the trip with him. The rest is easy. I'm on the blind, an' when the train gits acrost into Idaho, she opens the end door, an' I takes him. Only the damn fool tries fer a gunplay, an' I has to bump him. I pulls the cord, an' when the train slows to a stop, we scrams. But someone must of seen me, cause the next day the heat's on. I've got a record—see. So I slips this jane the stuff—sixty thousan', an' enough clear money so she don't have to spend none of the hot cash—an' tells her to meet me in Dawson. I hits acrost the line an' ships out of Vancouver after laying low fer a while. She's s'posed to take the stuff with her, an' go out through Seattle. Well, she's had plenty time to git to Dawson—but she ain't there. The damn skirt played me fer a sucker an' lammed with the sixty thousan'. Good clean money in fives, tens, an' twenties—easy to shove out when the heat dies down an' them numbers gits cold. Like I said—she ain't in Dawson—but she's somewheres in this country, all right. I got a line on her—she passed through Skagway. A bird I know'd in Soapy Smith's mob passed me the word. 'She's gone on inside,' he says. An' believe me, I'll find her! An' when I do, it'll be a damn cold day before she tries to double-cross another pal—an' you kin bet yer last stack of blue ones on that. Kin you imagine a woman givin' a man the run-around, like that?"

"Well," said Cush, "they've been doin' it fer a long time. What did you want to see John about?"

"I want to find out if this jane has showed up on Halfaday, er if mebbe he might know where she's at. I'll cut him in on that sixty thousan' if he kin locate her. An' I'll sell him the balance of them hot bills at a discount. They're good money—an' when the insurance is paid an' the heat dies down so the numbers is fergot, a man could pass 'em anywheres. But I need the money right now; I'm about broke. That offer goes fer you, too—how about it, brother? Has she showed up on the crick? It'll be money in yer pocket to tip off her hand."

"What might her name be?"

"Name! Hell—she's got a string of 'em. Didn't I tell you she'd be'n on the make! Frisco Nell, some calls her. She's known as Nellie Lovall, an' Marie Donart, an' prob'ly a lot of other names. You'd know her—she's a baby-faced blond—big innocent lookin' blue eyes, an' the prettiest yaller hair you ever seen, with streaks like red gold in it. She stops 'em all—that kid! She's thirty—but she looks twenty. An' she's plenty wise. How about it? Is she here, somewheres?"

"I couldn't say," answered Cush. "But I don't mind slippin' you the word that Corporal Downey of the Mounted was through here a few days ago lookin' fer you."

"Lookin' fer me? How do you know he was lookin' fer me?"

"Well—his description fitted you like a glove. Britton, he said the name was. The American police give him the description. What was botherin' him most, though was some prospector that got stuck up down below Whitehorse. Bein' in his deestrict, that-a-way, that job shore had him peeved."

"It's a damn lie!" exclaimed the man uneasily. "I never stood up no prospector. Where's this corporal, now?"

"He went on up the crick," lied Cush. "He ought to be comin' back most any time now. He's lookin' the boys over pretty thorough on account of that prospector job."

"You mean, he'll be comin' back here?"

"Shore he will. He ain't got no other way to git back to the river."

"Mebbe," ventured the man, "if I laid low in that cabin you was tellin' about he'd pass it up, goin' back. He must of looked in it comin' up, didn't he?"

"Yeah. Downey, he don't miss no cabins when he's prowlin' around after some miscreant. Most likely, though, he'll look 'em over on his way back, too. Downey's like that. There ain't many gits by him when he's on the prowl. Course, it's you that's takin' the chanct. You kin suit yerself. It ain't none of my business, one way 'er another."

"But where in hell kin I go, if I don't go there?" inquired the man with a swift glance over his shoulder. "I mean, where could I lay low till he goes back down the crick?"

"WELL," CUSH replied, after a moment of deep thought, "there's the Alasky Country Club. You might go over there an' hole up fer a few days. It's over on the American side, only a mile er so beyond the line. We built it so the Yukon wanteds would have some place to slip to when there was police on the crick."

"There must be some of the boys there now, then, eh?"

"No," answered Cush. "It jest so happens that you're the only Yukon wanted on the crick jest now. The rest is all dodgin' the American authorities."

"But—I tell you I ain't wanted in the Yukon!" declared the man, in a tone that somehow lacked conviction.

Old Cush shrugged. "In sech case," he said, "why don't you jest stay where yer at?"

"You said this here corporal was huntin' me fer that Idaho job, too," reminded the man. "Hell—I don't want to git picked up fer that. I'd git the rope back there."

"That's so. I expect, if I was you, I'd hit out fer the Country Club. There's grub there, an' blankets, an' licker to make a man comfortable fer as long as he's a mind to stay."

"But you say this here club is on the American side—what's to prevent some American marshal from walkin' in on me?"

Old Cush wangled the corner from a plug of tobacco, nested the quid comfortably, and spat accurately into the box of sawdust. "The len'th of the walk, mostly," he replied. "That, an' the fact that most of them Alasky marshals is plumb adverse to takin' even a short walk, er to doin' anything when they git there. The Country Club has still got its first time to be invaded by the American Law, seein' as there's several hundred mile of damn rough goin' betwixt it an' the nearest marshal."

"Over there alone like that—how would I know when the Law was off the crick, here, so I could come back?"

"Well," Cush replied, "here on Halfaday we always aim to give a man about what's comin' to him in the way of friendliness. I could slip you the word when it's deemed advisable fer you to come back. Chances is, Black John will be here then, too."

Ten minutes later, after pointing the way up the dry gulch that led to the boundary line, Old Cush watched the pack-laden man out of sight, and returned to the saloon.

"I shore don't like that party's looks, nor nothin' about him," he muttered, as he lifted the Bible from the back bar and adjusted his spectacles. "An' I'm hopin', fer the good of the crick, that that there female he mentions stays away from here. Not that I'm bemoanin' this damn cuss's loss none whatever, but seems like every time some woman shows up on the crick, somethin' happens."

III

WHEN BLACK JOHN appeared two days later, old Cush regarded him sourly as he set out the bottle and glasses. "Seems like," he growled, "you always pick out a hell of a time to go kihootin' off on a prospectin' trip."

"Hell, Cush—this is a good time. The flies an' mosquitoes is pretty well down, an' the weather's been even better'n what a man could rightfully expect."

"Flies, an' mosquitoes, an' weather is small worries compared to what's liable to hit Halfaday," retorted Cush. "This here Britton that Downey was huntin' has showed up on the crick."

Black John grinned. "Well—what's one more malefactor, amongst friends?"

"It ain't him I'm worryin' about—it's the woman."

"Woman! You mean the one that worked with him on that Idaho express job?"

"Yeah. Her."

"So they're still together, eh? Is she a good looker, like Downey claimed?"

Old Cush filled his glass and emptied it at a swallow. "Accordin' to Britton's tell she's got even that there Della in the Bible backed off'n the map fer looks, besides bein' twist as ornery. Accordin' to the Book, Della only took the big Swede fer his hair, but this here female took Britton fer the sixty thou-san' they netted on that express job. An' they ain't together, none whatever. It's the gittin' together I'm feared of. Believe me, John—if that there woman should come trouncin' in on Halfaday hell will pop, an' sparks will fly. Britton don't take his loss none easy. Blood show's in his eye when he mentions her. She's his main thought—an' don't you fergit it."

"Where's this Britton at, now?"

"He's over to the Country Club. I didn't want no murder to happen on Halfaday whilst you was away, so I lied to him about Downey bein' still on the crick, an' huntin' fer him on account of the Idaho job, an' also that prospector stick-up. I told him about the Country Club, an' he's hidin' out there. I aimed to keep him there till you got back. It would be a hell of a mess if a woman got murdered, even if she's a thief."

"Did he own up to them jobs?"

"He mentioned the Idaho one plenty—claimin' he give the money to the woman an' told her to hit fer Dawson with it, an' meet him there. He come through by way of Vancouver, an' slipped down to Dawson—but she wa'nt there. She come inside, though. He got a line on her in Skagway. He claims he never pulled no prospector stick up, but whilst he wasn't lookin' I got out my pencil an' figgered he lied about it."

"Yer pencil! How in hell could you figger it with a pencil?"

" 'Rithmetic, His pack hit the floor like a hundred pound—but it bulked awful small. Thirteen hundred ounces, I figgered was eighty-one an' a quarter pound. That's what the prospector lost. He's prob'ly got nineteen, twenty pound of other stuff mixed with it. He had another pack, but he didn't regard it none, havin' left it in his canoe. This heavy one he kep' plenty clost."

"The sum is worth contemplatin'," observed Black John, "an' as fer as I kin see you done about as well as I could, myself. That lie about Downey bein' still on the crick was nothin' short of an inspiration."

"I don't know nothin' about that," grunted Cush. "But it was the only lie I could think of that would fit the case. I don't want no woman butchered in this here saloon."

"Cheer up, Cush," grinned Black John. "She might never show up on Halfaday."

CUSH SHOOK his head sombrely. "That would be jest too damn much luck fer us to have," he replied. "She's a crook—same as if she was a man. An' you know jest as well as I do, John, that sooner er later every crook in the Yukon shows up on Halfaday. It's owin' to them damn fools down along the big river claimin' we're outlaws."

Black John nodded slowly as he refilled his glass. "I contemplate with sadness on the reputation we've got amongst the misinformed," he said sombrely.

"If them big words means anything, John, you've wasted every damn one of 'em," replied Cush sourly. "An' besides which, them two last drinks is on you. An' on top of that, what the hell are we goin' to do if this woman shows up on the crick?"

"Well, of course I couldn't stand around an' see her murdered any more than you could. An' yet, we can't keep this infamous wretch, Britton, hangin' around the Country Club indefinite, neither. Likewise, we can't cross no bridge where there ain't none. So in case she afflicts us with her presence, we'll jest have to cherish her—an' let nature take her course."

"Is that some form of hangin'?" asked Cush. "Hell, John, I wouldn't want us to hang no woman, no more than to see one git murdered in here."

"The abysmal depths into which ignorance kin plunge a man is shore dismal to contemplate."

"Which, if that answers my question, you might as well of kep' yer mouth shet," grumbled Cush. "An'—well, lookit comin' up the bank!" His eyes were fixed upon a figure that was negotiating the last few steps of the steep trail that led down to the landing. "It's her," he breathed, with an air of surrendering to the inevitable. "An' now mebbe you'll do somethin' besides jest stand around an' say big words," he added, with just a trace of malice in his tone.

The figure stepped lightly to the doorway and paused, smiling, a light pack dangling from her shoulder. Red lips smiled as her baby blue eyes met the gaze of the two men. "Hello, boys!" she greeted. "My guide tells me that this is Cushing's Fort, on Halfaday Creek."

White teeth gleamed from behind Black John's heavy beard as his eyes swept in a glance of approval from the small pac-shod feet to the shapely legs that showed below the short skirt of heavy serge, and upward to the mass of golden hair that gleamed beneath the tam that surmounted it at a jaunty angle.

"You was rightly informed," he replied, as his glance shifted momentarily to the Indian who stood behind her leaning stolidly upon his paddle. "An' if you'll step inside, Miss, the house will buy a drink."

The woman's smile widened, as she crossed to the bar. "How do you know whether it's Miss, or Mrs.?" she asked, with a daring flash of the blue eyes.

"I'm a man who hopes fer the best," smiled Black John. "Meet Mr. Lyman Cushing, proprietor of this haven of rest an' comfort, who will be glad to mix you up any drink you kin mention—providin' it's straight whisky."

"Whisky suits me," laughed the woman, resting a foot on the brass rail, as she swung the light pack to the bar. "I'm hunting for Black John Smith."

BLACK JOHN swept the hat from his head and bowed low. "I've been hunted on numerous occasions, an' fer various reasons," he smiled, "but I was never caught up with by a lovlier pursuer." And the smile widened as, out of the tail of his eye, he caught the glare of grim disapproval with which Cush was regarding him.

"So, you're Black John?" said the woman, with a warm glance of the blue eyes. "I've got a proposition to put up to you."

"Well—I'm only human. Any proposition you'd care to make would doubtless be favorably received."

Behind the bar a glass dropped to the floor with a sharp jangle of shattered glass. "Remember Samson," growled Cush, as he stooped low to pick up the pieces.

"Who's Samson?" asked the woman.

"Oh," replied Black John, "he's jest a feller that had bad luck, a while back. Cush, he always remembers him when he breaks a glass. About that proposition you mentioned. My cabin's only a short piece from here. Mebbe you'd like to—?"

"Listen, big boy," interrupted the woman with a smile. "You've sure got a line, but don't get me wrong. I'm here for business—and business only. I know all about you—picked it up down around Dawson; how you're all outlaws up here, and you're king of the bunch. Well—I'm on the run, myself, and I've got something to unload. Are you interested?"

"A man couldn't hardly help but be—what with them eyes, an' that yalla hair."

"This is a money proposition—big money. I've inquired around, and I know I can talk to you boys. Whether we deal or not, I know you won't let me down. Me and my boy friend took an express car for sixty thousand and I've got the stuff here with me. It's all good stuff—fives, tens and twenties—easy to shove. But it's hot right now—and I need the dough. I'll make a good proposition to the right party."

Black John nodded. "An' this boy friend you mentioned? Where does he come in?"

A hard look flashed in the baby-blue eyes and the red lips tightened at the corners. "He don't come in," she said, in a brittle tone. "He's a rat. He made me take the stuff so if he was picked up he'd be in the clear. I was to meet him in Dawson and we'd split; but I know what kind of a split I'd get—and I did most of the work. Put in a month playing the poor sucker of a messenger. He wasn't a bad guy, at that—and Britton knocked him off. There was no sense in that. But Britton's got a record, and he was afraid to let him live."

"How come you didn't connect up with this Britton in Dawson?"

"I got there first. I didn't dare to stay in the States—with that hot stuff on me. Then he hit there and before he'd located me he fell for a dance hall jane and told her what they'd do when he got that sixty thousand. It was plenty—and she told me. I knew then where I'd get off at. In the meantime I'd heard all about Halfaday Crick—so I hired an Indian to bring me here. I figured that if I could deal with you boys, if you'd take the stuff off my hands and give me some dough that I ain't afraid to shove, I'd hit back for Frisco, and let Britton have his dance hall baby—the dirty rat!"

"About how much of a sacrifice would you be willin' to make on this hot money?" Black John asked.

"Well," considered the woman, "how about giving me fifty thousand? That would give you a clean profit of ten thousand on the deal. A year from now, when the heat dies down, you could shove it to the bank it was shipped to and they'd never spot it."

"Mebbe," admitted Black John. "You say you've got the stuff with you, let's have a look at it."

The woman opened the pack and dumped the packages of bills onto the bar. "There you are," she said. "Right in the original packages with the bank bands still on 'em."

PICKING UP a package, Black John riffled the bills through. He picked up another package, and another, until he had counted it all, as Old Cush leaned over the bar and watched, now and then picking up a package and examining it on his own account.

"Sixty thousan' is right," announced Black John. "But like you say, sister, this is hot money. Mebbe the heat'll be off'n it in a year—mebbe not. Anyhow, a year is a long time to tie up fifty thousan'. I wouldn't hardly care to take you up on the proposition."

"Ten thousand profit on your fifty thousand is twenty percent," reminded the woman. "What more do you want? Make me a proposition."

Black John cleared his throat. "Drink up," he invited, "an' I'll buy one. As the glasses were refilled, he caught a glance of warning from Cush. Ignoring it, he turned to the woman. "Percentages don't mean much to us, up here. It's lump sums we deal in. I'll make you a proposition. You kin take it er leave it. It's all the same to me. I don't aim to stand here an' dicker. Yer goin' to think I'm hoggish—an mebbe I am. It's my nature. If you don't like the proposition, all you got to do is turn it down—an' the incident will he fergot. You could prob'ly do better almost anywheres else.

I'll give you thirty thousan' fer the sixty. I make it a p'int never to deal, in a case like this, without I can double my money."

"It's a damned outrage!" exclaimed the woman, glaring at the big man angrily. "You don't look like a man that would take advantage of a girl that way!"

"I've took advantage of a lot of 'em, in my time," replied Black John evenly, "an' most always to my own detriment. I'm concludin', then, that the deal is off?"

"Make it forty-five—or even forty."

"Thirty was the figger I mentioned," reminded Black John, as behind the woman's back Old Cush was wagging his head in a vigorous negative.

"Give me the thirty, then—and to hell with you!" spat out the woman in a tone of deep disgust. "It's all I'd have got out of it from Britton, if he'd have come clean—and that dirty rat couldn't come clean, if he tried. I'd have been lucky to get ten."

"That's lookin' at it sensible," agreed Black John as he turned to Cush. "Jest count me thirty thousan' out of the safe, Cush, an' I'll pay the lady, so she can be on her way. She better be hurryin' out of the country before this Britton comes up here lookin' fer her. Ain't that right, Miss?"

"I'll say it's right. Give me the dough, an' I'm gone."

THE MONEY was counted and stowed in the woman's pack, and she left as abruptly as she had come. When she disappeared over the edge of the bank, Cush, who had been regarding the pile of new bills with a frown of disgust, raised his eyes to the face of Black John.

"Of all the damn fool deals I ever seen, that takes the cake," he growled.

"What do you mean—damn fool deals? I doubled my money, didn't I?"

"Doubled yer money! You give out thirty thousan' good dollars fer a bunch of junk that wouldn't fool the greenest bank clerk there is! Damn it, John—couldn't you see that stuff is counterfeit? Couldn't you see me shakin' my head? What the hell did you expect me to do—yell out about it?"

"Downey was shore right," muttered Black John, "she was a mighty good looker. Cripes, Cush—did you see them reddish glints in her yella hair?"

Old Cush snorted his disgust. "Yeah, I seen that fer nothin'. It cost you thirty thousan' to look at it. Er mebbe part of it was fer lookin' into them blue eyes. I told you some woman would make a fool of you, yet! But I didn't think you'd be took in so damn easy as all that. Cripes—couldn't you see that stuff is queer?"

"Oh shore, Cush—I seen that at a glance. But hell—queer money is as good as good money, if you keep it movin'. I still figger I doubled my money. Tell you what I'll do, Cush—jest charge half of that thirty thousan' up again' yerself, an' I'll go you fifty-fifty on the profits."

"Not by a damn sight! I don't want nothin' to do with shovin' queer money—an' yer a damn fool to tackle it, yerself. Believe me, John—you'll be money ahead, if you chuck that stuff in the stove there an' touch a match to it."

Black John shook his head. "No, I'll git rid of it, all right. I ain't worryin' none. Did you notice them lips of hers, Cush? Hell, mebbe I ought to give her forty thousan' instead of the thirty—a man don't git the chanct to see a woman like her every day."

"It's a damn good thing you don't, er you'd be broke in a month's time. You've got plenty, John, but you won't have long, if you shuck it off thirty thousan' to a crack—jest because some woman's got yella hair an' blue eyes. Hell, my first three wives was all like that! The last one was darker. Accordin' to them Bible pitchers, Eve was one of them blondes, an' that there Della, too. I guess all them gyp women is."

"Yeah," grinned Black John, "the on-morality of blondes has, from time to time, caused me more or less trouble without runnin' to the Bible fer it. But I don't begrudge them bygones none. A man learns from experience."

"It don't look like you've learnt no hell of a lot—the way you shoved that thirty thousan' to that dame. Where you goin'?" he added, as the other turned from the bar.

"Oh, jest projectin' a round a little. If that there Britton should come before I git back, you might tell him his woman showed up here an' sold out them sixty thousan' to me for thirty thousan' in cash. He'll prob'ly take out after her, an' Halfaday'll be shet of both of 'em."

"I hope he don't ketch her," Cush replied. "I'd rather she got them thirty thousan' than him. I don't like his looks. He ain't no one you could trust."

IV

PROCEEDING TO HIS cabin, Black John grinned to himself as he produced a shiny piece of metal from a recess behind his bunk and polished it on his sleeve. "I know'd damn well I could make use of this here badge sometime, when I took it off'n that marshal," he muttered. Pinning the badge conspicuously on his shirt front, he thrust a forty-five revolver into his belt, and proceeded up the dry gulch that led to the Alaska Country Club.

Slipping along the wall, he removed his hat, and applied his eye to a corner of a window. Both doors stood wide to allow free passage to whatever air was stirring, as the afternoon was sultry. Near the front door, seated comfortably in a chair, a man sat reading an old magazine. Beside him, within easy reach on the table, stood a bottle and a glass. Toward the farther end of the big room, near the back door, a pack lay at the head of a bunk. Stealthily Black John moved along the wall to the back door, and drawing the revolver from his belt, he cocked it, and stepped abruptly into the room. As his figure darkened the doorway, the magazine fell to the floor as the man sprang from the chair and faced him.

Black John leveled his gun. "The jig's up, Britton," he said. "You might as well come along peaceable. This is a rough country, an' dead men is hard to pack."

"Who—who the hell are you?" gasped the man, his hands elevated above his head. And then, as his gaze centered upon the badge, he croaked: "U.S. Marshal!"

"Yup—from Fairbanks. We got word that you'd prob'ly headed north, an' to be on the lookout fer you. I s'pose," he added, with a glance toward the pack on the bunk near where he stood, "that the sixty thousan' you gathered when you knocked off that express messenger is in there. Yer goin' to swing fer that job, Britton. That's why I don't want to have to cool you up here." Lowering the gun, he turned toward the pack, and in that instant, with a lightning-like leap the man vanished through the front door.

Yelling loudly at him to halt, Black John reached the door just as the man vanished around the first bend of the trail leading across the line to Halfaday and—safety. He fired three or four shots from the doorway, and turning back into the room, lifted the pack from the bunk, carried it to the table, and proceeded to examine its contents.

OLD CUSH looked up from his reading, as a form plunged through the doorway and catapulted to the bar. The man's face glistened with sweat, and his heaving chest drew the air into his lungs in great sobs as he glared angrily across the bar.

"You claimed," he panted accusingly, "that there couldn't no U.S. marshal git to that there Country Club!"

Shoving his spectacles from nose to forehead, Cush regarded the man sombrely. "I don't rec'lect makin' no sech claim," he observed. "I told you that, owin' to slothful habits, there hadn't none showed up there yet—"

"The hell there ain't!" interrupted the other. "There's one there right now. An' believe me—he took me fer plenty! He'd of got me, too, only I ducked when he took his gun off'n me fer a second."

"I thought you said you was about broke—what with offerin' to discount them express bills to us fer ready cash if you could locate the woman that had 'em," Cush reminded. "How could he of took you fer plenty?"

"I had right around twenty thousan' in dust, besides," moaned the man, "an' the hell of it is, he didn't have no right to take me fer that job. I pulled that down on the Yukon."

"You might go back an' p'int out the mistake," suggested Cush. "Mebbe h'd give it back to you. So it was you that stuck up that prospector Downey was tellin' about?"

"Yes, it was me all right," snarled the other. "I told you I didn't do it—but a man don't have to tell all he knows to strangers. I'm in a hell of a spot now! No matter which way I jump, I'm picked up. I ain't even got an outfit. Did that corporal come back down the crick yet?"

"No, he ain't showed up since you was here. He's liable to, any minute."

"What the hell can I do? Of all the tough luck a man ever had—I'm havin' it!"

"Yeah," agreed Cush, "an' you don't know the half of it. That there woman you was huntin', she showed up on the crick after you'd went acrost the line an' on-loaded them express bills onto Black John fer thirty thousan' in cash—an' then beat it back down the crick with a Siwash paddlin' her canoe. She claimed she was headin' fer Frisco. She was sore as hell at you on account she claimed you'd throw'd in with some dance hall jane down to Dawson."

"You say she got the cash? Thirty thousan' in good cash?" demanded the man excitedly.

"That's what she got—an' by the look in her eye when she spoke of you, she aims to keep it."

"How about an' outfit?" cried the man. "Damn her! I've got to ketch up with her. That's every cent I've got in the world—now! Stand me off fer a canoe an' some grub, will you? If I don't ketch up with her, you lose. If I do, I'll come back an' pay double. Is it a deal?"

Cush nodded. "Yeah, I'll take a chanct. There's a canoe at the landin' you can have—an' I'll stake you to some flour, an' pork, an' sugar, an' tea. If you go like hell—at least you might be able to keep ahead of Downey. Come on an' help fetch the stuff down to the canoe."

V

AN HOUR AFTER the man's departure, Black John showed up at the saloon and Old Cush set out the bottle and two glasses as he approached the bar.

"That there Britton, er whatever his name is, ain't over to the Country Club," he announced. "I sort of sauntered over to size this fella up—an' there ain't no one there."

"Not even a U.S. marshal?" asked Cush.

"No. Why would you think a U.S. marshal would be there?"

"Well, he must of pulled out in a hell of a hurry, then," Cush replied. "Damn near in as much of a hurry as Britton did. Britton, he come bustin' in here a couple hours ago damn near winded on account of he'd ran all the way down the gulch. He claimed a U.S. marshal show'd up there an' took his pack—which did have that there prospector's dust in it, jest like I figgered it did. He owned up about it when he was bellyachin' about his loss. Claimed the marshal didn't have no right to it on account he'd pulled the job on this side of the line. He was shore sore about it, but it wasn't nothin' to the rage he flew into when I told him his woman had show'd up an' onloaded them bank bills onto you fer thirty thousan' in cash."

"Where is he now?"

"He's goin' hell-bent down the crick after her. I staked him to an outfit. I figgered it was a cheap price to git shut of sech a character—him an' the woman both. Halfaday Crick shore don't need no sech people as them livin' on it."

Black John nodded. "Yer right, Cush. But at that, yer out a canoe, an' that grub. Looks to me like you was a kind of a sucker."

"Sucker!" snorted Cush. "You callin' me a sucker 'cause I let go of a hundred dollar canoe, an' mebbe twenty dollars worth of grub—when that woman took you fer thirty thousan' in cash. It's you that's the sucker, this time, John. You ought to listened to me. I tried to warn you about them queer bills. Sucker—hell! But, at that—I know'd that some woman was bound to take you, sometime. Mebbe yer lucky to git off with a thirty thousan' loss. Anyhow—it learnt you a lesson."

"Mebbe," grinned Black John. "Wait till I fetch in a pack I found over to the Country Club, an' we'll see."

Cush's eyes widened as the other swung the sack to the bar. "Why, that's Britton's sack!" he exclaimed. "It's the one he had with him when he come—the one I figgered he had that prospector's dust in!"

"Yeah," Black John admitted, "an' it's in here yet—every damn ounce of it."

"But—how did you git it off'n that marshal?"

"What marshal?"

"Why—the one that show'd up at the Country Club an' draw'd a gun on Britton an' run him out of there?"

Black John's grin widened. "Oh, hell—that wasn't no bony fido marshal, Cush. That was me. It was more er less of a natural mistake on Britton's part, under the circumstances, on account of me wearin' that badge I took off'n that marshal, that time down on the big river. If he'd stayed there an' demanded to see my papers, he'd have had me in a hell of a spot. But what with the badge, an' the gun an' all, he seemed a bit nervous, an' pulled out in a hell of a hurry, without even tryin' to salvage his pack. An' by the way, Cush, you was pretty near right about the weight of this pack. The rest of it is bills; sixty thousan' dollars in good bills—the ones they took in that Idaho train robbery. Here they are—jest look 'em over. They took the bank bands off'n 'em to wrap around that fake currency the woman sold me."

OLD CUSH'S eyes fairly bulged from their sockets, as he stared at the bundles of bills that tumbled from the sack, as Black John emptied it onto the bar. He moistened his lips with his tongue. "But them other bills, John—them fake ones? Where in hell do they come in—an' why did you buy 'em?"

"Merely as an investment, Cush," grinned the big man. "I offered to let you in on the deal—but you wouldn't come. You see, when I seen that queer stuff, I rec'lected that Downey mentioned that this Britton had worked with queer-shovers, an' that give me an' idea. Them two crooks was workin' a game on us. They wasn't sore at each other—that was part of the set-up. They figgered on takin' us fer what they could git on that fake money, an' still keep the sixty thousan', an' the prospector's dust in the clear. But—they didn't have no luck at it."

Cush nodded slowly, his eyes on the heap of bills and the little sacks of dust that reposed on the bar. "Yeah," he admitted, "but still I don't see why you bought that there fake money. What in hell you goin' to do with it, now you've got it?"

"Like I told you, Cush, counterfeit money is as good as any other money, jest so you keep it movin'. I aim to keep this movin'—I'm turnin' it in to Corporal Downey, along with this here dust that was stole off'n that prospector. I'll bet that pore devil will be glad to get his dust back—what with his wife an' kids, an' all. I'm glad I was able to locate it fer him. Downey'll be glad too."

"Shore, Downey'll be glad to git the man's dust back—but what's he goin' to think about them fake bills? He'll know them crooks never got them bills off'n no express car."

"That's where the woman claimed they got 'em," grinned Black John. "It ain't my fault if she lied. Any way, Downey gits 'em. What he thinks about 'em ain't losin' me no sleep."

"An' these here good bills—what you goin' to do with them?"

"Oh—them. Why they constitute my profit on the deal. Don't you rec'lect I told that jane that I never touched a deal without I doubled my money?"

"But—s'pose Downey should pick these here crooks up, later?"

Black John shrugged. "I hope he does. Folks like them ain't got no business runnin' around lose amongst decent people. Figger it out fer yerself—are they goin' to squawk? They'd only git in worse, no matter what they said. An' anything they could say would involve some U.S. marshal; which would complicate matters till I doubt if even Downey could ever figger out the straight of it."

Old Cush wagged his head sadly as he stowed the packages of good bills into the safe, and credited Black John's account with sixty thousand dollars. "An' I could of had half of it," he muttered regretfully. "But I figgered that there dame was gyppin' you, John. I figgered you'd fell fer that yaller hair, an' them blue eyes, an' them red lips. I kep' thinkin' about that there Samson, an' how that woman gypped him, an' I figgered that if she could git Samson, which he's in the Bible, this woman could shore git you, which you ain't in no Bible—so I wouldn't have nothin' to do with it."

"Yeah," grinned Black John, "but you ought to have noticed that I didn't give this here woman of Britton's no chanct to cut off my hair. Come now, drink up, an' I'll buy one."

BLACK JOHN INTERVENES

OLD CUSH, PROPRIETOR of Cushing's Fort, the combined trading post and saloon that was the headquarters for the little community of outlawed men that had sprung up on Halfaday Creek, close against the Yukon-Alaska border, scowled at the dice as Black John Smith returned the leather box to the bar with a flourish.

"That's a horse on me," he admitted. "But next time roll them dice out, instead of slidin' 'em out."

Black John grinned. "I'm surprised that you'd mention a thing like that, Cush. Last time, them three aces you throw'd never even come out of the box at all. You was holdin' 'em up ag'in the bottom of it with yer little finger—an' I didn't even comment on the fact."

"Huh," grunted old Cush, "I wouldn't neither, if I aimed to come right back at me with them four sixes—slidin' 'em out of the box as slick as what you done. That's a horse apiece—let's make the next throw honest."

So engrossed were the two cronies with their good natured bickering that neither had noticed a man who had watched the proceeding from the doorway, and now advanced into the room, a broad smile on his thin lips.

"Honesty, gentlemen, is always the best policy," he announced, ranging himself beside Black John, and elevating a foot to the battered brass rail. "And especially so in manipulating the little cubes." Reaching for the leather box, he scooped the dice from the bar with a single deft motion, and rattled them audibly in the box. "If you will permit me, I will endeavor to demonstrate how easy it would be for a dishonest person who had the required dexterity to fleece the unsuspecting. For instance—you both saw me gather the dice from the bar—if not, I'll do it again—so. Now, gentlemen, you will both admit that there are dice in this little box that I hold here in my hand—you saw them enter the box—you can hear them rattle as I shake it back and forth—but do you know how many dice are in the box? Tell me, gentlemen. I'll give you each a guess. And please note that I am holding no dice in my hand. I grasp the box only with my thumb and two fingers."

"Five, I s'pose," ventured Cush. "There was five layin' there on the bar."

"And you?" the man turned to Black John. "How many would you say were in the box?"

"Well, five goes fer me, too."

"Five," repeated the man, shaking the box so that the dice rattled loudly. "They both say five—so five it must be. But—let's see—we cast them—so—and to our vast surprise we find the box is empty. There are no dice in the box—though we all saw them go into it, and we heard them rattle as I shook it."

"Well I'll be damned!" exclaimed Black John, as he gazed with interest at the empty box. "I was watchin' clost, an' I never seen them dice go up yer sleeve at all."

"Up my sleeve! Oh, nothing so crude as that, I assure you. See—my sleeves are free of dice—examine them yourself."

"Where in hell be they, then?" asked Cush, a look of bewilderment on his face.

"Look in the pocket of your shirt—the right hand pocket."

Hooking a thumb into the edge of the pocket, Cush, pulled it open and peered down into it. "There ain't no dice in there," he said.

"What? No dice? Maybe, then I'm wrong—let's look in the other pocket." Reaching a long arm across the bar, he felt the left hand pocket of Cush's shirt, and shook his head. "No dice in that one, either—but surely I can't be wrong—look again in the right hand pocket, just make sure."

Again Cush peered down into the pocket, and his eyes wide with surprise, he reached in and laid the five dice upon the bar. "Well—I'll be damned!" he muttered. "Them dice wasn't there the first time I looked—I'd bet my life on it!"

"Never bet on the other man's game," smiled the man. "You're bound to lose. But permit me to introduce myself—Professor Leonidas Dykes, practitioner of the art of legerdemain, commonly called sleight of hand, a form of deception, gentlemen, that is based upon the fact that the hand is quicker than

the eye. Take this silver dollar that I hold before you in my hand—now you see it—and now you don't see it—and here you see it again."

Old Cush watched the deft manipulation of the coin in the man's hand, and turning to the back bar, produced a bottle and three glasses. "This un's on the house," he said. "Drink hearty."

As Black John reached for his glass, he caught sight of a figure beside the door. "Who's the lady?" he asked abruptly.

"Ah pardon me, gentlemen," said the newcomer suavely. "May I present Mrs. Dykes?" He turned and beckoned to the woman with much the same motion he would have summoned a dog, although he spoke in a honeyed tone: "Come in, darling. Don't be afraid. These gentlemen are friends. Meet Mr.—er—"

"Smith," supplied the bearded man before the bar, "known fer reasons more er less obvious, as Black John. An' that there's Lyme Cushing."

Cush acknowledged the introduction with a bob of the head and set out another glass. "Fill up, mom," he invited. "The drinks is on the house."

"Thank you," she said, "but I don't drink."

Dykes smiled, and Black John noted that behind the smile the man's thin lips held much of cruelty, and little of the milk of human kindness—a trait that was further accentuated by his beedy, close-set eyes.

"No," he said, "Mrs. Dykes has small regard for the demon rum. He turned his thin-lipped smile upon her. "Go sit down while we talk business—sweetheart," he ordered, and Black John sensed venom behind the honeyed tone. As the woman crossed to a chair beside one of the card tables, the big man noted that she would have been beautiful but for the tragic hopelessness that shone from the large dark eyes—a haunting look, half-fear, half-blank despair."

He turned to Dykes. "What's the nature of this here business we're s'posed to talk?" he asked.

THE MAN swallowed his liquor, and motioned toward the bottle. "Drink up, and have one with me," he invited. "The fact is, gentlemen, as you may have guessed, I'm a showman. I have no superior, and few equals in the realm of legerdemain. I put on a show lasting two hours and a half, and guarantee satisfaction, or your money back. I instruct. I amuse. I mystify."

"You mean you want to pull off a show here on Halfaday?"

"That, gentlemen, was my thought—providing of course, that it meets with your approval—and I could find a building that would house the audience."

"This here saloon will hold everyone on the crick," observed Cush, "an' room to spare."

"Yeah," agreed Black John, regarding the man intently, "there ain't only fifty, sixty of us here on Halfaday. Even if the boys all come to yer show at say, two, three, er even five dollars a throw, an' Cush was to let you use the saloon, rent free, fer the performance, you wouldn't make no hell of a lot. It wouldn't hardly pay you fer the trouble an' expense of comin' up here."

"Anyway, it would be something."

"But not enough to justify swingin' clean up here off'n the big river," persisted Black John. "I s'pose you show a lot of card tricks, too, eh?"

The man's thin smile became even thinner, as he allowed the lid to drop slowly over his left eye. "No. No card tricks. Any dexterity I may have with the pasteboards is reserved for—er—I may say, special purposes. And therein lies the real reason for my appearance on this creek. The fact is, gentlemen—I have heard of you both. It is common knowledge along the Yukon that Halfaday Creek is an outlaw community. It is also common knowledge that Black John, here, is king of the creek—and that you, Cush, are a sort of prime minister."

"I read in the Good Book, now an' then—but I ain't no minister," disclaimed Cush. "I run the tradin' post, an' saloon."

"Even so," smiled the man, "I believe I am safe in assuming that the destiny of Halfaday rests largely upon you two. It has also come to my ears that the per capita wealth of Halfaday is probably greater than that of any other creek in the Yukon—and that poker and stud games are almost of nightly occurrence." The man paused, and Black John, who had been regarding him intently, asked abruptly:

"An' so what?"

"And so, my friends, it occurred to me that an alliance might be formed which, with your prestige and my dexterity, would prove extremely profitable to each of us."

"Meanin'?" queried Black John.

"Why—simply that you two sort of sponsor me—just see that I'm properly introduced, and allowed to sit in these various games of chance, and in case of certain misunderstandings, or accusations, see that I got a—shall we say, a fair break? The profits, of course, to split three ways."

"Oh, shore—we'll see that you git a fair break all right," agreed Black John. "But let's see if I've got this straight—your proposition is that me an' Cush sets you in the games so you kin rob the boys by crooked card-playin', an' then you split the stealin's with us, an' besides that, if you was to git ketched in yer crooked work, we're to see that you don't git what's comin' to you. Is that it?"

"Well—er—putting it that way—yes—that's about what it amounts to."

BLACK JOHN regarded the man thoughtfully. "This here common knowledge that you gathered down along the Yukon seems fairly accurate as fer as it goes. But if you'd of delved further into the founts of this knowledge you'd of come acrost the axiom that there ain't no crime permitted on Halfaday. You would have learnt that along with sech crimes as murder, larceny, an' claim-jumpin', we've got a cardinal sin called skull-duggery which includes all known forms of vice which we deem on-desirable, an' that card-cheatin' comes under this head. You would also have learnt that our one an' only punishment fer any of these crimes is hangin', an' that, in our rather uncouth administration of jestice, there ain't no sech loopholes as, demurrers, stays of execution, paroles, pardons, appeals, or reversals of sentence. In other words, if a man's convicted by a miners' meeting on Halfaday, his longevity practically ceases right then."

"I know," the man replied. "I heard all that, of course. But I've been around some. I know that no matter how strict a set of laws are, contact with the proper people can—shall we say?—mitigate their enforcement. I also know that every man has got his price. It occurred to me that with all the ready cash and the dust that's here on the creek your price could be met."

"Sech occurrence," replied Black John evenly, "is based on fallacy."

"Hell!" exclaimed the man. "You're an outlaw, aren't you?"

"Oh, shore—that part of it's all right. That's the reason I've got to keep an eye on my ethics—so's to keep my record clean. Cripes—I couldn't look no one in the face if I'd stoop to sech lousy forms of skullduggery as aidin' an' abettin' a card shark. My advice to you, Perfesser, is to git sech part of yer anatomy behind you as belongs behind an' head fer Dawson before it gits bruised by the toe of someone's boot."

"You mean," persisted the man, "that you won't play ball with me?"

"Not ball, nor no other game—'specially poker, er stud. You better head fer Dawson an' hook up with Cutter Malone He'd welcome a bird of your ilk."

"I can't go to Dawson," replied the man. "I skipped out of Dawson. The police warned me not to come back. That's why I came to Halfaday. I figured I'd be safe here."

"A man's as safe on Halfaday as his actions permits him to be," replied Black John.

"But—I'm broke. An' I've got my wife to look out for. I can't starve."

BLACK JOHN glanced toward the woman who sat out of earshot across the room, elbow on the table, her chin resting in her palm. "Under the circumstances," he said, "we ain't got no objections to yer remainin' on the crick providin' you don' set in no card games. What with most any claim payin' wages er better, a man can't starve here."

"You mean—go to work? Dig in the gravel for gold?"

"That's the way we git it," Black John replied. "But there ain't no prestidigetators amongst us. Mebbe you kin figger some way to juggle it out."

"It might take me quite a while to get used to it," said the man, "an' in the meanwhile, we've got to eat."

"That part could be easily arranged. You kin put on a show—an' you might as well throw in some card tricks fer good measure, seein' that you won't be needin' 'em fer no other purpose. Besides, it would serve to warn the boys as to what you could do with a deck—jest in case you might try to coax some of 'em into a private game. Cush'll loan you the saloon, an' I'll spread the word along the crick, so you'll have a crowd. The boys would prob'ly welcome an entertainment of that kind. It'll be right interestin'. You'd ought to take in enough to finance you till you kin take out some gold. You kin move into One Eyed John's cabin. It's empty now—sence we hung One Eyed. It's jest a little piece down the crick."

"What did you hang him for?" asked Dykes.

"He held out an ace in a card game one night, so we went ahead an' hung him," Black John explained gravely. "Later, it developed that he didn't hold this ace. Cush found it on the floor next mornin' when he swep' out. But the thought was there. An' the hangin' served as a warnin' to the rest of the boys. One Eyed broke even on the play, at that; he'd held out a card onct before, an' be in' as there wasn't no quarum present, we had let him off with a warnin'."

"Do you let first offenders off with a warning?" asked Dykes, a gleam of hope in his eye.

"Yeah—he was it. Sence then, we hang 'em."

II

STARVED FOR ENTERTAINMENT, Halfaday Creek turned out almost to a man a few nights later, and at five dollars a ticket witnessed a very credible performance which Professor Dykes, assisted by his wife, gave on an improvised stage at one end of the saloon. As master of ceremonies, Black John introduced the pair, and shrewdly shattered any lingering hope that Dykes may have had of profiting at the gambling table by calling upon the audience to pay special attention to the man's uncanny dexterity with cards, and then figure what chance any one of them would have facing him across a poker table. He concluded with a tribute to the principal actor. "But the perfesser don't gamble, boys. His standard of ethics bein' sech that he scorns to take advantage of his skill to the detriment of his fella man.

And now, boys, the perfesser will proceed with his show—an' I want you to take partic'lar of notice how easy it would be fer him to make a sucker out of any one of us with cards, dice, coins—or in fact, most any damn thing he could lay his hands on."

Despite Black John's encomium, he was to find out a few days later that Professor Dykes' standard of ethics did not include wife-beating among its taboos. Passing along the trail, late one afternoon, he heard the woman scream and, peering through the brush, saw her crouching on the small gravel dump with arm upraised, trying in vain to ward off the rain of blows that Dykes was administering.

Crashing into the clearing, Black John caught the man's upraised arm and hurled him backward with a force sent him rolling almost to the door of the cabin. Instantly he was up on his feet, his eyes blazing with insane fury.

"Damn her!" he shrilled. "I'll teach her to spill sand down my neck! I warned her the first time—and she did it again!"

"I—couldn't help it," explained the woman. "I asked him not to fill the bucket so full. It's so heavy to crank up, and when I go to swing it to the dump, I can't help spilling some of it."

Black John nodded, and advanced toward the man, his huge fists doubled. "He won't fill it so full when I git through with him," he said, "nor neither he won't beat you up no more if you happen to spill some sand on him."

The look of fury in the man's eyes changed to one of abject fear, as he cowered against the wall of the cabin.

Before Black John, his huge fists doubled, could strike a blow, the woman slipped between them.

"Oh—don't—please!" she pleaded. "He didn't hurt me badly—and maybe I was a little careless with the bucket. Please don't hit him."

Black John's fists relaxed, as he regarded the cowering man from beneath scowling brows. "All right," he said. "As a favor to yer wife I'm lettin' you off with a warnin'.

But it's a warnin' you'd better heed. Only one other man has been ornery enough to abuse a woman on this crick. Stamm his name was. His slab is next to One Eyed John's in the grave yard—an' there's room fer yourn on the other side.

"Woman beatin' is inclooded in our skullduggery law, Dykes. It's a hangable offence on Halfaday—an' I might add fer yer further enlightenment that any bruise, bump, contusion, er abrasion on the person of sech woman is primo facial evidence of sech assault, even if she refuses to testify. These facts, coupled with the idee that we've got plenty of rope up to Cush's, an' that the name DYKES ain't overly hard to cut in a softwood slab, should furnish you food fer thought."

A SHORT time later, as he entered the saloon, Cush greeted him with a question. "Where in hell you been? There's a new fella show'd up on the crick. Claims his name is John Brown, so I didn't make him draw none out of the can. There ain't no more Browns on the crick, right now."

"What fer lookin' is he?"

"Well—he don't look like nothin' anyone would be proud of. 'Bout like the common run of chechakos you see along cricks. From what he says, I figger he's moved into Olson's old shack. I told him it was onlucky, but he didn't seem to mind."

"Quite a few has made that mistake," opined Black John. "Where's he at now?"

"He was askin' fer you, so I told him where yer cabin was, an' he went out. Why'n hell can't you be around here when strangers comes?"

Black John grinned. "I've been adjustin' certain serious conjugal eventualities in the cosmos of the Dykes's."

"Down to Dykes's, eh? Why'n hell couldn't you say so without stringin' in all them big words? They seem to be gittin' along fine down on One Eyed John's claim, don't they?"

Black John's grin widened, exposing white teeth behind the heavy black beard. "As a medium for the transference of thought, words of more than one syllable are plumb wasted on you, ain't they, Cush?"

"Huh—it takes a damn sight more'n a lot of big words to make me think you had any reg'lar business down to Dykes's. You allus claim yer a woman-hater, John, but I take notice that whenever one shows up on the crick, you ain't never no hell of a ways off."

"I happened to be goin' past, an' he was beatin' her up, so I made him quit—an' promised him a hangin' if he done it ag'in."

"That's good," approved Cush. "Did he bung her up much? Even if he did, them fist scars heals up quick. That claim of One

Eyed's ain't so bad. They ought to do right well if they work. An' after the warnin' you give Dykes, she ought to be happy."

Black John shook his head. "Like you said, scars on the body heals up an can be fergot. But there's scars on the heart, Cush, that don't never heal. She'll be game all right—but not happy."

"Here comes Brown now. He prob'ly didn't find you to home."

"Most likely not," grinned Black John, eyeing the stranger that was just entering the doorway.

He greeted the man cordially. "Good evenin', Brown! Cush was jest tellin' me about you. Sorry I wasn't to home when you called. Step up an' have a drink. The house is buyin' one."

"The house bought the last un," observed Cush, setting out bottle and glasses, "this un's on you, John." Reaching for his day-book he made an entry, as the newcomer regarded the big man appraisingly.

"So you're Black John Smith, eh? Well—here's mud in yer eye. I heard about you down on the river."

"Yeah?"

"Yeah. Heard all about you, an' the haul you made off'n the army over in Alasky, somewheres—an' how Halfaday Crick lays right up agin' the line where it's handy fer a man to slip acrost when the police shows up. Drink up, an' have one on me."

As he refilled his glass. Black John glanced past the other to the open doorway where the figure of Dykes appeared for a moment, then vanished. But in the brief moment that the man had stood poised in the doorway, Black John saw his beady eyes fixed on the newcomer, saw them widen in surprise and then narrow as his mobile features contorted in a grimace of venomous hate. Neither Cush nor the man who called himself Brown, had noticed the incident.

Black John toyed with his glass. "Figgerin' on locatin' on the crick?" he asked, casually.

"Yeah—if there ain't no objections. I stopped comin' up an' throw'd my stuff in an empty cabin a few mile down the crick.

Cush, here—he was tellin' me how the cabin was onlucky. But I don't go much on luck."

"Some don't," observed Black John. "I'm kind of open-minded, myself. Here's how."

"I'll buy this un," said Cush, as the glasses were emptied and refilled. "As fer as a claim goes, Olson's hadn't ought to be bad. There ain't never been no hell of a lot of dust took out of it. Seems like everyone that's tried to work it, his luck ketched up with him before he could git agoin'."

"I'll take a chance," blustered the man, the strong liquor loosening his tongue. "You bet—that's me, every time. Hell—Columbus took a chance. An' me—I've took many a one in my time. Drink up, boys, an' have another on me." He paused and tossed a limp sack onto the bar. "Weigh her out of that," he told Cush, "an' don't be afraid—there's plenty more where that come from. I don't only carry ten, twelve ounces around with me fer spendin' money—but I've got plenty. I've heard all about you boys, an' how everything goes on Halfaday."

BLACK JOHN cleared his throat. "Jest a word on that p'int to avoid any misonderstandin'," he said. "It ain't none of our business what a man done before he come to Halfaday, but after he gits here he's got to refrain from crime of any kind, no matter what his tendencies might be. Bein' outlawed like most of us is, fer one reason er another, it ain't nothin' to our advantage to have the police come snoopin' around to clear up some crime, so we save 'em the trouble by promptly hangin' anyone guilty of murder, claim-jumpin', any form of larceny or skullduggery. Which last offence is flexible enough to include whatever I deem advisable. If a man minds his own business, he gits along fine on Halfaday; if he don't it's all the same to us—except fer the nuisance of buryin' him."

"Oh, that's all right with me. I ain't no small time crook that would foul his own nest fer the sake of a few dollars. Hell—I jest pulls off a job that nets me right around forty thousan' dollars.

You bet—twenty-five hundred ounces in good dust, the Consolidated's last month cleanup on Quartz Crick. You see I trust you boys. I ain't afraid to talk right out, bein' outlaws yerself, you wouldn't dast to squawk if you wanted to."

"We won't squawk," Black John assured him. "Twenty-five hundred ounces, eh? That's a good haul. Did you pull off the job alone? Or did you have to cut someone in on it?"

The man laughed uproariously and ordered another round of drinks. "I had help, all right, but I didn't cut no one in. Git an' earful of this," he confided in a loud blatant voice, punching Black John familiarly in the ribs with his forefinger, "it's rich. There's a guy hangin' around Cutter Malone's in Dawson that was a mighty smooth article when it came to pullin' off tricks with dice, er cards, er coins, an' stuff like that. Why say—he could take a deck of cards in them long, slim hands of hisn, an' make it do anything but talk; an' he could pick yer pocket while yer lookin' at him. What I mean, he was slick. He was makin' a damn good livin' rookin' the boys at poker an' liftin' their pokes, till some of 'em put up a squawk. The police really had nothin' on him—he was too slick fer that—but they got him to one side an' gave him twenty-four hours to git out of Dawson—er else. Malone got scairt of him, too, an' fired him out of the Palace, so this guy had got to lam out. But he'd got all caked in on a gal that worked in a restaurant, which he'd told he was an actor of some kind—a sleight of hand guy—an' that ain't no lie, 'cause he was, at that. He didn't tell this gal the police had put the finger on him. He showed her how to help him with some of his tricks an' told her they could make big money givin' shows up an' down the river. But she wouldn't pull out with him onlest they were married. This guy was already married, an' he didn't want no bigamy on him, so he slipped me a hundred to pull off a fake weddin'—me bein' able to do it on account of havin' stole a priest's outfit out of a mission up on Teslin, figgerin' it might come in handy fer a disguise sometime. Well, this hundred he slipped me left him about broke—but he didn't dare pull nothin' in Dawson. In the meantime, I'd cased the Consolidated's layout on Quartz Crick, an' I found out where they kept the dust till it's sent to Dawson onct a month. It was a cinch, providin' I could git holt of the key to the room where they left it. This key was on a ring with a lot of others, which was kep' in a desk. I gave this guy the lay, an' he agreed to go along with me. We made up a bunch of keys an' this guy went in to see about a job, an' damn if he didn't switch bunches of keys right in under this Consolidated guy's nose. I told him to go back to Dawson an' git his woman, an' throw his stuff in a canoe, an' cross the river, an' I'd meet him the next day, an' we'd split. Well, he's waitin' there yet fer all I know. I got the dust that night—an' hit out upriver. I'd heard of Halfaday Crick, an' I headed fer here, but I got lost an' went up the wrong river—Ladue Crick, they call it—an' I wasted a couple of weeks. But what the hell's a couple of weeks?"

BLACK JOHN'S eyes rested on a clean-cut shadow that appeared for a moment against a little patch of sunlight that showed on the bare ground beyond the doorway. It was the shadow of a tall thin man, and he knew that just outside the door Dykes had been listening. "A couple of weeks might make a hell of a lot of difference in a man's luck," he opined. "You mean, you couldn't find them folks acrost the river, next day?"

"Find e'm! Who the hell wanted to find 'em? I didn't go acrost the river—me. Why in hell should I cross a river to hand some guy twelve hundred and fifty ounces of dust when I could keep the whole haul fer myself? He don't dast to squawk.

He's slick as hell with his fingers, but he's a damn sap when it comes to usin' his head—er he'd never of let me pull a fast one like that."

"Guess that's right," agreed Black John in a loud hearty tone. "But I'll bet if that fella ever ketches up with you he'll hang right on yer tail till he gits his half of that dust—what was it, twenty-five hundred ounces you said? That's quite a heft of dust to leave layin' around loose. Up here on Halfaday, most of us that's got dust banks it in Cush's safe."

"Not me," replied the other with a crafty leer. "I've got that dust cached where I kin git holdt of it in a hurry, if I've got to. If the police show up, I kin pick it up in a dozen jumps an' be on my way. No one gits to handle that dust but me. I earnt it fair an' square—an' I aim to keep it!"

"Oh, shore," agreed Black John in a placating tone, "I jest suggested the safe, in case that, mebbe, you'd left the dust layin' around where it might be a temptation fer someone to rob you."

"The dust's safe," retorted the man. "If anyone thinks they kin git it, they're welcome to try. What the hell do you do around here fer excitement?"

"Well, after supper the boys'll be driftin' in fer a session of stud. The game generally gits excitin' enough fer most of us."

"Sure, stud's all right," agreed the man, "but the fact is—what with the drinks I've bought, I ain't got enough dust on me to set in no game onlest I win the first couple of pots. I could go back down the crick an' git some dust out of my cache, but it would be midnight before I'd git back."

"That's right," agreed Black John, "but you don't need to worry none about the dust. I kin generally tell an' honest man when I see one. I wouldn't mind lendin' you a few ounces till tomorrow on yer I.O.U., seein' yer apt to be located on the crick, permenant. I'm takin' yer word that you've got dust enough in yer cache to pay me."

"Yer damn right I have! An' I'll pay you tomorrow—sure. Cripes, do I look like a guy that would double-cross a pal?"

III

THE GAME LASTED through the night, and in the dim light of early dawn the man who called himself Brown paused for a moment in the doorway of the saloon and called to Black John who stood at the bar:

"I'm slippin' down to the shack now to ketch me some sleep. But I'll be back this evenin' an' fetch them ten ounces I'm owin' you—an' plenty more along with 'em. You boys sort of took me this time, but I'll git it all back an' plenty more along with it. You fellas thinks that's a tough game—but I'll show you!"

Black John nodded. "We'll be lookin' fer you. But I wouldn't figger much on winnin', if I was you. Before you git through with Halfaday, Brown, yer goin' to find out that the game yer settin' in is a damn tough game to beat."

The man uttered a laugh, half amusement, half derision. "Yeah? Well, take it from me—you birds ain't as hard as you think you are. I was jest kind of feelin' you out, last night. When I really git to goin'—you watch my smoke." With which parting retort he was gone.

Stepping to the door, Black John watched him disappear down the trail. A moment later he descended the steep path to the landing, stepped into a canoe, crossed the creek, and with his revolver under his shirt and an empty pack-sack dangling from his shoulder, struck out at a brisk pace on a trail known only to himself and One Armed John, that shortened the distance to Olson's old cabin by nearly a mile.

Recrossing the creek at a shallow rapid, a short distance below the cabin, he worked up through the thick bush, and concealed himself behind a young spruce at the edge of Olson's clearing. Fifteen minutes later the man, Brown, stepped into the clearing, paused for a few moments to scrutinize the back trail, and satisfied that he had not been followed, moved swiftly to the base of the wall of rim-rocks, pushed aside a flat stone that concealed a crevice, reached into the cavity, and drew out a heavy moosehide sack from which he hurriedly filled the empty pouch he drew from his pocket. Securing the larger sack, he returned it to the cavity, replaced the flat stone, and after another careful scrutiny of the up-creek trail, crossed the clearing and entered the cabin.

Smoke rose from the stovepipe as Black John crept through the brush to within a few feet of the man's cache. "He's cookin' him some breakfast now," he mused, his eyes on the cabin. I'd ruther wait till he got to sleep, but I've got to take a chanct. He can't see the cache without he steps outside—so here goes. If Dykes shows up, an' all that dust in Brown's cache there's no tellin' what'll happen. The damn cuss might pull of'd a larceny of some kind. It shore beats hell the bother I'm put to to keep Halfaday moral."

EDGING SWIFTLY along the base of the rock-wall, he removed the flat stone from the crevice, lifted five heavy sacks from the aperture and placed them in his pack-sack. Then he replaced the stone, picked up the pack-sack and slipped silently into the bush. A hundred yards farther along the wall he buried the sack beneath the loose rocks of a talus and returned to his spruce tree at the edge of the clearing. "Brown, he ain't so fer off in figgerin' that dust at twenty-five hundred ounces. Them sacks'll go right around thirty, thirty-five pound apiece. Generally damn cusses like him lies about their haul till you can't believe nothin' they say. But at that, he shore talked too much with his mouth back there in Cush's. From the viewp'int of human nature, it's goin' to be interestin' to see what partic'lar form of revenge Dykes' ire will lead him to."

Half an hour had passed before a slight crackling of brush drew Black John's gaze to the opposite side of the clearing where the first rays of the morning sun to creep over the rim-rocks played with startling distinctness upon a lean white face with thin lips and beady eyes that devoured the cabin in a gaze of burning hate. The face drew swiftly back into the bush as the door of the cabin opened and Brown stepped out, water pail in hand. Pausing for a moment to glance toward the cache, the man proceeded to the creek, to return a few moments later carrying his pail of water.

Suddenly Dykes stepped into the clearing, a nickel-plated pistol pointed at the unsuspecting man's broad back. Close beside him Black John heard a sound—like the gasp of a suddenly indrawn breath, and peering through the branches of his spruce, saw Mrs. Dykes, her eyes staring in horror at the two in the clearing, her hand pressed tightly against her lips as though to stifle a scream. The woman's approach had been noiseless, and although she was within a few feet of him, Black John saw that his presence was unsuspected. "There's all the ingredients of a drayma here—the way things is shapin'," he breathed softly to himself. "It's goin' to be interestin' to see how it'll turn out."

A dry twig snapped in the clearing and the man whirled, dropping his pail so that the water splashed over his boots—whirled to stare in wide-eyed horror into the thin, fury-distorted face behind the shining pistol.

"What? What the hell?" he croaked in a voice hoarse with fear.

"It's me, Meeker," answered Dykes, in a voice that crackled brittlely from between his thin lips. "I've come to collect my half of those twenty-five hundred ounces."

"Oh! Yeah! It's you, Dykes, eh? Where in hell was you at that day? I couldn't locate you nowheres acrost the river. I didn't dast to hang around. I know'd the Consolidated would miss that dust in the mornin'. So I hit fer here, figgerin' on gittin' word to you later."

THE THIN lips behind the gun twisted into a sneer. "You're a damn liar, Meeker! You never crossed the river. An' you never figgered on gitting word to me—you dirty, double-crossing skunk! I've got a mind to shoot you where you stand."

"An' leave yer half of that dust lay where it's at, eh? An' git hung besides. They hang men fer murder on Halfaday, Dykes—a damn sight quicker than the law would. You got me wrong, Dykes—honest to God you have. You'll git yer share of the dust all right. Take that gun off'n me, an' we'll talk it over."

"You're damn right I'll get my share of that dust—and I'm holding the gun on you till I do. Don't try to kid me. Meeker. I stood outside the tradin' post door yesterday evening and heard every damn word you told Cush and Black John about how you'd gypped me out of my half of that dust. You were right about one thing—I was a sap to trust a damned yegg like you out of my sight—but I'm not sap enough to make the same mistake twice. If there's any talking to do we'll do it when we get to your cache. Get going—and keep your hands in plain sight. This gun's loaded and cocked, and I'd a little rather shoot you than not."

Only for an instant did the man hesitate. "All right," he said, "but you only git half of that dust. They hang men fer robbery the same as murder on this crick—an' don't fergit it."

"My half is all I'm looking for. Meeker. I wouldn't double-cross a pal."

Turning abruptly, the man led the way to the foot of the rock-wall and, stooping, slid the flat stone from its place. The next moment he whirled and faced Dykes with blazing eyes. "It's empty!" he shouted, his face white with rage. "You damn dirty double-crosser! You follered me down the crick this mornin' an' watched when I come here to fill my poke—an' then robbed the cache when I went in the cabin!"

Dykes regarded him with a sardonic grin. "That's too thin, Meeker. Come across. I didn't come down here to look into an empty hole. Come on—you've had your little joke. Now take me to the real cache."

"By God, this is the cache!" cried Meeker. "That dust was in here less'n an hour ago. You got it—damn you—you got it all!"

Dykes shrugged. "Don't be a fool," he said. "If I'd got the dust, why would I be here, now? Come on, I'm tired of this Stalling."

Meeker's eyes widened in sudden panic. "Yer here to knock me off!" he cried in a voice thin with terror. "To croak me, so I can't squawk to Black John about the robbery!" And, with a motion incredibly swift for a man of his build, he hurled himself upon Dykes, who was caught momentarily off guard. The two forms struck the rocks together, the pistol in Dykes' hand being discharged with a loud report. For several furious moments the struggle went on, but Meeker's superior weight gave him the advantage in the rough-and-tumble, and sitting astride the other he reached for the gun. There was another loud report, and Meeker leaped to his feet as the long, thin form of Dykes writhed convulsively for a moment, and lay still. Then deliberately Meeker fired another shot into the silent figure just as the woman leaped out into the clearing with a shrill scream of terror.

Meeker whirled, gun in hand, to face her as she stood at the edge of the brush, staring wide-eyed into his face. "Who—who are you?" she cried. "Where have I seen that face before?"

Meeker grinned. "You ought to know, baby," he retorted. "You ain't been a bride long enough to fergit the priest that married you."

"But—surely—you're no priest!"

"I'll say I ain't! But you didn't know the difference—so what the hell?"

"You mean our marriage was a—a sham?" cried the woman in a tone of horror. "That we never were really married?"

"It don't make no difference if you was, er wasn't. Yer a widder now. Dykes, he learnt the hard way that it don't never pay to double-cross a pal. Thought you was pretty slick, the two of you, didn't you? Slipped down an' robbed my cache, an' then figgered on knockin' me off, an' then either hidin' my corpse where no one would find it, er claimin' you croaked me in self-defense, an' gittin' away with the hull twenty-five hundred ounces."

"What do you mean—robbed your cache? I know nothing about any twenty-five hundred ounces. Twenty-five hundred ounces of what?"

"Horse feathers!" sneered the man. "What was it you an' Dykes was waitin' fer acrost the river the time you pulled out of Dawson?"

"Why—for the man who was to finance our show trip, up and down the river. But he didn't show up, and we came on here."

"Well, he's showed up now, baby! But he ain't financin' no show trips. Come acrost with that dust an' you an' me won't git along so bad. Yer smart enough to trail along where the dust is. I ain't hold-in' this play agin' you. Dykes figgered it out—an' it damn near worked. You ain't got the brains to. But yer lucky—you win, no matter which way the cat jumped. Throw in with me, an' show me where the dust is, an' we'll leave things jest as they be an' go fetch Black John an' show him how I knocked Dykes off with his own gun whilst he was robbin' my cache." Meeker stepped toward the woman who was staring at him in horror. "Come on," he demanded gruffly. "Come acrost with that dust, er I'll—"

With a shrill scream of terror, the woman turned and leaped into the brush. The man raised the pistol and fired at the spot where she had disappeared, and with the shot, Black John heard her body crash to the ground and then the thrashing of brush as it rolled into a narrow ravine. Lowering his pistol, Meeker ran cursing toward the spot, reaching the edge of the clearing just as Black John, a cocked .45 in his hand, stepped from behind his spruce.

"Drop that gun," the big man roared. "Quick!" For a single instant the man stood staring into the muzzle of the big six-gun, then the nickel-plated pistol clattered upon the rocks at his feet and he was staring into the cold eyes that glittered like blue ice above the black beard.

"Dykes was robbin' my cache!" Meeker yammered, the words crowding each other upon his lips. "I shot him with his own gun. It was self-defence!"

"Yeah? An' shootin' the woman in the back—was that self-defence, too?"

"Sure it was! They'd follered me down here—the two of 'em—an' robbed my cache. They figgered on knockin' me off, to boot, but I shot Dykes with his own gun—an' then I had to git her er she'd of gone up to Cush's an' swore a murder onto me! Sure, it was self-defence—anyone kin see that. With her loose on the crick, I wouldn't of had a show! You boys would of hung me sure!"

"I'm inclined to agree with you on that last p'int," Black John retorted, eyeing the man with the utmost contempt. "An' it's my duty to warn you that yer goin' to have to talk God-awful fast to convince a miners' meetin' that shootin' a woman in the back is self defense in any man's language."

"But they'd of hung me!" whimpered the man.

"They would," opined Black John, "an' they will. Git over to the cabin, now, while I find a piece of rope to tie you up with while I git the woman's body."

BINDING THE man securely, hand and foot, Black John stepped into the bush, descending the steep bank of the narrow ravine, lifted the inert form in his arms and carried it to the clearing. As he lowered her gently to the ground, she opened her eyes and stared intently up into his bearded face. Her lips moved.

"You?" she whispered, raising a faltering hand and passing it across her eyes. "I—I thought— Oh— It's like a horrible dream—that man—and—"

"Take it easy, mam," interrupted Black John. "It wasn't no dream. Where did he git you?"

"Get me? He didn't get me. He started toward me, but I—I ran—and then I tripped and fell—and there was a loud crash—like a shot—and that's all. I—I must have fainted—but I never fainted before."

Black John was searching her with his eyes. "I don't see no blood, nowhere," he admitted. "Yer shore he didn't git you when he fired?"

The woman rose slowly to a sitting posture, and then, with the help of Black John, to her feet. She moved her arms, and took a step or two. "I seem to be all right, except for a few slight bruises," she said. "If he shot at me, he must have missed."

"Yer lucky," opined Black John, with a smile of relief. "When I heard you go down, an' roll through the brush into that holler, I thought he'd got you shore."

"By God, she ain't the only lucky one! You can't hang me now," cried Meeker, who, lying trussed like a turkey, had been an interested listener.

"No?" Black John shot the man a glance of contempt. "You wait an' see."

"I never touched her. I only shot to scare her."

"Yeah?"

"Sure I did—an' I shot Dykes in self-defence!"

"Ye're in error," replied Black John. "I mean that rookus. It ain't self defence, on Halfaday, when a man gits a man down, an' gits straddle of him, an' reaches fer a gun an' shoots him through the head, an' then stands up an' fires another shot into him fer luck. Sech actions savors of murder."

"But," shrilled the man, "I tell you he robbed my cache!"

"It would take more than you're tellin' to make me believe it. But even admittin' he did, fer the sake of argument, that didn't give you no license to murder him. You had him down. You're stronger'n him. You should of fetched him up to Cush's, so we could try him by miners' meetin'. If you could of proved yer case, we'd of hung him—same as we'll be hangin' you tonight. We don't play no favorites, on Halfaday."

"But I tell you it ain't a murder!"

"Mebbe the boys'll look at it that way," replied Black John with a shrug. "But I wouldn't bank much on it, if I was you. Remember—Cush told you this cabin was onlucky. Even if they concede the p'int, it wouldn't have no bearin' on the hangin'. Any man with ethics sech as yourn, would be hangable on Halfaday—if he never fired a shot."

IV

MEEKER'S FOOT-BONDS WERE removed and he was marched up the trail ahead of Black John. As they passed One Eyed John's cabin, the big man turned to the woman who accompanied him.

"You better wait here fer a bit. I'll send some of the boys down to fetch Dykes up so we kin give him a decent burial. I've got some arrangements to make with Cush, an' then I'll be back to kind of talk things over. You'll likely be wantin' to git back to Dawson."

The woman nodded, her eyes filled with tears. She attempted to speak, but her voice broke, and she turned abruptly away, and a moment later the door of the cabin closed behind her.

In the saloon Black John found One Armed John. "Slip down to Red John's," he ordered, "an' tell him an' Pot Gutted John to go down to Olson's old shack an' fetch Dykes' corpse up here for burial purposes. They'll find a canoe there. It'll save back-packin' him. Then you hustle up an' down the crick an' tell everyone you see to show up here at eight o'clock tonight fer a miners' meetin' to try this here John Brown, alias Meeker, fer murder, an' skull-duggery, an' hang him. Git agoin' now, but first help me an' Cush drop this here defendant in the hole, after he pays me back them ten ounces he owes me."

With the prisoner safely lodged in the log-lined cell beneath the floor of the storeroom, and a barrel of pork rolled onto the trap door, Black John turned to Cush.

"Jest count me out twenty thousan' in bills—make 'em twenties," he said.

Cush opened the safe, counted the money out onto the bar, and made an entry in his book, as Black John made the bills into a thick packet and thrust it under his arm. Then he regarded the other across the bar. "What you goin' to do with all that money, John?" he asked.

"Oh—jest a personal matter," the big man replied evasively.

Cush shoved his square, steel-rimmed spectacles from nose to forehead. "From what you told One Armed John," he said, "about us havin' to bury Dykes an' hang Brown, I s'pose he must of murdered him."

"Sech supposition is well founded," grinned Black John, "an' does credit to yer powers of preception. It turns out that Brown come amongst us under an alias, his real name bein' Meeker. He accused Dykes of robbin' his cache, an' murdered him by way of retaliation. Then he took a shot at Dykes' woman, fer good measure—but he missed, that time."

"Brown claimed he had twenty-five hundred ounces in his cache," said Cush. "Did Dykes really rob it?"

"I give you Brown's, er rather, Meeker's version of it," replied Black John. "The woman claims she don't know nothin' about the dust nor the cache. Dykes is dead, so if Meeker sticks to his story, I s'pose we've got to accept it, much as I'd hate to believe a man of his calibre."

"That's a hell of a lot of dust to have layin' around in a lost cache," observed Cush regretfully. "Mebbe me an' you could go down there an' find it, sometime."

"We could try," Black John replied, "if we deem it worth while."

"What about the woman—now Dykes is dead? What's she goin' to do? I don't believe they've took out no hell of a lot of dust."

"That was my thought," agreed Black John. "I'm goin' down an' have a talk with her now. She'll probably be wantin' to git off'n Halfaday."

"You mean," exclaimed Cush, eyeing the packet under the big man's arm, "that yer goin' to give her them bills? Cripes sakes, John—it's all right to help someone out, if they're down on their luck—but twenty thousan' dollars, that's goin' a little too fer!"

"I feel kind of sorry fer her, Cush. Anyone could tell she's had a hard break—jest lookin' into them eyes of hers."

"Yeah—but you think in too big figgers, John. Hell—give her a thousan' if you want to—that'll git her back where she come from, an' some left over."

"She's a nice woman," argued Black John. "I'd like fer her to have enough to start her up in some little business—a store, mebbe, er a restaurant. She's took a lot of hard knocks, Cush—an' she's game."

"Huh, you claimin' to hate women!" snorted Cush in disgust. "An' all one of 'em's got to do is to pull a hard luck story an' you dig down an' shove 'em a barrel of money."

"Oh, well—jest charge it off to tenderheartedness on my part—er mebbe it's worth twenty thousan' to git a woman off'n the crick."

A FEW minutes later, with the pack-age concealed beneath a slicker he had carelessly thrown over his arm, he knocked on the door of One Eyed John's cabin and was admitted by the woman, who had evidently been crying. She indicated a chair, and seating himself with the slicker on his lap, Black John began, awkwardly:

"Now, mam, I wouldn't worry none, if I was you. I know you got quite a jolt, this mornin'—what with seein' Dykes murdered, an' findin' out about you an' him not bein' married, an'—"

"You know that?" asked the woman.

"Oh, shore—I couldn't help but hear you an' Meeker talkin'. I'd went down to Meeker's to collect a little debt, an' was jest on the edge of the clearin' when Dykes steps in an pulls the gun on him. So I hung back in the brush an' took in the whole proceedin'. That's how I come to be there when you come to. I seen Meeker take a shot at you, an' after I tied him up, I went an' fetched you out in the clearin'."

"Oh," cried the woman, "then if it hadn't been for you, he'd have found me and—and—" Her voice broke, and she shuddered.

"That's all right. I didn't do nothin' anyone else wouldn't, under the circumstances. We'll tend to Meeker's case, tonight. An' tomorrow we'll bury him an' Dykes in the graveyard. But what I come down fer, in particular," he continued, "is to find out how yer fixed."

"What do you mean?"

"Well, I figger you won't want to be stayin' along on Halfaday, the way things has broke fer you. An' I sort of thought that if you didn't, mebbe, have enough dust fer to git back where yer goin', the boys would all chip in an' see you through. I could mention it to 'em at the miners' meetin', tonight. They'd all be glad to help."

"Oh—I—I'd hate to accept charity. We've got some dust—I don't know exactly how much. Maybe it's enough to get me back to Dawson."

Black John nodded. "S'pose we weigh it up, an' see," he suggested.

"I'll get it," the woman replied, and stepping outside, reappeared after some five minutes carrying a limp moosehide sack.

"It isn't very much," she explained. "We've paid for our supplies as we went along. This is what's left of the dust we took in from the performance we gave, and we've added what we panned out every day."

Black John nodded, as he eyed the sack on the table. "It ain't very much, at that," he admitted. "Ten, twelve ounces, mebbe. But—why did you cache it outside?"

"Why—I don't know. We found a hollow place in the rocks, and put the dust in there and covered it up with other rocks. Isn't that the way people generally cache their dust?"

"Well, a few careless ones might. Meeker did—an' you seen what happened. He claimed Dykes robbed him."

"Oh but he didn't!" exclaimed the woman hurriedly. "He went to the saloon last evening and came home later, white with rage. He told me he had just seen a man who owed him a lot of money—and that in the morning, he was going to collect it. As soon as we'd finished breakfast he loaded his pistol, put it in his pocket, and told me to keep my mouth shut, and when he came back he'd have plenty of dust to last us the rest of our lives. I was afraid to ask any questions. He was in a cold fury, his eyes glittering like a crazy man's. He started off down the trail, and I followed him. I don't know what I expected to do, but I just couldn't stay here in the cabin. I felt that something terrible was about to happen. I'd never seen him quite like that before. He went on and on down the trail, and I followed just out of sight. I think if he had known I was following, he would have killed me. Then he came to the clearing—and stood there for a few moments, looking at the cabin, Then the man stepped out to get the water, and—and I guess you know the rest."

"Yeah, I know the rest."

"So, you see—he couldn't have robbed that cache."

"That's right, Mam—he couldn't. I'm glad to git the straight of it. But I wouldn't of helt it agin Dykes' mem'ry on the onsupported word of a man like Meeker. But gittin' back to this here cache of yourn—didn't Dykes tell you about the inside cache?"

"Inside cache? What do you mean?"

"Why, when I fetched him down to this cabin, the first day he hit Halfaday, I show'd him about this cache. You see, I put up this buildin', myself—an' I fixed a section of log so it'll come out when you twist the right peg. I showed Dykes how to work it, in case he'd be wantin' to cache somethin.' But I s'pose he didn't want no one should know where his cache was—even me. It's a sight handier 'n an outside one, though—I'll show you." Rising, Black John tossed his slicker onto the table, and stepped to the opposite wall where, grasping one of the wooden pegs used as clothes hangars, he moved it sidewise a bit, and lifted a two-foot section of log away, exposing a deep cavity beneath. "There you are," he said, thrusting his arm into the aperture. "Nice an' handy—an' right where you kin keep an eye on it, night an' day. But what's this?" he asked. "Dykes shore must of stuck somethin' in here, 'cause it was plumb empty when I show'd it to him—I could take my oath on that," He withdrew a paper-wrapped package and laid it on the table. "Better open it," he said. "Funny he didn't say nothin' to you about the cache."

THE WOMAN removed the paper wrap-ping and gasped audibly as she stood staring at the pile of currency. "Money!" she cried incredulously. "Twenty dollar bills—thousands of them!"

"There's a sight of 'em, all right," agreed Black John. "We'll count 'em an' see." Deftly he counted the bills. "Jest an even thousand of 'em," he announced as he returned the last bill to the table. "I guess we won't have to ask the boys to take up no collection, after all. It's funny you didn't know about all them bills."

"I certainly didn't know about them!" exclaimed the woman. "He told me he was broke. He didn't want me to know that he had them. He's lied, and lied, and lied—from the first—and I was fool enough to believe him!" she cried. "I can believe now that he did intend to rob Meeker—and he told me he was going to collect a debt!"

"Well," placated Black John, "you can't hardly blame him none fer that. It wouldn't be nothin' a man would care to brag about to his wife. Any man that would rob, would ondoubtless lie now an' then—he'd pretty near have to."

"But—where did this money come from? Where did he get it? How do I know he didn't steal it from someone?"

Black John shook his head. "Nope," he decided, "that there has got all the ear-marks of honest money. If it had be'n stole, like from a bank, or some-wheres, them bills would be numbered consecutive—an' they'd have bank bands around 'em. I know, because located up here clost to the line like we are, me an' Cush meets up with quite a few outlaws of one stripe an' another, an' we've got kind of expert in spottin' stolen money. This here looks to me like money that had be'n saved up fer a long time. Dykes, he prob'ly made it in the show business, an' kep' saltin' away them twenties fer an ace in the hole."

"It's more money than I had ever hoped to see," breathed the woman, running her fingers over the bills as if to assure herself they were real.

"Yeah, it's a right snug sum. It would set you up in some nice little business, somewheres."

"I—I'll take it and go back home—back to Iowa and buy back my Dad's farm!" cried the woman. "They took it away on a mortgage—and I had to go to work. I came to Dawson, because in Seattle I heard of the high wages."

"That's a fine idee," agreed Black John. "You do jest that. I'll see that you git put safe aboard an upriver steamer."

"Oh—how can I ever thank you?" cried the woman. "And just to think— Leonidas Dykes told me you were an outlaw!"

Black John grinned. "Oh, well—pore fella. He's dead, now. We hadn't ought to hold it agin his mem'ry. Prob'ly jest another one of his lies. Even at that—he might of believed it."

"You're an honest man," replied the woman, with conviction. "You could have had all this money—and I'd never known the difference. But I can't help thinking about that poor Meeker. Will they really hang him, tonight? Isn't there something else you could do?"

"Well—we might burn him to a stake, like the Injuns used to. Er we might feed him to some varmint, like they done the early Christians. But on Halfaday we're more civilized. We've sort of standardized, you might say, on hangin'."

"I mean—must you kill him? Even if he is a murderer—it seems somehow—terrible."

Black John read compassion in her eyes. "Well now. Mam—don't you go worryin' about Meeker. He'll git a fair trial—an' mebbe the boys'll turn him loose. You can't never tell. After hearin' the evidence, if they think he done right, they'll acquit him. Anyhow, he'll git all the breaks he's got comin'. I'll be goin'. Some of us'll see you git started fer the big river tomorrow."

V

THE FOLLOWING MORNING old Cush faced Black John across the bar. "Well," he opined, pouring a drink, "Brown, er Meeker, er whatever his name was, hung pretty good, at that. We've had consid'ble trouble with some of them thick-necked ones. But he hung nice."

"We're gittin' more used to it, I guess," Black John replied. "Pot Gutted is tyin' a prettier knot than he used to. An' that reminds me—I want to arrange with him an' Red John to take that woman of Dykes' down to the big river an' see that she gits on an upriver boat."

"Huh-an' twenty thousan' dollars of your money along with her!" snorted Cush. "Cripes—I wisht I was a woman. All I'd have to do is to git around somewheres where you was an' look sorriful—an' you'd shove me a bale of bills."

"Try it an see," grinned Black John. "I'll bet I'd git good interest on my money. But kin I believe my eyes—look who's here!"

Cush raised his eyes to the doorway where Corporal Downey of the Northwest Mounted Police was just entering the room. "Jine up, Downey," he greeted, "The house is buyin' one."

"Busy as ever, I see," grinned the young officer with a wink at Black John. "How's yer health?"

"Well," the big man replied, "I ain't permittin' myself to do no hard work these days. I've had a little trouble with my spleen—er mebbe it's my epiglottis. How you be'n? An' what you doin' on Halfaday? You ain't favored us with no call in quite a while."

"I'm fine. I swung up this way on the chance of pickin' up a couple of birds that robbed the Consolidated's Quartz Crick layout of twenty-five hundred ounces of dust."

"Twenty-five hundred ounces, eh? Not sech a bad haul, at that. Was they professionals—er jest a couple of punks?"

"They were good enough to get away with it, anyway. I've got a line on 'em, though. One of 'em's a bird by the name of Meeker. He hung around pretendin' to hunt fer a job till the day before the robbery when he shows up with another cuss that had been hangin' around Cutter Malone's, pickin' pockets an' fleecein' suckers at cards. We'd got on to him in Dawson, an' warned him out of camp jest the day before. I suppose he throw'd in with Meeker fer a last big play. He's a slick article all right, but I wouldn't have played him to pull off a job of that size, at that."

"He wouldn't be a party named Dykes, would he? A kind of a long, skinny fella that does tricks with cards, an' hats, an' things?"

"That's the man!" exclaimed Downey, "Is he here on Halfaday?"

"Yeah—he's here."

"An' this other one—Meeker? He's a heavy-set man, around five-foot, ten. Straw-colored hair, an' blue eyes. They separated, I guess, because a man of Meeker's description was seen around Indian River the day after the robbery. He headed upriver in a canoe, alone. I hadn't got track of Dykes till jest now."

"Yeah, they separated, all right," agreed Black John. "There wasn't no one with Dykes but a woman."

"A woman?"

"Yeah—his wife."

"Where is he now?"

"Well—on the basis of past performances, accordin' to the theologians, he's most likely in hell by this time. Bein' open minded, I wouldn't dispute the p'int with 'em. I might add, though, that if he ain't there, then hell's plumb futile."

"An' you don't know nothin' about Meeker, eh?"

"Not much—beyond the fact that he's a damn yegg that robbed a mission on Teslin, stole a priest's outfit, an' posin' as this priest, pulled off a fake weddin' in Dawson, marryin' this Dykes to a young woman who thought Dykes was an actor an' that the deal was on the level. Then him an' Dykes pulls this Consolidated job, an' he lams out, leavin' Dykes holdin' the bag."

Downey looked astounded. "You know a lot more than I do about the case," he grinned. "Where did you pick it up?"

"Oh, I jest come by the information casual—partly from things Dykes let drop, partly from Meeker, an' partly from the woman. They all had more er less to say."

"Where's Meeker, now?"

"He's in the back room—along with Dykes. That is, their corpses is. We aim to bury 'em this afternoon—providin' enough of the boys shows up to make grave-diggin' a mere pastime, rather than a chore."

"You mean—they're both dead?"

"That was Cush's diagnosis of their status—an' he's a coroner."

"How did they die?"

"Dykes hard; an' Meeker easy."

"I mean—what killed 'em?"

"A bullet—an' a rope."

"A murder an' a hangin', eh? You might as well give me the story."

"It's a sordid tale," began Black John. "But it ended happy—except that the weather's come off hot, an' we've still got them tombs to excavate. Dykes got here first—him an' the woman. Then Meeker shows up, an' Dykes gits his gun an' slips down to Olson's old shack where Meeker's livin', an' pullin' the gun on him, demands his share of the dust they got off'n the Consolidated. Meeker seized up the gun, an' agrees to divide the dust. He leads Dykes to a cache which proves to be empty—whereupon he accuses Dykes of robbin' this cache. Dykes repartees that Meeker is a damn liar, an' threatens to fill him full of lead if he don't come clean. Meeker takes umbrage either to the epithet er the threat, I couldn't rightly say which, an' makes a sudden an' successful attack on Dykes, finally gittin' holt of the gun an' placin' it agin Dykes'es head, he blasts what few brains Dykes had all over the rocks. Now, scannin' Dykes' past, sech act couldn't be considered no more than a tort, at most, an' nothin' to hang a man fer. But Meeker ain't satisfied. He compounds the tort into a felony by accusin' the woman of aidin' an' abettin'

Dykes in this cache-robbery, an' then takin' a shot at her when she denies it. He'd of got her, too, if she hadn't ketched her foot in a root an' fell down jest as he shot. Jedgin' matters had gone about fer enough, I intervenes at this p'int, with the result that Meeker got hung last night by a miners' meetin'."

"An' the twenty-five hundred ounces of dust? What became of them?"

Black John shrugged. "Well—like I told you, Downey, Meeker claimed Dykes had removed it from his cache. An' Dykes accused Meeker of double-crossin' him by showin' him an empty hole. From the nature of the case, they can't both be right. One of them parties, mebbe both, is bound to be lyin'. I'd say that somewheres between them two statements, lays the truth."

"Yeah," grunted Downey, "an' the dust."

"That's right. An' except fer the fact that the Consolidated is a damn outfit that's guttin' this country as fast as it kin, an' has already took out so much dust they don't know what to do with it, it would be sad to contemplate."

"Who do you think got it?"

"Me—I wouldn't take sides, one way er another. I'm open-minded on the subject. I wouldn't believe neither one of them two birds under oath. I'd bet my last blue chip, though, that if Dykes did git that dust, his woman don't know nothin' about it. She's square as hell, Downey—an' she's game."

"How does it come that you was on hand jest at the right time to save this woman?"

"Oh, that's jest one of them lucky coincidences that happens every now an' then. Fact is. I'd strolled down the crick to speak to Meeker about a little debt he owed me—triflin' matter of some ten ounces he borrowed in a stud game, but worth lookin' after, Downey—worth lookin' after."

"I don't s'pose it would be any use huntin' fer that dust?"

Off hand, I'd say it wouldn't. Them caches is hard to find—what with all the places there is to look. A man might spend a month at it, an' then not have no luck. Fer's I'm concerned, the Consolidated's the one to worry about that dust. Anyhow, you ought to be satisfied. You kin write the case off the books. An' by the way—when you go back, take that woman of Dykes' along with you. She's got twenty-thousan' in bills on her, that Dykes left. She wants to ketch an upriver boat."

BLACK JOHN FILES A STOVE LEG

OLD CUSH FINISHED his bar chores just as Black John Smith crossed the floor and up-ending an open pack sack, dumped a miscellaneous collection of objects upon the bar. There was a splash, and stooping swiftly, Cush rescued a slipper the color of gold as he scowled at Black John. It was a small slipper—a woman's slipper, dripping wet, and he held it gingerly by the heel.

"Where an' the hell did you git that junk?" he demanded. "An' besides, I don't want no women's shoes in my rinse tub."

"This," explained Black John, "constitutes the bag of tricks of the late Professor Dykes, slain a couple of weeks ago, as you may rec'lect, in a fit of anger by the man, Meeker, or as he would have it, Brown."

Cush nodded, shook the water from the slipper and returned it to the bar. "Yeah, I rec'lect," he replied with elaborate sarcasm, "an' I'm shore glad you fetched this stuff in to show me, John. I didn't know a man could buy that much fer twenty thousan' dollars."

"What do you mean—twenty thousan' dollars?"

"Well, I rec'lect that was the amount you give the widow Dykes 'cause you felt sorry fer her on account of him gittin' knocked off."

"Yeah," grinned the big man, "I figger I jest about doubled my money."

"Doubled yer money! Hell—I wouldn't give you five dollars fer all that junk."

Black John picked up a gown of flimsy golden material and held it up for inspection. "Them slippers an' this dress was the ones she wore on the stage when she helped Dykes with this act," he explained. "Pretty, ain't they?"

"Oh, shore," Cush agreed. "You'll look swell in that dress, John—an' them slippers, too. Take it this winter on a moose hunt, them high heels will keep you from slippin' down the hills. Er mebbe you figger on savin' 'em to wear to dances in Dawson."

Ignoring the jibe, Black John dropped the gown into the pack sack and picking up a deck of cards shuffled them and extended them toward Cush.

"Draw any card you want—look at it, an' shove it back in the deck." Cush complied, and placing the deck on the bar, Black John picked up a light bamboo wand or baton, made a few mysterious passes over the pack, touched it lightly with the wand, and eyed Cush. "I'll now turn yer card off'n the top of the deck—fer the drinks."

"Turn it," replied Cush, reaching for bottle and glasses.

"I'll not only turn it," grinned Black John, "but I'll name it in advance. The card you selected was the jack of diamonds—and there he is." He flipped over the top card, and Cush stared in astonishment at the jack of diamonds.

"Well I'll be damned," he exclaimed. "That's right—the drinks is on me. But jest the same, John—it'll take you a hell of a while to git twenty thousan' dollars back bettin' the drinks."

Black John returned the deck to its case, and produced another. "I'll bet you the drinks I kin—"

"No more bettin' the drinks with me on them card tricks," retorted Cush. "You got me onct, an' that's enough. All you got to do now to double yer money, figgerin' drinks at fifty cents, is hunt up about seventy-nine thousan' other folks to bet with."

"There's a lot of this stuff that I don't know how to work," said Black John, "these here glasses, an' boxes, an' balls, an' I'll bet I couldn't never git four dozen eggs in that high hat, like Dykes done. An' here's a big magnet, an' a bottle of gold paint. She prob'ly had the paint to touch up her shoes with when they'd git dull."

"Uh-huh," grunted Cush, eyeing the objects sourly. "It's a great bunch of stuff, John. It would be even better if you know'd how to work it. When you figger it out I s'pose you'll be goin' around the country givin' shows. At that though, I wish you'd show me how in hell you got that card I draw'd on top of the deck. I shoved it right in the middle, an' I kep' my eyes on 'em every minute."

"Well," grinned Black John, "seein' yer a friend of mine, I'll show you this one trick, providin' you'll buy another drink."

"Fill up," replied Cush, "an' let's see it."

ONCE AGAIN Black John extended the deck and Cush selected a card, glanced at it, and then at Black John who grinned. "I see you got the same card, didn't you? Take another."

Cush drew another, and Black John's grin widened. "Simple, ain't it, Cush—when you know how to work it? Every damn card in the deck is the jack of diamonds. You've shore got to hand it to us prestidigitators."

"Huh, I know'd it was some kind of a damn fake," grunted Cush. "But I'm shore glad I ain't got no twenty thousan' dollars tied up in it. It looks like Dykes's woman made a good trade."

"She left the stuff down in One Eyed John's shack when she went back with Corporal Downey," said Black John. "I was sort of pokin' around down there, so I fetched it along. I'm takin' it over to my shack. I might find use fer it, sometime.

"A man can't never tell what'll come in handy. An' that reminds me—I've got another pack out by the door." Stepping outside, he returned with a heavy pack sack which he swung to the bar. "Jest, slip this here stuff in the safe, Cush," he said. "It's twenty-five hundred ounces of dust—runs right around forty thousan' dollars. You'll rec'lect my investment was twenty thousan'."

Old Cush's eyes seemed about to pop from his head as he stared at the sack. "Them twenty-five hundred ounces that Dykes an' Meeker stole off'n the Consolidated!" he exclaimed.

"That's merely a conjecture on your part," retorted Black John. "Both Meeker an' Dykes are dead. I found this dust in a cache down near Olson's old shack."

"Well, I'll be damned," grunted Cush. "An' here I figgered you was crazy!" He paused abruptly and glanced toward the door, at the same time swinging the heavy pack sack to a place of concealment behind the bar. "But here comes someone. It would serve you right if it would be Corporal Downey after them twenty-five hundred ounces."

Black John turned to survey a young man hardly out of his teens who had paused uncertainly in the doorway. "Step up," he invited. "The house is buyin' a drink."

"Is this Cushing's Fort on Halfaday Crick?" the newcomer asked, as he advanced to the bar where Cush had set out another glass.

"This is the place," Black John replied. "An' back of the bar, there, stands Cush, hisself—an' I'm Black John Smith."

"I heard about this place in Dawson, and about you, too," said the youngster, as the drinks were poured, and then paused as though at a loss to proceed.

"Yeah," encouraged Black John, "an' this here news you got about us—was it good, bad, or indifferent?"

The other smiled. "It was good news to me, all right. I heard that you men up here were all outlaws, and that the police didn't dare to bother you."

"Sech report bein' erroneous, but about as accurate as news is apt to be. The facts is, some of the boys along the crick is outlawed fer one reason er another—but to say that the police don't dare to bother us is shore takin' truth by the forelock an' yankin' hell out of her. The only reason they don't bother us is because we don't give 'em no cause to. Not because they don't dare. The Mounted dares to go anywhere. But why would anyone of your age be hankerin' to consort with outlaws?"

"Because, I'm an outlaw, myself," the youngster replied, and Black John noted that the words were not uttered boastfully, nor was there any hint of swagger about the lad. Rather, the admission had been made in a tone that indicated bitter acceptance of fact.

THE BIG man shrugged. "What any man done before he come to Halfaday ain't none of our business," he said. "But after he gits here he's got to refrain from murder, larceny, claim-jumpin', er any form of skullduggery whatever—er git hung. So if yer contemplatin' launchin' out on a long life of crime, yer shore out of luck. There ain't no crime on Halfaday." He and Cush swallowed their liquor, and with his own glass untouched upon the bar, the youngster hastened to reply.

"I never committed any crime—and I never intend to. But I'm an outlaw, just the same. There's a United States marshal hunting me, right now."

"Mistake, eh?" suggested Cush.

The other shook his head slowly. "No, not a mistake. A man was killed one night in a saloon in Rampart—and I'm the goat." He paused and glanced from Cush to Black John. "I don't know whether you men will believe me or not, but I'm telling you the God's truth. I didn't kill that man in Rampart, and what's more—that marshal knows I didn't kill him. Either he, himself, or some of his friends killed him—and to protect whoever did it, this marshal fastened the murder on me. You probably won't believe that a marshal would do a thing like that—but it's true, every word of it."

Black John grinned. "Son, when it comes to U.S. marshals, I'm plumb credulous. What I'd believe about one of 'em is surprisin'. S'pose you go ahead an' git it off yer chest, if yer so minded. Me an' Cush both has had more or less experience in sortin' out truth from lies. We'll prob'ly know, before you've finished, whether yer handin' it to us straight, er not."

"Joe Leatherby's my name," began the lad without hesitation. "I live in Ottawa, Illinois, and when my chum and I heard of all the gold they were digging up north we decided to get some of it, too. We were broke but we beat our way to Seattle and when we got there we heard that the Mounted Police wouldn't let anyone into the country who didn't have a year's supply of provisions with him. My chum gave up and I guess he went back home. I knew there would be some way to get into the country, so I stuck around, and finally got a job as coal passer on a boat bound for St. Michaels. Then I got another job firing on a river steamer. I handled more cordwood than I thought there was in the world going upriver. We tied up nights, and when we'd be at some town, like Anvik, and Tanana, and places like that, the boys would go ashore and get drunk. I don't like whiskey and only went along because there was nothing else to do, but I didn't get drunk till that night we tied up at Rampart. There was a big dance going on with Indians and white people all mixed in together, and we danced, and after every dance we'd buy our partner a drink. I don't remember much about the last part of the night.

"I got sick and went out and wandered around and into another saloon where some men were playing poker. It was quieter in there and I remember of sitting down in a chair. I guess I went to sleep because the next thing I knew it was daylight, and I was lying on the floor with a pair of handcuffs on. I was awfully sick, and my head ached terribly. I sat up, and a man stepped over from the bar and jerked me to my feet. He said he was a United States marshal, and that I'd killed a man. I recognized the marshal as one of the men who had been playing poker, and he jerked me to the back of the room and drew back an old blanket that had been thrown over a dead man, and pointed down at him. He was a horrible sight—his face covered with blood that had flowed from a bullet hole in his forehead. He was another one of the poker players, and so were the men who stood drinking at the bar. I told the marshal he was crazy, that I never saw the dead man until I saw him at the poker table that night, and I couldn't have shot him because I never owned a pistol—never even fired one more than half a dozen times in my life. He hit me in the mouth with his fist, and the others laughed. I told him I was a fireman on the steamboat and had just come up to the dance with some of the crew, and that I had to get back to the boat. They all laughed again, and the marshal said that the boat had pulled out hours ago. I denied killing the man, and they all told me I was too drunk to remember what I did—they said I came in sometime after midnight and stood behind the man's chair and began tipping off his hands, and when he called me for it, I pulled a gun and shot him. The marshal showed me a pistol which he claimed he took away from me. They said they all jumped up when I shot the man and overpowered me, and the marshal put the handcuffs on me and I was so drunk I fell asleep and they laid me on the floor. They were pretty drunk, the marshal and all, and he insisted on taking me down to Tanana in a canoe. I protested and he hit me again, and told one of the men to go get a canoe ready, and we'd pull out. He slipped a bottle into his pocket and after a while the man came back and said the canoe was ready, so he told the men he'd let them know when they'd be needed as witnesses at the trial, and then yanked me down to the river and told me to get into the canoe and lie flat, and that if I tried any monkey business he'd put out my light.

"**I LAY** there on my back so sick that I didn't care much what happened to me. He paddled slowly, letting the current do most of the work, and every little while he'd take a pull at the bottle. Toward noon he began to get sleepy. His chin would drop lower and lower and his paddle would trail along in the water until the canoe would swing around broadside to the current, and I'd get to wondering whether I could swim with the handcuffs on if she tipped over. Then his head would come up with a jerk, and he'd take another drink and then after a few minutes paddling the same thing would happen again. After this had happened a dozen times or so, he said he'd been up all night, and that we'd land and take a little rest. By that time he was so drunk he could hardly talk, and he nearly tipped the canoe over landing it. He told me he was going to chain me to a tree, and after fumbling around in his pockets he found the key and unlocked one of the handcuffs. He'd forgotten to pick up his pistol from the bottom of the canoe where he'd laid it within easy reach in case I started to make trouble, so when he finally got the handcuff unlocked, I jerked away, stepped back and swung the loose cuff as hard as I could. It caught him on the side of the head and he went down and out. I found the key and unlocked the other cuff and threw them in the river. I left him lying there, and jumped into the canoe and pad-died across the river after tossing the pistol overboard.

"I found I couldn't make any headway upstream, so I landed on the other side, but the banks were so rough I soon saw that without any grub I'd never get anywhere. I felt a little better and after I'd drunk a lot of water my headache eased off and I sat down on a rock to try and figure what I'd do. I could see smoke down around a bend so I got in the canoe and paddled down, keeping close to shore. As I swung around the bend I saw a steamboat tied up to the bank at a wood yard. She was headed upriver so I landed and found her short handed. The captain hired me on the spot, and in a couple of hours we finished wooding up, and she pulled out. I sure was scairt until we'd passed the place I'd left that marshal. I was afraid he had waked up and would signal us to pick him up. But he didn't, and after a while I breathed easier. When we pulled into Rampart, I took good care not to show my face for fear someone would recognize me. But we pulled out and I came on through to Dawson.

"I quit the boat there and got a job in the sawmill. I don't know anything about mining, and I figured I'd better get a little stake and keep my eyes and ears open till I got onto the ropes. I hung around the saloons evenings and listened to the talk and asked questions about mining when I'd spot a man I thought would give it to me straight.

"Then, one evening I saw the marshal who had arrested me in Rampart. I slipped back to the shack where I was living with a couple of other fellows, and in the morning I drew my pay at the saw mill and bought a canoe from an Indian, and some grub, and hit out upriver. I had heard about Halfaday Creek, and that everybody up here were outlaws. I didn't know where it was, except that it was up the White River, and I didn't dare ask about it in Dawson, so I paddled on up to Indian River, and was told how to get here. I'm afraid, though, that that marshal will hear about Halfaday, too, and come up here, when he don't find me in Dawson."

BLACK JOHN nodded. "Yeah," he agreed, "he might."

"It would be tough luck to be hung for a murder I never committed," the lad said.

"Yeah," Black John agreed again, "it's kind of tough luck on a man to git hung, even fer a murder he did commit. I believe you've told us the truth, son. A man of your years couldn't hardly tell a lie that long that would hold water from start to finish. Fer as I kin see yer only crime was gittin' drunk, an' that can't be considered hangable. You ain't drank yer drink yet—an' it's gittin' about time fer another."

Leatherby eyed the liquor in his glass sourly. "That time at Rampart was the only time I was ever drunk, and it made me so sick I nearly died. Even the thought of whiskey makes me kind of sick to my stomach yet. But—here goes."

"Hold on, son," said Black John. "There ain't nothin' compulsory about takin' a drink on Halfaday. Most of us uses whiskey up here because we're habited to. A man kin git jest as drunk, or stay jest as sober as he likes, providin' he refrains from crime in either case. So if you don't want that drink, jest shove it over here an' I'll keep it from sp'ilin'. A man ain't thought none the less of amongst us because he don't drink."

"I don't think I could ever learn to like it," smiled the lad, pushing the glass toward Black John. "Somehow, it don't seem to agree with me. But it ain't going to make much difference whether I'm guilty of that murder or not, if that marshal comes up here and takes me back to Alaska. With that bartender and all those others to swear I killed that man, I wouldn't have a show."

"Most likely not," Black John admitted. "You better jest stick around an' see what happens. He might never come up here—but even if he does it don't look to me like a man of his stripe would have much luck on Halfaday."

"Could I get a job of some kind? I can't jest lay around idle."

"I've got several good claims along the crick. I kin use a man at an ounce a day, er I'll go fifty-fifty with you on what you take out—either way suits me. You could work fer me till you git onto the hang of it, an' plenty of room fer more locations. In the meantime you might throw yer stuff in my cabin. I've got an extry bunk in there an' you kin make yerself to home."

II

"**HOW'S YER NEW** hand doin'?" asked Old Cush, some two weeks later, as he and Black John stood shaking dice for the drinks at the bar.

"Pretty good. He was green as hell, to start off with, but he's willin' an' smart to learn. He'll make a damn good man."

"What does he do with hisself evenin's?" asked Cush. "He don't hardly ever show up in here."

"He's so damn tired he goes to bed pretty quick after supper. He reads some, but it ain't long before he's asleep."

"What does he read? I didn't know you had any books, except that law book you stole off'n that crooked lawyer that time down to Dawson."

"That's the one he reads in. An' besides I never stole that book. I merely replevined it, you might say, on account of ketchin' him cheatin' in a card game. It ain't what I'd pick out fer light recreation, but I s'pose it's better'n nothin' if a man hankers to read. Them law books, though, is plumb pernicious in the hands of the young."

"You mean they're mean fer to hold up on account of the heft?"

"Well, not exactly," grinned Black John. "What I meant was that it bodes no good fer their future. Jest stop an' think—what's the first thing a man does when he reads a law?"

"I couldn't say I don't know as I ever read none."

"Why, nach'lly, he starts in figgerin' how to circumvent er evade it. What I claim—give a man a book of statutes, an' plenty of time, an' if he's at all smart he'll figger out a way to git around nine out of ten of 'em. The result is, you've got a potential criminal."

"I wouldn't know what kind that is," Cush replied. "Is it some form of skullduggery? But how about lawyers? They read all them laws."

"Yeah," agreed Black John, "an' look at 'em. But you better shove out another glass. Here comes some one."

A heavy-set, rather squat man crossed the open space and stepped through the doorway, pausing only for an instant for a swift survey of the room before advancing to the bar. He was an unprepossessing man, with thick lips, a wide red-veined nose, and little blood-shot eyes that darted here and there in a series of quick, intent stabs.

"This is Halfaday Crick, ain't it? An' I s'pose this here's Cushing's Fort? An' I guess you're Cush, there behind the bar? An' you'd be Black John Smith?" he said, turning to the big man beside whom he had ranged himself.

"A man," replied Black John, "which he's right every time he guesses had ought to do pretty well fer hisself, in the long run."

"Yer damn right. I don't make many mistakes. Can't afford to."

"You shore can't on Halfaday."

"How do you mean?"

Black John shrugged. "Well—today's mistake might well be tomorrow's hangin', as a poet would say."

"Who was in here before I come?" the man demanded abruptly, eyeing the third glass on the bar.

"Everyone on Halfaday, an' a lot of folks that ain't on the crick no more."

"I mean right now—jest before I come in? An' what did he duck out fer?"

"Askin' questions seems to be yer main holt," observed Black John. "An' I might add that it's a form of conversation that ain't favored in these parts. Ignorance of local customs has got lots of folks in trouble, before now. But I don't mind tellin' you that there ain't be'n no one in here fer the last couple of hours except me an' Cush."

"What's that other glass doin' there, then?"

"It ain't doin' nothin' that I kin see. Cush jest shoved it out when he seen you headin' fer the door. He figgered that mebbe you'd jine us in a drink. It's another local custom that the house always buys the first one when a newcomer appears amongst us."

"Guess yer right, at that," admitted the man, picking up the glass and examining it. "This un's dry; an' the other two is wet." He reached for the bottle and filled the glass to the brim. "Sure, I'll have one with you boys. Brown's the name—John Brown. Here's how."

"John Brown, eh? That's a kind of an onlucky name on Halfaday."

"What do you mean—onlucky?"

"Well, the last man that claimed it got hung. That was a couple of weeks ago, though. Times might of changed sence then. An' besides, he lied about it. His right name was Meeker."

THE MAN grinned. "I guess names don't mean nothin' on this crick, nohow. I heard about you boys in Dawson—how yer all outlaws up here. An' how this place lays right up agin the line so you kin slip over into Alasky when the police shows up. How fer is it to the line? An' which way?"

"About twenty minutes of fast walkin' up that gulch yonder."

"I always like to git the lay of the land when I hit a new crick," said the man, with a meaning wink. "I might want to leave in a hurry."

"You might, at that."

"Yer damn right. When the law's trompin' on a man's tail he's got to be ready to jump. Fill 'em up an' have one on me." He tossed a well-filled sack onto the bar, and refilled his glass. "Yes sir—when I heard about you boys all bein' outlaws up here, an' how a man kin do as he damn pleases without no law to bother him, I says 'that's the place fer me,' I says—an' here I be."

"A man kin do as he pleases on Halfaday," observed Black John, "only as long as he don't please to commit no crime. Murder, all forms of larceny, claim jumpin', an' general skullduggery is hangable offenses on this crick, an' the interim between the crime an' the hangin' ain't hardly worth mentionin'. The easiest way to put this thought acrost to a total stranger who might have criminal tendencies would be a trip through our graveyard. It lays jest back of the saloon on the flat between here an' the rimrocks, an' we take a sort of civic pride in keepin' it systematic an' orderly—not so much in the way of a tribute to the dead, as a lesson to the livin'. Fer instance, we use three check letters: M, H, an' D. These letters is burnt in the slab under the name of the deceased. If you see the name, John Smith with an M under it, you know he was murdered. If there's an H under it, he was hung. An' if the letter's a D he jest died without no assistance from anyone. A careful analysis of these grave slabs will show an H fer every M, an' quite a few left over on account of its owner bein' deemed guilty of some other malfeasance. There's a scatterin' of Ds, too, fer folks that died miscellaneous—but it's well to note that H is the predominatin' letter amongst them slabs."

"Looks like yer damn handy with a rope, fer a bunch of outlaws," grunted the man. "What does the police think of all these hangin's?"

"They're in hearty accord with the bulk of 'em," Black John replied, "bein' as they know they was arrived at by the quasi-legal intervention of a miners' meetin'. A hangin' on Halfaday has saved Corporal Downey many a laborious trip back to Dawson with some prisoner."

"I s'pose U.S. marshals don't bother you much up here."

"No—we don't consider 'em much of a bother. One shows up, now an' then—but he don't never have no luck. You see, he's on the wrong side of the fence, so to speak. He ain't got no authority on this side of the line, an' when you come to strip a U.S. marshal of his authority he's sad to contemplate."

"If he located his man here, he could wait till he cross the line some day, an' then nab him," suggested Brown.

"Yeah," admitted Black John, "but sech degree of astuteness is way beyond the capabilities of any marshal we've saw, to date. Besides, it would require considerable patience."

"What do you fellas do, up here?"

"We dig gold fer a livin', an' fer recreation we indulge in sech simple pastimes as is afforded by whiskey an' stud, with a little draw poker throw'd in by way of variation."

"How's chances to locate a claim on the crick?"

"Most anywheres a man would stake he could take out wages. Some claims pays considerable better than wages—an' a few is real strikes."

THE MAN turned to Cush. "Could you put me up 'til I find a location that suits me?"

Cush shook his head. "I don't keep no boarders, nor yet no lodgers. Why don't you throw yer stuff into One Eyed John's shack? It's be'n empty, off an' on, sence we hung him."

"You mean that empty shack that I passed six er eight mile down the crick? Hell, that's too fer away. I kind of like to mingle around with the boys evenin's. Whiskey an' stud suits me fine."

"No," replied Cush, "that's Olson's old shack you mean. One Eyed John's shack ain't only a little piece below here. You didn't see it from the crick on account of the bank bein' too high. It's right handy—an' his claim ain't so bad, neither, in case you didn't find none you liked better."

"Why ain't it be'n took up, then?"

"It has," replied Black John, "one time an' another. But the ones that took it didn't seem to have no permanency to 'em. Professor Dykes was the last one. He got murdered by Meeker, the one that claimed his name was John Brown. Their graves lays right side by side—them two fresh ones. Wait till I slip over to my cabin an' git some tobacco, an' I'll show you One Eyed's shack."

Proceeding swiftly to his cabin, Black John paused beside the new shaft that young Leatherby was sinking nearby. "Slip over into the storeroom the back way, son," he said, "an' foller along the back wall of the saloon till you come to where some pork bar'ls stands agin the wall. Then look through the slot you'll find there into the saloon, an' see if the bird I go out with is anyone you know. Then you come back an' start supper cookin' an' I'll be along in a little while."

Half an hour later he returned to his cabin to find the table set, and a savory moose steak frying in the pan. Besides his bunk young Leatherby was hastily stowing his few belongings into his pack sack.

Black John accorded him scarcely a glance. "Goin' somewhere?" he asked casually.

"Yes, I've got to move on—and move quick. That man was the marshal who arrested me for that murder in Rampart. I was afraid he'd follow me up here, when he didn't find me in Dawson."

"Yeah, it seemed likely he would," admitted Black John. "I kind of mistrusted he was him when he first come into Cush's. An' sech suspicion was practically confirmed when he admitted he was a crook, an' give us an exhibition in shrewdness by pickin' a dry glass out from two wet ones—after havin' made one wrong guess about 'em. Come on, let's eat."

The lad shook his head. "I won't wait to eat. I've got to get going."

"Where to?"

"Why—I don't know. I'm not going to stick around and let that marshal take me back to Alaska. I'm pulling out."

"Pullin' out! Without no grub in yer belly, an' none in yer pack?"

"I thought you'd slip me some grub from Cush's to take along, and give me the balance of what I had coming."

Black John shook his head. "Nope. I ain't slippin' you no grub, nor neither I ain't payin' you what you've got comin'. Yer gittin' along fine, right where yer at. But you've got to stick at it awhile longer. There's quite a bit you still got to learn about this minin' game before yer ready to go on yer own."

All color drained from the youngster's face as he stared into the big man's eyes. "You—you mean—you won't help me get away from that marshal?" he asked in a dry voice.

Black John shook his head. "I can't do it, son. Jest think—what kind of a man would I be to help a fugitive git away from an officer?" He seated himself, and reaching to the stove for the pot, poured a cup of black tea. "Come on, now, an' eat—an' set that fryin' pan on the table before that meat's cooked to a frazzle."

The lad set the pan on the table, but remained standing. "I—I can't eat," he said. "I ain't hungry."

Black John regarded him attentively. "Ain't hungry after doin' a hard day's work? What's the matter, son—you ain't sick, are you? Ain't, mebbe, worryin' about somethin'?"

"Worrying! I guess you'd worry if you were going to be hung for a murder you never committed!"

Black John shook his head. "Nope. Sech cases is far too rare to worry about. Set down an eat yer supper. Let this here marshal do the worryin'. He's the one that's huntin' someone—not you."

"But—what'll I do?"

"Jest like you been doin'. Yer gittin' along fine. In a month er so, when you git the hang of buildin' sluices an' flumes, you kin locate a claim of yer own. Yer too smart a young fella to be wastin' yer time workin' fer someone else."

"But what if he should see me?"

"He ain't apt to if you stay away from Cush's, evenin's. But s'pose he does? What of it? He ain't got no authority this side of the line."

"He might pull a gun on me and force me to cross to the Alaska side. He could arrest me then."

BLACK JOHN grinned. "Sech act would jestify all the worryin' he ever done in his life, son. It's jest one of them things that couldn't happen on Halfaday. Set down an' eat an' quit pesterin' about that marshal. Now that I'm shore of his identity I've got a kind of a hunch that his sojourn amongst us ain't goin' to be onduly prolonged. Of course the obvious an' simple way of reddin' the crick of a varmint of his ilk would be hangin'. But we've got to kind of go slow in a case like this an' proceed along lines that wouldn't disturb the delicate balance of international relations, as a lawyer would say. It would be best if his departure was entirely voluntary. I'll consort with this marshal this evenin' in the hope of locatin' some weakness he might have. Jest remember that, son—if you want to handle a man, find out his weakness an' then govern yer-self accordin'. Every man's got from one to a dozen of 'em. They ain't hard to find."

"You mean," asked the lad, "that you can make the marshal leave Halfaday without takin me with him?"

"I wouldn't go so far as to say I'd make him leave. I'm jest predictin' that the chances is he'll pull out voluntary—an' in more er less of a hurry. It's jest a hunch I've got—that's all."

As the big man talked the strained and hunted look had left the lad's face. He slipped into his chair, and speared his half of the steak from the pan with his fork and transferred it to his plate. Somehow, the very tone of Black John's voice, even more than his words, carried comfort and reassurance. "I'll do just as you say," he said. "Gee it would be great if I didn't have to worry about that marshal! I'm sure interested in this mining business."

"Worryin' don't git a man nothin' but discomfort," Black John replied, and a few moments later finished his supper with another big cup of black tea and rose from the table. "I'm leavin' you to clean up the dishes alone, tonight. Guess I'll loaf down to the marshal's shack before he gits up to Cush's. You kin generally git better acquainted with a man if you' git him alone than if he's in a crowd. An' when you git done with the dishes you might kind of red up the shack a little. Take it about onct in so often a man ought to sweep out in under the bunks an' the stove an' around in corners where his broom don't reach every day. It's a good thing to remember, son, that when a man begins lettin' dirt ketch up with him, it's a shore sign he's slippin'. A dirty man ain't never a good one."

PAUSING AT the saloon only long enough to procure a quart bottle of whiskey, he proceeded on to One Eyed John's shack where he found the marshal in the act of preparing supper. "Hello, Brown," he greeted from the doorway, "how about a little drink before you eat? Things is kind of quiet up to Cush's, so I got to thinkin' about you bein' a stranger an' all—mebbe you'd be kind of lonesome."

"Don't care if I do," said the marshal, setting a couple of cups on the table. "Nothin' like a little snort er two fer an appetizer."

"That's right," agreed the big man, pouring a drink. "Here's mud in yer eye."

They drank, and as the empty cups were returned to the table, Black John glanced toward the stove where water was boiling in a tea pail beside a frying pan in which a can of beans was warming. "Ain't you got no meat?" he asked.

"No, Cush didn't have none to sell an' I didn't stop to kill none on the trail. I'll do a little huntin', onct I git strung out. Beans stays by a man pretty good when he ain't got no meat."

"Beans an' tea's a hell of a supper, though," Black John replied. "I've got part of a hind quarter left. I'll slip over to the cabin an' fetch you a chunk."

"Have you et yet?"

"No," lied the big man, "I'll go back an' cook me up somethin' later. It's kind of lonesome eatin' alone, an' I sort of put it off till I git damn good an' hungry."

"Hell," said Brown, "fetch enough meat fer the two of us an' eat here! I've got plenty of beans an' tea, an' there's some extry plates an' knives an' stuff there on the shelft."

"Yeah, them was some that One Eyed John left one time when we hung him. I'll go after the meat, but we better have another drink. A man can't walk on one leg. Fill yer cup up good—there's plenty more where that come from. I'll be back d'reckly."

When Black John returned with the meat, the two liberal drinks of liquor on top of those Brown had consumed at the saloon were taking effect. He waxed loquacious under the stimulus of a third drink that the big man poured and offered him as he sliced the steaks.

"I heard about you back in Dawson," he confided. "Yump—fella was tellin' me about you down in Klondike Palace. Says how you've got plenty of guts—robbed an army er somethin', one time, he claimed."

"Only part of one," said Black John deprecatingly; "it wasn't so much of a job."

"Huh—anyone that could rob even part of an army is good enough fer me. You know, I've took a kind of likin' to you. Yup, 's a fact. Mostly I don't like strangers. I mistrust 'em. But take you—you're different."

"Yeah—a man wouldn't hardly want to have nothin' to do with someone he'd mistrust. Have another drink. Little licker before supper goes kind of good, now an' then."

"You bet! What I claim—if a man won't take a little drink onct in a while, look out fer him. He might be a preacher er somethin'. But take you—anyone could tell you ain't no preacher, jest lookin' at you. You got a different look—an' you'll take a drink."

"Oh shore, I don't mind a little snort when I'm dry. An' like you p'inted out—there's a hell of a lot of preachers I ain't be'n mistook fer. Better have another, while that meats fryin'."

THE MAN poured another and surveyed Black John a bit unsteadily. "Y'know—take a fella like you, with plenty of guts—me an' you might do pretty good fer ourself."

"You mean, hook up pardners on a claim?"

The man laughed. "Claim—hell! Y'know I been around some—down river, on the Alasky side. I know my buttons, all right. What I claim, a man's a damn sap that breaks his back shovellin' gravel. There's other ways of gittin' it that's quicker, an' a damn sight easier, if a man's got the guts."

"Yeah?"

"Sure. Hell—I know a couple of jobs, right now that you an' me could pull, an' split a damn good haul betwixt us. There's a saloon keeper down to Rampart that's got twenty, thirty thousan' on hand all the time—an' I know where he keeps it. You could slip in there some night, an' stick a gun on him, an' if he tried to tell you he didn't have nothin' except, mebbe, what's in the till, you could tell him right where it's at—me puttin' you wise first—an' then if he didn't come acrost with it, you could plug him an' git away with it, an' we'd split, fifty-fifty."

"Yeah," admitted Black John, "it sounds easy enough. But in a case like that, I'd be the one that would have a U.S. marshal on my tail with a swell chanct of gittin' hung when he ketched up with me. Mebbe it would be better if we both stuck this guy up."

The other shook his head. "No it wouldn't. If I went along we'd have to croak this bird fer sure. He's a friend of mine, an' he'd spot me in a minute. It's got to be someone he don't know—like you. I wouldn't like fer him to git croaked onlest you had to, bein' a friend an' all."

"Well, of course, if a man's sentimental about friendship, that way," Black John admitted, "mebbe it would be better to git a stranger to do it. But it kind of looks like a fifty-fifty split would be givin' you a shade the best of the deal, seein' I'm the one that would be doin' all the work an' takin' all the risk, to boot."

"It's me that knows where he keeps his money," reminded the man.

"Yeah, but it would be me they'd hang when the marshal ketched up with me."

Brown grinned fatuously, and poured himself another drink. "There ain't no marshal goin' to ketch up with you, pal," he said. "I'll guarantee that you won't git hung even if you knock this guy off."

Black John looked skeptical. "Who the hell are you—the jedge, er somethin'?"

"No," replied the other, "I'm the marshal."

BLACK JOHN grinned. "Couple of more drinks an' you'll be the president, er at least the attorney general. In the saloon this afternoon you give out the impression that you was jest another outlaw, with the police on his tail."

"Sure I did. A marshal don't never tell all he knows—a good one don't. How would I git my man without I pretend to be a crook, myself?"

"Sech pretense wouldn't be no strain on yer imagination, at that," observed Black John.

"How do you mean? You think I ain't no marshal, eh?"

"Well, a man's always entitled to a reasonable doubt, ain't he?"

"What would you say if I'd prove it?"

"A man can't fly in the face of proof."

"Well—here you be, then." Opening his shirt, the man turned it back to show a United States marshal's badge pinned on its inner surface. "There's the badge, an' here's my papers." Drawing a wallet from his hip pocket, he produced his commission, duly signed and attested. "Everett Druker, that's my real name," he explained. "John Brown, that was jest the first name I happened to think up to tell you fellas."

Black John nodded, and returned the paper after a careful perusal. "It savored slightly of an alias when you mentioned it," he said. "How does a man go about gittin' a job as marshal, anyhow?"

The man winked, and poured another drink. "Politics," he uttered thickly. He was weaving slightly, so that he held onto the table with one hand to steady himself. "It's easy if yer smart—git somethin' on someone, an' then pull yer wires—that's all. A man don't have to work, if he uses his head. I guess now you kin see where I earn my fifty-fifty split, can't you? After we divide the stuff, you hit back upriver, an' the marshal—that's me—I hit downriver, hell-bent after the one that done it—see?"

"It looks like a good scheme," admitted Black John, "providin' you played square with me. I'll think it over."

"Played square!" exclaimed the other, drawing up in a drunken attempt at dignity. "I'll have you to know I'm the squarest guy in Rampart!"

"Oh, I wouldn't doubt that none."

"Lishen, pal," said the man, in a tone meant to be confidential, as he lurched forward and laid a hand on the big man's shoulder. "Yer—hic—yer a frien' of mine—she? D'w' I look like a guy that would—hic—double-crosh a frien'? Do I? I'm ashkin' you, man to—hic—man if I do?"

"No, no!" Black John assured him. "You don't look like no one that would ever double-cross me. Not in a thousan' years, you don't. But if yer a U.S. marshal, what are you doin' on Halfaday?"

"I'm huntin' a prishner. He knocked me on the head an' got away. I trailed him up to Dawson but he skipped out ahead of me, an' I'm bettin' he come here. Ain't shaw him, have you—young gaffer, name Leatherby?"

"What did you arrest him fer?"

"Murder."

"Was he guilty?"

The marshal leered drunkenly. "The jury'll shay sho, anyhow. Tha's all I give a damn. Lishen—yer my pal. Ain't you my pal?"

"We're jest like brothers. Hell, you know that, marsh. There hadn't ought to be no secrets between us."

"Sure—jes' like—hic—brothers. Well—I plugged that damn cuss in Rampart—plugged him right in the middle of the head. He was cheatin' in a game. But me bein' a marshal thersh liable to be a stink about it. So—hic—thish young gaffer comes along, stewed to the gills, so I nabs him fer the murder—she? The boys in the game's all good frien's of mine—they're jes' like I am—do anything fer a frien'—they'll all swear this young punk shot this guy—an' the saloon keeper, too—he'll stick by me." The man paused and winked elaborately. "He's the one we're goin' to—hic—rob."

HE WEAVED uncertainly on his feet and Black John took him by the arm. "Better let me help you over to the bunk, yonder," he said. "Seems like yer gittin' a little bit onsteady on yer feet."

"Onstidy! Who—me? I—hic—I kin walk jes' shtrait's you kin. That li'l drink I took might of—hic—went to my head fer a minute, but—hie—she that crack there in the floor. I'll walk it. Look." The man balanced himself carefully, his eyes fixed glassily upon a crack that ran from where he stood beside the table to the door. Then he started to walk—but not toward the door. One step he took, then another—backward. Then he paused, weaving uncertainly on sagging knees, his eyes fixed in a do-or-die stare on the floor. "How'n hell—hic—kin I walk a crack when you keep pullin' it away?" Again his legs got into motion, and as before, they carried him backward, despite his ludicrously strenuous effort to control them, and the next instant they came into violent contact with the edge of the bunk, and the marshal collapsed onto it in a heap.

When Black John stooped over him he was breathing heavily, sound asleep. The big man shoved the frying pan to the back of the stove, and eyed the quart bottle that stood on the table, only a scant inch of liquor showing in it. "Jest another marshal tryin' to git along," he commented. "He didn't do so bad, at that, on an empty stummick. I only had a couple of swallers out of that bottle."

III

RETURNING TO HIS own cabin Black John found young Leatherby busily engaged in house cleaning. Everything from the shelves was piled on the bunks. The floor had been freshly scrubbed, and the lad was standing on a chair scrubbing the shelves with soap and hot water. The big man grinned.

"Hell, son, I didn't mean you should run hog-wild with yer cleanin'."

"I thought a good scrubbing wouldn't hurt the floor any, and when I finished that I noticed that the paper on the shelves had got pretty dusty so I thought that I'd change it. I found some old newspapers under your bunk."

"It'll look right nice," agreed Black John. "I been aimin' to change them shelft papers fer a year er so, but I never seemed to git around to it, busy as I've been. You've got to remember though that even cleanliness kin be overdone. A finnicky man ain't no better than a dirty one—an' a damn sight harder to git along with. A sort of middle course between filth an' clenth is best in the long run."

The lad grinned. "Did you have any luck finding that marshal's weakness?" he asked.

"Yeah, I didn't do so bad, in the time I had. Near as I kin figger his weaknesses consists of drunkenness an' theft, with a lib'ral dash of perfidy an' murder throw'd in fer good measure. He ain't no man I'd want to be associated with."

"Do you think you can make him leave Halfaday without—without taking me with him?" the youngster asked anxiously.

"Oh shore. Like I told you, bein' a U.S. marshal, we can't jest go ahead an' hang him like an ordinary citizen. This here situation havin' an international angle, it's got to be handled diplomatic. Them diplomats always finds a way of puttin' somethin' acrost that leaves the other fella thinkin' he's got the best of the bargain—but they ain't got nothin' on me when it comes to onder-handedness. Don't you worry, son. I'll find a way, onct I set my mind to it."

Young Leatherby folded newspapers, covered the freshly washed shelves, and began to return the objects he had removed from them. He paused and held up a pair of gold colored slippers.

"I'll bet there's a story behind these, and that dress hanging there in the corner," he ventured.

Black John's eyes assumed a far-away, reminiscent expression; and there was an unwonted softness in his voice as he answered. "Yes, son—a sad story, an' a long one. I might tell you about it some time—but not tonight. They say a man never loves but onct—an' I guess they're right. It was long ago—she was my first an' only love." He paused and heaved a long and bitter sigh. "But another man got her—an' all I've got left is them pore little mementoes fer to remember her down through the lonely years."

"I'm sorry," said the youngster, a note of sympathy in his voice. "I oughtn't to have mentioned it."

"Oh, that's all right, son. It don't hurt a man, now an' then, to set an' contemplate his woe."

"And this gold paint. I suppose you keep this to touch 'em up when they get dull and tarnished?"

"Gold paint? Oh—in that bottle. I'd fergot about that paint. Yeah—shore—to touch 'em up, now an' then—it sort of keeps her mem'ry bright an' fresh like."

"But—how did you come to have her dress, and her shoes for mementoes?"

"Eh? Why— I hadn't thought of that. How did I? Damn if I know—onless I jumped up in a hurry one night an' grabbed the wrong pile of clothes."

"Here's a magnet, too—what have you got that for?"

"Magnet?" The big man's eyes rested for a moment on the large horseshoe magnet that the lad held in his hand. "Hold on!" he exclaimed suddenly. "Gold paint—magnet! By God, the germ of an idea's beginnin' to tickle my skull! Put them things back on the shelft an' leave 'em there. I'm goin' over to Cush's!" He leaped to his feet and vanished through the doorway, leaving the youngster staring after him in amazement.

STEPPING INTO the saloon, he called Pot Gutted John aside and entered into a long and earnest conversation, after which he mingled with the others until closing time.

"Kind of funny that fella, Brown, didn't show up this evenin'," said Cush, after the others had departed.

"Yeah, it is kind of strange, at that. Mebbe he don't care nothin' about licker."

"Huh—the way he throw'd them drinks into him this afternoon, it didn't seem none hateful to him. An' that nose of his'n with all them blue an red veins showin' on the end of it—he never got that nose on crick water. That nose cost him somethin'."

"It cost someone somethin', all right, but I'm doubtin' it was him."

"Guess you sized him up about like me," observed Cush. "Somehow, I don't like his looks."

"He ain't what you'd call prepossessin'," admitted Black John.

"An' that reminds me," said Black John, "give me a couple of files—ten er twelve inch flat ones'll do."

When Cush disappeared into the storeroom to get the files, Black John stepped out of doors and returned with a sizeable stone.

"What an' the hell you goin' to do with that rock?" asked Cush, eyeing the stone dubiously.

"Prop up the corner of the stove with it," Black John replied.

"What ails the corner of yer stove?"

"It ain't my stove I'm goin' to prop up—it's yourn."

"My stove! Hell, it's settin' level. It don't need no proppin'."

"It will when I take the leg off."

"The leg?"

"Yeah. I need a piece of cast iron—an' my stove legs ain't nothin' but sheet iron."

"You ain't goin' to take no leg off'n my stove," said Cush, eyeing the big man belligerently.

"Shore I am," replied Black John. "Don't tell me that long as I've know'd you, yer goin' to start in at this late day an' hog stove legs on me."

"What the hell would you want of a stove leg?"

"I bust my gun, an' I need a piece of cast iron to fix it with—that's what I got them files fer. To file out a piece so it will fit."

"Cripes, you can't fix no gun with a stove leg! What part's broke?"

"Why it's a—a little dingus in the lock somewheres. I don't know what you call it. It's a kind of a small piece. Hell, I won't likely use the whole leg. There'll prob'ly be enough of it left to put back. Even if there ain't, that rock will hold up the stove—look—it's solider'n it was before. Them legs is kind of spindlin'."

"Huh," grunted Cush. "It might be solid, but it looks like hell."

Black John eyed him pityingly. "Are you runnin' this saloon fer looks, er utility?" he asked, and before Cush could reply he had vanished through the doorway, carrying his files and the stove leg with him.

IV

HE RETURNED TO the cabin to find young Leatherby sound asleep in his bunk. Tip-toeing in, he procured a sheet of old newspaper, and retiring to a rude bench just outside the door, seated himself, spread the paper over his lap and set to work with a flat file.

A few minutes later a voice sounded above the sound of the filing, and he looked up to see the lad, standing naked in the doorway regarding him with puzzled concern. "It's long after midnight. What in thunder are you doing?"

Black John paused, his eyes on the silvery ripples of the rapids that showed beyond the eerie black shadows of the spruce trees. "Don't mind me, son," he replied, accompanying the words with a deep sigh. "Go on back to sleep. I'm only settin' out here filin' a stove leg in the moonlight."

"Filing a stove leg! What for?"

"I don't know as I could explain it—jest in words, son. It's a sort of a habit I've got, that's all. Whenever I git sort of sad, an' low like I go off by myself somewheres an' file a stove leg. Somehow there's somethin' comfortin' about filin' a stove leg. Try it sometime when yer feelin' downhearted an' sad. I s'pose it was you mentionin' them gold slippers that started me off. It fetched up vivid an' painful mem'ries of my lost Cinderella?"

"Cinderella! Was her name really Cinderella?"

"Well, partly it was, an' partly not, son. As I rec'lect it, her name was Eller—an' I used to call her Cinder, on account of her color. It was a kind of a pet name I had—me bein' young an' kind of foolish, them days. Go on back to sleep, son, an' leave me alone with my sorrow."

The youngster withdrew into the cabin, and white teeth gleamed in the moonlight behind the heavy black beard as the man grinned broadly to himself. Finally, with a goodly pile of gray iron filings on the paper, he laid aside his file and regarded the stove leg.

"Didn't hurt Cush's stove leg none, filin' around the edges like I done. It's a little slimmer'n the others, mebbe, but I didn't shorten it none, an' there's still plenty of it left to hold up his stove." Reentering the cabin without disturbing the youngster, he removed the bottle of gilt paint and the slippers from the clock shelf and returning to the bench busied himself with the gold paint and the iron filings. Returning the slippers and the bottle to the shelf, he waited a while for the gilded filings to dry before making them into a small package which he pocketed and proceeded to the cabin of One Eyed John.

The marshal still lay on his bunk, and as Black John lighted the tin bracket lamp he stirred and mumbled heavily something about supper.

"It's jest about ready, now," reassured the big man, stepping to the table and pouring the remaining whiskey from the bottle into a cup which he carried to the bunk. "Here," he said, "we'll have one more little drink before we eat. That steak's about done, now. You must of dozed off fer a second. Throw this into you, an' lay back, an' I'll holler when it's ready."

With the help of Black John, the man raised his head, and drained the cup which the big man held to his lips, then sank back, and in two minutes, he had passed again into his alcoholic coma. Deftly Black John removed the sack of dust from the man's pocket, extracted a certain quantity from it, replacing the amount with the gilded filings from the package. Then he returned the sack, proceeded to his own cabin, and went to bed.

Next morning when the youngster awoke it was to find the big man snoring contentedly in his bunk. He noted that the slippers on the clock shelf had been freshly gilded.

"Poor fellow," the lad muttered. "I'm sure sorry I stirred up those old memories. I won't wake him for breakfast. He was up most of the night filing away on that stove leg. Queer sort of a mental kink—filing a stove leg. But I suppose it made him feel better to regild those slippers. Sometimes, from some of the things he says and does, I kind of wonder if he's all there. But he's a mighty fine man—even if he is a little queer."

V

THE NEXT EVENING Black John greeted the marshal vociferously as he entered the saloon shortly after supper time. "Hello, Brownie, old pal! Say—we must of had quite a session down to your place, last night! I don't rec'lect us ever eatin' that supper we was fryin' up—do you? Hell, way along towards mornin' I woke up with my neck about broke from bein' doubled agin' the back of my chair where I'd fell asleep. You was snorin' away in yer bunk, so I blow'd out the light an' hit fer home to git me some real sleep. Had a hell of a time findin' my cabin. We must of been soused to the gills."

"God," uttered the marshal quickly, "I guess we must of be'en—the way I feel. That must of been damn powerful licker you fetched along. Hell—that's the first time my half of a quart bottle ever throw'd me plumb down an' out. We never et no part of that supper. It was all on the stove yet when I woke up, a couple of hours ago. I tried to eat some of it, but I didn't have no luck makin' it stick—the way my guts feels."

"Oh shore. I felt the same way till I'd had a couple of drinks. Here, fill up an' throw a couple of jolts down you. The hair of the dog is good fer the bite, as the Good Book says—an' believe me some of them old prophets know'd what they was talkin' about. I feel fine, now. The boys'll be droppin' in d'reckly an' we'll start a session of stud."

The man poured his drink but when he tried to raise it to his mouth his hand shook so that all the liquor slopped from the glass.

"I've got the shakes," he said. "I couldn't set in no card game."

"Hell, don't let a little thing like the shakes bother you. I'll show you a trick. Throw him a bar towel, Cush. There—pour out another drink. Now fetch the towel up around the back of yer neck an' then pinch one corner of it agin the glass when you pick it up, an' git holt of the other end of the towel with yer left hand an' draw the drink up to yer mouth, same as a pulley."

The man did as instructed and had no trouble in conveying the glass to his lips. "There—what did I tell you?" approved Black John. "Cripes, what I claim, if a man's goin' to persist in drinkin' licker, he might's well know all the tricks. Time you git three, four more hauled into you, you'll be able to h'ist the rest of 'em without a tremble."

Several other drinks followed the first, and an hour later when a stud game was started, the marshal was among the players. Along about ten o'clock the game was interrupted by the arrival of Pot Gutted John, who burst into the room with the announcement that his cabin had been robbed that afternoon while he was off on a moose hunt.

"What was stole?" asked Black John, folding the four cards that lay face up before him and tossing them into the discards.

"A sack of dust. Not a full sack—but damn near it. I keep it in my cabin an' keep addin' my day's clean-up to it till it gits full, an' then I fetch it up an' have Cush stick it in the safe. I been doin' that-a-way right along, an' never had none stole before. What I claim—it's a hell of a note when a man can't leave his dust lay around on Halfaday. We'll be gittin' as bad as Dawson, if we don't look out."

BLACK JOHN nodded agreement. "That's right. But rec'lect, Pot Gutted, I warned you last week when I was down to your shack an' seen that sack layin' there on the shelft, that some sneak thief might pinch it off. Some black sheep is liable to show up—even on Halfaday."

"That's right," admitted Pot Gutted John. "I rec'lect you tellin' me that. An' I rec'lect you claimed how you'd fix it so's if anyone did steal it, you could locate the guilty party. The poke's gone, an' now it looks like it's up to you to do the locatin'."

"That's right," Black John agreed. "It shore looks like I'm fetched up, face to face, with my own promise. An' do you rec'lect what I done with that sack?"

"Why shore. You took down the scales an' weighed out a couple ounces of dust an' put 'em in yer own sack, an' then you weighed out some dust out of another sack in yer pocket an' put it in my sack to make up fer what you'd took out. But hell—I can't see no sense in that. Yer dust ain't no different than mine. All Halfaday dust is the same."

"Er so you think," replied Black John glancing into the faces that now rimmed the table, for a theft on Halfaday was a matter of grave concern for all. Leaning back in his chair, he included the whole assembly in an expansive glance. "You know, boys," he began, "when I was a little shaver I always wanted to be an actor. The stage, somehow, always appealed to me. There was sort of mysterious glamor that attached to them actors an' actresses that ketched my fancy. But I never got no chanct to be one. Next to bein' an actor I wanted to be a lawyer, er a detective, but certain circumstances that developed subsequent rendered it impractical fer me to fool around with the law—from that angle. So I went from one thing to another, an' from one place to another—sometimes fast, an' sometimes more leisurely, accordin' to the circumstances, till I wind up as you see me—a simple delver fer gold. But, boys, there's certain yearnin's an' instincts in every man's soul that won't never down. Fer instance, if I know there's a thief loose on a crick, I want to know who he is. I don't seem to git no rest till I locate him. That's why, boys, that I bend so much of my time an' my energy to the elimination of crime. It ain't that I abhor crime fer crime's sake, like some you might think. It's only that I'm actin' accordin' to this here primordial urge that's in me—that, an' the fact that we don't want no damn thief loose among us. So when I seen Pot Gutted John's sack layin' around that way, I jest nach'ly figgered it was good thief-bait, providin' of course there was anyone on Halfaday so degraded as to have larceny in his soul. So I set my trap. You all heard Pot Gutted explain how I traded some dust with him. Well, boys, there was method in that trade. It was bony fido dust I took out of his sack; but it was gilt iron filin's I put into it. Yes, sir, the widder Dykes left behind all that junk that the perfesser used in his tricks, amongst which was a little bottle of gold paint an' a magnet. Now you all know that a magnet won't draw gold—but it will draw iron. Do you see the p'int? Someone on Halfaday has got Pot Gutted's dust—but part of that dust is yaller iron filin's." The big man paused and glanced about him triumphantly as he drew the large horseshoe magnet from his pocket. "I don't know what use the late but not lamented perfesser had fer this thing—but in my hands it's a crime detector. Boys, some one on this crick has got iron filin's mixed with his dust—an' here's the little instrument that will reveal his perfidy an' earn him a much required hangin' to boot. That man might not be here in this room at present—an' then agin' he might. Detectin', like charity, begins at home, as the Good Book says, an' here goes! Every man in this room is hereby required to line up to the bar an' lay his poke in front of him. I'll step behind the bar, an' as each man opens his poke I'll insert the magnet. If he ain't got nothin' but gold dust in it he ain't got nothin' to fear—the magnet will fetch 'em out—an' a miners' meetin' will do the rest. Providin' the thief ain't located amongst us here present, we'll continue the investigation up an' down the crick till we find him. Line up an' lay yer pokes on the bar, boys. I'll examine my own first, jest to show you I don't play no favorites."

THE MEN lined up and laid their pouches on the bar amid expressions of hearty approval, as Black John passed from one to the other inserting the magnet into the mouths of the sacks and drawing it forth clean.

The marshal was standing well toward the end of the line, watching the proceeding with interest, his own sack ready for inspection. He even expressed his approval to Long Nosed John, at his right. "That's what I call pretty slick work," he said, admiringly. "I must remember that one. It might come in handy, some time."

"You bet," agreed the long nosed one, "Black John, he's smart. A man could learn a lot of tricks from him."

Then the magnet was thrust into his own poke and came out clean. He was returning it to his pocket when a loud chorus of exclamations and invective filled the room, for as Black John drew the magnet from the sack of the man who called himself Brown it came out heavily incrusted with yellow iron filings.

"I'll say you'll remember it!" roared Long Nosed John, in the man's ear as his long arms closed about him. "But you won't remember it long!" Others crowded about and laid hands on the man who was staring in wide eyed horror at the encrusted magnet. Suddenly, the man found his voice.

"It's a damn lie!" he shrilled. "I never stole his poke! I don't even know where he lived! I never seen him before. It's a frame-up! I tell you I never stole no poke!"

Picking up a bungstarter Black John pounded the bar for silence. His frowning gaze turned from the face of the marshal to the others.

"Is there anyone in this room," he asked, "that thinks I would frame an innocent man?"

A loud chorus of "nos" greeted the question.

"Call a miners' meetin'," demanded someone, "an' while we're tryin' him, Pot Gutted John kin be cuttin' a len'th of rope an' tyin' the knot."

Again Black John pounded the bar to quiet the loud voiced approval of the men. "Miners' meetin' called," he announced, "fer to try this here alias John Brown fer larceny, said crime havin' took place agin the peace an' dignity of Halfaday Crick, Y.T. It won't be necessary to repeat the evidence agin this prisoner, you all havin' heard how Pot Gutted's poke was pinched, an' seen the tell-tale iron film's draw'd from this defendant's poke. But in fairness to the thief, he will now be give the chanct to try an' lie out of his trouble—with what success it will be up to you boys to determine. He turned and eyed the trembling prisoner sternly.

"Do you promise to tell the truth, the whole truth, er any part of it, s'e'lp'e God? What's yer name?" he demanded.

"Why it's—er—John Brown."

"Where was you at, to wit, this afternoon when Pot Gutted John's poke was stole out of his cabin, which it's only two claims down the crick from One Eyed John's shack where you're livin'?"

"I was asleep in my bunk,"

"Got any witnesses to prove it?"

"No—but you know damn well I was drunk. Hell, you give me the licker yerself!"

BLACK JOHN regarded him quizzically. "Me! You shore can't be referrin' to that one quart me an' you split between us last evenin' before supper."

"That's what I'm talkin' about. After finishin' that quart I don't remember nothin' till I woke up with the shakes jest a little before suppertime tonight."

Black John allowed his glance to travel over the faces of the others and then back to the prisoner. "Boys," he said, "you're the jury. I'll ask you all to take a look at this here craven defendant. Look him over good. In fairness to him I'll say that him an' I did split one quart before supper yesterday. But I'm leavin' it to your judgment an' common sense—would his share of a quart of Cush's licker have sech dire effect on a man with a nose like his, to put him down an' out fer nearly twenty-four hours? That nose ain't the nose of no novice in the art of licker drinkin'—it's the nose of a master. An' besides that, when there was only one drink left in the quart, this man positively stated that he was sober—an' demonstrated his contention by walkin' a crack—an' not only that, boys—he walked it backwards! I'm leavin' it to you to decide, bearin' all these facts in mind. Kin a drunk man walk a crack backwards? Does this man's story sound reasonable?"

Unanimous negation answered the question, and Black John pounded on the bar. "You've all heard the evidence, pro an' con, an' I might add that this here defendant was dooly warned when he first showed up on the crick that larceny an' all other major crimes is hangable offences on Halfaday. We'll now put his guilt er innocence to vote. All in favor of conviction signify by sayin' 'Aye'."

A lusty "Aye" roared from every throat.

"Contrary—'no'."

The silence that greeted the words was broken by the voice of the condemned man which rose, shrill with terror. "I never done it! I tell you you can't hang me! I never done it—an' besides, I'm a U.S. marshal!"

An astounded silence greeted the announcement. Men stared into each other's faces, and then at Black John, who seemed momentarily at a loss for words. Finally he spoke:

"You all heard what the prisoner said. If his contention is true we'd be more er less flyin' in the face of providence to go ahead with this hangin', much as he deserves it. We can't afford to focus the attention of the whole world on Halfaday by promulgatin' no international incident. Boys, if this man kin prove his contention, we'll have to dispense with the hangin'."

"I kin prove it! Here's my badge—an' my papers!" Hastily he produced his evidence, laying it on the bar for all to see. He turned to Black John. "You know'd who I was! Hell—I show'd you them papers last night!"

The big man smiled. "If you was drunk as you claimed you was," he retorted, "you couldn't of showed nothin' to no one." He picked up the paper and examined it. "This here commission is made out in the name of one, Everett Druker," he said. "I thought you claimed yer name was John Brown. Kin you explain the slight discrepancy?"

"Sure I kin! Hell, I jest give out that name because I didn't want to use my own. But that's my right name there on the paper—Ever't Druker—that's me. An' I never stole that poke!"

"A man," observed Black John, "who would lie about a simple thing like his own name, wouldn't hesitate to lie about stealin' a poke of dust. This here paper might be spurious; er it might be good. Anyhow, we ain't goin' to take no chances of gittin' in trouble over you, much as you'd ought to be hung. The revised sentence of this miners' meetin' is that you be give a packsack full of grub, which you'll pay Cush fer, an' then be escorted to the line by this here assembly, in toto, an' kicked acrost it into Alasky where you belong. This grub, if used frugal, will be sufficient to see you through to some p'int on the upper Tanana, if you're lucky. If you ain't then, some day someone's goin' to kill some grizzly, er some wolf with a U.S. marshal's badge in his belly, which oncommon happenin' will ondoubtless give him food for speculation. An' I'll add, as part of the sentence, that if you ever show yer face agin' on Halfaday, you'll be shot on sight—not as a marshal, but as a common nuisance."

THE SENTENCE was duly carried out as amended, and late that night, after all the others had left the saloon to return to their homes, Black John laid a flat file on the bar. "I only used one of them files, Cush," he said. "You kin take this one back an' don't fergit to give me credit." Walking over to the stove, he removed the stone that supported a corner, and replaced the leg.

Old Cush watched him in detached silence. "By Cripes, John!" he exclaimed, "I'll bet, if that son of a gun was really a U.S. marshal, he was the one that kid busted away from that's workin' fer you!"

"Well," grinned Black John, returning to the bar and pouring himself a drink, "the idea hadn't occurred to me—but I believe yer right!"

Noting the grin, and the twinkle in the blue-gray eyes above the black beard, Cush turned his sombre gaze upon the filed stove leg.

"Did you git yer gun fixed?" he asked abruptly.

"My gun? Oh shore. Yeah it shoots good now—jest as good as ever. It pays, now an' then, if a man's mechanical-minded."

SLANG IS NOT AS DATED AS ONE WOULD THINK

SUCH SEEMINGLY MODERN terms as 'taking it on the lam,' 'on the up-and-up,' 'taking a rap,' 'fall money,' etc., are quite in order in my story 'Three Birds With One Stone,'" writes Jim Hendryx. "Most, if not all the crook terms, now so familiar to the average reader, were in common use in the underworld long before they came to the surface—that is, to the attention of society in general. For instance, the word 'racket,' meaning an illegal or shady business, was practically unknown to the public at large until prohibition brought it out into the limelight—yet this was a common term in underworld parlance, both in this country and in England, a hundred years ago. 'Hooch,' meaning liquor of any kind, was a word in common use in the Yukon country in '98, undoubtedly derived from the Indian word 'Hutchnu,' or 'Hoochnu.'

"The boys that are 'on the make,' are many of them very clever in eluding officers, planning and pulling off jobs of various sorts—but few of them are clever in inventing terms that stick. A great many of the slang terms of crookdom are of British origin, and have been in use these many years.

"In my younger days in Sauk Centre, Minnesota, I was a frequenter of the 'jungles,' the hobo hangout near the 'stone arch bridge' in close proximity to a railway junction where, in the days before block signals, all trains had to stop and whistle, making it an ideal spot for the itinerant gentry to hop on and off the trains. There collected as fine an assortment of hoboes, bindle stiffs, boomers, and yeggs as one could hope to meet, and many's the good mulligan and can of Java I've had with 'em—meanwhile, learning about everything except women from them. I have found out in later life that this was about the only part of my early education that was worth a damn. Later knocking around, of course, added the finishing touches—I referred merely to the primary education. But as I was going to say, during the course of my matriculation in the jungles, I heard nearly every term that I have heard since—and I've played around with some pretty rough boys, too.

"Prohibition brought most of these terms to light, because prohibition, and the alleged attempt at its enforcement, brought the type of men who used them to light. When the boys found out that they could violate the prohibition laws with impunity, and financial success, they became bolder along other lines—hence the vast increase in bank holdups, snatch jobs, and all other forms of skullduggery.

"Jim Hendryx"

www.ingramcontent.com/pod-product-compliance
Lightning Source LLC
LaVergne TN
LVHW091032080826
845145LV00002B/465

* 9 7 8 1 6 1 8 2 7 5 6 4 6 *